I love you, Amanda...

He kissed her tenderly, dizzyingly, endlessly, until she felt her knees threaten to buckle under her. The flames reflected dancing lights on her face, and she felt herself melting into his embrace.

"Oh, Josh," she said, "I'm so happy."

He stroked her dark hair. "I'm going to make everything all right."

She laughed. "Can you? We barely know each other. You don't know anything about my life and I know nothing about yours."

"You're so wrong," he said, and swiftly drew her into his arms again. He looked deeply into her dark eyes, knowing only the beauty and luster he saw there, *forgetting the promise he had made to himself a long time ago!*

Golden Days, Silver Nights

Rochelle Larkin

A Dell Book

Published by
Dell Publishing Co., Inc.
1 Dag Hammarskjold Plaza
New York, New York 10017

ISBN: 0-440-13051-4

Printed in the United States of America
First printing—April 1982

This is Jonathan's book.

And in our dearest treasure-trove
Where crystal shines with jewel lights
There shall we bide our constant love
Through golden days and silver nights.

DARRELL FAIRFIELD

Chapter 1

Amanda Parrish pulled her smartly tailored coat a bit closer to her. It was cooler than she had expected from the bright sunshine pouring through the window of her office inside Pembroke's. She stood just outside the famous wide double doors of the store, the most prestigious jeweler in the world, and the store that carried her designs exclusively.

She made a striking figure as she turned into Fifty-seventh Street; her straight dark hair whipped by the wind, her bright red coat fitted to her slender frame and flaring slightly at the hemline, complimenting her strong, shapely legs. Men looked at her, but if Amanda was aware of that, she gave no indication. She walked briskly to her destination, a car rental agency a few blocks from Pembroke's. She filled out the necessary forms and was handed the keys to the waiting car.

She moved the vehicle, a shiny red subcompact, quietly and efficiently, heading cross town to the East River Drive and to the Connecticut Turnpike.

What a perfectly divine time for a weekend in the country, she thought. The weather was crisp and beautiful, sunshine dappling the remaining leaves into mosaics along the highway. Normally Amanda loved listening to music as she drove. But today her mind was so busy with her thoughts that she never noticed she hadn't turned on the radio.

There was very little traffic and it seemed to her no time at all until she reached Connecticut. Autumn had come early to southern New England, and the trees were already bare. What had been lush stretches of emerald green grass were now scrubby patches of tans and yellows. Still, there was a serenity to the landscape, even shorn of its green, the softly rolling hills and stone embankments giving an air of solidity that Amanda always felt secure in.

Her head was so full of everything that had been troubling her lately, so many stirring and conflicting thoughts about Tommy and Alan, Marshall and his needs, all of the problems at the store, that the miles flew by quickly and she almost missed her turnoff. Quickly commandeering the little car, she swerved toward the exit she had almost missed, the one that would take her from the turnpike and onto the road that led to Paolo Aldobrandini's house.

The views were prettier here on the less frequently traveled country road. It would be fun to bring Tommy up here with her as she had in previous years, she thought, when the weather turned warm and he could romp in the sunny outdoors, enjoying the pool of Paolo's house and the ponies that a neighbor kept stabled at a nearby estate. She felt a small pang, missing him already. *That's dumb,* she thought, smiling to herself; she had kissed him and left him waiting for the school bus only a few hours earlier that morning. Under the terms of their divorce agreement, his father, Alan, had Tommy every other weekend. It was a pattern she had lived with for almost two years now. Yet she had that undeniable sense of loss when Tommy was with Alan.

You're being silly, she told herself. This weekend with friends, in the quiet, uninterrupted country hours, was exactly what she needed—to be away from the hectic holiday madness that turned Pembroke's from a usually dignified old dowager of a store into a frantic hurdy-gurdy. A small line formed unconsciously between her eyebrows. Marshall Strang, her fiancé, would be among Paolo's other houseguests this weekend. Dear Marshall, so kind and attentive, she thought. She wondered why she felt a slight annoyance at the thought of spending the weekend in his company.

Any woman in her right mind would welcome the attention of Marshall Strang. He was attractive and distinguished, the president of a major Fifth Avenue store. He had the kind of quiet command that bespoke old money and long-standing traditions. He was quietly effective, so different from Alan, her ex-husband. That was one of the reasons she had been so attracted to Marshall at the beginning. Now, she was forced to admit, she was finding him ever so slightly boring.

It could be that was a factor in the composition of good men. Maybe the exciting, dashing ones were bad for a woman. *At least this woman,* she thought grimly, tightening her grip on the wheel as the car topped a small hill and began its descent. She steeled herself hard against the back of the seat as the car suddenly gained momentum. She pushed on the brake, panicking when it didn't respond to her frantic pumping motions. She screamed as the old stones of an embankment wall loomed abnormally large in front of her. Over the sound of her own voice she could hear the loud impact of the car crashing into the wall and the sickening noise of screeching, crumpling metal.

She was thrust forward, seeing only a blaze of silver hurtling past the windshield. She went forward, her head falling on the steering wheel. Her cheek lay against it, as if it were a pillow.

Amanda felt herself being lifted out of the car. Pain was shooting through her head, and she could feel the softer hurt of bruises on her face. Her body felt limp and lifeless. She knew she was being carried from the car, but she was too numb to know or care whose arms were holding her.

When she opened her eyes, she was in a totally strange car, lying back on the front seat, which was covered in such a meltingly soft fabric that she was almost unconsciously aware of it in spite of her dazed mind and aching body.

She turned her head slowly toward the driver's seat, grimacing with clenched teeth at the wrenching pain she felt when she moved her neck.

A man sat there, a blond and total stranger, looking at her closely, his deep blue eyes filled with concern as he scanned her bruised features.

Amanda found her voice. "Who are you?" she asked. "What have you done to my car? Couldn't you see where you were going? You—you might have killed me!" Her voice rose shrilly as realization of the accident broke over her. She felt terribly confused. She had never had the slightest accident before; now it felt as though her whole well-ordered world had fallen down.

"Calm down," he said in a voice that was pure and quiet New England. "You've had a nasty shock and so has your car, but I think mine has suffered a lot more damage than either of you."

Amanda was livid. "That wasn't my fault!" she protested hotly. Her head was starting to pound. "As far as I can see, you deliberately ran into me! There will be all sorts of problems and red tape with that car. It's rented—"

"That's a relief," he interrupted. "I couldn't

imagine that your taste ran to red Pintos." He smiled at her.

Amanda felt her temper soar, but she tried to keep it in check. "It's a valuable piece of equipment, and the company is certainly going to want a good explanation of what's happened to it." She glared at him for a moment, then lowered her eyes. Looking at him only added to her confusion. The concern he had shown only moments before seemed to her to have swiftly turned to amusement instead.

"I'm relieved that you're not badly hurt," he said, again smiling. "Otherwise, you wouldn't be doing all this complaining." He turned the ignition key gently and tested the motor. His carefulness was soon rewarded by the low purring of the still-functioning motor. "That's good," he said, and his relief was obvious to Amanda. "I was afraid this poor baby wasn't going to turn itself over. Good girl."

Her ears perked up at the words. "Me, or your stupid car?" she asked before she could stop herself.

Her outburst was rewarded with a chuckle from him. "I guess whoever taught you that a Jaguar is a stupid car also taught you how to drive," he said.

"There's nothing wrong with my driving!" Amanda contested hotly, "and I don't care what kind of car this is, you deliberately ran it into me and smashed my car into that wall!"

"Yes, I did drive into you." She was surprised to hear him agree. "I had just turned in behind you going over the hill and saw you going out of control. I swerved ahead to stop you and keep you from smashing head-on into that embankment."

"That's your version of it." Amanda was unconvinced. The pains in her legs and torso were getting worse, now that some of her initial numbness had subsided. She glanced at the landscape quickly going by. "And where are you taking me?" she demanded, realizing that they had been moving all the time they were arguing.

"To the closest hospital," he said. "We should be there in another couple of minutes. As soon as I know you're all right I'll take you to wherever you were going. Then when I bring this wounded hulk to my garage, I'll have them pick up the Pinto."

"That is very kind of you," she said, "but I really don't need any favors. I'm quite capable of—"

"Walking the next several miles to the emergency room?" he finished the sentence for her, grinning.

Amanda looked straight ahead and tried to keep her voice as even as her gaze. There was something infuriating about him. His eyes had been sparkling with amusement ever since she had started yelling at him, and his strong square jaw had not hardened into that attitude of anger that she knew her own had assumed. His whole lean body seemed totally at ease. His touch on the car was featherlight, yet everything he touched responded immediately to him as if he controlled its inner workings with the surest command. Damaged as the car was, and Amanda could plainly see the totally crumpled fender in front of her, it moved under him with a grace and precision she had never before associated with an automobile.

She wondered who he was, curious in spite of herself, wondering in spite of the anger she still felt.

They drove on in silence, both staring at the road in front of them. Amanda felt her hostility slipping away. The accident had happened for reasons she could not understand, and her aches added to her confusion. And she could not deny, even to herself, that there was something intriguing about him. The easy assuredness, the well-bred good looks, the sleek and expensive car—these were not the properties of a back-roads country bumpkin. So many wealthy New York people, like her friend Paolo, kept weekend and summer houses here that her rescuer could be anybody, but she couldn't give him the satisfaction of knowing she was the least bit curious about him.

"You mentioned your garage," she said lightly, daring another glance at him. "Are you by any chance a mechanic?"

He laughed. "You might say that," he said, and she knew immediately that he was no such thing.

"Well, you mentioned a garage and you certainly know how to get this thing moving," she gestured lightly with her hand, stopping in midair as pain shot from her shoulder to her fingers.

"Did that hurt?" he asked, his voice all concern again, even though his eyes never left the road. "Don't worry," he went on without waiting for her answer, "it's only a very short way from here."

"Thank goodness," Amanda said, rubbing her arm and lapsing into silence again.

"You know, you really should have more respect for this vehicle," he said. "Aside from the fact of its having rescued you, it's scarcely a 'thing.' As a matter of fact, it's quite unique in the world. There are hundreds of people who would gladly change places with you if they could."

"I can scarcely believe that," Amanda grumbled, trying to shift her weight from one hip to the other as the pain in her side continued. "Unless it was someone terminal." She tried to smile.

"Hold on," he said as he brought the car easily from the straightaway into the curved driveway of the hospital entrance. "I'll pull right up to the emergency room. You won't have far to walk."

"I can manage just fine," Amanda said, reaching for the door handle to let herself out.

"Now just sit still like a good girl," he commanded, opening his own door and getting out. "You're not going to be able to manage that."

Amanda sank back into the velvety gray seat, angry at herself for needing his help. As he stooped and opened the door he tenderly put his hand under her elbows and drew her out of the badly damaged vehicle. Amanda stood up, not caring to have his arm around her, helping her, but too worn out to argue about it or shrug it off. She glanced momentarily at the crippled car poised at the curb. Only now, from outside, could she see how extensive the damage was.

It bore mute witness to what he had said. The damage was all along the passenger side of the car, where he had deliberately swerved it to stop her own lurching vehicle. That the motor was still functioning was due to both his skill in maneuvering the Jaguar and the sturdiness of the sleek silver car's construction, a strength belied by the delicately sculptural sweep of its body.

Amanda saw everything around her with a keen designer's eye. Pained as she was and loath to admit it, the wrecked car was, or had been, something of real beauty, and she felt a sudden melting of her anger toward its owner, who had knowingly damaged this precious possession in order to help her.

She leaned gratefully on his arm and almost smiled at him as she gave the admitting nurse her name and other data. A young, white-coated resident physician led her into an examining room before she had a chance to turn to her rescuer to thank him and tell him it wasn't necessary for him to wait.

"Please," she said to the young doctor as she hobbled down the corridor after him, suddenly feeling very bruised and tired, "couldn't I please call my friends to let them know where I am?"

"Just give the information to the nurse," he replied as he motioned her onto the examining table. "She can make the call for you."

"Tell them it's nothing serious and not to worry," Amanda said to the starched and efficient young nurse, who wrote down Paolo's phone number.

"Ouch!" she said sharply, turning toward the doctor who was probing and feeling her arm.

"Disrobe and put this on," he said, reaching out for a dull green hospital smock. He turned away discreetly, studying her admissions form on his clipboard.

Amanda found reaching back for the zipper of her dress, and struggling to get out of it, a difficulty she had never encountered before. Her bones were aching throughout her body. She wondered suddenly if she had been badly hurt in that stupid accident after all, although her rescuer hadn't thought so. Still, he had brought her to the hospital. She hadn't been in a hospital since Tommy had been born. Tommy! She thought suddenly. What if she were really hurt and couldn't get back to the city on time? She'd have to call her mother and make some kind of arrangement, but where was Sylvia this weekend? Amanda couldn't remember. Her thoughts were scattered all at once.

She felt the doctor's fingers gingerly touching her face, his gentle probing almost a caress. She thought suddenly of the man who had brought her there and blushed angrily. There was no reason to be thinking of him, no reason at all. Unless she was really in this mess because of him. Maybe he had invented his version of what had caused the accident to cover up his own mistake. That seemed likely. His account of rescuing her from additional injury could have been pure fabrication. Certainly his claiming that his car was totally unique sounded like fancy, for all that it was a Jaguar and Amanda knew that they were less than commonplace, especially in the countryside.

"I'd like to take some X rays," the doctor's voice broke into her thoughts.

"Why?" Amanda asked, suddenly fearful again. The cold, antiseptic atmosphere of the white-and-steel hospital room frightened her.

"Just as a precaution, Mrs. Parrish," the doctor assured her. "You have been pretty badly shaken up and you're going to be feeling those bruises for a few days. I don't think you've injured anything seriously, but in cases like this we want to be very cautious."

Amanda started to protest, but she bit her lip and stopped herself. If nothing was serious, it was silly of her to make a fuss. What the doctor was saying made simple good sense. She slipped off the table meekly and stood against the wall-mounted X-ray machine as the nurse instructed. In a few minutes it was all over, and she was told she could get back into her clothes, sign a release, and be free to go.

Amanda thanked them both, dressed hurriedly, as best she could, and went back through the corridor to the waiting room.

"Oh, I'm so glad you're here!" she cried.

Two men jumped up, almost hitting each other. They exchanged puzzled glances.

Marshall Strang kept his gaze on the handsome blond man, obviously several years his junior. He couldn't imagine why this total stranger thought Amanda was addressing herself to him.

Amanda put her hand on the sleeve of Marshall's dark cashmere coat. "This gentleman," she hesitated only slightly over the word, "brought me here. Although I'm still not quite sure whether to thank you or blame you, Mr.–"

She hesitated more fully this time, as she realized she didn't know his name.

"McKay," he replied, "Josh–Joshua–McKay."

They held their glances for a moment until Marshall interrupted. "Amanda, are you all right?" he demanded. "What in the world happened?"

"I'm not quite sure." Amanda couldn't quite help laughing slightly. "It seems there are two versions to choose from."

Josh McKay grinned. "Not really," he said, turning slightly to Marshall. "The lady's car went out of control. Luckily I was behind her and was able to stop it before it went into an embankment."

"I see," said Marshall slowly, although he wasn't quite sure he did.

"I'm not really sure that my car was out of control," Amanda said evenly. "I'm a pretty good driver, and nothing like that has ever happened to me before. Besides, the car was supposed to have been thoroughly checked before I took it out."

"We were just coming down a hill," Josh explained, as though he were addressing a classroom of students. "Had you been the good driver you say you are, and had your vehicle been functioning properly, you would have slowed down on level road and not accelerated off the shoulder." The words were simple, but spoken with a tone of such authority that Amanda felt defensive.

"How can you be so sure?" she argued. "You weren't inside my car to know what was happening."

Josh smiled. "I've been inside enough cars to be able to tell," he said in the same quiet but firm voice.

He's probably just some car mechanic, Amanda decided furiously, *and trying to show off.* She glared at him, wanting to end it all there, but a nagging reminder told her that was impossible. There was all the business about getting the car towed that he had promised to see to, but there would still be the red tape of straightening it out with the rental agency. She was going to have to put up with his insolence for at least a while longer.

"If she was really going so fast, how were you able to catch up and stop her so quickly?" Marshall asked.

Amanda squeezed the arm she was still leaning on, wishing she could hug him for the nice supportive question.

"I was road testing a prototype of a new Jaguar," Josh said. "It wasn't very difficult to outrun, outmaneuver, and outthink that little red rented Pinto."

"I see," Marshall said, this time without any hesitancy. He extended his hand. "I want to thank you very much, Mr. McKay, for your quick action—and your car's. Thank you for bringing Mrs. Parrish here."

He turned toward the door, leading Amanda along with him. He held the door open for her, and led her the few steps to a long black limousine that took up most of the curbside. The black-suited chauffeur jumped out to open the door, and Marshall handed Amanda into the comforting recesses of its wide back seat. The chauffeur closed the door smartly after them and jumped back into his own seat, speeding them swiftly away, in the now dark evening. None of them looked back to the hospital entrance, where Joshua David McKay stood thoughtfully watching them through the large glass door.

Chapter 2

After the antiseptic atmosphere of the hospital and the quiet drive in the dark countryside, it seemed to Amanda that Paolo's small house was exploding with light and warmth and noise. The chattering, laughing conversation of houseguests modulated into murmuring tones of concern for her and curiosity about the accident. Amanda found herself drawn into her usual circle. Answering their questions and allaying their fears made the whole strange afternoon seem nothing more than a new anecdote. She tried to play down the incident, brushing aside any intimations of curiosity about her rescuer.

It wasn't until later, when she was alone in the flowered chintz of the main guest room, that she found herself thinking about the man she had met so unexpectedly. Using her bumps and bruises as excuse for an early bedtime, she had begged the others to have dinner without her. She had undressed and soaked in a hot, hot tub, letting the warmth of the water soothe her aching body. She had dried herself in the moist air of the bathroom, its cheerful fittings matching those of the bedroom to which it belonged. Amanda slipped into a long white cotton nightgown, its eyelet lace trimmings very much at home in the old-fashioned decor of the room. She was about to turn out the bedside lamp when she heard a light tapping at the door. Drawing the coverlet up to her chin for modesty, she called out, "Come in."

It was Paolo with a tray.

"Oh, darling, you shouldn't have," Amanda said. "What is all that?"

"Just what you need to sleep," Paolo smiled. He was tall and lean, dark-haired, and with the air and manner that comes from not generations but centuries of noble breeding. His taste, his clothes, everything about him was impeccable and understated. He had a natural and undeniable authority that let him turn his back on his titles and lands and focus his attention instead on the world of fashion, where he set the style for women who could afford his clothes and advice. He had been surrounded by hordes of servants all his life, yet here he was, Amanda marveled, bringing her a bedtime tray.

"It's just what the doctor ordered," Paolo said as she studied him. He set the delicate white wicker tray on its legs, straddling her lap. A tantalizing but unfamiliar aroma came from the white porcelain teapot as Paolo poured a steamy brew into two tiny matching porcelain cups.

"My doctor didn't order anything," Amanda said, smiling gently, as if admonishing him for bothering.

"The doctor in this case," Paolo declared in his liltingly accented English, "is my Italian grandmother who prescribed exactly this for your condition."

"As if you had a grandmother who wasn't Italian," Amanda reminded him, "But what is it? It smells absolutely dreamy."

"It's an herbal tea," Paolo explained. "Comfrey, hyssop, chamomile. The first two are to ease your aching bones, the chamomile will help you get to sleep."

"You shouldn't be waiting on me like this," Amanda demurred.

"Would you rather have had Laura bring it?" he asked mischievously. "They're all dying to know about your charming rescuer on the white horse and you know I'll be much more subtle than she ever would."

They both laughed. "It wasn't a white horse, it was a silver Jaguar," Amanda reminded him. "Not quite that romantic, I'm afraid."

"But lots more expensive and therefore just as charming," Paolo insisted. "Was he very good-looking?"

"How do you know he was good-looking at all?" Amanda parried.

"Simple. By the look on Marshall's face," Paolo laughed. "You know we all love a good bit of gossip, and except for your bruises, this is the most intriguing thing to happen in this dull countryside in quite a long time." He touched the bandage at Amanda's cheekbone, and she winced involuntarily.

"See, it does hurt, my darling," Paolo said soothingly. "So you must drink some of Grandmama's tea."

Amanda smiled and sipped slowly. The warmth of the tea spread quickly through her, and Italian grandmother's efficacy or no, it did feel good.

Paolo stared at her carefully. "I wish I had not invited the others, *cara,*" he said softly. "I do not think you are in the mood for all the busyness of this weekend."

"Oh, no," Amanda hastened to reassure him. "I'm sure that all I need is a good night's sleep. I'll be alive and well in the morning."

"Well, do not look *so* eager," Paolo warned playfully. "Laura is not going to give up too easily. I know she has a thousand questions to ask you."

Amanda laughed. "Really," she said. "There's nothing to tell. It was just an unfortunate accident, and I'm lucky that I wasn't really hurt. A few days, and the whole incident will be completely forgotten."

Paolo rose from the floral-padded wicker armchair he was sitting in. "Well, get your good night's sleep, and I'll try to keep Laura from pouncing on you." He touched his lips lightly, blowing her a good-night kiss.

Amanda snuggled under the welcoming blankets. She switched off the light, but didn't fall asleep immediately as she had been so sure she would. She had been grateful to escape to this quiet room, away from the questions and laughter of the other weekenders. Laura Summers was a very social creature, the on-again, off-again wife of the international playboy Diego del Rayamonte. Diego was a constant topic of Laura's conversation; indeed, it seemed as though her whole existence pivoted around him. But except for occasional excited declarations from Laura that he was in town, or a blurry candid on the social pages of *Vogue* or *Town and Country,* nobody Amanda knew had ever really seen Diego. Still, Laura was amusing and a well-meaning friend, although she had an insatiable need for gossip.

Besides Marshall, Paolo's other weekend guest was Colby Brookes, a man whose company Amanda usually enjoyed. He had been a bit of a matinee idol on Broadway decades before and had had a less successful fling as a second leading man in Hollywood. Although he had never quite become a household name, he had been privy to the comings and goings of all the legendary stars and was the bearer of all sorts of information about the great studios in their heyday. It was the rare dinner party that wasn't ignited by the still-handsome Colby's recounting the escapades of the old Hollywood greats. He was so distinguished in looks and manner that, telling the raciest stories as he did, in a quiet, low-key way, the dowdiest dowager could not have taken offense.

Amanda reflected on the concern she had read on Marshall's face when he had picked her up at the hospital and several times again at the house when she had caught him looking at her. She had been wearing his ring, a large, flawless diamond, for several months now. He had been her friend and escort almost from the time of her divorce from Alan. They had not made definite marriage plans, even after their engagement, and Amanda was grateful for that. Her future with Marshall wasn't a subject she was able to think about. Not yet.

The next morning it wasn't Laura but Marshall who drew Amanda aside. Her night's sleep had not been quite the cure-all she had bravely foretold, but she had forced herself to come down to midmorning brunch with the others. She felt as though she could draw a map showing every bump and bruise on her body. It wasn't unbearably painful, but she felt the aches everywhere and, to her shock, found herself hobbling hesitantly down the stairs.

When Paolo searched a narrow hall closet and drew out a stout wooden walking stick, the others protested he was going too far, but Amanda grasped it and found it was a help.

"Wherever did you get that?" Laura asked. "It's the most nineteenth-century-looking thing I've ever seen in my life."

Paolo, whose patrician tastes ran more to classical antiquities and mementos of Renaissance art, agreed. "Actually," he exclaimed, "it's blackthorn. English gentlemen always kept them at their country houses. See how the top has been shaped, almost like a knob, from the pressure of hands resting on it?"

"It's really quite a good-looking example," Marshall said. "I remember my grandfather having one quite like it. May I ask where you got it?"

As Paolo told them about the country auction where he frequently picked up such oddities for the house, Amanda found herself studying the group of friends. Something she hadn't realized before struck her quite forcibly now. Paolo was ageless in the continental way that kept him from being identifiable as belonging to any particular generation. Colby Brookes had been at the peak of his success back in the 1940s, Laura Summers, or del Rayamonte as she seemed to be again, at least for this season, was an international jetsetter who frequently retreated for weeks at a time into the health spas and rejuvenation clinics of three continents, keeping herself at other times in the hands of the most practiced and expensive facialists, masseuses, and cosmetic practitioners. Yet behind all the practice and artifice there was no denying her age.

And Marshall, Amanda realized with sudden awareness, when he gently turned aside from the others to talk to her privately, had been at the helm of his family's stores for at least twenty years and showed it.

She was by far the youngest person in the house. She had never noticed that. It was true among her whole circle of friends. She had never even thought of it before. It was only now that something was stirring inside her, bringing it all home.

Marshall was talking to her in a low voice, but all of Amanda's perceptions were held by the sudden flash she had of the lean, muscled body she had been sitting next to, and the clear blue eyes and firm square jaw when he had turned to her.

She turned back to Marshall as if waking up suddenly from a dream. "I'm sorry," she murmured, "I–I didn't hear you, dear, what were you saying?"

His voice was gentle. "I just wanted to know if you felt up to taking a few turns outside. The temperature isn't too bad and the sun is nice and bright." There was a veil of hesitancy in his eyes, but the sudden rush of eagerness in his voice made up for it. "I'll go upstairs for your coat and things. I don't want you up and down the stairs unnecessarily, but a little walk might do you good."

Her face was bright with gratitude as she smiled up at him, accepting. It would do some good to be in the fresh air, she thought as she watched him go up the narrow staircase. The thoughts that had been rushing through her mind had made her feel suddenly closed in; the house, usually so charming and cozy with its provincial country decor, now seemed positively claustrophobic. She welcomed the idea of sunshine. When he came back and helped her with her coat, it took a little doing to get her arms inside, and Paolo and Laura insisted on helping to bundle her up with hat, scarf, and gloves against the cold.

Paolo lifted the blackthorn stick, handing it to her as if it were a scepter. Amanda took it happily and walked slowly out of the bright red front door that Marshall opened for her.

The noonday air felt good as they walked slowly around the flagstone path that circled the house. Down the back lawn, sloping toward a running stream, there was a small lattice-roofed gazebo. In summertime, when the now tarp-covered pool was busy with swimmers and sunbathers, it was sometimes used for lunch or tea. Now the gazebo stood quietly deserted, at one with the somber landscape. The sun shining through the latticework made a linear pattern on its floorboards and seats.

"Do you think you'll feel too cold sitting out here for a while?" Marshall asked tenderly.

"No," Amanda answered, "it looks perfectly fine. The sun seems strong enough to make it warm."

Marshall helped her up the two small steps, and they rested in the shelter of the weather-beaten wood. Amanda sat back with a sigh. The walk, short though it was, had taken some of her strength. She sat quietly, breathing deeply.

"I hope this isn't going to be uncomfortable," Marshall fretted. "I hope it's not too cool, but it was the only place I could think of to get you alone."

Amanda looked at him questioningly.

He plunged right in as though the tide of emotion that had built inside him was too powerful to be contained. "When the call came from the hospital last night, I was beside myself," he confessed. "I was almost mad with not knowing how badly you had been hurt. I'm sorry"—and his tone dropped to one almost of apology—"that it took something like an accident to make me open my eyes and to realize how I feel about you, Amanda."

"Marshall," she murmured his name, not in affirmation or surprise but merely to confirm that she was there, that she heard him. She also—she couldn't help thinking and had to bite her lip to keep from smiling—had to give him at least a microsecond to catch his breath. Marshall had never sounded so emotional, so charged and breathless, so out of keeping with his usual self.

"I think I've always been in love with you, Amanda," he went on, his voice stronger and surer now. "Only now it's been driven home to me with such force that I cannot deny it. I can't express the way I felt when you came into the waiting room last night. I was filled with gratitude that you were all right, and yet angered and alarmed at the sight of your bruises." He lifted his hand awkwardly to the bandaged cheekbone and, barely touching her, quickly dropped it. "I love you, Amanda dear, and I want to marry you."

"Marshall, I don't know what to say." It was true she had known for some time now that this moment would come, but now that it was here she was totally unprepared to deal with it. Gone were all thoughts of the cold and the aches in her bones. Clearly she had to tell him, but above all, she had to not hurt him, this dear man who was so concerned and caring. "I'm just not ready to make that commitment," she said, her eyes searching the dappled pattern of the wooden floor. "You're very dear to me, but I must have at least a little time. There are so many questions."

"It's been two years, Amanda," he reminded her gently.

"Yes, I know," she said, but it was only two minutes since he had proposed. All the time in the world since her divorce and until that moment didn't count at all. It was new time she needed, Amanda thought desperately. New time to think out all of the details and complications that Marshall was presenting to her. All the things she hadn't wanted to think about.

As soon as these thoughts formed she knew, and realized it sadly, that she wasn't enough in love with Marshall Strang. If she were, she wouldn't be looking for excuses now. She would be laughing and hugging him, throwing herself in his arms, happy and lit from within.

Again a strange and unexpected image pierced her thoughts. Blue eyes, steely blue, but bright with something that she couldn't yet identify, only recognize. She brushed the image from her mind. All of this had nothing to do with him, she insisted to herself.

It was her independence that was at stake here, Amanda thought, two solid years of being on her own, making all of her own decisions, being scheduled only by Tommy's needs and the demands of her job. Within those parameters she had found a kind of contentment, a satisfaction with life that she felt was healthy and productive. She had her son, she had her work. There was a busy and entertaining social life as well. She hadn't felt the need for anything else, certainly not the need to have a whole new set of imperatives put to her. Clearly she needed time to think.

She put her hand on his arm and looked up gratefully, trying to show him how pleased she was at his asking for her, and trying at the same time to read his thoughts. The most important thing, she reminded herself again, was that Marshall was not to be hurt. However she framed her answer to him, that was the most important point.

"Please, can we go inside now?" Amanda begged. "It is getting rather cold, and you'll have to admit that you've given me a great deal to think about." She rewarded his acquiescence with the brightest smile she could muster, and he helped her as they walked slowly back around to the front of the house.

Once inside, Amanda pleaded tiredness as her excuse to flee once more to the refuge of the flowered bedroom.

Marshall Strang was distinguished, successful, and

attractive, she admitted to herself, resting on the bed. He would make an excellent husband and could be a good father for Tommy. But what about her work? It was impossible to imagine the wife of Marshall Strang going to a job every day.

Her experience with marriage had not been so terrible. True, she and Alan had ended in divorce, but many of their years together had been happy ones. The marriage had brought Tommy, whom they both adored, and it had enabled Amanda to start the work she was so happy in and devoted to. And yet ultimately the marriage had not been enough, had never been enough. The amount of time that Alan had devoted to his businesses made real companionship impossible. Even the most glorious vacations, the farthest destinations, the most sparkling beaches and brilliant landscapes, found him with a telephone at his elbow. It had become part of him, she had argued bitterly, an extension of his arm and, more importantly, his mind. No matter how hard she tried, Alan's head was always someplace else, buying up or selling off, but always, always on business.

It had undermined their relationship to the point where she felt she'd be better off on her own. At least if she accepted a dinner invitation or bought benefit tickets, she could be sure of showing up. With Alan, that had been impossible. Their marriage had been pockmarked by the disappointments and broken dates that were usually the hallmark of a crumbling courtship. Marriage, Amanda had felt stubbornly, should put an end to all of that. Marriage was certainty and security and always knowing where you were. With Alan all that was simply nonexistent.

She had been struggling with the idea of separation for a long time before she actually asked for the divorce. She had great qualms about managing on her own and providing for Tommy. Marriage to Alan wasn't without its benefits. She was afraid she had gotten too used to the conveniences of the bills always being paid, a car always at her disposal, charge accounts in all the stores, a magnificent apartment in the city and a beautiful old rambling house in the country, and all the best in schools and help and everything else for Tommy.

It had been a great relief to find Alan as magnanimous in divorce as he had been in marriage. He had kept the country house but he had readily agreed to continue to pay all of Tommy's expenses and to sign over the apartment to Amanda so that she and the boy could continue living there. He wanted as little disruption in his young son's life as possible, and he never stinted in providing for him. For that, Amanda was everlastingly grateful to him, but now, with two years of being on her own behind her, she had to admit that she hadn't really had much of a struggle. Alan's financial support eliminated most of the rough spots she had anticipated, and her own growing success made everything else she wanted for Tommy and herself easily obtainable.

Along with her growing life of independence came her deepening commitment to her work. She had always been fascinated by jewelry, as much from an aesthetic point of view as from an inquisitive one. She didn't lust after expensive baubles as objects to own; rather, she experienced and appreciated the brilliance of gems in and of themselves. The subtle properties of the precious metals, gold and platinum and even silver, fascinated her. She loved the way gold could be warm and cool at the same time, the way the play of lights on carved and worked silver could make it at once subtle and brilliant.

She had taken courses in gemology in the Museum of Natural History, more to take up some of the time that Alan was away from her than with any definite goal in mind. But as her knowledge increased, so did her appreciation, and so did the creative sparks that had long lain dormant but now came bursting to the surface.

In class or at home she found herself constantly sketching: a ring, a brooch, and sometimes the most elaborate settings for necklaces of diamonds and emeralds, which she knew would cost a king's ransom to create.

She had laughed a little at herself, but she couldn't stop. The next step had been to take jewelry-making classes. There what had been an innocent pastime burst full-blown into a talent that her teachers marveled at and told her must be exploited. "You only need to learn all the technical stuff," her last teacher had said, "and if you're not going to be crafting the pieces yourself, you'll only need to know what can and can't be done. There'll be somebody else to do the actual work."

Amanda had been thrilled but couldn't quite believe it. When she told Alan what her teacher had said, for once he showed some interest in what she was doing, and asked to see her sketches. Amanda blushed but showed them to him. He was duly impressed, impressed enough to insist that he show her work to people who could evaluate it.

The rest had been really like a dream. Alan, with his first-rate contacts, had shown her work to Willis Haviland, the crusty tastemaker and guiding spirit of Pembroke's. Willis had insisted on meeting her.

Although the occasion was set up more as a social meeting than a business one, Amanda had been unaccountably nervous. She had sat, hands folded quietly, and answered Willis's probing questions. She had mentally thanked her instructors, grateful for having learned the answers to the technical questions that Willis Haviland was putting to her. He seemed equally satisfied and offered her not a job but a commission. He asked her to undertake designing a piece for him, and gave her the option of executing it herself or entrusting it to his own incomparable workrooms.

Amanda, if she knew anything, knew that the training of the master jeweler took many years. She had only the very beginnings of that training. What she did have was the taste and sense of style that were the hallmarks of a designer. In a moment she answered that she would prefer only to design the piece. Willis Haviland nodded sagely. She had made the right decision.

After the piece—a gold button, suitable for men or women, that Willis used as an award to key employees of Pembroke's—had been executed, they sat down, Haviland, Alan, and Amanda, to discuss terms.

The two men did most of the talking, Amanda confident that Alan would handle her affairs in their best interests. The outcome was a contract with Pembroke's under which she would design a line of jewelry exclusively for the store, to be executed by Pembroke jewelers but to be identified with her name. A name that, Willis Haviland assured her, would be quickly known to the jewelry-buying and fashion-conscious public, as he intended to promote this new line with advertising and publicity and a counter of her own on Pembroke's dazzling main floor.

That had been three years ago, one year before the divorce and two since. Although she wasn't a household word like Halston, or Cardin, Amanda Parrish was a name that appeared with growing frequency in the Pembroke advertisements, the editorial pages of *Vogue, Harper's Bazaar,* and *Town and Country,* and the gossip and news columns of *Women's Wear Daily* and *W.*

Thinking about it all now, Amanda wondered if Alan, with all his astuteness, hadn't seen both her growing success and the eroding of their marriage and had helped set in motion all these forces that had enabled her to be happy and independent without him.

She smiled. He was just shrewd enough to have done that, and concerned enough about her, as well as Tommy, to have helped her along. Surely otherwise no one of her then amateur status could have signed so advantageous a contract as she had with as important an institution as Pembroke's.

Amanda thought of Tommy. At six he had many of the traits of both his parents, plus the advantages of being brought up in a smoothly run household that never knew financial problems. He was old enough now to realize what it meant that Mommy and Daddy didn't live together. He had seen little enough of Alan during his baby years, and the divorce meant that he was with his father every other weekend and some holidays. Amanda knew that the time that Alan spent with Tommy was truly spent with him, and she was grateful for that. Usually, she knew, he took the boy to the country house, a place Tommy loved no matter what season of the year it was. Somehow Alan had managed to find more time for Tommy since the divorce than he ever had during the marriage. Of course, there was no way of Amanda's knowing how often the phone rang or how long the business conversations ran. Still, Tommy always seemed pleased after a visit with his father, and Amanda had to admit that Alan was very precise in taking Tommy for every bit of visitation time the agreement entitled him to.

Could it be possible, she wondered, that divorce had made Alan a better parent than marriage had? Sometimes she had to admit that she felt it was quite true of herself. Knowing that Tommy didn't have his father close by made her extra careful about the amount of attention and time she gave him. It was probably a question of compensating, and if she was doing it, there was no reason Alan couldn't be also. The important thing was that Tommy suffer as little as possible from the incompatibility of his parents.

Amanda wished that there was a way to make the weekend fly. Thinking about her son always made her lonesome for him, even when they had only been separated for a day or two. She had to admit to herself that there were reasons other than Tommy that made her wish that the weekend she had begun so eagerly were now over. It wouldn't be fair to keep Marshall dangling too long, yet she knew she couldn't give him the answer he wanted.

All of these thoughts were floating and mingling in her mind as she felt herself drifting off to sleep. A daytime nap was unheard of for Amanda, but she didn't fight the feeling this time. The circumstances were unusual, she convinced herself. The accident alone was justification for her needing more rest and, she had to admit, sleeping most of it away was one way of making the weekend go quickly.

When she woke, it was totally dark. The small bedside clock told her that it was nearly eight. She couldn't believe that she had slept so long, and she was grateful that the others hadn't disturbed her for dinner.

She yawned and stretched and smiled to see that moving her body caused her much less aching than it had that morning. She realized with a giggle that she was hungry after all. By now, she thought, all of the others had probably finished and were having drinks around the old stone fireplace in the living room. She threw off her bedclothes, splashed water on her face, touching it only here and there with makeup, and pulled on a pair of corduroy jeans and a matching sweater. Combing her hair, she gave herself a deep appraising look in the bathroom mirror. She felt almost her old self again, and she looked it too, except for the bandage on her cheek.

Amanda touched the gauze hesitantly and then picked at the tape until she had taken it off. The bruise was dark, with a bright red glow around it. She discarded the old frayed bandage and replaced it with one of the extras the doctor had given her. She went downstairs to join the others.

"Welcome back, darling!" Laura called in greeting as Amanda appeared on the stairs. "We had almost given up on seeing you again today."

Colby sprang up to take Amanda's arm as she reached the final steps. He moved so quickly he was at her side before Marshall could get there.

Amanda murmured her thanks and sat down on a small, well-upholstered love seat. "I feel so much better," she declared. "Almost as if I've been on vacation."

"Sleep is always a great restorative," Paolo said, "the best medicine."

"That's what Diego always says," Laura added. "He says it's why movie stars never get up before noon."

"How would he know?" Colby asked jokingly. "I don't think he ever gets up before three himself."

"Diego has got rather a reputation for spending a lot of time in bed," Laura admitted wryly. "Although I can't really say how much of it he spends in sleeping."

"Catherine the Great of Russia stayed in bed all the time," Paolo said. "My grandmother said she held court there. She would even interview her ministers and foreign ambassadors from her bed while she had them served tea."

"How did your grandmother know that?" Laura asked. "Was she there?"

"Of course not, darling," Paolo replied. "That was long before her time. She used to tell us about it, because she thought it was totally decadent."

"Your grandmother sounds like a very moral woman," Colby said. "Had she ever been connected with any court?"

Paolo replied in great detail, delineating the royal and noble houses of Italy with much embellishment and risqué anecdotes and scandal.

Amanda listened, mildly amused, unable to help noticing that Marshall was even more withdrawn from the general conversation than she was. A great guilty feeling settled on her. She would have to tell him her decision, and tell him soon.

Games and conversation continued far into the night. Amanda was grateful, not feeling the least bit sleepy after her long nap. She faced Marshall across a backgammon board, but they both concentrated on the game, saying little.

At last everybody started drifting up to their bedrooms, agreeing to head back to the city after midmorning Sunday brunch. It was a busy time of the year for those with business concerns, and socially hectic for all of them. Monday mornings signaled the start of a brand new week and made quiet Sunday evenings and early nights an imperative.

They got into the city-bound cars in the early afternoon coldness, Amanda going back alone with Marshall in his car.

The glass partition that kept the chauffeur from hearing their conversation was in place. Amanda leaned back against the soft upholstery and turned her face slightly toward Marshall.

Amanda felt herself melting toward him. He was such a good, kind person, such a dependable and good friend to have. She thought of all the evenings they had spent together. The opera and the ballet, the elegant dinner parties and the chic gallery openings. He was always wonderful to be with, an impressive arm to be on in any social situation. She frowned slightly, angry at herself. Marshall Strang was an important man, she reminded herself crossly. He was heir to a sizable fortune and a very respected person in the life of the city. It was wrong of her to be reducing him to the function of an escort, even if it was only in her own mind that she was doing it. Marshall was so much more than that, so much better and so much more substantial than the young men who did little more than make a profession of taking ladies places.

The thought of Basil Hemmings flashed into her mind, and she frowned again. Her young assistant at the store could almost be characterized that way, but in his case it was worse. Basil loved escorting the rich and fashionable women whose presence would get his name in the columns, while his real preference was for his own sex and, Amanda suspected, activities that would be startling for even the most gossipy tabloids. But Basil was something she would have to deal with on Monday; he was of no moment in the problem she had now.

"Marshall, I'm sorry." She said it quickly and simply. "The first consideration I have in the world must be to my son. Frankly, darling, I don't see how our lives would even begin to mesh properly. It wouldn't be fair to you, Marshall. You've never lived with a young child. It would be so different from what you're used to."

There was a moment of silence. When he spoke, his tone was subdued and had in it something that Amanda had never heard before.

"Don't you think I would be a good father?" he asked, his hurt almost visible.

"It's not that," Amanda rushed to answer. "It's just that it would be so different from the life-style you're used to." Her words came quickly, but she stumbled over them, handicapped both by not quite knowing how to express herself and by not wanting at all to hurt him. Yet, difficult as it was, his very question reinforced Amanda's recent feelings. There was an incompatibility here, not so much between herself and Marshall, but between the facts of her life—and his. Tommy was the most important factor, but there were others.

They rode most of the way back to the city in silence, the heavy atmosphere in the car expressing what neither of them wanted to articulate.

When they reached Amanda's apartment house, the

chauffeur brought the long black limousine to a smooth, gliding halt, then jumped out to open the door for her.

Amanda turned to Marshall. Her eyes were brimming with tears. She put her hand on his and squeezed hard. "Good-bye, Marshall, dear," she said softly. She wanted to add something about seeing or talking to him again soon, but somehow the sentiment didn't seem the right one to express at just that moment. He murmured good-bye, and Amanda got out and walked quickly inside past the doorman.

In the elevator she dabbed at her eyes with her fingers, unmindful of the black kid gloves getting all wet. She turned the key into her front door, glancing at the pretty wall clock in the foyer. She would barely have time to change and freshen herself before Tommy would be back. She didn't want him to see her all teary-eyed like this, it would be too difficult to explain.

Amanda drew off her coat and gloves and threw them on the bed. She wanted to get rid of the cheek bandage and camouflage the bruise so that Tommy wouldn't be alarmed. She felt well enough and free enough from the ache of her bruises not to tell him about the accident at all.

She scrubbed her face, wincing as she inadvertently touched the cheek bruise. She applied makeup carefully, as if she were at the beginning of the day instead of the end of it, using more foundation than usual and glad she had touch-up cream to help conceal the bruise. She looked at herself in the mirror when she finished. Her eyes were bright and her cheeks glowed with blusher. Her natural flush came to her as she realized that she looked as though she was preparing to meet a lover, not a six-year-old boy who would probably be totally oblivious to the way she looked.

She wondered if Alan would send him up alone in the elevator or come in with him. Her ex-husband was sharply observant, and he would be bound to notice the bruise even if Tommy didn't. She hoped she wouldn't have to face him.

The intercom from the doorman buzzed, and Amanda ran to the foyer to answer it. It was Tommy, being very insistent on announcing his arrival himself and telling her that he was coming up alone.

But when Amanda opened the door, there was a tall, familiar figure standing behind the little one. She knelt down to scoop Tommy in her arms. She looked up at Alan in surprise.

He grinned back rather sheepishly. "I know Tommy said he was coming up alone," he said almost apologetically. "But I haven't seen you in a little while and thought it would be all right if I just popped in to say hello."

Amanda regained her composure. "Of course it is," she said warmly, extending her hand. "Come on in and take your coats off, both of you." She closed the door behind them and followed Alan into the living room.

Alan Parrish looked around the large, beautifully furnished room that was so familiar to him. If he regretted not living there anymore, he didn't show it. His own apartment, which Amanda had never seen, was in a comparable building, just a few blocks south.

"I wasn't sure you'd be back this early," Alan said, turning from the window to face her. "I just figured I'd check and see before I brought Tommy to my place and then had to bring him out again." He smiled at her, and if he noticed her injury, he said nothing.

"I'm glad you did," Amanda said.

"I've always loved this view," he said, turning to the window again. "The expanse of the park, the buildings all lit up, the feeling of having all of New York at your feet."

"Does your apartment face the park?" Amanda asked.

"No, unfortunately," Alan replied. He seemed almost at a loss for words, which was unusual for him, and Amanda felt the weight of the whole weekend suddenly pressing in on her. She felt too weary to try to make small talk, and besides it was a school night and close to Tommy's bedtime. If this conversation with Alan became much more drawn out, she wouldn't have the time she wanted for Tommy.

"I guess I'd better be going." Alan seemed to sense her mood.

"It's almost his bedtime," Amanda said apologetically as she handed Alan his coat. "I always want to spend a little time with him when I tuck him in. Especially when I haven't seen him for a while."

"Of course." He looked at her with what Amanda thought was almost sadness in his eyes. It was not an emotion she had ever associated with him before. Alan was too solid; his grooming was always perfect, his dark hair and clean-shaven face always—she groped in her mind for the right word—always businesslike, always ready for what the situation was or might be. His looks and demeanor, except for his eyes, told nothing about him. It was those eyes, dark, large, always searching, always busy, that did the most to reveal him. Perhaps that's why she found the prospect in them so troubling now. It was so different from his usual look.

"I'll call you during the week," he said almost

brusquely as she walked him to the door. "Maybe we can plan something for Tom for the holidays."

"That would be nice," Amanda said with all the warmth she could muster. "Good-bye, Alan."

She was relieved when she closed the door behind him, glad, too, that Tommy hadn't seen anything of this rather troubling scene between his parents. Nothing had really been said or done, but there was a strange underlying tone that puzzled Amanda. She stopped for a moment on the threshhold of Tommy's bedroom, took a deep breath and composed herself, a bright smile on her face as she knelt down to help him undress.

She helped him with his bath, brought him milk and cookies, and tucked him into bed while she listened to his account of his weekend.

She bent over him to kiss him good night. He suddenly stretched out his arm and touched her cheek. "Did somebody hurt you, Mommy?" he asked.

Amanda drew back momentarily. Then she laughed and bent again to hug him close to her again. "No, darling," she said. "Mommy just got a little bruise, like you sometimes do. It's nothing." She kissed him again, smoothed the blankets around him, and snapped off the bedside light.

She left his door slightly ajar, as she did her own. Slipping into bed at long last, she tried to think ahead to all of the problems that would be waiting for her at Pembroke's in the morning. She drew her own covers around her and shivered slightly despite the warmth of the room. In her mind's eye she saw other eyes, all peering at her: Tommy's, round, dark brown, troubled at seeing her bruise; Marshall's, gray, uncomprehending, hurt and confused; Alan's strangely saddened look, so unusual for him. They all came at her, moved away, merged and floated away again, all pushed to the background of her consciousness, pierced again and again by a pair of laughing blue eyes that threatened to disturb her peace.

One way or another, Amanda thought grimly, it had been a weekend full of men, and tomorrow, tomorrow there would be another collection of them to deal with at the store.

She sat up in bed and turned the light back on. She reached for a book and tried to read. She turned to her sketchpad and tried drawing. She threw the book and pad to the floor, switched off the light, tossed and turned and tried to remember why she should forget someone named Josh McKay.

Chapter 3

Amanda waved good-bye as Tommy waited for the school bus the next morning. She began the brisk twenty-block walk downtown that formed her daily constitutional and got her to Pembroke's. The morning was cold, but in her dark mink coat and high black boots, she was dressed for it. The city was coming alive. Already Fifth Avenue was choked with cars and buses. By the time she had reached Fifty-seventh Street the combined stimulation of exercise, cold morning air, and the bustle of the city around her had her invigorated and ready to work.

Henry, Pembroke's doorman for as long as anybody cared to remember, tipped his hat and swung open the huge glass panel for her. Amanda smiled back. Henry was like a touchstone at the beginning of her workday. It was said that he had started at Pembroke's the very same day as Willis Haviland himself had first reported to work. Henry had never risen from his position of doorman, while today Willis ran the store. It was a story shrouded in legend, as were so many things about Pembroke's, but both men were nearly as venerable as the store itself.

Once inside, Amanda took a deep breath. She felt as though she drew inspiration out of the very air at Pembroke's. Its glittering wares, counter after counter of fabulous jewels and kings' ransoms of gold, were unequaled anywhere in the world. At this time of year especially the store was crowded with customers. But even at the busiest times, there was an air of subdued hush at Pembroke's. There was never the noise and clamor of the bigger and busier stores that dominated Fifth Avenue and gave the street its character and prestige. Even when the counters were crowded three-deep with waiting customers, everything at Pembroke's seemed to flow with quiet, efficient ease. Selections were made, transactions in the thousands of dollars, yet the loudest sound was that of a salesclerk rapping with a pencil on a glass counter to signify that a sale had been made and a page's presence was required.

Amanda walked across the floor, glancing at the expensively dressed women and impeccable men. Everyone in Pembroke's bespoke good breeding, the carefully chosen salesclerks as well as the customers. Some of the older salespeople had been with the store for twenty-five, thirty years and more. And many, especially among the younger staff, were from social register families, there because the Pembroke imprimatur made even selling behind a counter prestigious work.

Amanda loved the store when it was like this, the massive crystal chandeliers lit and shining, the mahogany walls and counters gleaming with reflection in their rich color. She cut across until she could see the aisle to the counter where her work was sold. A joyous feeling bubbled up inside her at seeing how busy it was. She didn't dare go any closer. If any of the customers recognized her, and some of them would be certain to, they would clamor for her help in making their selections. As much as Amanda enjoyed doing that, now was the wrong time. There was new work to be created, waiting for her presence upstairs. Only when the new items were ready could she take the time to mingle with customers again, getting their reactions and helping make sales. It was a part of the work that she truly loved—being in touch with her followers—and she regretted having to forgo the fun of it this morning.

But there was too much on her agenda that had to be done. She ducked into the small elevator at the rear of the store, just before the door slid closed, and got off at the fourth floor, where her tiny office workroom was located, behind Pembroke's huge silver department.

The office door had a tiny plate with her name on it, and Amanda smiled at it as always when she turned the knob to go inside.

"Amanda darling! Good morning," Amanda heard herself greeted.

"Good morning, Basil," she replied. "How are you?" It was a question she didn't enjoy asking, especially right after a weekend, for Basil Hemmings delighted in taking the question quite literally and answering her extensively on his most recent doings.

Basil Hemmings was Amanda's assistant, less talented than she but clever and massively ambitious. He knew all of the right people and cultivated all of the wrong ones. He was very shrewd about getting his name in the columns, always at the parties, openings, and clubs where the action was and reporters and photographers would be too. He ran with a very fast set, newsmakers in a way, that Amanda felt uncomfortable about. Aside from stalking the aboveground social and show business worlds, Basil existed in a nebulous sort of netherworld where talents and types and sexes often blurred indistinguishably. Basil's dark, sardonic looks, his frame, lean almost to the point of gauntness, and the cachet of his Pembroke's connection, were the unusual combination that made him a leader of his strangely assorted clique and granted them entree almost everywhere. Amanda viewed the whole thing with a degree of reserve that she kept to herself. Basil was good, enormously good, at his work, and he was a great help to her. But just as she concealed her feelings about his life-style, she knew he concealed his notion of one day overtaking and supplanting her. He had ambition enough to want it, but not the talent, and Amanda never considered him the threat he thought himself to be.

Willis Haviland did not put up with a great deal of nonconformity among his employees, even the most creative ones, and Amanda was sure that Basil would one day overstep the bounds.

As she went through the papers on her desk, and the mail that had piled up, she glanced at her appointment calendar and saw that she had a short meeting with Willis scheduled for midafternoon. The telephone's ringing interrupted her. It was one of the saleswomen from her boutique. "There's a gentleman here to see you, Mrs. Parrish," the saleswoman said. "He's interested in your designing a piece for him."

"At this time of year," Amanda said, groaning inwardly. "Tell him—" she hesitated for a moment and glanced over at Basil. "Tell him that Mr. Hemmings will be down in a moment, thank you." She replaced the receiver on the hook.

Basil stood up smiling. "Irate customer needing placating?" he asked, grinning.

"No," Amanda said, "a customer wanting a new design."

"And you're sending me?" Basil asked in a half-mocking tone.

"I'm sure you can handle it," Amanda said smoothly. She was not going to let him ruffle her feathers this morning.

He bounced out of the office and returned in what seemed to Amanda to be too quick a time to have conferred with the customer properly. She looked up inquiringly.

"He wants you," Basil said, spreading his hands and shrugging in a gesture of mock admiration. "The obviously well-to-do, unexpectedly gorgeous man wants you."

Amanda was annoyed. "Why wasn't it something you could handle, Basil?"

"I'm sure I could have," he snapped. "Whatever it was. I never got to find out. The gentleman"—and his voice underlined the word—"wants you."

Amanda could see the mounting jealousy, but she couldn't help wondering, from the extravagant words Basil had used to describe the man, whether his mockery was based on professional or personal irritation. "I'm really too busy to go down now," she said.

"I don't think so," Basil replied, in a voice that

caused Amanda's eyebrows to raise slightly. "I think you should take yourself downstairs, Mrs. Parrish."

Amanda got up slowly. Basil never called her by her married name unless he was extremely irked or wanted to provoke the same emotion in her. "Very well," she said evenly, "if you think I should, Mr. Hemmings, I certainly will." She walked out of the office and pushed the elevator button, wondering about the customer waiting below.

When she got to the counter, the questions melted in her mind. She recognized him immediately as he stood leaning easily against a mahogany column. He was dressed in a beautifully cut beige cashmere coat whose classic lines were the perfect complement to his understated good looks. Even in the crowd of thronging shoppers, he stood out. When he saw her, he smiled, and Amanda gasped. What was he doing at Pembroke's? How had he known to find her here? Why in the world, especially after that terrible beginning, had Josh McKay decided to come back into her life?

"Good morning," he grinned.

"What are you doing here and what do you want?" Amanda asked. She felt a sort of strange fright rising in her, and she fought to keep it down.

"Didn't they tell you?" he asked. "I've spoken to a salesperson and to your assistant, I believe. It doesn't speak very well for the efficiency of this store."

"What do you want from me is what I mean," Amanda said.

He stopped smiling. "I have a picture here of something I'd like to have copied and made in silver as a pendant," he explained. "You do that sort of thing?"

"Yes."

"Then why should my being here seem to cause you so much confusion?"

"How did you find me?" Amanda couldn't help the question.

"There was nothing difficult about that," Josh explained. "You're Amanda Parrish of Pembroke's. Everybody knows that."

"Everybody?" she echoed.

"You mean," he said, and the grin was back, "that you're surprised at a garage mechanic knowing who you are?"

She knew now that he was parrying with her, but somehow it still didn't feel like a game, at least not to Amanda. Of course he was no garage mechanic, she knew that, and he knew that she knew it. "What is it you want, Mr. McKay?" she asked.

"You remember my name." He seemed genuinely surprised and touched. "Let me show you this." He reached into his pocket. "Is it all right to do it here?"

Amanda thought for one fleeting moment of her small office space and the leering Basil in it. There was a small, beautifully appointed private salesroom where important customers were accommodated and designs and commissions discussed, but she didn't want to take him there. It would be better to see what he wanted and get the whole thing over as quickly as possible.

"This will be fine," she said.

He unfolded a brightly colored photograph. Amanda looked at it as he held it toward her. On a yellow field was a prancing black stallion balanced on its two hind legs, mane and tail blowing wildly in the unseen wind. It was fanciful and powerful all at once, caught in a moment of majesty and freedom.

"It's lovely," Amanda said admiringly, "and I think I know what it is, but I'm not sure."

"It's the symbol of the Ferrari," Josh told her. "It appears on all of their cars."

"And you want a copy of it made to wear?" Amanda said slowly. "That might bring in some questions of copyright. Besides"—and she frowned slightly—"I don't like the idea of copying someone else's work. I've never done anything that wasn't entirely original."

"I quite understand," Josh said. "And that's really why I've come to you. I don't want an exact replica of the prancing stallion; rather, I want your interpretation of it. Very close to the feeling of the original, but your interpretation."

Amanda studied the picture thoughtfully. Recreated in silver, in miniature, the stallion would indeed make a charming piece. The lines of the animal were strong, yet delicate. Casting it could be quite tricky. She had done some modeling along those lines, but nothing since she had completed her classes. It was not like anything she had designed since, and her apprenticeship had been a rather limited one. It was too busy in the shop for any of the silversmiths to do it now, and there was something of a challenge in it that tugged at her. If he wanted it quickly, there was no way of the shop's handling it.

"How quickly do you need it?" she asked, and she knew she was looking for an out that would take the problem and the stallion and Mr. McKay off her hands once and for all.

"There isn't any particular time limit," he said, "although of course I would like it as soon as possible."

Amanda's heart sank. "I thought perhaps you

needed it for a gift in time for the holidays," she said.

He grinned. "No," he said. "The gift is from me to me."

"I really don't know if I can," Amanda faltered.

"Part of the gift is that it's made by you," he said firmly. "I'll wait as long as I have to."

Amanda flushed lightly, and studied the picture again so that she wouldn't have to look at him. "I really don't know," she said, "it represents a lot of possible technical problems."

"Do you mean that you can't do it?"

"Of course I can!" Amanda snapped. His doubting hit her like a slap in the face. "Yes, I'll do it for you, Mr. McKay."

"That's all I wanted to hear," Josh said. "What happens next?"

Amanda felt a sudden sense of elation she couldn't quite explain. Later she would tell herself it was the joy of going back to working with her hands again, to solving the problems of the drawing board and the modeling wax that would precede that actual casting. Now she explained the paperwork necessary in contracting such a commission. "It's a beautiful concept," she said, "and I'm sure it's going to make a wonderful piece of jewelry."

Josh laughed. "If it really works out well," he said, "I may even want another one made to present to the genius behind all of this."

Amanda looked interested, and so he went on. "When Enzo Ferrari raced his first car, he used the same mascot as a World War I flying ace named Barracca for good luck. He won that race, and the prancing horse has been the symbol of the greatest racing cars ever since. The yellow field and stripes are the colors of the city of Modena, where the cars are made."

"Are you a racer, Mr. McKay?" Amanda couldn't help asking.

"I race once in a while," he replied, "but I'm not really good enough at it to stay in Formula I competition all the time."

Amanda didn't know what that meant, but she said nothing. Her continued silence led him to go on.

"I guess I still have it in my blood. But I also work with racers and other cars, besides racing myself. Team Ferrari is the most expert when it comes to building and racing, and I'm happy to be able to make some small contribution."

"Do you work exclusively for them, then?" Amanda asked.

"Nope," he said, "I free-lance. I work with Ferrari, Jaguar, and once in a while some other special situations. Usually it's for these and other foreign carmakers who need someone familiar with American laws and roads to modify their original prototypes for export to us."

"How fascinating," Amanda, who had never even conceived that such work existed, couldn't help saying. This unusual work of his explained a great deal about him; that, she finally had to admit, he had been just the right person, in just the right moment, to save her life, probably, four days ago. "Mr. McKay, you'll hear from us as soon as the piece is ready for your inspection," she said. "It's been very interesting, but I really must go now."

"When will I see you again?" he asked.

"When the piece is ready," she repeated.

"Not the piece," he said gently, lowering his voice. "You."

Amanda smiled and stepped back a little. "When

it's ready, Mr. McKay, I'll be glad to discuss it with you personally so that if you're not completely happy you can tell me what changes to make." She paused for a moment. "Will that be satisfactory?"

"Not unless it will be ready tonight," he said. "Can you have dinner with me?"

"That's impossible," she said, her voice sounding slightly breathless to her own ears.

"Oh?" His eyebrows raised just a little. "How about tomorrow night, then?"

Amanda shook her head.

"Later in the week?"

"No, I don't think so," she said softly. She was suddenly aware of all of the people around them. The traffic at her counter had not slackened the entire time that she and Josh had been talking. So engrossed had she been in their conversation that she had blanked out everyone else around them. Now she felt suddenly self-conscious, as though everyone in the store had been listening to them.

He raised his hands in a gesture of defeat. "Well, that's it, then. I'm leaving for Florida at the end of the week."

Amanda didn't know whether that thump she felt inside was relief or disappointment. "Palm Beach?" she asked, trying to cover her feelings, whatever they were.

"No, Daytona," Josh answered.

"Why Daytona of all places?" she asked.

"Your Palm Beach is the playground of the idle rich," he said. "I'm going south to work. Daytona happens to be the site of an important racetrack where my brother and I have a lot to do."

Once more, in spite of herself, she was curious.

"Oh, is your brother in the same line of work?" she asked.

For the first time an expression akin to worry clouded those blue eyes that had been disturbing her so. "He races."

"Oh, I see." Amanda said. She waited for him to pick up the conversation, but he seemed to have become suddenly distracted. His whole expression seemed to have changed.

"Look, I'll be gone about a month," Josh said, his tone almost brusque. "I hope the piece will be ready for me when I return."

Amanda started to say something, but just at that moment a woman from the contract department appeared, to complete the paperwork. Amanda watched as they walked to the elevator. She stayed at the counter for a few moments until she was sure they had gone up.

She wondered when she was going to see Josh McKay again, and realized how much she wanted to. Something about him had melted all the anger she had felt at their first encounter.

She would have something new and exciting to tell to Willis Haviland at their meeting later in the afternoon.

She looked at the picture of the stallion again. The piece of jewelry would certainly suit its owner. There was something so free about both of them, such a feeling of grace along with strength, that both man and symbol shared. A prancing stallion and a racing car driver. Both free, both fast. That was their world, so different from her own. Perhaps the task he had given her would create a bridge between.

Chapter 4

A half hour later Josh was back outside being jostled by the holiday crowds shopping Fifth Avenue. He was glad that he would be leaving the city soon, although he found it hard to account for the sudden change in mood. It wasn't caused by anything he could admit to himself. He had planned this expedition to Pembroke's very spiritedly, convinced of its happy outcome.

From the moment he had lifted Amanda Parrish out of her damaged car, something he had not felt in a very long time stirred in him. At first he had been taken by her loveliness, her face so pale against the softly curling long dark hair. Even when she recovered from the initial shock of the accident and grew angry and accusing, he had been amused and not offended by her imperious manner. He could tell that she was a cultivated and spirited woman, and he had always admired spunk. Perhaps that was a strange word for her, covered as she was by so much polish. But he had guessed at once that there was much more than surface to her.

She was beautiful, she was spirited, and the man who came to get her at the hospital was all wrong for her. Josh guessed that instantly. They didn't look right together. She was too vital, too fiery, to belong to the staid old world that that man represented. Only she didn't know it, at least not yet.

But Josh did. When he had watched them drive away in the big limo, it was as though she was being carried back to a world that hid behind careful manners and heavy draperies, expensive and studied, structured and orderly. She was too alive for all of that, and what she needed was someone to open the doors and windows of her life, someone to bring in the sunshine and the air and the wind. Someone like Josh.

He had handled all the business about her car before coming into the city. He had known who she was from the time he took her into the hospital, and he knew just where to find her. He had fantasized her reaction at seeing him, anticipated her elation over the stallion. He grimaced. He had been right about that, at least, but she had looked as if she couldn't care less about seeing him again.

Now he was on the street, being pushed this way and that, and wondering where he was going, and what it was all about. He started walking downtown feeling more at odds by the minute. His eye was caught by a travel agency sign, and impulsively he went in.

"Can you take care of a change in an airline ticket for me?" he asked the young woman at the first desk.

She examined the ticket he drew from his inside pocket. "When do you want it changed for?"

"Tonight," Josh said. "Get me on the first possible flight out of here." He had a small duffel packed at his hotel nearby, he realized. He could pick it up and be out at La Guardia in half an hour.

The travel agent made some hurried calls and at last announced success.

For the first time since he had entered the office, Josh relaxed noticeably.

The flight was ticketed and the paperwork done swiftly, much to the disappointment of the travel agent, who hadn't had such an attractive customer in a long time. It wasn't until he had checked out of the hotel and was halfway to the airport that Josh realized he should have called his brother, Dutcher, to let him know of the change in plans. Maybe there would be time to phone before the plane took off. Otherwise he might find himself in Daytona without a place to sleep. *Well,* Josh thought, *worse comes to worse, I can always bunk with Dutcher.* But as soon as the thought crossed his mind he realized how improbable it was. His younger brother had already been in Daytona for a couple of weeks, and that meant there were probably at least six young women already competing for the spare-time attention of Dutcher McKay. Josh's mood had lifted with his decision to leave for Florida immediately, and now he could grin to himself at the thought of the kid brother he was fond of referring to as the young Casanova.

At the terminal he checked in and made the call to Daytona. Dutcher wasn't in—not that Josh expected him to be—but he was able to leave a message with the arrival time of his flight. He hung up the phone, walked to the boarding gate, and settled himself for the few minutes till flight time.

He picked up a magazine that someone had left on the next seat. It was a news weekly, and as he glanced at the articles in the table of contents, he wondered how Amanda Parrish had gotten so quickly and firmly under his skin. No woman had done that in a very long time.

It was no use trying to read, nor was it any better once he was on the plane. The flight itself was uneventful, but Josh's mind was full of thoughts of Amanda. When they landed, Josh flung his duffel over his shoulder, wavering between hailing a taxi and renting a car to take him out to the motel near the track. As he approached the terminal exit, still undecided, he spotted an unmistakable figure lounging against one of the pillars. The somber mood that had been oppressing him for much of the day suddenly lifted. His younger brother's infectious grin was immediately mirrored on Josh's features.

Unconcerned about anyone else in the terminal, the two men exchanged a bear hug, grasping each other in warm embrace. Although they were brothers, only half a dozen years separating them, Josh had been playing the part of father to Dutcher ever since they were small children and their real father had been killed in a spectacular racing smashup. Dutcher had grown up idolizing his older brother, following in his footsteps as soon as he had been old enough to get behind a steering wheel.

When Josh had given up racing, Dutcher had declared that he would carry on the family tradition. Although Josh tried hard, he wasn't able to dissuade the young hothead from pursuing that course. It was the first time that Dutcher had rebelled against his brother's authority, and although it had taken a long time for the rift to heal, they were as close now as they had ever been. Their chosen careers enabled them to be together frequently, and Dutcher still looked up to his older sibling for guidance and advice.

Josh had to admit to himself that recently his counseling had been becoming more and more restricted to racing matters. And while Dutcher spent much of his spare time exploring the world of women, this was an area he didn't think he needed coaching in.

They made a striking pair, the two McKay brothers, as they got into the low-slung green hatchback that Dutcher had waiting for them. The younger McKay was as blond and lean as his brother, although he stood a few inches shorter. Josh always teased him that he tried to compensate for that by being faster.

"This thing moves well," Josh said admiringly as Dutcher swung them out onto the freeway. "Are you planning to race her?"

"Only from here to the motel," Dutcher replied, grinning.

He sat in the compact car in the classic racer's posture: his arms straight out from the shoulders, hands clutching the top of the steering wheel. Although the car wasn't meant for racing, it had the close-to-the-floor seats that enabled the driver to maneuver it like one.

Josh was pleased to see that Dutcher's reply was light; he watched the road carefully, taking no chances, maneuvering the car conservatively, as though he were very aware of his older brother's watchful gaze.

They drove in silence for a few moments. Then Dutcher broke in. "Would you like to meet someone?" he asked, trying to frame the question in the least objectionable way.

"Tonight?" Josh asked.

"Sure. Why not?" Dutcher answered offhandedly. He knew in advance how Josh was most likely to handle the situation of Dutcher's having a roommate while he was in training. Setting Josh up with a friend of Bootsie's might ease things considerably, but his big brother wasn't having any of it.

"Come on, kid," Josh said, "give me the whole story. What's really happening?"

Dutcher broke out in a grin. "It's sort of this way," he began slowly.

"Never mind the sort of." Josh interrupted what was sounding suspiciously like the beginning of a long, complicated narrative. "Just give it to me straight."

"It's Bootsie," Dutcher said.

"Bootsie Farr?"

"Yes," Dutcher answered. "I see you remember her." He shot his brother a quick sidelong glance.

"Bootsie is beyond forgetting," Josh said wryly. "And she has a sister."

"She doesn't have a sister, exactly," Dutcher said, "but she's got this sort of cousin."

"And you've got this sort of brother," Josh reminded him. "Thanks, but no thanks."

"You're not in training," Dutcher shot back.

"And you are," Josh said quietly.

"So the shoe should be on the other foot, as well," Dutcher said.

"Whatever that means," Josh said. "The point is, you shouldn't be and I don't want to be."

Dutcher grinned. "Don't want to be what?" he teased.

"Up to my ears and bothered by Bootsies, Tootsies, or any other brand of female distraction," Josh said. "The stuff we're working on now is too critical, Dutcher, and you should be the first to realize it. Fun and games have got their place, but this isn't it."

"A man's got to relax some time," Dutcher argued.

"Sure," Josh agreed, "You can relax with a TV set, or a good hot tub, or even a couple of beers. But there's too much to concentrate on to treat this time as though it were a vacation."

Dutcher shot him a look. "Man, I have been *working*," he said with a drawled-out emphasis on the last word that made Josh chuckle in spite of himself. The young brother kept his eyes straight on the road now, as if those of his guide and mentor were watching him as closely as if they were out on the track. Dutcher loved Josh, and making Josh proud of him was more important to him than he would have been able to admit. When he was a kid and his friends had been wrapped up in their sailboats and ski weekends, he had followed Josh to the racing circuits. Both boys had treasured the yellowing newspaper and magazine clippings that their mother kept in a large, leather-covered scrapbook, mementos of their father's illustrious career. Dutcher could remember turning those pages for hours, wondering about the man who lived there, in words and pictures, but who had died before his younger son had ever seen him.

The pictures showed small resemblance to the boys who studied them: oddly enough, both favored their mother's blond hair and blue eyes, slim profile and straightforward gaze. But the man in the photographs, his hair covered by the leather aviator's helmet of the early racers, so different from the modern crash helmets his sons were protected by, his clipped moustache so like the style of the English aristocrats of that era, his eyes as dark as theirs were light, had left them a legacy stronger than the physical one that shaped their faces. The senior McKay's love of speed and cars had shaped their lives.

Although Josh had been old enough to remember his father, the heritage was no less strong with Dutcher. If anything he was even more determined to be the best—and the fastest. For Josh, each race was a test of the car and himself. For Dutcher, the car, important as it was, was merely the instrument with which he tested himself. To be fast. To be good. To be best. He started hotdogging the car, pushing it hard, making it respond. Just thinking about racing made him feel as though he really were. He leaned forward almost unconsciously, trying to get more out of the little compact than it was capable of giving.

"Hey, what're you doing?" Josh asked as the formerly well-behaved car started bucking under them.

Dutcher flushed. "Sorry," he said, grinning sheepishly, "I forgot." He decelerated.

The car went back to its normal speed with what sounded almost like a sigh of relief to Josh's practiced ear. Dutcher was a racer, he thought to himself, right down to his bones. If he ever made a mistake, it would be a driver's mistake. He knew how his kid brother felt about him, and sensed Dutcher's embarrassment at having done something silly with Josh in the car. "Hey, good buddy," he said in the accents and phrases of the Southern drivers who populated the stock-car tracks like Daytona, "how about stopping for a couple of beers? I'm feeling a little dry since that flight."

"Great!" Dutcher agreed, happy to have the tension broken. "I know just the place."

I'll bet you do, Josh started to say, but he let the remark pass. He didn't want to say anything that would sound like criticism. Not over something trivial. Starting the next day, when they were out working in the pits, he would have to assume the role of teacher and critic. Dutcher would have to be in a receptive mood, and listen. If Josh came off sounding negative now, Dutcher might be less inclined to listen then, when things would be so much more important; he could disregard something significant as meaningless. That was too much a risk to take, especially in their business.

Dutcher pulled into the parking lot of a brightly lit tavern, and the brothers piled out. Dutcher was eager for the chance to pal around with his big brother and Josh was keyed up.

As they walked in the greetings came to them from the men gathered around the paying side of the bar. Josh recognized the usual collection of racing mechanics and track types, a rough-and-ready crowd of guys whose off-track antics belied the deadly seriousness with which they regarded and performed their work. Men who worked in the pit stops were almost as highly trained and proficient as the drivers they serviced. They were a particularly American phenomenon, even the classiest Formula I Grand Prix having no equivalent of crews who vied with each other in making record-breaking changes during races. They were good, and they knew it; that knowledge and a deeply ingrained love of cars and racing made them a fraternity, competitors during races, comrades after, living a fast-moving, pressurized life, traveling like gypsies from race to race, knocking themselves out in a grueling existence in order to be close to greatness.

As New Englanders, the McKays were outsiders. As drivers, they eradicated the differences in background and breeding and became part of the inner circle. Josh greeted the men he knew and quickly was introduced to those he didn't.

The room was hazy with smoke, thick with the smell of beer and men who worked hard for their living. The talk was cars, and Josh was drawn right into it. The flight down quickly receded from his mind, and suddenly New York felt even farther away than it actually was and Josh felt good for the first time in hours.

And hours later they were still talking, ordering

beers and arguing results of races that had long since passed into history, trading shoptalk about new products and parts, comparing results on some levels, tight-lipped and ungiving on others. Finally Josh looked at his watch. It was much later than he had thought.

Dutcher, seeing him, took the hint immediately and stood up without Josh saying anything. They made their good nights and walked back out to the parking lot.

"I didn't realize it was so late," Josh said, as if blaming himself. "I didn't think we'd stayed so long."

Dutcher opened the door on the driver's side. He looked at his brother over the low roof of the car. "I think that did you a lot of good," he said evenly. "I think you needed it."

Josh scowled. Were his feelings so transparent, then? "Maybe I did," he said, getting into the car, staring straight ahead.

"New York can do that to you," Dutcher sympathized. "It does it to me sometimes too." He turned the key. "I think you're going to feel better, now that you're here."

"I think you're right," Josh said, somewhat gratified by Dutcher's perception but still a little angry at himself for letting his feelings show. Especially to his kid brother, who had other things to worry about, like a Formula I race the next month. Maybe the kid was growing up after all.

But when he registered at the motel, Josh wondered if it was the press of tourists or his brother's adroitness that had his room two floors above Dutcher's. As they rode up in the elevator together Dutcher again sensed Josh's mood. "Are you sure you don't want to say hello to Bootsie?" he asked. "Or to meet her cousin? She's a peach."

"I'm sure she is," Josh said. "They're all peaches." He thought of the kind of girls who hung around racetracks and drivers. Racing groupies, he always thought of them, and they were usually very much alike—tall, thin young girls, their hair usually blond and long and streaming, their knowledge of cars limited to makes and speeds, their knowledge of the drivers profound down to the last intimate detail. He had enjoyed that kind of adulation when he was younger and still driving; now he could only think of them as children.

If he wanted a woman, it was going to be a real woman, like the fierce and independent dark-haired beauty he hadn't been able to get out of his mind since he had carried her from her smashed car.

He didn't want to be thinking about that, he reminded himself forcefully, after he had bade Dutcher good night and was alone in his room, stowing away his gear. The car, the embankment, the metallic crumple of the wreckage, reminded him all too much of another wrecked vehicle, one he hadn't been able to stop, one he hadn't even seen, until it was all over and too late.

He lay back on the still made bed, the darkness of the room closing in on him but unable to shut the awful images from his mind. All the old feelings came crashing down on him—love, conflict, pain, forgiveness, and the final, ultimate tragedy that had come and made the forgiveness too late.

Elizabeth. How young she had been, no older than Bootsie and her friends, but how beautiful, with a delicate, ethereal loveliness that had touched him deep inside every time he looked at her. She had always seemed so fragile to him, as though she would break in his arms if he held her too tightly. He remembered the first time he had seen her, really seen her, that is, as a grown woman. Their families had known each other since both of them were children. They shared the same Connecticut background, the same country clubs and Ivy League and Seven Sister colleges. Elizabeth had gone to Bryn Mawr, and the time that Josh always thought of as the first time he had really seen her was the summer she came home after her junior year.

She had grown from a skinny, straw-haired little girl into a woman of incredible beauty. There was a porcelain quality about her, like a Dresden figurine who all but carried a sign that said "Don't touch." Her coloring was pale, as if even that had been applied with the lightest touch. Her blond hair was almost more silver than gold, and her skin paler than ivory. Her eyes were the only really vivid thing about her—deep blue, fringed with thick dark lashes that made the searching pupils look even more intense. He had been mesmerized by those great dark eyes and had failed completely to read what was behind them. That was the irony of it, so bitter that even now, eight years later, he could still taste it like gall in his mouth.

He had come up from New Haven, trying to decide whether or not to go back for his last year at Yale. He had been racing for several years by then and had gone home for a few days to see his mother before taking off for the excitement of Monaco and his first Grand Prix. He wasn't going to race, of course: he was still a long way from that. But he had never seen the crown jewel of all world-class racing, and he was almost jumping with excitement.

He had agreed to accompany his mother to a dinner dance at the country club where she still maintained membership, although she had dropped almost all of the others since his father had been killed.

His parents had been a rather oddly matched couple, their backgrounds similar but their interests worlds apart. His mother had always clung to the security of their Connecticut country club existence and the social milieu they had been brought into and brought up in. His father had been totally at home but never satisfied with the same endless rounds of golf and drinking and dinners and parties. He had become interested in cars when he was still a boy and had started racing in his late teens. His first racer had been a gift from Josh's grandfather, more a bribe than a gift, really, a compromise that meant he would finish school in exchange.

Josh would never have had to strike a similar deal with his father. Jack McKay had encouraged his son in his love of cars, and Josh's racing was expected and understood, except by his mother. She saw in it only the same restless pattern that would leave her a widow with two small sons to raise. But the pattern was already too strong, and there was no way she could keep her boys away from the cars. Josh's decision about Yale was made mostly to please her.

But there were no more bargains to be made. After college, he would race.

Then, just a few days before he was to leave for Monaco, there was the new complication—Elizabeth. The very next day after they met, he drove around to her house without even phoning first. He stopped at the doorstep of a large, white-columned Colonial and announced that he had come to carry her off.

She laughed and was pleased when he helped her

into the car he had then, his first Jaguar. He had bought it secondhand and had spent the previous two summers tinkering with it, changing parts, customizing it almost from the floorboards up, so that when he was at last almost finished, he felt that he had recreated it. That was exactly the way it felt under his hands, as responsive to him as though it knew how much love and soul he had put into it.

Elizabeth admired the car but shuddered visibly when Josh began to take the back-road turns at ever accelerated speeds. He raced along the deserted straightaway, giving the juicy little Jaguar the kind of workout that both he and the car were made for. He loved the feel of the Jag and the wind whistling around them as he drove faster and faster. And now there was the added element of this beautiful girl, as finely tuned as the car, sitting beside him. Josh remembered the exhilaration, the happiness that had lasted until Elizabeth had started screaming, screaming so loud that he had lost all sense of the road and everything around them. He had brought the Jag to a quick stop on the shoulder. He had turned to her helplessly, trying to stop the uncontrollable sobs that were wracking her body. She hid her face in her hands, crying into her fists as if to stop the outburst that had overtaken her.

Josh had put his hands on her shoulders, trying to comfort her, but it was difficult and awkward trying to maneuver in the bucket seats. Finally she brought herself to a halt.

"I'm sorry," she said in a voice still wavering, "I didn't mean to spoil your fun, but you had me terribly, terribly frightened." Those bottomless eyes had looked up at him almost accusingly. "I don't think I've ever been so frightened in my life."

"I'm terribly sorry," Josh said, feeling miserable. "I thought you would enjoy it. Most girls love–"

She interrupted him. "Please, Josh," she said, her voice still soft but carrying a different tone now. "Don't ever confuse me with other girls. That is, if we're going to be friends. I don't care what other girls like." She stuck out her chin almost defiantly, staring straight ahead at the green fields they were parked beside. "I know what I like and what I don't like. What I don't like is being frightened or being in any kind of danger. That might be thrilling for some people, but it's not for me."

He had been so dazzled by her that he thought he understood, and empathized at once. Of course she was too delicate, entirely too fragile for the bone-rattling, nerve-testing nonsense that he loved. Elizabeth was very special. He was going to have to remember that and concentrate on what she did like, forgetting about what she didn't.

"What do you like?" he asked slyly, trying to put his arm around her and bring his mouth close to hers.

But she had moved away from him, protesting lightly. "Please, Josh, I hardly know you."

All his reminding her that they had known each other since first grade was to no avail. Josh had turned the ignition key and driven slowly, very slowly, back to her house. He didn't call her again until he came back from Monte Carlo, so full of the excitement of witnessing his first Grand Prix that he had completely forgotten her aversion to racing.

He went around to see her, and it seemed as though she had forgotten it too, so glad was her greeting. She had even welcomed the idea of going for a drive.

But then he had remembered and was careful to keep the Jag under tight reins.

They had started seeing each other frequently. He had taken to calling for her in his mother's station wagon, explaining that he was still making a lot of modifications on the Jag. He had been planning to go to the raceway at Lime Rock for a week to test the car, time it, and make final adjustments. They were sitting in the dark garden behind her house one evening when he told her about it.

"I'd like to come with you," she had said.

Josh was surprised. He had tried to keep Elizabeth and the Jaguar totally out of each other's way. He was spending his days with the car and his evenings with her, not liking to compartmentalize his life that way but knowing it was the best compromise.

"I thought you didn't like fast cars," he reminded her.

"I don't," she admitted. "But it is a pretty place and I've—I've sort of gotten used to you, in these last few weeks."

Josh squeezed her hand and leaned over, lightly brushing her cheek with his lips. "I'd love it," he confessed. "Love to have you with me."

She had edged away from him slightly. "Not to race, Josh," she reminded him. "You can do whatever you want to, just so I'm not involved."

"Fair enough," he replied in agreement. "Most of my time is going to be spent on tinkering with the car and then in time trials. You certainly don't have to be on the track with me then, and when we do drive, I promise it will be just that—driving, not racing."

Two days later they had fitted their bags into the Jag's small trunk and headed for the state park where the raceway was located. They checked in at the Interlaken, where Elizabeth would be able to spend her days using the resort's facilities while Josh worked on the car. She stood away from him with her back turned when he signed the register "Mr. and Mrs." and looked uneasy when they were shown to one of the town-house accommodations away from the main building.

As soon as they were alone in their room Josh had put his arms around her, but she had shrugged him gently away.

"I'm going to put my things away," she said, "and then freshen up a bit."

They were close enough to the track for Josh to sense the sounds and smells of the pits and mechanics and other drivers. The urgency to be part of it welled up in him, and he left Elizabeth to herself, giving her time for herself until he'd be back for dinner.

The track was swarming with people. Josh raised his arm in greeting to those drivers and mechanics he knew. The pungent aroma of gasoline permeated the air; small black liquid pools dotted the paved area of the pit. Here and there the gray pathway was blazened with long black scars—burned-rubber reminders of sudden stops. The air rang with the mostly good-natured gibes of the drivers, taunting each other in advance with the beating they were going to administer on the track as soon as the racing began. He walked over to the partitioned area where his silver Jag sat shining pristinely. He patted the hood, and then got himself a small wooden dolly. He used it to cushion his back and propel himself under the Jag where he could tinker with some of the wiring he had been concerned about, holding a huge flashlight in his left hand while he carefully probed with the right.

He saw that there really wasn't much that needed doing on the car; he certainly would not have been able to accomplish anything much anyway, encumbered as he was by the need to hold his light by himself. But he loved getting under the car: understanding its workings was as pleasurable and as important to him as racing it. Whatever time was spent under the chassis or deep inside the hood was imperative and, he was sure, would pay off. His intimacy with the car was sure to be reflected in his handling of her on the track. When he got up, there was a smear of grease across his cheeks and an inordinate amount of the same stuff buried under his fingernails that would take a great deal of scrubbing to get out. He grinned thinking how awful he would look presenting himself to Elizabeth this way, but knowing that he himself didn't mind the dirt at all. It was almost a badge that identified him as a member of the driving fraternity.

What he was doing was more important than mere fun. Josh wasn't yet at the level where he could afford the services of a mechanic to help him. In this he was not so much different from most of the other drivers. None of them were full-time professionals, and most of them had to do most of their own tinkering and repairs, whether they wanted to or not. The tasks of caring for their vehicles were too enormous to be avoided. Josh was lucky, he conceded to himself, that he loved it as much as he did and never thought of the car's upkeep as a task.

He spent the rest of the afternoon under the car, surprised when he finally remembered to look at the watch he had left on the front seat at how late it had gotten. He had to hurry to get back to Elizabeth. He was glad that there was a sink close by so that he wouldn't have to go back to her looking like this. He took out his clean-up kit—an admittedly ragged towel and a can of Gre-Solvent—and headed for the washup. He wanted a few more days of tinkering with the Jag. Then he would be ready, when he was sure that everything was as finely tuned as he could make it, to take her out on the track.

He stowed his cleaning gear away, gave the car a final pat of approval, and went back to the room where Elizabeth waited for him.

That was the pattern of the first few days there. Josh had never been so happy in his life. Elizabeth had finally succumbed to his caresses and they had made love, tenderly, for the first time. She seemed strangely quiet, but he attributed that to her timidness at being there with him.

Before long he was ready to enter the Jag in the time trials. The Jag had performed beautifully, bettering the time of everything else on the track that morning. Josh felt triumphant. He threw his helmet onto the seat, locking the car and deciding to call it a day. He realized he had been neglecting Elizabeth somewhat, although she hadn't said anything about the amount of time he spent away from her. He thought she was enjoying herself nonetheless.

He expected Elizabeth to be at the pool or somewhere on the grounds, but figured he'd better go up to the room to wash and change before looking for her.

He turned his key in the door. Elizabeth was on the bed, her pale nude body pressed against the darker one of a man Josh recognized only as the owner of a red Corvette.

She jumped up, throwing her hands in front of her breasts, her body trembling as she began screaming even more than she had that first time in the Jaguar.

Almost without thought he returned to the Jaguar and drove it slowly out of the raceway and onto one of the roads paralleling the park. He drove for hours, driving slowly, not racing, changing direction every time the sun was in his eyes, not knowing where he was going or even noticing the highway markers that would have told him which road he was on. The sun was setting when he finally noticed a sign indicating Lime Rock. He turned off and headed back there.

All the mindless driving had convinced him of only one thing: he had been wrong, wrong to bring Elizabeth to the track with him, wronger still to have left her alone for all of those hours. She had warned him, she had told him not to treat her like other girls. That she was different and knew what she wanted. Josh had almost laughed at himself, remembering. Too bad he hadn't realized what she had meant.

He didn't understand what was driving Elizabeth. She had not been all that responsive to his own advances until the last few nights. At home she had denied him everything but the lightest of kisses and caresses.

Maybe that was it. Maybe she had to be away from the confining influence of her house and parents before she could give in to her real needs. Or maybe it was just anger at him.

Whatever it was, Josh blamed himself. He cared enough for her not only to forgive her but to take all the blame on himself.

He brought the Jag back to its resting spot and walked to the town house. It was dark inside, and when he turned the key and went inside, it was empty. Her things were still there, but Elizabeth wasn't.

By now it was dark, and time for dinner. Josh had locked the door and gone back to the Interlaken restaurant to look for her.

But she hadn't been there either. He gazed around the large dining room, looking at the people who sat laughing, chattering, and eating. There was no sign of Elizabeth, nor of the man who had been with her.

Josh felt no hunger, only a churning in his stomach that he couldn't identify. He walked out into the bar, sat down, and ordered a bourbon. He had positioned himself in a place where he could watch people coming into the cocktail lounge and the restaurant beyond. He had downed three bourbons in as many hours and she still hadn't appeared. He pushed some money over to the bartender and walked out.

He had let himself back into their room. She wasn't there. He peeled off his clothes and threw himself on the bed and fell into a dead sleep.

He had been awakened the next morning by the dual shocks of bright sunlight streaming across his face and a loud knock at the door.

Josh had jumped up to answer it, realizing for the first time that he had slept in his clothes. He forced a smile on his face and was forming welcoming words for her, only to be confronted by a distinctly nonsmiling pair of policemen.

Josh was totally confused by their appearance and their questions. He followed them meekly into the squad car that was waiting. He blinked in the early morning sunlight as they drove to the opposite end of the state park.

He drew in his breath at the sight of the crumpled

metal mess that had once been his prized car. Then, as he got out of the squad car and walked toward it, he felt the restraining hand of the policeman beside him.

"She isn't in there," the policeman had said softly. "I'm sorry. Your wife is dead. She must have died immediately on impact."

Everything went black. Josh felt the ground swaying under his feet. Only the firm grip of the policeman kept him from falling. "She wasn't my wife," he said dully, "she was a girl named Elizabeth."

They had taken him back into the squad car then, and on to the state trooper station, where there were a lot more questions waiting for him.

His mouth was dry, he felt grubby and unshaven, the grease of the car pit still under his fingernails and filling the lines in his hands. "Has anyone else been notified?" he asked. Elizabeth had carried no identification, they explained. They had traced her to him through the car. "Her family—her mother—will have to be told." Every word was like a groan being forced out from deep within him.

The officers were very courteous and concerned. They asked if he wanted to tell the Staffords himself, or if he wanted one of them to do it for him.

Josh shook his head. He had brought their daughter to this, he would bear the responsibility for telling them.

Josh was in a sweat. The thick Daytona heat was closing in on him. He had forgotten to turn on the air conditioner when he came into the room. He had also forgotten, he thought wryly, to find out until what time room service delivered. He hadn't had a bourbon in all the years since that night, but he suddenly felt the urge for some Jack Daniel's and ice.

He didn't feel like going down to the bar. He picked up the phone. The switchboard operator informed him that room service had closed two hours earlier. *Oh, well,* he rationalized, *I'm probably better off without it.*

He had not been able to stand the thought of bourbon: it always triggered the nightmare of Elizabeth when he even saw a bottle or an ad. He wondered why he wanted some now. Maybe it was a sign that he had finally gotten over the tragedy or at least blaming himself for it. He wondered if this new emotional freedom had to do with Amanda Parrish. He hadn't been able to save Elizabeth; he had been able to save Amanda.

Maybe the long years of emotional penance were over. Maybe he could just start to enjoy his emotions instead of cursing them.

Not that the dark-haired beauty had given him much encouragement on that score, Josh admitted to himself. She acted very distant toward him, yet Josh believed he had read something else in her eyes. There was a conflict going on inside Amanda Parrish, whether that lady knew it or not. Josh wasn't misreading this time, he was sure of it. Amanda had more stops and starts in her than a car running on a low tank of gas. Every time she started to acquiesce, she pulled herself back. There was no mistaking that, any more than there was mistaking the thoroughbred lines of her beauty. Something else intrigued Josh. She had made a name for herself in a craft that she obviously loved. That there was no husband in her life he was quite sure; the arrival of her friend at the emergency room had confirmed that.

It also confirmed, for Josh, that there was really

no man in her life, either. The obviously successful gentleman who called for her in his chauffeured Cadillac was no more than a friend. He could read that on her face and in the way they greeted each other. No matter what they might think, Josh knew they weren't in love. The man, though obviously wealthy, was no match for that woman. Amanda herself had to be as aware of that as he was. Otherwise there was certainly a great deal of unhappiness in store for her.

A woman like that needed someone very special. Someone, he thought very honestly, like Joshua David McKay. Anything else, he decided solemnly, would be a big mistake.

And besides, he thought a little wickedly, he hadn't saved Amanda in order to lose her to anybody else.

He left for the pits bright and early in the morning, glad that he hadn't had the bourbon after all. He felt more alive than he had in a long time. The welcoming sun seemed to be shining just for him. He hadn't stopped to rouse Dutcher.

That could have been awkward, Josh grinned to himself. Better to set a good example by being up early and already hard at work whenever Dutcher did appear.

His work took him all over the world, but the immediate foreground was always the same: dirt tracks, test runs, machine shops, and pit stops. Monte Carlo had been his first Formula I race. But since that beginning as a spectator he had set cars racing through the mountains of Europe, the deserts of Africa, even hilly medieval villages. Ferraris were road tested amid houses that looked as old as the invention of the wheel. He could not remember when he had taken a vacation that was just a vacation—where there hadn't been a track nearby or an important race going on.

Not that Josh felt deprived. On the contrary, Formula I races especially were great events that brought out holidaying crowds and all the glamour and excitement that one could expect at any world-class event. It was just his own choice to spend what leisure time he felt the need for close to the work of his life. He had tried once, when he was feeling tired and dispirited, to take himself off to a Caribbean beach and lose himself in a blur of sea, sand, piña coladas, and rum punches. But it hadn't worked. In less than three full days he had thrown all of his stuff back into his bag and caught the first plane out. As a matter of fact, he smiled in remembering, he had flown to Miami and rented a car and driven straight up the coast right back here to Daytona. He had not been able to educate himself to prefer the fragrance of hibiscus to motor oil. It was damn lucky that the Grand Prix races took place amid champagne parties, all-night galas, idolizing spectators, and the other trappings of the sybaritic aspects of racing. Otherwise he might easily forget what those pleasures were.

He adored the racing, the swift, reckless side of driving, but he had developed a deep sense of the seriousness of a world that went everywhere on wheels. The sobering up that Elizabeth's death had forced him into had never left him. Now he was as engrossed in that aspect of his work—adapting foreign cars for safe use in America—as he was by the more glamorous side.

He wandered into the pit area, greeted by a smiling Dutcher.

Josh grinned back, pleased to see him there so early. It was a good sign. He didn't think he could ever get his brother really concerned about the nonracing aspects of cars. He had all he could handle just in keeping Dutcher from behaving utterly recklessly with regard to racing. Josh felt again the worry that came with his knowing that Dutcher was interested only in racing the best cars he could as fast as he could, leaving the specifications of building and design to others like Josh, whose approach was that of the engineer, conservative and scientific. Dutcher had cast himself in the mold of earlier heroes of racing, men who had made their reputations not only on the track but as the playboy darlings of the international set. Still, he worked hard and was, in his brother's opinion, a good kid. He studied his car, as if unmindful of the glittering scenes worlds away from the grease and dirt of the early morning Florida track. Josh shook his head, hoping fervently that Dutcher's recklessness wouldn't cost him dearly some day. But right now Josh was approving as Dutcher threw himself into the work with all of the concentration Josh could wish for.

With them were some of the Southerners they had been drinking with the night before, the good old boys, living only for cars and racing, the girls this would get them, and the rowdy carousing and beer drinking in country music bars and honky-tonks at night. They too were far removed from the grand scenes of international Formula I racing, just as far from the cultivated New England Ivy League background of the two McKay brothers. It was something of a miracle how such different types melded so closely into a perfectly functioning team. Josh understood it, knew that what brought them all together was the great equalizer that took no notice of background or education. Racing. Racing only cared what you could do to or in a car. Where you were born and what else you knew didn't matter.

The mood on the track when they worked was like that of a professional sports team's locker room. If there was any joking at all, it evolved around inside stuff pertaining to their work and themselves.

It was a world adored and admired by women, but here at the core females had no place. It was only on the fringes as spectators and relaxation that they existed. It wasn't until later that evening, after they had scrubbed and scraped the day's grease from their hands and bodies and were relaxing in the motel lounge, that Josh realized there were almost no women around at all. He wasn't surprised. This was off-season for Daytona, when no big races were scheduled and the track was mostly used for working and testing. There were the usual barmaids and local women around, but except for Bootsie Farr, who finally had made a sleepy-eyed appearance, there were no racing groupies in evidence.

"Hi, Bootsie," Josh greeted her.

"Sit down, babe," Dutcher said, making room for her next to him in the little booth they were sharing.

Bootsie smiled slightly at Josh, and then sat down. It was obvious that she had eyes for, and interest in, only Dutcher.

"Are you tired, honey?" Dutcher asked, his voice all concern.

Josh wondered what Bootsie had been doing all day to warrant the question and care from his brother.

"It's a tough circuit," Dutcher said, looking at Josh and frowning, as if he were reading his mind. "It's only a couple of weeks before we leave for California. Then, before you know it, there's Spain and Belgium before Monte Carlo." He paused for a moment, shaking his head. "That's really jamming it up, three races in one month."

"August is going to be just as tough, remember," Josh reminded him. "Germany, Austria, and Holland."

"Yeah," Dutcher concurred, "but there isn't as much moving around as we're going to have during the spring. The summer circuit seems easier to me somehow."

"It isn't even Christmas, and you guys are complaining about the summer already," Bootsie interjected. "It's such a long time away, I can't even think about it."

" 'If winter comes, can spring be far behind?' " Josh quoted. He knew the idea would probably go right over her head. Bootsie lived for the moment and the day and could scarcely think about what would be necessary in a week, let alone a month or a season. The instant-gratification generation, he thought to himself, if they don't have something that minute, it doesn't exist.

Dutcher, at least, knew the need for planning and thinking ahead. The Grand Prix circuit wound its way from January through October, and a man had to fit himself to its demands. If, on the one hand, racing gave Dutcher an excuse for his recknessness, the stringencies of Formula I also imposed a structure and a schedule on his life.

Josh broke the silence. "Did you go to the beach today, Bootsie?" he asked, thinking that she looked rather pale and could use some sunshine and fresh air.

"No, I didn't," she was pouting slightly. "Dutcher promised he would come back and take me, but he didn't."

"I said I would if I could, Bootsie," Dutcher said softly, "but there was too much work to do. You can ask Josh if you don't believe me."

"But this isn't any fun at all!" Bootsie retorted, ignoring his suggestion completely.

"I told you back home that it wasn't going to be a vacation, hon," Dutcher went on. "I knew it was going to be boring for you, but it was your idea to come along anyway."

"Boring is right," Bootsie said grimly. She cast an imploring glance at Dutcher. "It's been so awful, you can't believe it. My cousin came down a few days ago and she left this morning, she couldn't stand it so."

Josh tried to control his impatience. He was angry at the girl's obliviousness to Dutcher's real reason for being in Daytona. Yet at the same time he was grateful to her for the light she was casting on the situation. Clearly it was at her insistence that she was there at all, and not at Dutcher's. Josh could see that his brother was trying to make the best of a difficult situation. He had let himself in, it seemed, for lots more of the same, since Bootsie was part of Dutcher's plans for the rest of the season. Of course, there would be lots more to occupy Bootsie's time once the racing started, but until then she was bound to be more trouble than was warranted.

For all the recklessness and derring-do of the professional driver, he was basically a superbly conditioned and finely attuned athlete who was responsible for not only his performance but his own life as well. To have potentially disruptive elements like Bootsie inserted into what should be as untroubled a time as possible for Dutcher was more, much more, than Josh wished to see his brother burdened with.

"Maybe this was the wrong time of year to come to Daytona," Josh said, trying to be as tactful as possible.

"But Dutcher said he had to be here now!" Bootsie wailed, missing the point completely, not realizing that its intent was focused on her.

"What Josh means, honey," Dutcher said softly, "is that he and I have to be here now, but maybe it's just the wrong time for you. There's really nothing going on that you can enjoy." He smiled at her.

"Unless you want to come down to the pits and get your hands dirty," Josh added, trying to alleviate some of the gloom that had fallen since Bootsie's arrival in the lounge. He could not understand how she could spend so much time with Dutcher and not realize how vital their work was. But her mind seemed to be on nothing but her own pleasures and Dutcher's role as the chief provider of them.

In spite of his annoyance with the whole business, Josh was impressed by the patience Dutcher was showing toward Bootsie. It was unfair, it was wrong for her to create a problem like this for Dutcher, to be selfish and silly at a time when Dutcher needed support and understanding from those around him.

That settled it in his mind. Somehow the problem would have to be resolved. He would urge Bootsie to leave Daytona the very next day.

He sipped his beer slowly, not really wanting it, and thought of Amanda. How out of place she would be here, he couldn't help admitting. Her world was also someplace far away, and for her there wasn't the lure of racing to smooth out the differences and make up for the change. He wondered what part of his life, if any, she could fit into. Surely someone with her appreciation of beauty and craftsmanship could learn to love the Ferraris and Jaguars, the sleek, sometimes perfect, jewels of his world. One could not look at a racing Ferrari and not appreciate it as a stunning piece of sculpture, a masterpiece that also performed its function superbly. To Josh's mind there was little art that was more significant than that. It was like Amanda's own art—to be used and not relegated to museums.

He wished he could show Amanda such cars and teach her to love them as he did. But, he reminded himself, that was exactly what he promised himself he would never do. Never again would he risk another woman's meeting the same tragedy as Elizabeth had. No, he thought firmly, his first intuition was the right one. Amanda Parrish was no part of this and never could be. And much as he might feel he was attracted to her, this was his world, in his blood, something he never could or even wanted to get away from.

The whole thing just didn't make sense. There was no way to make it add up. He knew he had to forget her, and he knew he couldn't. It was going to be the longest month of his life.

When it was over and he was back in New York, the little silver horse would be waiting for him. And what else, he wondered. What else?

Chapter 5

Amanda adjusted the light over her worktable. She bent slightly, scrutinizing the tiny model. The prancing horse had turned up more problems than she had anticipated. The body was a large mass, relative to its size, and that was all right, but the delicacy of the flung-out legs, and especially the tiny hooves, worried her. There wouldn't be any point in making the piece only to have one of the delicate limbs break off easily.

She leaned back in her chair for a moment, brushing her forearm across her brow to get the hair out of her eyes. She stretched slightly, with more than a touch of annoyance that the twinge in her back had steadied itself into a real ache. She didn't know how long she had been working; she was oblivious to the time. She was alone in the office, Basil having long since left for one of the endless parties that filled his social calendar, especially now during the holiday season. Amanda felt grimy and knew that she should have left earlier too. She liked to be home for Tommy's dinner, but that hour, she was sure, was long past. Naomi, their housekeeper, would have already put him to sleep.

The shrill ring of the telephone interrupted the silence. "What are you still doing there at this hour?" Marshall asked in surprise, after Amanda had said hello. "I just called your apartment to see if you were ready. I was coming to pick you up."

"Oh, dear!" Amanda exclaimed. "I got so caught up in what I was doing, I completely forgot the time." Forgotten too that he had been set to escort her this evening, a plan made weeks before their last meeting.

"Cara Langford would have you drummed out of the universe if you ever dared to forget one of her dinner parties," Marshall said. "Hurry home and dress, and I'll make excuses for your being late."

When Amanda finally arrived, breathless and flushed, at the Langfords' Sixty-eighth Street town house, the others were still having their predinner cocktails. The forty or so beautifully dressed guests clustered in shifting, informal groups in the rather formal marble foyer. The floor was authentic Carrara marble, and the far wall echoed the classic theme, painted entirely from floor to ceiling in a trompe l'oeil effect that gave one the feeling of standing beside a marble-columned ruin on a Grecian hill and gazing off to islands set in a distant sea. The other walls were draped and swagged in the classical, festooned manner. Excellent antique furniture, Empire chairs and tables, continued the motif.

Amanda had the fleeting thought, as she always did when entering this room, that the women should all have been dressed by Madame Grès; the flowing Grecian togalike draperies for which the famed couturière was known, would have fit the Langfords' East Side house perfectly. Amanda smiled happily. Her own dress, a heavy silk design by Mary MacFadden, was a contemporary draped and corded version of that look. Glad that she had arrived before her tardiness could be taken for rudeness, she murmured apologies to her hostess and kissed Marshall lightly before going over to link arms with Paolo, who was standing with a small group of people.

"Darling, you look wonderful," he said after kissing her on both cheeks and then looking at her appraisingly. "Slightly tired, but wonderful. Tell me what exciting things you've been doing."

"Working," Amanda said, but there was something in her voice that made it sound like something more than that.

"Really!" An older, regally dressed woman at the edge of their group exclaimed. "I know it's become quite the thing for women to be suddenly signing their names to all sorts of things, but I didn't realize that one would take it quite so seriously." She shuddered snobbishly.

"I take mine very seriously," Amanda said.

"Well, darling, I didn't mean anything disparaging about you," the woman replied. "You, after all, are selling at Pembroke's, and your things run into the thousands. I really meant those women who, for the life of me I can't understand why, are making everything from underwear to workmen's clothes," insisted the dowager firmly as she turned her back and walked over to another group.

"How odd," Paolo declared, "she's rather boring, don't you think?" He addressed his question to Amanda and Laura, but was answered by a man who identified himself as the woman's husband.

"Yes, quite, absolutely," the man agreed. "I've lived with her for thirty-seven years now, and she's always been boring."

Laura was enchanted. "Even as a young woman?"

"Even as a girl," came the reply. "If she ever was a girl. I can't say I really remember."

They all laughed helplessly at that. "Well, I can never say I find my husband boring," Laura said. "I never know where he is or what he's up to."

"How long have you been married?" the man asked, as if that was the point.

"Do you mean this time? Or altogether?" Laura asked.

They all laughed again, this time at the older man's expression of surprise at the unusual question.

Laura was starting to count on the fingers of her heavily bejeweled hands, and Amanda guessed that it was more for the sake of displaying those diamonds than for pinpoint accuracy in answering the question. In any event Laura's computations were interrupted by the Langfords' butler announcing that dinner was served.

The doors that separated the dining room, living room, and salon had been folded back to expose an enormous dining table that accommodated all of the guests. It was brilliantly set with sparkling Irish crystal and fine Minton china, with individual silver salt and peppers at each place. Guests found their seats, and the waiters began pouring what would be the first of the three wines served with each course. Low masses of floral arrangements were set along the entire length of the table, and the flames of the fat, waxy candles in each bouquet added to the glitter of the room. Amanda preferred to entertain large dinner parties at smaller, separate tables scattered about the two large reception rooms of her apartment, but she had to admit that there was a touch of stateliness in the formality of the Langfords' arrangement that was rather grand. The waiters began serving the first course, giant mushroom caps stuffed with savory crabmeat. This was followed by vichyssoise, braised pheasant with exotic vegetable accompaniments, and a cool sorbet to clear the palate before dessert was offered. Busy, experienced hands poured Muscadet, Chablis, gold red Burgundy. Amanda had been seated toward one end of the table, and Marshall was placed somewhere near the center, certainly too far from her for convenient conversation. That suited her mood perfectly, strained as any conversation with him would be. She would have to confront him soon enough, she knew, but the stress of appearing with him in public might be her undoing. She smiled nervously across the table at Paolo, and turned slightly to face her dinner partner.

Amanda was pleased to find herself seated next to

the hitherto unknown gentleman. He and his wife were the only two at the party that Amanda did not know. She liked the idea of having someone new to talk to, especially this very charming gentleman who obviously said whatever was on his mind. It was a refreshing quality and quite a change from the usual arch and sophisticated conversation at such dinner parties.

His wife had known who Amanda was, but he seemed totally oblivious of her work and was merely pleased at having a beautiful and attentive young woman to address his outrageous remarks to. Amanda knew that their name was Sargent, that his wife was the heiress to an enormous midwestern manufacturing fortune but considered herself an art connoisseur and had lived in various parts of Europe for most of her life. Her husband seemed as unintimidated by her airs as he was by her fortune. He delighted in darting barbs about both and her personage in general.

But even his sprightly conversation was beginning to pall on Amanda. She found herself becoming restless and bored, when she suddenly heard Mrs. Sargent say something that drew her sharply attentive.

"It's the most beautifully preserved town, I dare say, in all of northern Italy. The great tenor Pavarotti comes from there."

"I know Modena well," Paolo was saying. "It's in the Romagna."

"Ferraris come from there," Amanda heard herself saying, and found all of the other guests looking at her.

"Diego had a Ferrari once, it was red," Laura said, trying to fill up the awkward silence.

"Yes, I remember," Paolo helped along. "It was a 5-liter, 12-cylinder sports model."

Amanda turned to him and whispered, "I didn't know that you knew about cars."

"And I didn't know you cared," Paolo whispered back, at once amused and puzzled. "Every Italian has something in his blood of Ferrari or Maserati"—he raised his voice for the benefit of the table and then lowered it again for Amanda—"but I didn't know that you did."

She flushed and found herself telling him the whole story of the little silver horse.

"So that's why we haven't seen anything of you for the past two weeks," Paolo said. "You really have been devoting yourself to your work." He gave her an affectionate look. "Regardless of what some of the others might say, I thoroughly approve. Even"—and he scrutinized her carefully as he said it—"the real reason behind this fervor."

Amanda started to protest, but he was having none of it.

"When will it be finished, and when will your dashing patron be calling for it?" he insisted on knowing.

"It should be done in two weeks," Amanda said, "when he gets back from Florida."

Paolo nodded. "You must keep me informed of everything that happens," he insisted. "I am absolutely enchanted by the whole thing. It's a marvelous modern fairy tale."

"Please, Paolo," Amanda implored. "Don't make so much of it. It's really nothing."

"Not at all," he smiled. "Handsome young gallant rescues maiden as he charges the countryside in his silver Ferrari. It's absolutely fascinating, and besides"—he gave her a conspiratorial wink—"I can help you with the technical details."

"Whatever are you talking about?" Amanda couldn't help laughing.

"I know a great deal about Ferrari," he said solemnly. "Even technical details."

Amanda teased him but she was impressed. She had never associated Paolo Aldobrandini with anything other than the ephemeral fashion world of which he was uncrowned emperor. For him to know about motors and models and such came as quite a revelation.

"The picture he showed you," Paolo pressed. "The horse was on a background of yellow, yes?"

Amanda thought for a moment. "Yes," she said. "That's right. How did you know?" She had fleetingly thought that the background color was that of the car on which the emblem was placed.

"Up until the last century, when Italy became unified, Modena was the seat of an independent duchy," Paolo said. "Yellow was always its color, and Ferrari used it when he introduced his marque."

Gone was Amanda's amusement with the garrulous Mr. Sargent, who had turned his attention to the lady seated on his other side. It was fascinating to her to hear her close friend speak so knowledgeably about something that was so new to her, and she listened to him attentively. She was not ready to grant even to herself, let alone to Paolo or anyone else, that the soon-to-be-owner of the silver prancing horse was the real reason for her obsession with the piece. She explained her design problems to Paolo, detailing the dilemma she had been in at the very moment that Marshall had called to remind her of this party.

Paolo listened sympathetically. but the amused sparkle in his eyes told Amanda that he was less than convinced that the commissioned piece was the only object of her enthusiasm. Right now, though, she was restless again and wished that coffee and brandy would be served quickly, so that she might make an acceptably early escape. She had brought the clay casting home with her and wanted to spend some more time on it before she went to sleep.

She didn't dare reveal this to Paolo. He would just use it as more evidence of the feeling she was trying so hard to deny.

At last the party was over, and Marshall insisted on seeing her home. He hailed a cab for the short ride, and he held both her hands in his.

"I've barely seen you these past few weeks, Amanda," he said slowly. "I've missed you terribly, my dear."

"Oh, Marshall, I've been so busy, and–" Amanda started to apologize.

"Your work never came between us before," he broke in quickly but hesitated over the words. "We've always been able to make plans and spend a great deal of time together."

Amanda thought deeply. What Marshall was reminding her of was exactly what she knew she had to get out of. The structured social life, all the evenings like the one that had just passed that were still so important to Marshall and had become so meaningless to Amanda. He was a dear and she knew he meant well, but everything that he and his world represented was suddenly closing in on her: its routines and demands threatening to rule her life, lock her in, closing out the sunlight and blue skies and open opportunities that Amanda realized all at once meant–freedom.

That was it. With Marshall she would be safe, secure, protected. The days and then the years would come in orderly procession, filled with all of the conventional notions of what the good life was all about.

There would be the parties and premieres in town, the necessary charity functions, the vacations even as predetermined and routine and peopled with exactly the same crowd as would constitute her clique in the city. There would be no surprises, no adventures, no extraordinary forays out of the usual. There would be no such thing as throwing a few clothes into a bag to catch the next plane out, or race down unknown roads to wherever they might lead.

That was the romance of life, Amanda realized in surprise. That and not a square-cut diamond on her finger, no matter how large the carat count or how perfect the clarity and color. She had left Alan in order to be free to live her life more fully and to pursue her work more completely. She knew now, with a slightly painful sadness, that accepting Marshall would be a giant step backward to that same safe place she had chafed in and fought so hard to get out of. No more did she want a life surrounded by chauffeurs and doormen. She wanted a life open to blue skies and freedom. Like the freedom that was so perfectly realized in the stance and pride of the little silver horse. Perhaps that was the secret of its majesty.

No one spoke in the taxi, but Amanda's mind was working thunderously inside her head. All of these realizations were coming home to her at once. She pressed Marshall's hand that still held hers, the gesture a mix of affection and good-bye.

It wasn't Marshall and his world she wanted. It was Josh McKay and his.

"I'm sorry, Marshall," she said softly. "But I realize it just wouldn't work for us. It's me, Marshall, believe me. I could never make you happy. Not the way I feel." She drew the magnificent ring slowly off her finger, placing it into his hand, from which she had removed her own, and pressing his fingers over it to protect the precious gem. She kissed him lightly, and as the cab drew to a slow stop in front of her building, Amanda opened the door herself and got out, feeling as she went through the lobby to the elevator as if she were floating, as if an enormous burden had at last been lifted from her, so happy was she when she walked alone into her own apartment.

Amanda threw her clothes off and, hastily donning a smock, ran to the room that had been Alan's study and where she now kept an almost complete replica of the tools and paraphernalia she had at the store. She drew off the cloth she had placed over the tiny clay horse and studied it again, becoming completely absorbed by it, working far into the night until at last she thought she had exactly what she wanted.

But she was so tired she doubted her own judgment and decided it would be better to sleep and reappraise the work when she got up in the morning.

After waking Tommy at eight, she walked quickly to the study, still in her bare feet. She uncovered the tiny clay figurine and held it up to the clear light of morning.

She hadn't been wrong! Even in the dull gray nocolor of the thick clay, the spirit and animation of the little horse could be seen. Once it was translated into silver, it would be perfect. She had solved the problem of the fragility of the outflung limbs by extraordinarily careful tapering and proportioning. Now as she turned the clay round and round in her hand, reexamining it from all angles, Amanda felt confident that it was going to work. Josh had been right, and so had her feelings of the night before. There *was* a lot of Amanda in the piece.

When she got to the store later that morning, she

didn't go directly to her office. She detoured to another floor, to the palatially elegant suite where Willis Haviland held court.

She told his secretary that she had no meeting scheduled, but wanted to see their boss for just a moment, if it was at all possible.

After quick, buzzed inquiry, Amanda was told to go in.

She entered the inner sanctum with only slightly less of the awe she still felt even after all the times she'd been in there. The room was almost square, but large enough to have contained her own cramped quarters perhaps four times over. The walls were the same lustrous, hand-rubbed mahogany as the main floor, and the antique porcelains and bronzes that stood on equally valuable furniture were all of museum quality. Willis Haviland had been a collector all his life, not only for his customers but for himself. There was something of the paradox in this man, roughhewn and outspoken even at seventy-eight, who was so drawn to objects of beauty he could not be without them day or night.

He sat behind a Louis XVI desk, all deeply carved turnings and brass fittings. His deceptively cherubic face was a scrubbed pink color beneath the thatch of white hair whose slightly longer length was the only concession Willis Haviland made to contemporary style in either his person or the objects that surrounded him.

"Good morning, my dear," he intoned in the deep voice that still carried traces of the Midwest. "You look lovely this morning, and happy."

"I am, Willis," Amanda said, addressing him by his first name, a guarded privilege of a special few. "I want to show you this." She drew the jewelry box in which she had placed the clay model from her handbag, and held it out to him. "You remember that commission I told you about for the silver pendant," she said. "The one that was giving me so much trouble? I think I've got it licked."

"The little Ferrari horse." Willis Haviland picked up the figurine carefully, examining it much as Amanda had earlier, turning it every which way in the light. "Charming, extremely charming."

Amanda sighed a deep sigh of relief. It meant so much to her to win approval for her work from this most difficult of men to please.

He handled the figurine a few more times. "When are you going to have it cast?" he asked.

"Immediately," Amanda said quickly. "The finished piece is promised for two weeks. That's why I did the modeling myself rather than give the sketches to the workroom."

"This gives me an idea," Willis said slowly. "We might be able to do a very sizable piece of business in reproducing the emblems of the prestige marques. The Jaguar, of course, and some of the more obscure ones. Did you know that Bugatti had a very limited edition, a car they thought they would sell to the kings of Europe in the 1920s, that had a trumpeting elephant on its hood?"

"Oh, no," Amanda groaned aloud. "Not you, too."

Willis looked up at her in surprise. "What's the matter?" he asked.

"Ever since I accepted this commission, I seem to have been running into car enthusiasts everywhere," Amanda explained. "Everybody seems to know the names of cars I've never even heard of, and they talk about their races and backgrounds as if they were pedigrees."

Willis smiled. "They are," he said softly. "Have you ever been in a really classic or antique car, Amanda?"

She shook her head slowly.

"Then you haven't seen the perfect marriage between art and function," Willis declared. "The Italians made most of them, but the British have their Rollses and Bentleys and others. The granddaddy of them all was the German Mercedes-Benz, and when I was a young man in the Midwest, the dream I shared with everyone I knew was to some day own a Duesenberg."

"I've never even heard of that," Amanda admitted.

"Probably the finest car ever produced in America," he said slowly. "Forgive me, my dear," he added, looking up at her with an expression she had never before seen on his face. "But I still get nostalgic every time I think of it."

"Did you ever get to own one?" Amanda asked sympathetically.

"No, my dear, I didn't," he answered half sadly. "By the time I could afford them, the company was out of business and my attention was in other places."

"Are they completely gone, then?" Amanda was curious.

"There are some still around, surprisingly enough," Willis replied. "The going rate is about $150,000, if you can find one."

Amanda was flabbergasted. "For that kind of money," she said, "it should be a work of art."

"It is, I assure you," he said. "I want you to think about this idea a little bit. It could be very interesting. The Duesenberg logo was set in a red-winged eagle, and they used a hood ornament for many years that's a perfect piece of Art Deco." He looked at Amanda straightforwardly. "It might do very well today."

Amanda laughed. "If car fever is contagious, I hope I don't catch it."

Willis shook a friendly forefinger. "Be careful, my girl," he said, "there's something about great cars and the men who drive them that can be irresistible."

Willis knew nothing about Josh McKay except that he had commissioned a piece of jewelry. Nevertheless Amanda felt a warm flush, and she knew that telltale color was suffusing her cheeks. There would be no fooling a sly old fox like Willis Haviland, and she knew she had better keep her emotions in close check. "Well, I've taken more of your time than I had intended to," she said, rising. "Thank you for looking at the model and for all the information."

"Be sure I see the silver as soon as it's done," he reminded her. "You might be starting another one of your famous trends."

Amanda smiled and thanked him. How kind he was, she thought as she made her way back to her own office: that understated compliment to the success of her earlier, much copied pieces was characteristically thoughtful and gallant.

She let Basil know that she was on the premises and then ducked right out of their office to take the clay to the silversmith, who would cast it for her. She spent most of the day working on it with him. The casting of the mold and the pouring of the silver would be done by the shop; then, the master silversmith and Amanda agreed between them, the rough silver would come back to her for engraving and the final polishing that would give the piece its finished form. She would select a suitable chain from the dozens that the store carried, and that would be it.

He agreed on a timetable, and Amanda went back to the office, satisfied that everything was working as planned.

She had forgotten how deeply gratifying the work of one's hands could be. She had been too long at her sketchbook, committee meetings, and promotional appearances. All of the work she had been doing to get the clay model perfect reminded her of the joy she always experienced in working directly with the materials of her art. Now she had it to look forward to again, when the rough piece came back to her for the work and attention that would perfect it.

The timing was good for another reason, Amanda had to admit. The alternate weekend arrangement with Alan, which was the crux of their separation agreement, meant that Alan was going to have Tommy for the Christmas holiday. Amanda had already turned down Paolo's invitation to have a country Christmas with him and a few others of their friends. She just hadn't felt in the mood at the time that his invitation came, and she knew that the gaiety of the season was going to spell a lonely time for her.

But now that she would have the silver horse to work on, she knew she had made the right decision. Instead of having to put up with the silly chatter and frivolity of Laura and the others, she would spend Christmas at home with herself and her work. She suddenly felt much better about everything. Josh would be back to claim the horse, and she could apologize for the curtness she had shown him. She could tell him . . . Amanda stopped short. How could she tell him all the things she was really thinking now?

Chapter 6

Pembroke's closed its huge front door promptly at noon on the Saturday before Christmas Eve. The last-minute shoppers who had not bought their baubles on time would have to make do at a lesser emporium. Amanda joined the hubbub of employees wishing each other the greetings of the season and then made her way home alone, stopping only to duck into a liquor store for a split of champagne that she would refrigerate and celebrate the holiday with.

Even her mother was out of town, Amanda reflected as she hailed what she was sure was the last remaining taxi in New York City, to take her up Madison Avenue and curve around to Fifth. Sylvia had called earlier in the week, both to announce that she was leaving for an extended holiday in Palm Beach and to insist that Amanda have dinner with her before she went.

Sylvia Firestone was a formidable lady who spent more time worrying about her only daughter than she liked to admit. She gloried in the fact of Amanda's success, preened amid her friends whenever her daughter's name or work received media attention, and despaired over the divorce that had shorn Amanda of the one element in life that Sylvia considered the prop on which all the others depended—a husband. Having gone through several of her own, always claiming to be "between marriages," Sylvia had never reconciled herself to the thought that

Amanda had done the right thing in divorcing Alan. No matter how successful Amanda became, her mother felt work should have been an addition to her life, and not a substitute.

Amanda had dutifully gone to dinner at her mother's sumptuous apartment as summoned. She listened to a repetition of all of what Sylvia considered the facts in her case and was told, moreover, that she looked decidedly peaked, was working too hard, needed a vacation, and even more, needed a new love interest. Amanda had been grateful that she had never told her mother about the accident with the car. That would have given her another theme to worry over constantly.

Now Amanda put aside all thoughts of what everyone she knew was trying to do for her. Once home, she drew out of her bag the prancing horse, now at last in silver, and hurried to her worktable to absorb herself completely in her task.

The prancing horse looked almost woebegone as she studied it. It was blotchy and discolored from the casting. Pieces of plaster still clung in some of the grooves that had been sculpted to show details in the mane, tail, and legs. Only when she was finished with the incising that she wanted in order to make those details even more real, would she begin the final polishing that would strip the figurine of all the extraneous matter from the modeling process. Then it would become the perfect, finished, shiny charm that Amanda felt was going to be among the best, if not the very best, that she had ever done.

She bent over her work for hours on end, scarcely knowing night from day. Occasionally she would turn on the radio to have some music while she worked, but as soon as a human voice broke in with news or weather or commercial announcements, she found it too distracting and flipped it off.

By the next morning the prancing horse was finished. It glowed with a sheen that could only be achieved by the hours and hours of hand rubbing that Amanda had given it. Every detail was clear and exact. The deep incisions she had made were thrown into shadow by the surrounding silver, giving the tiny piece an extraordinary depth and breathtaking vitality, almost as if the tiny horse were prancing with real energy coursing through him.

Amanda propped him up against the base of the lamp, letting the light shine fully on him, almost sending sparks flying, so right was the finish on the round flanks, deep chest, and noble throat of the stallion.

She went into the kitchen and uncorked the refrigerated champagne. She poured herself a brimming glassful in her best Waterford crystal, tucking the small split bottle under her arm and taking it back to the study with her.

She stood in front of the worktable, looking happily at her accomplishment. She raised her glass, toasting the silver figurine. "To you, silver stallion," she said out loud, "may you shine forever the way you do now. And may you be as happy with your owner as I am with you."

Her own words gave her pause. She had intended, silly as it might have been, to share the moment only with the stallion and herself. The thought of his owner had come unbidden. Yet once there it was not to be denied. She couldn't wait to see the expression in those blue eyes when he contemplated his precious toy. Amanda wondered what his attitude would be toward *her* when he claimed her creation.

Suddenly Amanda felt totally frustrated. It was only Sunday. Pembroke's wouldn't reopen its doors until Tuesday morning. There was no one with whom she could share her accomplishment for two whole days. She didn't even know when Josh would be back.

Everyone she knew or liked was away from the city. For the first time she could remember, she felt completely isolated and alone. The very walls and familiar furnishings of the apartment seemed withdrawn and quiet. She walked from room to room, not feeling warmth anywhere. The champagne's elation had lasted as long as its bubbles.

She knew she could call Paolo, catch a train out of Grand Central and be among friends in less than a couple of hours. Yet she didn't really want to. She couldn't think of anything she really wanted to do at all. Just somehow make the hours leap by, instead of dragging as they would now, until the store opened and she could show the piece to Willis Haviland and the others.

Tommy wouldn't be getting back until Tuesday night. Since it was Christmas vacation time, and he had no school, she had agreed to let Alan keep him in the country for an extra day.

She wondered what Josh was doing at that very moment. He was probably still in Florida. She wondered if he stopped to observe such nonautomotive events as holidays. She stood at the living room window, looking out at the park. It seemed dark and deserted, even at this early hour. All of the stores and shops on Fifth Avenue and the rest of the city would be closed. The great apartment houses lining Fifth Avenue seemed to have locked their doors, curtained their windows, and withdrawn into themselves. Whatever merrymaking was going on would be inside and private. Amanda walked back to the study and picked up the prancing stallion. She brought it back into the bedroom with her and put it again in a circle of light, propped up against her bedside lamp.

Then she remembered something. She bounced out of bed and ran back to the study, searching among the floor-to-ceiling shelves of books that Alan had never taken to his new apartment. She leaned over to a tall shelf that held a selection of large-sized, brightly jacketed volumes. Quickly she found the one she was looking for and, as happy as if she had discovered a great treasure, lugged the outsize volume back to the bedroom. She propped herself up this time, among the many pillows that she loved to rest on, and opened the book, glancing first at its brilliant photographs of the living pieces of sculpture that Willis Haviland had so lovingly described. Then she turned back to the beginning and settled back to read the text of this book she had remembered being in the study. She didn't understand a lot of the words. Right from the very beginning it seemed very detailed and technical about the endless series of cars it was describing. But Amanda concentrated hard, learning new names and new words, grateful when the cumbersome text was broken every few pages by pictures of the undeniably magnificent machines that had sent men's hearts soaring. She skipped over the paragraphs about the technical parts—gearshifts, shoebrakes, twin chain-driven overhead camshafts with twin choke carburetors were another language. She read instead about the marques, a word she remembered Willis Haviland using and that she now learned designated a manufacturer or brand name. She read about the races that had been going on, she was surprised to realize, from the late 1890s, almost simultaneously with the creation of the automobile itself, an attention-getting device that carmakers used to promote their early products. She was absorbed in the accounts of how quickly both the cars themselves and the racing aspects of the business had evolved with sophistication and expertise that drew more spectators than the older and more genteel sports of yacht and thoroughbred horse racing ever had.

A glance at the clock told her that it was just past midnight. Amanda marked her place in the book with a velvet ribbon and set it aside for the moment. She stretched and yawned, unable to believe that she had been so absorbed in her reading that all of the day and half of the night had slipped away. *Well,* she thought happily, *that's exactly what I wanted—something to make this endless weekend go as quickly as possible.* All of the names and dates and events and terminology of the book were jumbled up in her head. She knew that she hadn't retained as much information as she would have liked, but some of the names in the pageantry of grand automobiles and racing had stuck firmly in her mind. As she studied the beautiful photographs she had made mental notes about the emblems she had seen, especially on the earlier cars, that might well translate themselves into the kind of jewelry Willis had been talking about. She glanced over at the closed book, regarding it almost fondly. She had been reading and making notes for hours on end, yet she hadn't even begun to skim the surface of the subject. A glance at the index told her that she had hundreds of pages to go through before the name Ferrari came up.

She fell asleep happily, knowing there was enough in the book to keep her occupied most of the following day. Then the holiday weekend would be over and she could get to the store.

She left extra early on Tuesday morning, anxious to see Willis Haviland and show him the horse. Anticipating his compliments was something she had been savoring all through the long hours since its completion.

Willis usually got to the store as early as any of the time-clock employees, and Amanda wanted to get to him before the press of the day's business had him all tied up. She hurried through the main floor, not even stopping to glance over at her counter. The store was beginning to fill up with the first customers of the day, but immediately after Christmas there would be more returning than buying, even at Pembroke's.

She went straight up to her office, but before she could even slip out of her coat, the phone began to ring.

It was Mrs. Burroughs, head saleswoman at Amanda's counter. "Mr. McKay is here, Mrs. Parrish," she said. "I didn't know if you were in yet."

Amanda couldn't believe her ears. How had he gotten there so early? "Yes, of course," she said. "I'll be right down." Here was the rightful owner, and Willis's appraisal would just have to wait! If, she realized, she ever got it back from the doggedly determined man who was claiming it his already.

His Florida sojourn had left him tanned, a perfect complement to his blondness, and made his eyes even more intensely blue.

He smiled at her, extending his hand. Amanda took it. "How are you?" she asked, striving for a polite, noncommittal tone.

"As fine as you look," he said. "You're really very lovely, Mrs. Parrish."

Amanda glanced around quickly, to make sure that no one could overhear him and to try to admonish him at the same time.

"Here it is," she said lightly, handing him the tiny drawstring jeweler's bag.

He turned to the counter, where a black velvet display board was sitting, and put the silver stallion on it.

He looked at it carefully for a few moments. Amanda couldn't help scrutinizing him, trying to read his reaction to it.

Then he picked it up, examining it and fondling it at the same time. "It's even better than I thought it would be," he declared.

Amanda let out a sigh of satisfaction that she hoped he didn't hear. "I'm very glad," she said.

"It's perfect," he smiled at her. "Now we have to go to lunch to celebrate."

"Lunch!" Amanda echoed in disbelief, glancing at the huge wall-clock at the back of the store. "It's barely past ten o'clock!"

"Brunch then," he compromised. "Can we go someplace where it's quiet?" he said hopefully.

"Would it be possible," she said hesitantly, "for us to meet later in the day?"

"Dinner?" He made the word sound as though he had scored a victory.

"No, not quite that late." Amanda was thinking. There was that idea of Willis's she had to discuss with him. "Could you meet me at about three o'clock?" she asked, desperately trying to keep the situation under control.

"Three o'clock at the Russian Tea Room," he said, "that will be fine."

"Why not here?" Amanda asked in surprise.

"I prefer neutral territory," Josh said. "I knew you wouldn't come to my hotel room, and Pembroke's rather intimidates me."

Amanda was elated.

"By three o'clock the lunch bunch will be gone and the cocktail hour won't have started. You don't have to be afraid that anyone you know will see us," Josh said.

"That isn't what I was thinking at all!" Amanda protested.

"Whatever you are thinking," Josh said with quiet authority, "I'll meet you there at three o'clock." He bowed his head slightly toward her, grinning, and turned and walked out of the store.

Amanda stood dumbfounded.

Her saleswoman's voice interrupted her. "Mrs. Parrish," she said gently.

"Yes, what is it?" Amanda asked, as if she had been woken out of a trance. "The gentleman obviously loved the charm"—Mrs. Burroughs had kept a distance while Amanda and Josh were talking—"but he didn't take it."

Amanda glanced down at the black velvet cloth on the counter. In its center the little silver horse, immobile, caught in his fixed and frozen moment, pranced, oblivious to the unsettled atmosphere swirling around him.

"That's all right," Amanda said at last, "I'll take it to him this afternoon." She picked up the little charm and placed it carefully back in the soft drawstring bag, glad at least to have it with her for a few more hours and to show it to Willis, who was as approving as she thought he'd be.

She busied herself in the workroom for the rest of the morning and early afternoon. At ten of three she pulled on her bright red coat and told Basil she wasn't sure whether or not she'd be back that afternoon.

If Josh McKay was as disturbing to her sense of balance as she had so far found him to be, she might head straight home after their meeting.

She walked west on Fifty-seventh Street, huddling into herself against the chill afternoon air. The sun was palely visible, shining more silver than gold behind gray clouds that stretched across the entire sky. When she went inside the restaurant, he was waiting for her.

Amanda jumped, slightly surprised to find herself standing so close to him.

"I got here early," he said by way of explanation. "In case you did also. I didn't want you to be waiting for me." He took her arm and led her past the bar area and into the brightly decorated but quite deserted restaurant. "See?" He indicated the room with a broad sweep of his free hand. "I told you we'd be all alone."

A red-jacketed waiter bowed them to a table along the wall. He held out menus, but Josh shook his head. "We'll have blinis with red caviar and a bottle of champagne. Moet '73 or '74 will be fine."

Amanda looked at him in amazement. The restaurant, although convenient to Pembroke's, wasn't one that she frequented. She would have liked to have seen the menu, if for no other reason than curiosity. It was rather presumptuous of him to order for her, she thought. But she liked it.

"Did you bring it with you?" Josh asked, breaking into her thoughts.

"Of course I did," Amanda said. "Did you think I wouldn't?"

"It's possible," he said, with that grin that was by now his most familiar expression to her. "Since I haven't paid for it yet."

Amanda drew back sharply. "My God!" she exclaimed. "It never entered my mind."

Josh laughed. "I'm glad to see you trust me," he said.

"With everything from Pembroke jewelry to Russian restaurants," she observed dryly. "How do you know that I want what you ordered?"

"You're the caviar type," he said. "And they've a superb way of serving it here."

For some reason Amanda couldn't bring her gaze to meet his. She looked everywhere around the room, as if intent on analyzing the decor.

"Try to relax," the words were said softly, caringly. But they were admonition enough to cause Amanda to turn quickly around and face him at last.

"I don't know why you make me feel like this, Mr. McKay," she said. "If it's a game you're playing, or—"

"It isn't any game, Amanda," he broke in, interrupting the flow of words. "I'm falling in love with you. I don't know how you feel about things like that, but to me it's no game. Now"—and his voice grew almost sternly authoritative—"take off your coat, lean back, and listen to me. I have a lot of things to say to you, and all of them are pleasant. Now, please," and his voice softened again. "Relax and be happy. That's all I want."

Amanda smiled but sat primly in her seat. "Mr. Haviland asked me to discuss something with you," she said, trying to keep the conversation light, "concerning your charm." Everything was moving too fast for her, and she determined to move the conversation back to safe territory.

Josh grinned widely. "Mr. Haviland doesn't know me," he said. "How can he possibly know about my charm?"

"The pendant," she said, trying to get the conversation back to a business level. "Mr. Haviland is very pleased with the way it turned out—"

"Good," he interrupted her again. "You had mentioned that before, so I assume it's very important. I hope it means a promotion for you, or at least an increase in pay." He smiled playfully.

"I'm trying to be as serious as I can," Amanda laughed. "If you're still interested in the horse—"

"I'm interested in the horse, Amanda," he said, "but I'm even more interested in you. Why won't you let me talk about that? You still refuse to take me seriously."

"I'm trying to take you very seriously, Mr. McKay," she said, her delighted voice belying the words. "I am being perfectly serious and businesslike. How much more serious you can expect me to be, I cannot imagine. I am trying to ignore your frivolity and keep this meeting on the subject it was intended for."

He tried erasing the smile from his face, not quite successfully. "Very well, Mrs. Parrish," he said lightly. "We will attempt to get on with the business you mentioned. Ladies first, always." He bowed slightly at her. "Then we can take up the matter that *I* came here for."

Amanda's eyes danced. "Mr. Haviland is interested in having Pembroke's reproduce the prancing horse and offer it as part of my design group," she said. "Since you brought the idea to us and the piece is yours, he wants to have your permission for and cooperation in our doing so."

"No way," his answer came, swift and unmistakable.

Amanda stared at him. He wasn't joking anymore. "Let me explain it a little further," she said. "In a situation like this, although it is rather a precedent, Mr. Haviland would naturally expect you to share in whatever sales we realize, sort of a royalty to you. Considering the success that the line has had thus far, that might be a fairly nice amount of money."

He shook his head. "Still no deal," he said. "I want an Amanda Parrish original." He stared at her boldly, but Amanda held his gaze this time. No flinching, no looking away, she told herself sternly.

"As a matter of fact," Josh said, extending his hand across the table to her, "I'd like it right now."

Amanda clutched her bag tightly as if to keep it from him a little longer.

Josh quickly sensed her teasing mood. "I want my Amanda Parrish original," he repeated. "Or"— he hesitated slightly for effect—"the original Amanda Parrish. Either one will do."

She felt her senses reeling. "Either one?" she echoed, surprised herself by her flirting audacity.

"Well, really," Josh conceded, "I want both. But I'll take them one at a time, in either order."

Amanda flushed, glad when the waiter arrived with their food, expertly folding sour cream, melted butter, and rich red caviar into the buckwheat blinis. He uncorked the champagne, pouring some for Josh's approval and, at his nod, filling Amanda's glass and then Josh's. He covered the bowls that held the remaining blinis and departed discreetly.

"Have some," Josh said, indicating the rich, pancake-like concoction.

Amanda took a few bites, and then a few more, and to her amazement, because she didn't think she was at all hungry, the blini had disappeared.

Josh laughed. "Eat," he ordered, uncovering the dish. He lifted out another one for her and for himself, and then filled it for her.

As she watched his practiced hands Amanda reached for her champagne. Before she could bring the glass to her lips, Josh interrupted again.

"A toast," he said, lifting his own glass toward her. "To the prancing stallion."

Amanda raised her glass happily. "To the stallion," she confirmed.

"And to you," Josh said, gesturing with the glass.

Amanda sipped her champagne, saying nothing.

She looked up, conscious that he hadn't tasted the champagne yet. He gestured again. "To us," he said, and then he drank deeply of the sparkling liquid.

The bubbles first tickled, then warmed her, as champagne always did. She took another sip, happy to have the warm, mellow feeling spread out through her strained and watchful body. She leaned back from where she had been poised at the edge of her seat. The warmth of the room, as well as the champagne, reached her. She felt blissfully happy, for no real reason other than that she was with him.

"At last," Josh said as he glanced at her empty plate. "Have another blini," he said, again doing the honors of serving her.

"You are the most outrageous man," Amanda said, surprised at the sound of her own voice and looking at him in equal disbelief.

"And you are the most adorable woman," Josh said. "At last, we're both having the same conversation."

"I thought we'd been having that ever since we

sat down," Amanda said, suddenly feeling ever so slightly giggly.

"Are you kidding?" Josh asked. "Every time I tried to say something about you or me, all you would talk about was Mr. Haviland and the store. It might as well have been Portuguese and Swahili."

This time Amanda really did giggle.

"Better, much better," Josh said approvingly, filling her glass again before she could protest.

"We also talked about the horse," Amanda reminded him. "That was having the same conversation."

"Almost," Josh amended. "I was talking about my one and only, unique, exclusive charm, and you were talking about mass merchandising."

"No," she corrected him giddily. "I was talking about your impertinence, and Willis Haviland was talking about your charm."

"It should be just the opposite," Josh said.

"No," Amanda said boldly. "Mr. Haviland doesn't know about your impertinence and–I'm not quite so sure about your charm," she added flirtatiously.

"But you're thinking about it at least," Josh teased.

Amanda shook her head, staring down into the nearly empty champagne glass. "I don't know what I'm thinking about," she admitted.

"Did you have anything to eat today?"

Amanda stopped to think. "I'm not sure"–she tried to remember–"but I don't think so."

"My sophisticated lady!" Josh chortled. "She doesn't know how to fold a blini or not to drink champagne on an empty stomach. All this time you've been trying to outclass me and you don't know the simplest rules in life!"

"That isn't true," Amanda protested, "not true at

all. You wouldn't believe the things that I know." She struck a provocative pose.

"Tell me." Josh leaned across the table, his eyes almost dancing.

Amanda took up the challenge. "Well," she said, "there's Hispano-Suiza and lock-to-lock steering and half-liter Bentleys and Stutz Blackhawks, and Boxer Berlinettas and Targa Florio and fuel-injected, dry sump, single overhead camshafts, whatever in the world that means!" She finished with almost a cry in her throat, a mixture of triumph and joy that she didn't quite understand.

Josh threw his head back and laughed, laughed so long and so hard that the group of waiters who had been talking to one another at a far table at the other end of the room stopped and stared at them.

At last Josh controlled his laughter and looked at her.

"You've been studying," he said, his own voice a mixture of admiration and happiness. "Dammit, you've been studying. It may be all mixed up inside that gorgeous head of yours, but at least it's there, you *care* and it's there. Don't worry, darling, we'll get it all straightened out and you'll understand everything, I promise you will," Josh whispered, taking both her trembling hands in his and covering and squeezing them close. He looked deeply into her great dark eyes, knowing only the beauty and luster he saw there, forgetting the promise he had made to himself—and too late to someone else—a long time ago.

"I didn't know any New York hotels had suites with wood-burning fireplaces," Amanda marveled.

"Not many do," Josh said as he stoked the blazing logs. "That's why this place has become a sort of second home for me, considering that I barely have a first."

"Why not?" Amanda asked. She had taken her coat off as soon as they had gotten in, and now she stood extending her hands in front of the fire.

"Because I travel so much," Josh explained. "I'm all over the world."

"But when you're here," Amanda persisted. "Not in the city I mean, but where you were"—she groped for the words—"when we first met."

"I usually stay at my mother's place," Josh said. "I use the guest cottage."

"You mentioned you had a brother," Amanda said.

"Yes, his name is Dutcher, he's four years younger than I am and home even less," Josh laughed.

"He's involved with cars too, isn't he?" Amanda was remembering everything now. It was funny how those details he had mentioned long ago were so clear to her now, while everything that had happened from the time she agreed to leave the Russian Tea Room until they had arrived here was so hazy to her.

"Dutcher is in Formula I racing," Josh said. "I'm the only one in the family who sees anything of him these days."

"Formula I," Amanda repeated, concentrating hard. "Those are the really important races—the Grand Prix."

"Exactly right," Josh beamed as he stood up, putting his hands on her shoulders. "I love you, Amanda."

She was sober enough to try and stave him off. "That's silly," she insisted. "You barely know me and what you do know, even I have to admit it not very nice."

"Nice?" he echoed in surprise. "Lovely, marvelous, wantable, so much more than just 'nice,' Amanda." He drew her body against his.

"I've been absolutely awful, Josh," she nearly wailed. "I've been stubborn, arrogant, hardheaded, snooty, superior—"

"Kissable," he added.

"No!" she exclaimed. "I've been terrible."

His lips gave the answer that no mere words could. He kissed her tenderly, dizzyingly, endlessly, till Amanda felt her knees get shaky and threaten to buckle under her. As if he read the language of her body to perfection, he led her, without relinquishing his hold, to the small nearby sofa facing the fireplace.

The flames reflected dancing lights on her face, and she felt herself melting into his embrace. She tried to pull away. "Oh, Josh," she said. "I'm so happy."

He kissed her lightly on the forehead and drew back, scrutinizing her. "You are something, Amanda," he said. "Like that little list you threw at me back at the restaurant with the jumble of cars and drivers, and races and parts. Your emotions are just as tangled, darling. You're as soft and warm as a woman can be, and yet you fight being what you are. You are so full of love and so much need to give it, yet just as soon as you feel it, you pull away."

"You make me sound hopeless," she said glumly.

"Oh, no, not that," Josh rushed to assure her. "You've been hurt, perhaps, or at the very least, confused about important things. But there's nothing to worry about," he added as he stroked her dark hair. "I'm going to make everything all right."

She laughed. "Can you?" she asked. "We barely even know each other. You don't know anything about me except my name and where I work. You don't know anything about my life, and I know nothing about yours. It's—it's unreal to think there's anything we can mean to each other."

"You're so wrong," he said, and swiftly drew her inside his arms again. Amanda tried to resist the touch of his mouth on hers, tried not to kiss back as she felt the rest of her body yielding to his strong demand. But it was useless.

Something inside her sparked, as if an electric charge had brought all of her being to life after a long, cold stillness. *Why shouldn't I,* she cried to herself, *why shouldn't I let him love me?* All of the anguish and the loneliness of the Christmas weekend just past came rushing over her like a bad signal, a dark cloud blotting out the sun and dulling her senses. It was impossible now to believe that that loneliness had existed less than twenty-four hours ago, when now she was caught in as fervent an embrace as she had ever felt in her life.

Why shouldn't I, she thought again, as he gently lowered both of them to the carpeted floor. The warmth of the fire beating against her cheeks was no match for the heat spreading inside her. She felt his hand at her breast, then loosening her dress, then slipping it off her shoulders. She closed her eyes, but his very touch was as vivid as if she were staring at him, seeing it. It was as if her mind were standing outside her, coolly watching the movements of her hot body.

But it was movement, she knew, that was toward, not away, from Josh. It was fighting free from herself, from whatever it was inside her that might have held back from him now. She gave, and loved herself for giving, and suddenly loved him for showing her how. When she felt him inside her, it was more than a physical filling of her senses. Her emotions were bursting as well.

When it was over she looked up at him. Her eyes held all of the wonder and gratitude he could have wished for. She closed her eyes again, her naked body still flushed and reeling from the impact of an explosion that she had never experienced before. She shuddered slightly, feeling as if a cool draft had suddenly blown into the too-warm room. Then she realized it was Josh, poised over her, kissing her everywhere.

If before had been an eruption inside her, this was now a flurry of butterflies, gently touching down briefly and spontaneously before lifting and going on again. She laughed out loud.

Josh looked down into her eyes. He seemed more pleased than surprised at her unexpected outburst. "What are you doing?" he asked quizzically.

Again that peal of laughter. "I'm imagining all sorts of things," she answered, throwing her arms out recklessly as she arched her body toward him. "I'm visioning visions and seeing all sorts of things."

"And here I was, thinking I was bringing you back down to earth," Josh said.

"Oh, no!" Amanda exclaimed. "I'm going on and on like this forever. I don't want to stop, not ever!"

His voice was gentle. "It will go on and on, I promise you," he said gravely. "We have all of our lives together in front of us, but not right now." He touched her gently.

Amanda was puzzled. "Why not now?" she demanded with all the intensity of the, for once, truly selfish.

"Because you've got a curfew," Josh said.

"Curfew?" Amanda echoed.

"Yes," Josh said, "your son's bedtime. We don't want you home any later than that, do we?"

"No, of course not," Amanda said, swinging her legs around so that she was sitting on the sofa; he startled her with his concern, knowing and caring about Tommy and his bedtime.

He brought her her clothes, in an unexpectedly neat pile.

Amanda began dressing rapidly, just barely noticing that he had left her alone in the living room to get herself together. That was nice. *He has a sense of privacy,* she thought happily.

She was fully clothed and straightening her hair in front of a mirror when he came back into the room. He had his overcoat on, and he helped Amanda into hers. Under his arm was a small, bulky, gift-wrapped package.

They took a cab back to her apartment. Amanda rang the bell, rather than using her key, and after introducing Josh to the astonished housekeeper, took his hand and led him straight to Tommy's room. Naomi had already helped Tommy into his pajamas, and he was sitting on the floor playing with a small set of wooden trains.

"Nice trains," Josh said, hunkering down on the floor so that he was almost eye level with the sprawling child.

"But not very fast," Tommy complained. "I'm pushing them as hard as I can, but they just won't go."

"Maybe this will be faster," Josh said and handed him the package. He got up, taking off his coat and tossing it carelessly on a nearby chair as he watched the boy expectantly.

Amanda watched both of them. She was thrilled

when Tommy got the wrappings off and exclaimed wildly over the shiny model car inside the box.

"Gosh!" Tommy exclaimed, "It's the superest model I ever saw!"

Both adults laughed, and Josh leaned down again to explain it to him.

"See the tiny little horse on the hood," he said to Tommy while glancing up only for a moment at Amanda and smiling. "That means it's a Ferrari. Can you say that?"

"Ferrari," Tommy replied dutifully.

"Good! Now look at these back wheels," Josh went on. "You rub them against the floor, very hard, a few times like this." He demonstrated. "That's what makes the car run." He let go of the toy, and to Tommy's uncontained delight it sped all the way across the room in a flash of color that stopped only when it hit the baseboard of the far wall.

"Wow! That's the fastest model I ever saw," Tommy exclaimed. "Wait till I show it to the kids at school." He scampered over to reclaim his prize. "Can I try it now?" he asked Josh.

Josh laughed and tousled his moplike brown hair. "Of course you can," he said. "It's your car, so you can do whatever you like with it."

Amanda had never seen her son so happy nor felt so good inside herself. What was the magic this man had, she wondered, this brash, take-charge, totally unexpected stranger who had crashed so unceremoniously into her life?

He was as good with Tommy as he was with her and, she had to admit to herself, Josh *was* terribly good with her. Everything about him that she had tried to put down and push from her mind after their first encounter was utterly endearing to her now.

She couldn't for the life of her imagine what had impelled her to try to brush him aside so totally after the incident with the car. He was everything a woman could want. She felt ashamed for the coldness and superiority she had assumed when he came to Pembroke's looking for her. The fault, she realized, was not Josh's but her own. She had tried to brush him aside because she wasn't ready for him, ready for all of the challenge and energy and life force he embodied. Being afraid of all of that was her own shortcoming. She watched them as they played, man and boy, both sprawled on the floor, Josh as unmindful of his impeccably tailored suit as Tommy was of his old flannel pajamas.

Amanda realized that her son was being initiated into that worldwide fraternity of automobile infatuates, being pulled right in by a master member. Oh, well, she thought, it was probably inevitable, given Tommy's impatience with his clumsy wooden trains. It was only a matter of time before he, too, became engrossed in fast cars and their drivers. Who better to teach him than the man with him now, carefully and patiently explaining to Tommy how the frictionalized action of the back wheels of the model worked, with as much care as though he were explaining the intricacies of a 120-horsepower motor to a grown-up mechanic.

He looked up at Amanda. "Has Tommy seen my horse yet?" he asked.

"No, he hasn't, he's just come back from the country today. Look, Tommy." She tried to get her son's attention away from his new toy. "Look at Mr. McKay's Ferrari horse." She drew it out of her purse and, shrugging helplessly, joined the two males on the floor.

Tommy examined the charm. "Nice," he said noncommittally, and turned his attention back to the car.

Amanda glanced at the Snoopy alarm clock. It was already eight thirty and, she gently reminded her son, already way past his bedtime.

"But Mom," he wailed, "this is my vacation. I don't have any school tomorrow."

Josh's eyes were relaying the same message, and again Amanda felt helpless against the double onslaught. "Okay," she said, "ten more minutes. But that's it, you guys, and no extensions." But they were already absorbed in the intricacies of the scale model, and she wondered if either of them had heard her.

At nine o'clock she stood up. "That's it," she announced, in a voice that sounded serious enough for Josh to pat Tommy on the shoulder and jump up to join her in a more adult position.

"When can you come back?" Tommy demanded, squinting up at Josh, "and play with me again and teach me more about cars?"

"Any time you like, son," Josh answered, and Amanda jumped slightly at the word. Josh seemed to have sensed her reaction, for he quickly added, "As soon as your mom invites me back."

Tommy scrambled up to beseech her. "Can he come back? Mommy, can he?" he demanded.

Amanda hugged him and laughed. "Of course he can, darling. He can come back and play with you very soon. But only," and her voice drew a warning, "if you go to sleep right now like a good boy."

The words were barely out of her mouth before he had jumped away and dived into his bed, pulling the sheets and blankets almost over his head.

Amanda, her eyes brimming, walked over, pulled

the covers down, and tucked them under his chin. She kissed him lightly on the top of his head, forgoing the usual impulsive good-night hug. She suddenly felt shy at displaying that kind of emotion in front of Josh. She switched off the lights, and they tiptoed out of the room.

"Oh," Amanda said, "I forgot your coat in there." She went back to retrieve it. The expression in his eyes when she rejoined him stopped her, but only for a moment. "Would you like a drink?" she asked simply. "Or some coffee? I suppose it's too early to offer you a nightcap."

"Not at all," Josh assured her. "Only I very seldom drink coffee or alcohol. It doesn't go with the job."

She yearned to keep him there with her, never to let him go, but she knew she mustn't.

"I hope I'll see you again soon," she said, with almost formal politeness that she knew was artificial and inappropriate.

Josh sensed her confusion. "I'll see you forever," he reminded her, his hand holding her arm. "But I think you'll be more comfortable if we start forever tomorrow."

She looked at him gratefully, smiling but unable to say anything, returning the hug that suddenly enveloped her.

"I'll call you at the store tomorrow," he said, getting into his coat. "I have to pay for my charm, and sign the contract that I've duly received it, and all. Then we can go to dinner."

"Yes, dinner," Amanda repeated slowly as she followed him to the front door.

"Till then," he said softly, lifting her chin in his hands and kissing her mouth lightly. "Sleep well, my lovely Amanda."

Then he opened the door and was gone.

Amanda undressed slowly and eased herself into the steaming bath that Naomi had run for her. She lay her head back on the tub, closing her eyes and letting her mind slip back into the dream of the hours just past while the water soothed her body.

She was afraid to linger in its caress, feeling herself almost falling asleep. She got out quickly, letting the warm air dry her. She slipped into bed without putting on a nightdress, suddenly wanting to feel nothing on her tingling skin.

She shivered slightly, despite the warmth of the room, and drew the thin topsheet above her breasts. Now she was safe to let her mind wander where it would, to drift into sleep with the kisses and caresses of Josh still warm and alive on her body. She felt herself almost trembling with happiness. She knew now she had what she had always dreamed of, and she fell asleep dreaming of it.

Chapter 7

"How did your gentleman like his prancing stallion?" was the first thing that Willis Haviland wanted to know.

"He liked it very much," she smiled.

"Good, I thought he would," Willis said. "How far did you get with discussing its reproduction and the possibility of doing others?" he asked.

"Not very," Amanda admitted.

"That's good too," Willis Haviland said.

Amanda looked surprised.

"The timing would have been all wrong," he explained. "Something else entirely has come up."

Amanda waited for him to go on.

"You know I've been dickering for a while with Neimeyer's," he said. "They're wild about your things and want a setup in Dallas similar to what you have here."

"It seems to me that was all very on again, off again," Amanda said.

"'Yes, well, now it's on again," he said, peering intently at her. "Very much on, I must say. We've just about completed negotiations."

"You mean I'm really going to be in Texas?" Amanda asked, somewhat surprised that the protracted dealings had so suddenly come to a conclusion.

"Yes, literally and figuratively," Willis said. "I should say personally. We've got enough inventory to get them started, and they want you to come down there for an Amanda Parrish Week to get the whole thing started."

"When would that be?" Amanda asked, wondering where Josh would be.

"They'd like to have you there the last week in March," Willis said. "How would that be for you?"

"That should be fine," Amanda said slowly. By then Sylvia should be back from Palm Beach to stay with Tommy, and depending on how the weekends fell, she could let Alan have extra time with him, if he liked.

"Are you pleased?" Willis wanted to know.

"Yes, very," Amanda said. She knew how long he had been working on getting this deal for her. She felt very grateful, but wondered why it had happened now, of all times, now when a complication named Josh McKay had entered her life.

"I daresay the ladies of Texas who have had to come here to buy your things or who have only seen them in the magazines, will descend on you en masse and hound you to death. I'm pleased that you look so happy to be going, but I predict you'll be even happier to come back," Willis said.

Amanda laughed. Then she turned serious. "I'm sure you're right, Willis, just as you're right about everything. I don't know how to thank you for this. I know all the time and work it's taken to consummate the arrangement. I can never be grateful enough for this and for everything else that you've done for me."

"Nonsense," he brushed her gratitude aside. "You have a very superior talent, and I kiss the feet of talent. Your being represented elsewhere will earn us income as well, more than enough to cover whatever has been expended in making the arrangements."

"Neimeyer's has branches even outside of Texas." Amanda was thinking. "Will I be in their other areas as well?"

"We'll wait and see how Dallas works out," Willis said. "If they move as much merchandise as I suspect they will, we may expand the operation."

"What about the locations where we both have stores," Amanda asked, "like Palm Beach?"

"We can either confine certain items to each store, or battle it out and let the chips fall where they may," Willis said. "But we'll cross that bridge when we come to it. Let's demolish Dallas first."

"Aye, aye, sir," Amanda said, smiling. "I go to do battle as ordered. Although I must admit I've never quite pictured myself on the old frontier."

"Have you ever been to Texas?" Willis asked.

"No," Amanda admitted. "Alan had a lot of dealings down there and wanted me to come along on some of his longer trips, but I always managed to avoid it."

"Until now."

"Yes," Amanda echoed. "Until now, but now I'm fighting under my own standard, and not someone else's."

"Texas is going to surprise you, I think," Willis said, "but I guess you may be a bit of a surprise to them, too. I'll predict a draw, until the final verdict is in."

Amanda felt suddenly very confident and strong. "As long as they buy jewelry, preferably mine, we'll all be winners."

"That's the spirit exactly, my girl," Willis commended her, punctuating the sentence with an offhand gesture that told her their meeting was at an end.

Amanda rose quickly, thanking him again, and left the office. Tonight at dinner she'd tell Josh. But before that she had a million things to do—telephoning Sylvia, telling her closest friends like Paolo about her new contract, letting Alan know so that he could make changes in his own plans.

She was delighted with the expectation of being surrounded by admiring customers, something there hadn't been time for at Pembroke's all during the last busy season. Willis didn't encourage much in the way of such promotion; it was too disruptive of the staid and orderly conduct of Pembroke's. Amanda missed the customer contact she had learned to relish when her first line was initially shown at the store. Now she would experience it all over again, and she was sure that would lift her to further new ideas and revitalized concentration.

She wondered if she should discuss with Willis the possibility of quickly making up a few new items, possibly Texas-oriented, to bring down to Dallas with her. But the trip was so little time away, and new projects would put unbearable pressure on her and on the workshop. She dismissed the idea as impractical, but there were a thousand other questions bombarding her mind.

It was impossible for her to hide her excitement from Basil, so she decided to tell him at once. "It's finally happened, Basil," she said happily. "Willis has finalized the agreement with Neimeyer's. They're going to be carrying us as of March, and I'm going to go down there to help kick it off."

"That is good news," her assistant replied. "I'll have to admit, I didn't realize that was the cause of all our happiness this morning. I thought you were in love."

Amanda gave him a sharp look. "This could be as important for you as it is for me," she reminded him. "It's scarcely something to joke about."

"I agree entirely." Basil threw his arms up as if to ward off an attack. "It's just that I didn't realize it had happened, and when you marched in this morning, I knew there had to be something important behind the brand new look."

Amanda a little self-consciously touched the hair she had brushed back into a chignon that morning. "I've worn my hair like this before," she said.

"It wasn't the hair I was talking about, angel," Basil said, regaining his usual composure. "It was your whole demeanor this morning."

For once Amanda was grateful for the ringing of

the phone. She picked it up as Basil went back to his own work. It was Paolo. Amanda was pleased, anxious to share the news about Texas with someone so dear to her.

Paolo was delighted for her, as of course she knew he would be. But when he invited her back to Connecticut for the following weekend, she declined. She started to tell him about Josh, then stopped herself. They would all know soon enough. But when the phone rang a few moments later and she heard Josh's voice, she felt like telling the world.

"This is a test," he said, teasingly. "What are you doing for dinner tonight?"

"I'm having it with you," Amanda answered swiftly.

"Right! Now, what are you doing for the rest of your life?" His voice had become a caress on the phone.

"I'm having it with you," Amanda said softly, terribly aware of Basil hovering in the small office, but flushed with happiness as she was, she didn't care.

"I love you," Josh's voice came floating to her.

That was a little too close for comfort, much as she loved hearing it. "This is a business phone," she said lightly.

"Then I'll save it for when I see you," Josh said, getting the hint immediately. "Besides, I much prefer telling you face to your beautiful face." They quickly decided on a time for him to pick her up at the apartment that evening.

There would be time enough to tell Josh about Texas then, Amanda decided, and went back to the piles of work and phone calls she still had to make.

When he came to get her that night, she decided to stay in and make a meal of what Naomi had prepared before she had left. Not wanting the formality of the dining room, Amanda brought their food into the living room, and they ate from the small coffee table while sitting on the deep, cushiony love seats in the cozy little corner that Amanda favored.

Tommy, usually shy with strangers, squealed with delight when he heard that Josh was there, and while the adults ate he plied his newfound hero with question after question about cars and races.

Amanda watched them happily, again letting Tommy's bedtime slip past, only not so long this time, since he had school the next morning.

"Now we can talk," Amanda said with a laugh, coming back into the living room after Tommy had been tucked in. "There is so much I have to tell you about."

"Me too," Josh said. "There's really so much we don't know about each other, I hardly know where to begin."

"Well," Amanda said rather ruefully, "I'm afraid I'm going to have to begin with a little late news rather than general background. Something's come up."

Josh looked over at her inquiringly, taking her hand in his as he leaned toward her. "Nothing serious, I hope," he said, his voice full of concern.

"Well, it's serious, but it's good," Amanda told him quickly. "Only I'm afraid it's something that's going to keep me very busy for the next several weeks. Then," and she lowered her voice, looking at him earnestly, "I'm going to have to go away for a while."

Josh's jaw dropped. "Where to, and when?" he wanted to know.

"Texas," Amanda said simply, "on business."

She was overjoyed to see that he relaxed visibly.

"My God! From the way you said it, I thought you had to go to the moon to concoct some new design from those rocks!"

"No, it's not that bad," Amanda said, her eyes sparkling, "I–I just felt a little strange at having to go away so unexpectedly, especially after what I promised you on the phone this morning."

"We've got a long time, darling," he said softly. "I don't ever want you to feel pressured or uncomfortable in any way. I know how important your work is to you. And, as a matter of fact, I've got business in Texas myself. Maybe we can even meet there. But first," and he squeezed her hand again, "tell me all about it."

Amanda found herself explaining about the Neimeyer's opportunity. She was surprised at her own enthusiasm in telling Josh what it meant to her, especially in terms of the desirability of her designs and how much *that* meant to her. She had always been rather diffident, at first with Alan and then with Marshall, in talking about her work, but Josh asked as many questions and raised as many points, almost, as Willis Haviland had. There was no doubt about either his interest in or his admiration of her accomplishments. When she finished telling him about how long the fabled Texas store had been after her, there was no mistaking the pride shining in his eyes.

But she quickly learned there was another reason for that special sparkle she had come to love so much. "I've been kind of sought after in Dallas myself," he said in a voice that made the statement sound almost like a confession. "As a matter of fact, I've been postponing going down there because I've been so busy with Dutcher, but it's been in the back of my mind, and now I'll have a double reason for going.

I'll call my friend down there and figure out a way to coordinate our trips."

Amanda found herself almost squealing. "You mean you'll come to Dallas with me," she asked excitedly.

"Well, I can't promise anything," Josh said thoughtfully. "My friend Haskell is a mighty busy man, but he's been anxious to talk to me about an important situation that he wants my thoughts on. We might not be able to go down together, but I'll figure out some way to catch up with you during the week that you're there."

"That's the icing on the cake, then," Amanda declared with a grin of fat satisfaction on her face. "We've got time to be together before I have to go, and then to be there together, it's almost like a dream."

"Not quite." Josh put a warning finger lightly on her cheek. "You mustn't forget that you tied yourself up with a traveling man, honey," he said. "I'm not going to be in New York all the time between now and then. I've got a couple of jaunts in between."

"Where to?" Amanda wanted to know.

"Just a hop down to Argentina and then Brazil," he said casually.

"You're kidding!" Amanda was astonished at the news.

"It's the Grand Prix circuit, remember?" he said. "This is the first year that my brother is entered in every race. The only one I'll miss going to with him is South Africa."

Amanda's eyes widened even further. She had always thought of the Grand Prix in Monte Carlo as being an important race, never realizing that it was a continuing, worldwide circuit. Her reading in Alan's book hadn't brought her even close to an explanation of today's racing activities.

"Then, right after I squeeze Dallas in, I've got to go out to California, to Long Beach," Josh went on. "That's the first American race of the year. It's going to be a quick jump, getting there from Texas." He winked at her. "Maybe there's a certain lady I can convince to come with me."

"I'm not sure," Amanda admitted. "I'm still trying to catch my breath from everything else you've said. I thought I was going to surprise you with Dallas." She shook her head wonderingly.

Josh laughed. "This year is a particularly hectic one for me," he said. "But I promise you it won't always be like this. Once Dutcher's got a full year under his belt, he'll be a seasoned veteran and I can relax a little more. Of course, I'm still going to want to oversee his cars and be with him for as many of the important races as I can, but it won't be an all-year-long, worldwide way of life. There'll be plenty of time for you and me and everything we want."

Amanda had always considered herself a sophisticated traveler, but she knew that Josh had covered a lot more territory than she ever had. She settled herself in his arms, leaning back, her head tucked between his neck and shoulders. "Tell me about it," she said dreamily. "Tell me all about this great wide world of yours that's so new and strange to me."

He talked to her at length about all of his hopes and dreams and aspirations from his earlier years of wanting to follow in his father's footsteps. He talked about the joy of being in control of a car, a superb racing machine, an instrument that was at one and the same time as powerful and as delicate as anything devised by man. He talked about the thrill of competition, of the feeling of being totally alive and all the senses attuned, giving the ultimate of oneself that competition racing demanded. He talked about defeats as well as victories, about places she had scarcely ever heard of, about mobs of screaming fans and the camaraderie of the men who race and build the cars. And as he spoke, so tangible was the magic of his feeling for it, that Amanda felt it all come alive for her. If there was danger in racing—and of course there was, she knew there was—Josh didn't dwell on it. Instead he drew for her glorious pictures of blue skies, winding tracks, shining machines, and courageous men.

There was so much for her to learn, for her to absorb and to know about, to sense and experience with him. It was as though he had carried her through the threshold of a brand new world.

They drank Soave, glass after glass of the light white chilled wine, and talked deep into the night. Amanda was startled when she saw how late it had gotten.

"I want to make love to you," Josh said slowly.

She lifted her face to his and kissed him deeply on the mouth. They clung together for moments, until Josh broke away suddenly with a short laugh. "My working woman," he said with pride in his voice. "I guess I mustn't keep you up too late."

"No," Amanda whispered, smiling. "You mustn't. But just a little. Yes?"

"Yes!" Josh breathed into her ear.

She broke away from him, laughing, taking his hand and leading him into her bedroom. She stood as he undressed her, watching him watching her, feeling the excitement rising between them. She wanted him, with an open, admitted desire unlike anything she had ever known before. This, too, she realized as at last they lay down, was another world he had led her to, an awakening not to a new outside experience but to an awareness of something within her, something *inside,* that was as unexplored, as previously mysterious, as the dark side of the moon.

The inside of Amanda, she thought happily as she stretched toward him. He gathered her into his arms, bringing her close to him. She nestled against him, letting her flesh tremble as he ran his hands over her body, opening herself to him with joy. The thrill of anticipation rippled through her, and she reached for him, her fingers tentative on him, tracing the strong lines of his body, enjoying him.

He caught her hand, lifting it to his lips, kissing the tips of her fingers, teasing her palm with his tongue before he set it back down on him.

Amanda moaned softly, a shudder ripping involuntarily through her. She pressed herself against him, wanting the answering thrust of him on her, in her. He held her strongly, their faces touching lightly, his above hers, seeming to the love-intoxicated Amanda as though he were floating above her. But she felt the realness of him in every fiber of her being, and as he melted her with tiny kisses she gave herself up to his total embrace, knowing him as she had never known any man before, knowing herself as she had never been before, feeling the blush that suffused her skin, the scent of her gratification filling her nostrils.

Afterward she watched him as he dressed, admiring the sinews and muscles of his slim, proportioned body. It seemed to her he was as efficiently constructed as one of his racing cars, and she told him so. He chucked her under the chin. "I wish I could listen to that sort of talk all night," he said, "but I know I mustn't. Someday, Amanda, someday soon, I promise you, we'll have all the time together we could want."

"What are you doing with the rest of your life?" she teased him.

"Saving it for you," he said simply, taking her arms and drawing her up from where she sat on the bed to stand next to him.

They kissed again, fervently, and again, after she had led him through the apartment and opened the front door for him.

"I'll call you early tomorrow," he whispered his good-night promise.

"Yes," she smiled back at him, before reluctantly releasing the door and locking it closed.

The next few days flew by, a kaleidoscope of shifting shapes and colors as Amanda whirled through her hectic daytimes and the dreamlike nights with Josh. She watched approvingly as the relationship between her son and her love grew and deepened and strengthened. She watched herself in the mirror as she brushed her hair and put on her makeup and creamed it off again at night and marveled and laughed at the glow that no longer came or went with the jars, created instead from the happiness that Josh had planted deep inside her.

When the day came for him to catch his flight to South America, she found herself more composed than she thought she would be at his leaving. What was happening between them was so good and so strong she was able somehow, miraculously, to take the parting in stride. She wanted to go out to the airport with him, but Josh dissuaded her, telling her it wasn't necessary, that he preferred to say good-bye in the apartment, and reminding her, moreover, that the very next day she would be driving out there anyway to meet her mother coming in from Palm Beach. No one, Josh told her, should have to go back and forth and hang around airports any more than absolutely necessary. "We'll be doing enough of it together before long," he told her. "I don't want you to wear yourself out with it when we're not traveling together."

They kissed good-bye, reminding each other that it was only for two weeks and that when they were reunited they had Dallas and the rest of the world still ahead of them.

Amanda was excited at the idea of seeing her mother again. She felt it was only right that Sylvia be the first to know about Josh, and she had had to restrain herself to keep from telling anybody else about him. She was bubbling over with the happiness of it, and exploding with the desire to share it. Now that Sylvia was at last coming home, Amanda could tell her and then, when Josh got back, after those two formidable figures had met, Amanda could start bringing him around to meet Paolo and the rest of her friends. Having Josh on her arm was an idea that made her almost giddy with excitement. She fell asleep hugging her pillow, planning for the day when everyone would know that the romantic incident they had all alluded to at the time of the accident had *actually* happened, and was going to have precisely the happy ending that Paolo especially had wanted for her. It was such a beautiful prospect that Amanda felt herself almost crying with happiness at the thought of it. Josh loved her, he loved her work, he loved her son. There was nothing else in the world she could ask for.

When she met her mother at the airport the next day with the limousine she had grandly hired for the trip, Sylvia Firestone scanned her daughter's face carefully.

"What are you looking for?" Amanda asked, somewhat amused at feeling she was under her mother's microscope.

"Something more than Texas," Sylvia declared in her usual style, coming right to the point and mincing no words. "Something's happened."

"Lots has happened," Amanda exclaimed lightly.

Sylvia scolded, "Something is up and you're not telling me what it is."

"Everything is fine, Mother," Amanda insisted. "I'm very excited about going to Texas, and there's an awful lot that's got to be done before I go."

"What about Marshall?" Sylvia demanded.

"What about him?" Amanda was surprised by the question. She hadn't thought of Marshall at all.

"What's happening with him?" Sylvia persisted. "Are you still seeing him?"

"No, Mother, I'm not." Amanda lowered her voice.

"There! I knew it, something's happened. Now, what is it?" Sylvia asked.

"He asked me to marry him," Amanda said, as if the whole subject were of no interest to her. "And of course I said no."

Sylvia grew reflective. "Anyone else would tell you you're a darn fool," she said. "Perfect gentleman, excellent family, prestige, and a comfortable fortune."

Amanda shot her a warning glance.

"But I'm not going to scold you," Sylvia said, reaching over and patting her daughter's hand, which she noticed was clenched into a small fist. "I'm not going to tell you you were foolish, because I happen to think you were right." Sylvia smiled sadly. "Marshall sounds very good on paper," she said, "but honey, he never would have made the right husband for you."

"I'm glad, very glad, that you can understand that," Amanda said. "I really was afraid you were going to try to push me into it."

"Nonsense," Sylvia explained, "I'm your mother. I know what's good for you. Marshall Strang is very fine, but he's not for you."

Much as she disliked her mother's probing of her life, Amanda couldn't contain her curiosity. "Since the president of Strang's would have been the perfect son-in-law for you," she said lightly, "would you tell me what keeps him from being the perfect husband for me?"

"He's too old," Sylvia said without blinking. "Much too starchy and not enough energy. You need someone who's going to light a fire under you."

"Mother, really!" Amanda exclaimed. "I never could keep anything from you."

"Well, you have this time," Sylvia answered, "because I don't have the slightest idea of what you're talking about."

"That may be," Amanda said, "but somehow you guessed it anyway."

Sylvia's face brightened. "Darling! What is it?" she asked. "Are you holding out on me?"

"I'm not holding out!" Amanda insisted. "You've been doing all the talking and you haven't given me a chance."

"You look as if you're ready to explode," Sylvia observed.

"I am," Amanda admitted with a deep exhalation. "I didn't want to tell anyone before I told you first."

"Told me what?" Sylvia demanded.

"I've—I've found him!" Amanda said, suddenly at a loss for words now when she finally had the opportunity to use them. "The most fantastic, exciting, lovable, understanding, incredible man in the world!"

For a moment Sylvia was speechless. Then the questions came with the rapidity of machine-gun fire. "Who is he? Where did you meet him, what does he do, do I even know him, for God's sake?" Sylvia fired all at once.

"No, you don't know him," Amanda laughed, "but you will very soon. He'll be back in a couple of weeks."

"Back? From where?" Sylvia demanded. "Two weeks, that long, for meeting a man who has swept my ice cube of a daughter off her feet! Why can't I meet him now?"

"Because he's in South America, darling," Amanda said, finally able to catch her breath and get her bearings while Sylvia continued her fusillade.

"South America?" Sylvia sounded rather dubious. "What does he do in South America?"

"He's only there for a couple of weeks," Amanda explained, "for the races."

Sylvia looked at her as though she were slightly mad. "A horseplayer?" she asked dubiously.

"Oh, no, Mother." Amanda had to laugh in spite of herself. "He's an automotive engineer, sort of, and he's very involved with race cars. He's down in

South America because his brother is driving in a couple of very important races."

Sylvia looked no less startled. "Race cars?"

"Yes," Amanda sighed. "I know it sounds rather strange, but believe me, it isn't. He's the most sensible, most solid man I've ever met."

"Now we're back to Marshall," Sylvia said reprovingly. "He was sensible and solid, remember?"

"Not the way that Josh is," Amanda answered. "Josh is totally different."

"Josh? That's his name?" Sylvia said.

"Joshua David McKay," Amanda answered, giving equal weight to all of the impressive syllables. "He comes from a fine old Connecticut family. He went to Yale. He's wonderful."

"So what's he doing hanging around racetracks?" Sylvia demanded.

"Mother, you're impossible," Amanda exclaimed. "You're the one who wanted someone to light a fire under me, and now that someone has, you're all questions and doubts."

"Well, I can't help it," Sylvia pouted. "You're my only daughter, and most of the time you're very sensible, too sensible, as a matter of fact." She paused "And then, to make things even worse, when you're not sensible, you sound absolutely crazy."

"I am crazy," Amanda admitted, "crazy about a man who is everything in life I've ever wanted."

"Well, suppose you explain to me about the racetracks," Sylvia said. "I'm a modern mother, and I'm perfectly willing to listen."

They spent the rest of the ride back into town with Amanda expounding on the wonders and virtues of Josh, prodded now and again by an incisive question from her mother. By the time the limousine had pulled up in front of Amanda's building, Sylvia was nearly totally convinced that her daughter hadn't gone completely berserk.

"But mind you," she said warningly in the elevator, "I'm withholding final judgment until I meet him."

"Fair enough," Amanda agreed.

When they got into the apartment, Tommy leaped on his grandmother, greeting her as though she were a long-lost friend. She hugged the boy close to her and then put him at arm's length, turning him this way and that to see how he had grown, exclaiming over his strong new muscles, to Tommy's squealing delight.

Amanda watched them, musing on the eternal question of why grandparents and grandchildren got along so much better than children and parents ever did. She expressed the question to Sylvia later when they were seated alone in Amanda's bedroom.

"It's easy to love your enemies' enemies," came Sylvia's unexpected answer. "Skip the generation in between and you find natural allies."

It was hardly the kind of answer that Amanda expected from her usually flighty mother, but it seemed to make some sense. She could never imagine Tommy as her enemy or think that she would bring him up in a way that he would consider her his. Of course, he was still only six. The major battles of growing up and growing away still lay far in the future.

"I suppose you're right," Amanda said, "although I suppose my raising him makes it easier than if you were going through it all over again?"

"And just what do you think I'm going to be doing while you're gallivanting in Texas?" Sylvia asked.

"I'm going to be totally responsible for him and watching him like a hawk."

"That really won't be necessary," Amanda reassured her. "He'll be in school most of the day, and Naomi will be here to do most everything else."

"Nevertheless I expect to be very close to him," Sylvia said. "I'll listen to his problems, play with his toys, and help him with his homework."

"Homework!" Amanda thought she would explode with amusement. "What sort of homework do you suppose a six-year-old has?"

"Whatever it is, I'll help him with it," Sylvia insisted.

She was glad that Sylvia was back, even though the relationship between them often exhausted Amanda. She sometimes wondered where her mother's high-flown energy came from.

Somehow the next two weeks flew by, and at last the pandemonium of Amanda's life was punctuated by a phone call from Josh, saying he was at the airport and coming into town.

"How soon can you be here?" Amanda asked. "I've got someone just dying to meet you."

"If it's someone important, I'd better go to my hotel room first and freshen up. It's been a hectic couple of weeks, and a very long, draggy flight. Will you let me do that?"

"Of course I will," Amanda said, "even though it means it'll be that much longer before we see you."

"Who exactly is 'we'?" Josh asked.

"My mother," Amanda said lightly. And then added quickly, "Of course, Tommy is dying to see you too."

"I think I'd better freshen up first," Josh said. "Will two hours be okay?"

"Two hours will be perfect," Amanda said, although she didn't know how she was going to live through them. "And everything else will be too, I promise."

When the doorman announced Josh's arrival, Sylvia insisted on opening the door for him herself, although Naomi was still there to serve dinner.

"Well," she said, taking his coat when he came in. "She didn't tell me you were gorgeous."

Josh chuckled appreciatively. "Just what did she tell you?" he asked in a teasing voice.

"Very little," Amanda answered, coming into the room to greet him.

"Do we have any mutual friends?" Sylvia wanted to know, still sizing him up.

Again Amanda answered. "I don't really think so, Mother. When Josh goes to Florida, he goes to Daytona, not to Palm Beach. When he goes to England, it's to Coventry, and not London."

"And when I go to Monte Carlo," Josh picked up the threads, "I go for the racing and not the gambling."

Sylvia peered at him curiously. "Don't you like people, Mr. McKay?" she asked.

Josh laughed. "Of course I do," he said. "As a matter of fact, I'm beginning to like you very much. May I call you Sylvia?"

"Most people do," she answered, trying to sound very offhand but secretly tickled with the serious attentiveness he was showing her. There was something in his expression and manners that was almost old-fashioned in its courtliness, young as he was. The combination was irresistible to Sylvia.

Amanda could see her mother was quickly warming to Josh. Sylvia's tell-all face held no secrets. They were all sitting in the living room now, Josh and Amanda enjoying the spectacle of her mother's preliminary feinting, like a wary boxer sizing up the competition. Amanda knew it would be a short-lived phase, judging by the way Sylvia was already melting. Josh would have her in his corner before the next bell.

Which just happened to be the dinner bell, telling them that everything was ready. Amanda got Tommy from his room so that the youngster could join them for the meal.

"I understand you're from Connecticut," Sylvia addressed Josh again.

"Yes, but when I'm in Connecticut"—the amusement in Josh's eye was unmistakable—"I don't go to Westport."

"You go to Darien," Sylvia pounced immediately, sporting her own gleam.

"No," Amanda interjected with a laugh, "he goes to Lime Rock."

"I give up!" Sylvia exclaimed, throwing her arms down. "What in the world is Lime Rock? It sounds like a drink."

Josh explained his work, mentioning the various British and Italian cars he worked on, knowing that they would be much more significant to Sylvia than the places they were manufactured or raced and road tested.

"He brought me a Ferrari," Tommy broke in proudly when he heard the name mentioned.

Sylvia fell silent for a moment, the light of understanding coming upon her. "So that's the little car he won't be parted from," she said slowly, looking at her grandson fondly. "One night after he was asleep,

I went in and I found it under his pillow. It's a wonder he hasn't hurt himself with it."

"I won't hurt myself, Grandma," Tommy said earnestly. "I know how to take care of a car."

Amanda shot Josh a knowing smile. "He's hooked," she said helplessly.

"You're going to Dallas with Amanda?" Sylvia asked. "You aren't racing there, are you?"

"Oh, no," Josh reassured her. "This trip is really for business kind of business." Josh went on to explain that he didn't really race cars anymore, only tested them, leaving the dangerous driving to his younger brother.

Amanda followed their conversation without contributing much. She was on a peak of excitement she had scarcely known before. She enjoyed the parrying that was still going on, mostly initiated by Sylvia in her eagerness to find out everything she possibly could about Josh, his background, and his family.

When dinner was finally over, Amanda was ready to call it a draw, but after Josh had made an early departure, her mother declared that he was absolutely the victor. He had conquered her completely.

And it was a rather smug and happy Sylvia who kissed Amanda good-bye and wished her a good trip the next week when the doorman came up to get her bags and carry them to the limousine, where Josh was waiting to take her to the airport.

The city streets and the expressway out to Kennedy were clogged with the usual New York traffic, but Amanda already felt as though she were miles away. "This is nice," she said to Josh, her hand touching the soft upholstery, wanting to thank him for his thoughtfulness.

"I feel as if I'm riding in a bus," Josh said. "The bigger the car, the less I like it."

"Why?" Amanda was a little surprised.

"Less maneuverability, less speed, less fun," he answered.

"I hope this isn't going to be too unexciting for you," Amanda said lightly.

"Only the car," Josh whispered, gathering her into his arms and kissing her while the uniformed chauffeur watched approvingly in his rearview mirror.

They got to the terminal with time to spare, and sat at a little plastic table talking over cups of coffee that neither of them really wanted. They kissed goodbye in front of the Eastern terminal, and Amanda boarded the plane for Dallas. Josh would join her later in the week, he didn't know exactly when.

The flight was uneventful, the unfolding landscape below, which Amanda had hoped to see, was obscured by clouds almost the entire length of the flight. It was only when they were in sight of the city that the cloud cover lifted and she could see stretches of dun-colored land reaching out for miles, crisscrossed by the gray of highways and with occasional clusters of buildings that marked smaller towns.

The store had a car and driver waiting for her, and she was whisked downtown to the glittering, green-glass Hyatt Regency Hotel, where they had reserved a suite for her use.

In her suite she found two enormous floral arrangements. One simply held the card of the store's president, the other had a note from Fred Hamilton, the general merchandise manager and vice-president in whose bailiwick Amanda's jewelry would be. The note welcomed her to Dallas and expressed the writer's anticipation of seeing her at the store at three o'clock that afternoon.

Amanda took off her coat and tipped the bellboy, impressed with the tone and efficiency of Texas hospitality. "I'm going to enjoy this!" she promised herself out loud as she swung around the suite, noting where everything was. The hour of the meeting left her plenty of time to relax and get ready. The chauffeured limousine would be waiting for her, to take her to the store and back again and on all of the other rounds of the busy week-long schedule Fred Hamilton presented her with when they met in his office at the appointed time.

Amanda studied the closely typewritten pages, wondering how they were going to fit everything in. Somehow she knew they would; she would have little time to miss Josh before he got there.

She was totally delighted with the next items Fred showed her—copies of the full-page ads that would appear in the papers the next day and throughout the rest of the week, replicas of the announcements of the boutique and her visit that had already been placed throughout the store and its branches, and a beautifully rendered drawing of the boutique itself, which Fred explained had been framed for her and would be sent to her home for her to keep as a remembrance of the visit.

Amanda was overwhelmed by the elegance and thoughtfulness that were the hallmarks of everything that was being done for her. Even her treatment at Pembroke's had never been as regal as this. Willis Haviland had impeccable taste, but he exercised it with a restraint that was certainly conservative compared to the flamboyance of the Texans. Yet there was nothing in their presentations that she could fault.

Everything was perfectly done. Amanda lost no time in expressing that to Hamilton and thanking him again for the magnificent flowers that had been waiting for her at the hotel.

Then she was introduced to the buyer who would be directly responsible for Amanda's department, and to the key salespeople. Amanda spent some time talking with them, happy to observe their enthusiasm about her work and to convey her own excitement to them.

Fred drew her aside after the others had left, telling her that they had deliberately left this first evening open for her. "We didn't know whether you had friends down here that you wanted to see, or whether you would like to just rest before the big day," he said. "We open at ten, and you'd better be right on the button for these Texas ladies. We've got them all dying to meet you."

Again Amanda was compelled to thank him for the thoughtfulness, explaining that she didn't know anyone in town but indeed appreciated having the evening to herself.

"The food at the Regency is pretty darn good," he said. "You might like to explore the restaurants or relax and have something sent up. It's probably going to be the only chance you get to sample it."

Amanda turned the pages of her schedule again, studying it more closely. "I see what you mean," she said, smiling. There wasn't a single lunch or dinner, starting with the very next day, that wasn't accounted for. She would be taking meals with various store executives, local socialites, media representatives, and even at a reception with the mayor. There wasn't an angle that hadn't been thought of and thoroughly covered. When she wasn't in the store during the day, there were newspaper, radio, and television interviews scheduled. Several of those took up evening hours, it being of prime importance that she spend as many hours as possible in the store with her potential customers.

She looked up at Hamilton. "It's going to be quite a week," she said.

He spread his hands. "We do our best," he said modestly. "Most of the credit for your week has to go to our promotion and publicity people. You'll be meeting them before long."

He took her arm, telling her he wanted to give her a short tour of the fabled store and a chance to meet some of the people he had mentioned, before she went back to the hotel.

He took her from floor to floor, explaining that the great volume of business had spread to the suburban branches and to the stores that now reached both coasts, but the most expensive departments, like jewelry, were still centered in the narrow downtown store where it had all started.

Afterward Amanda thanked him and bade him good-bye and was sped the few blocks back to the hotel. How different it was from New York, she thought, with Fifth Avenue and the surrounding midtown area being so full of life and energy. Here, what were the main streets of the city seemed quiet and somber, not at all the bustling, roustabout atmosphere she had expected. There was fabulous wealth down here, and the people she was going to meet were wealthy, cultivated, and powerful. She hoped they were going to be her customers as well. One thing was certain—they were going to go all-out in showing her themselves and their city.

Back in the suite after her bath, Amanda propped

her legs up as she reclined on a small love seat in the living room. She reread the typed schedule. Her mornings started early, with the store opening, every day. Some of the evenings went very late, when there were parties and receptions scheduled at the homes of both the store's president and a prominent Texas socialite whom Amanda had never met but whose name she recognized from the newspaper columns.

It looked as if her first breathing space came after her early-evening dinner with the mayor and other city officials.

That was three nights away, four if she included this one, which hardly counted at all, since she had it all to herself and could do nothing, which was exactly what she wanted.

A couple of the store sessions were at branches, and Amanda was grateful to see that they opened an hour later than downtown. But before she could congratulate herself on gaining an extra free hour, she remembered that a good portion of that time, if not all of it, would be taken by getting out to the branch store. *Too bad,* she concluded, *but thank goodness for the limousine.*

It was hard to believe that the month had passed so quickly. She had been through her loneliest Christmas, her reunion with Josh, the elation before this Texas venture, and all the preparations for it. Now, at last, she was actually in Texas. And soon Josh would be here.

Amanda hadn't had time to pick up the automobile book since she had first read it, and she was pleased to think that she still remembered some of the terminology. She wondered how the Texans she was about to meet, wealthy sons of bronco-busting ancestors, felt about fast cars. She knew the answer as quickly as she formed the question.

Well, she thought, all to the good. If the conversation got around to car racing, she would at least be able to follow intelligently. If these Texans talked about their oil, their cattle, or their investments, she would be completely lost.

She was only slightly nervous in the morning, but all of her apprehensions quickly melted in the enthusiasm of the crowd that gathered around her. Several very beautiful young models, all dark-haired like Amanda, had been hired and were gliding around the main floor, wearing stark black dresses, bare at the top, and choice samples of Amanda's jewelry. They needn't have bothered, Amanda thought; it was the first, although unimportant, misjudgment the store had made. The customers paid little or no attention to the models; they wanted Amanda herself. The pieces were shown to perfection on the black velvet counters and trays of the boutique, which, with its slender stainless-steel fittings and sparkling glass shelves, was itself a gem.

What the women wanted, more than to see the jewelry worn by models, was Amanda's advice on what was suitable for them. Question after question was thrown at her, ranging from the appropriateness of diamonds in the morning to the particular shape of gem or colored stone most suitable for the prospective buyer's own shape and coloring. The women were concerned about the suitability of Amanda's rather formal designs even for less expensive pieces, for all the hours and places in their lives. She couldn't imagine why anyone would feel it necessary to wear jewelry to a tennis lesson, but after being asked the question for at least the third time, Amanda concluded with much amusement that it had to be one of the more popular issues of the day.

When her own day was at last over and she could relax at the hotel before her dinner engagement, she felt completely overwhelmed. People were enthusiastic, and friendly, and generous in their compliments. Women asked almost as much about her hairstyle and clothes as they did about the jewelry that was for sale. It had been the most hectic and exhausting day Amanda thought she had ever faced. But now that it was over, she confessed, she had loved every minute of it and couldn't wait to plunge right back in the next day.

Dinner, thank goodness, was a much more subdued affair, besides having the decided advantage to Amanda of being a formal, seated affair. After being on her feet all day, she had feared that this first night might be one of those great Texas barbecue buffet parties that the people here were so fond of throwing.

But this was an elegant sit-down dinner that might have taken place in any Fifth Avenue apartment: pâté en croute, cold poached bass, pears in brandy, and the appropriate accompanying wines.

The conversation didn't center on any of the topics Amanda had anticipated, but moved instead from art to theater to ballet, as available in both New York and Dallas, and then quickly on to the most universal of all dinner party subjects, the comings and goings of the international set, particularly those members whom the gossipers knew.

Her hosts seemed slightly surprised at the number of people they thought she would know whom she didn't. Marriage to Alan and her consequent involvement with her jewelry had kept her from being terribly active on the international social scene. But everyone, it seemed, knew Count Paolo Aldobrandini. Amanda regaled her audience with the description of how this most elegant man had furnished his country house, which none of the others had seen, with old castoffs from the Salvation Army and the scruffiest of Third Avenue thrift shops. Paolo and his escapades always produced the most scintillating dinner conversation, and this night and place were no exceptions. Amanda and her hosts and the other guests traded Paolo anecdotes back and forth, and Amanda was delighted to collect a few that she hadn't heard before and couldn't wait to confront him with.

One of the other women had already bought Amanda Parrish jewelry at Pembroke's, and she was lavish in her praise of Amanda's impeccable taste and flair for design. Fred Hamilton, who Amanda was quick to discern was as highly placed in local society as he was in the store, insisted that she had had a very rough day and that the evening must not be too protracted. He was seconded by his wife, the couple offering to see Amanda back downtown to her hotel.

They left a short while later, Amanda thanking her host and hostess sincerely for a most enjoyable evening. It would be more fun, though, when Josh got in and they could face these affairs together.

But it had been nice, she reflected, as she snuggled into the king-size bed that felt much too large for her alone. She liked being around new people and discovering both differences and similarities. She felt very much at home now, and was more than eager to tackle new crowds.

The next morning found her leaning over the counter, trying to figure out which of two adjacent rings a customer was pointing to. She saw something dangling somewhere near her and heard a masculine voice ask, "Do you think you can duplicate this?"

Amanda lifted her head to say that she was busy, but the sight of the prancing silver stallion stopped the words in her throat. She looked up into Josh's smiling blue eyes.

"Darling! You're here at last!" Amanda couldn't conceal her delight, almost oblivious to the crush of customers around them.

"I couldn't wait," he confessed. "I flew in this morning, left my stuff in the suite, and came right here. I hope that's okay?" The look in his eyes revealed he knew that of course it was.

"I'm going to have to be here all day," she said. "What are you going to do to amuse yourself until tonight?"

"I'm going to buy a cowboy hat, if you don't mind," he said seriously. "I've always wanted one when I was down here, but I never had the chance to shop before." He stroked his chin thoughtfully. "I have to admit I don't get into stores much."

Amanda laughed. "You had no trouble finding Pembroke's a couple of times," she reminded him.

"What's our schedule like for tonight?" he asked.

"An early ceremonial dinner with the mayor and city council," Amanda said, waiting for his reaction. She was expecting a groan and was quite surprised when he seemed pleased with the idea.

"Then I'm definitely going to need the cowboy hat," he said. "I'll mosey back and get you for dinner."

Amanda laughed. "At least you've picked up on the language," she said, "so I suppose it's only appropriate that you get the rest of the regalia."

He disappeared again until closing time, when he

scooped her up and the limousine brought them both back to the hotel, where they dressed for dinner, Josh insisting on wearing his new tan Stetson with its feathered headband. Amanda merely shrugged, knowing that he knew more about Texas modes and mores than she did, and was happily vindicated in her judgment when they arrived at the dinner to find most of the men there, the city officials, similarly attired.

The mayor and the council members turned out to be very gracious and when, backed by some of the prominent Dallas ladies she had already met, the key to the city was presented to Amanda at an authentic Texas barbecue with all the trimmings, she was absolutely delighted. Josh was next to her, all grins. She expressed her thanks to all of them, and the mayor gracefully turned around to thank her for bringing both her personal beauty and precious gems to their city, declaring that it was once more clear to the rest of the world that Dallas was up there with the best of them, in terms of culture, wealth, and beauty.

After the festivities the car was waiting as usual to take them back to the hotel.

"How long will it take you to slip into a pair of jeans and something?" Josh asked.

Amanda was astounded. "Why jeans?" she asked.

"My friends are sort of informal," he said.

"Give me just a few minutes," she murmured, reaching over to kiss him before she slipped into the bedroom to find something suitable.

Minutes later he was helping her into the passenger side of a beautifully low-slung, very solid-looking car. "No limousine tonight," Josh said. "I hope you like the change."

"I love this car," she stated when Josh had come

around and settled into the driver's seat. She marveled at the elegant smartness of the design and nestled against the sumptuous tan leather upholstery.

"You should," he said, "especially with your taste. This is a Jaguar XJS, with some very special custom touches."

"To your commission," she said teasingly.

"No," he said, "it's not my car. It belongs to this friend we're going to see."

She leaned back. She remembered also how assured he looked when he was driving a car, how he sat differently, arms ramrod straight, from any other man she had ever driven with. As they drove along he was interested in her reaction to Dallas, and what it was like to go through the heavy promotional schedule that had been set up for her. He was happy that she was once more at his side.

"Where are we going?" Amanda asked.

"Do you really want to know?" he asked her, reaching over and ruffling her hair.

She didn't really, Amanda realized suddenly. There was something so lovely about gliding smoothly through the dark and totally unfamiliar city without knowing. She felt relaxed and happy being with him, floating effortlessly through the night to an unknown destination. *This is silly,* she thought, *but somehow exciting.* She knew the real excitement was due to the man behind the wheel.

"This is the Highland Park section," Josh interrupted her thoughts. "Home of the very richest of the rich. They even have their own private police force, independent of the Dallas P.D." Amanda looked outside the window. The houses, while spacious, were not of the estate size she would have expected from Josh's description. Even more surprising was the proximity. They were easily within shouting distance of each other, not protected and isolated behind high walls and acres of sloping lawns and trees.

"People are very neighborly out here," Josh explained, as if reading her thoughts. "There's enough grandness inside to make up for the lack of pretentiousness on the outside," he said. "But they like being within easy reach of each other. It's really very informal."

"So you promised me," Amanda said, glancing down at her jeans. Well tailored as they were, she really wasn't sure that she should have followed his instructions in wearing them. Especially if this suburb was really as exclusive as he said.

But after they had parked the car and been welcomed inside the house by the apparent owners, Amanda was relieved. Her hostess's short but very round figure was also fitted into denims that tightly hugged her rump, although Amanda was quick to note that her upper torso, equally robust, was straining against a Roberta di Camerino sweater Amanda had seen at the Fifth Avenue boutique for nine hundred dollars.

Josh introduced her to Haskell Cates and his wife, Delma.

"But everyone calls me Del," the woman assured Amanda. "Come on in and sit down, honey. I'm so happy to meet you."

Amanda thanked her, smiling, and turned to smile at the equally if not even more rounded figure of Del's husband.

"She's much prettier than you said, Josh," Haskell admonished his guest. "You're a much better judge of horsepower than you are of women, my boy. What would you like to drink, honey?" he asked, turning his bulk toward Amanda.

She didn't want anything more than Perrier, but she wasn't sure if she should ask for it. She glanced up quickly at Josh.

"She's no better than I am, Haskell," Josh said. "Another mineral-water-on-ice person, I'm afraid."

Haskell stood in deep, disapproving silence. "You New York people," he grumbled, "you Yankees, supposed to have all the smarts and hustle in the world, but I haven't found a real two-fisted drinker among you yet."

"Now, Haskell, you stop that," Del interjected. "The only reason you won't let go of your bourbon is because the doctor says you should. You're only drinking to spite him."

"And challenge medical history," Josh added, laughing.

It was apparent to Amanda that a very easy, down-home relationship existed between Josh and these people. She wondered what the connection was and realized that it would certainly prove to have something to do with cars.

Just that moment Del sat down beside her. "I want to hear all about your jewelry, honey," she confided, "before these boys get started. Once they get going, it'll be cars, cars, cars, all night long and we women won't be able to get a word in edgewise."

"Oh, no," Josh corrected her. "Not Amanda. She knows dozens of words about cars, and she'll get them in any which way she can. One of these days, though, I'm going to have to teach her how to put them in the right order and what they mean."

Caught up in the spirit that warmed the massive,

stone-fireplaced living room, Amanda didn't at all mind his teasing.

"Well, cars are an important business as well as a great love of mine," Haskell began.

Del looked at the ceiling imploringly and then over at Amanda, as if in confirmation of what she had just said. "Haskell is not going to sit still until he gets his way," she confided to Amanda. "Until he can convince this handsome boyfriend of yours to drop everything and go over to England and buy Haskell some company."

"I know this is Texas," Amanda said slowly, "but I'm still a little–" she held her hands up in a gesture that signified total helplessness.

The other three all laughed. "It's very simple, honey," Haskell explained. "I've got a car that's the apple of my eye. I've wanted one of those babies ever since I was knee-high to a grasshopper. I finally located a beauty, thanks to your boy here, and now the dang company has got the nerve to go out of business."

It was the second time that one of the Cateses had referred to Josh as hers, and there was something about it Amanda loved.

"Carrington is one of the greatest marques in history," Josh picked up the threads of the story, "but the company has never been properly financed. Now, with the British economy going through so many changes, it's all but gone under. Haskell wants to buy it, get it going under no-nonsense American production techniques, and bring it back as a contender in world markets."

"To say nothing of being able to get parts for my little jewel," Haskell said, winking at Amanda. "That's what's really behind all this finagling." He looked across at Josh with an expression of unmistakable admiration. "What I need this young man for," he said turning again to Amanda, "is to go in and check the plant that they do have. Make sure that there's equipment and machinery already that's worth some of the money I'm willing to put up."

"Don't take him too seriously," Josh warned Amanda. "Three million dollars is a lot of money for anyone to spend on spare parts."

"Not Haskell Cates," Del Cates insisted.

They all laughed.

"Now can we talk jewelry?" Del asked earnestly. "Honey, I've been meaning to get down to Neimeyer's and get a whole drawerful of your stuff, but I haven't been able to get away this week. Besides, I don't rightly relish the idea of having to buck all those crowds the paper says you've been drawing."

Amanda started to ask her what sort of things she thought she wanted, but Haskell broke in. "Those baubles, not meaning any disrespect, Miss Amanda, but that's Del's idea of spare parts. She can spend with the best of them, and don't let her tell you otherwise."

"I know," Amanda said wryly, "I've noticed."

"If you just have old Neimeyer's send her up a bunch of stuff that you particularly like, I'm sure that'll be fine," Haskell said.

"I can do that easily enough," Amanda said. "It's called consignment, and we do it all the time in New York." She turned to Del. "If you show me the kind of thing you already have or know that you want, I'll be glad to make the arrangements at the store tomorrow."

Del stood up, delighted to lead Amanda off to her bedroom safe, leaving the men behind to talk shop.

Amanda had no idea of how long they had been at it when Josh knocked discreetly at the door, reminding her that it was getting late and she had to be at the store in the morning.

But he showed no such concern about time when they got back to the hotel. They rode up silently in one of the gliding all-glass elevators that were a prominent feature of the Regency. All Dallas lay at her feet, and Amanda thought that the lights twinkling below could be given in even exchange for the real diamonds in Del Cates's wall safe.

"How did you like Del and Haskell?" he asked when they were in the bedroom of the suite.

"I loved them!" Amanda said.

He talked about the Cateses, about how the folksy, down-to-earth appearances they both maintained belied one of the largest fortunes in the state, the whole country, in fact. Haskell, for all his roughhewn ways, was something of an electronics genius who had built one of the most important pioneering companies in that entire industry. Now his millions were spread in many other areas, almost too many to count. Where he and Josh touched base, of course, was in their common love of racing cars. "If Haskell makes this British deal, it'll be one of the biggest coups in history," Josh said, his expression bemused. "I'm getting a charge just out of being involved with it."

"But it sounds like you're much more than just involved," Amanda protested. "Haskell sounded as if he's depending on your judgment as to whether he'll make the deal at all."

"That's true," Josh conceded. "Haskell loves cars, but he doesn't know a damn thing about them. He knows how to run a company, though," Josh went on. "And if the deal goes through, he'll know just how to whip Carrington into shape. They may even start racing again."

There was a gleam in his eye that was infectious. "You mean they might develop Formula I cars?" Amanda asked, half slyly, and half shyly, a bit worried about whether she had it right.

Josh laughed and rumpled her hair. "Yes, smarty cat, Formula I racers, the greatest machines in the history of the world." Then he grew serious again. "But that's a long way in the future," he reminded her. "It's much too soon to even start thinking about that."

He smiled down at her, then lowered his head to kiss her deeply. Then he looked at her again, and there was a question in his eyes.

He looked straight into her eyes. "Will you come to England with me when the time comes?' he asked.

Amanda exploded. "Yes! Would I let you go without me?"

Then he took her and loved her with an intensity that left her breathless, until he remembered that she had to be up early and that she had forgotten it too.

Somehow the next day flew by. Every once in a while Amanda had to hug herself to conceal all the delight she felt. She hadn't yet decided whether she could take the extra time to fly to California with Josh, but something in her mind told her that she would. Then, there was going to England with him looming sometime in the near future, and she was so excited at that prospect she could barely contain herself. *Even if I don't go to California with him,* she thought, *there'll be England and everything else after that.* They would have to be separated at times, but that was almost natural. It was true for almost every husband and wife that she knew. Certainly it had been her lot when she had been married to Alan. She had understood and not minded the absences too much. With Josh the separations, as long as they were short, would be more than made up for at their joyous reunions.

The idea of flying on to California, actually to see a Formula I race and experience at first hand all that Josh had filled her head with, was very tempting. Even more than the excitement of the event was her anticipation of meeting his brother, Dutcher. From everything that Josh had told her about him, Amanda expected a younger carbon copy of Josh, with all of the McKay charm and good looks and a measure of boldness thrown in. She loved the way Tommy and Sylvia had taken to Josh, and the idea of meeting someone from his family thrilled her deeply. It made everything about their love so much deeper and more real to experience it in the company of those to whom they were closest. She knew she was going to love Dutcher, and even though she felt a little guilty about being away from Pembroke's a little longer, her desire to know Josh's brother was the factor that was going to tip the scales in favor of her going with him.

At last her time, hours in the sprawling suburban mall, was over, and the limousine whisked her back to the hotel, where Josh was waiting for her. She dressed quickly, selecting a brilliantly striped silk Missoni gown and some of her own silver jewelry. As much as Amanda had enjoyed the gala evening that had marked the beginning of her Texas visit, having Josh with her this night made everything infinitely more exciting. She had to admit to herself how much she enjoyed the inquiring and then coveting glances signaled by the other women at the glittering reception. It was good to see how easily Josh moved among this moneyed Dallas crowd; how he bantered charmingly with the women and was accepted by the men. He could be at home anywhere in the world, she told herself; she knew that she could be happy with him anywhere. She chatted with some women, watching Josh over the intervening shoulders of the beautifully dressed guests. Fred Hamilton smiled his way toward her and drew her slightly aside.

"I'm so glad you seem to be enjoying Texas so much, Amanda," he said. "I can't tell you how much we've enjoyed having you here. This is one of the most successful promotions we've ever had, and I'm sure it's as much due to your presence here as it is to your lovely jewelry."

Amanda reached up toward the tall Texan and kissed him lightly on the cheek. "Thank you, Fred," she said, smiling. "I can't tell you how happy I've been here."

It was all true, yet she was glad when the waiters had finally passed the last trays of smoked salmon and caviar and pâté, and the last rounds of champagne had been drunk, and she and Josh were at last on their way back to the suite.

Josh had one arm around her, his hand squeezing her waist, his other reaching for the wall switch that would throw dim lights into the suite.

Amanda started suddenly, her eyes caught by an unexpected blinking. It was the red light on the telephone, indicating that there was a message waiting. "I wonder who that can be," she said, frowning, "calling at this hour of the night." She disengaged herself gently from Josh and walked to the phone.

She picked it up, identifying herself and listening for a moment. Then she turned toward him. "It's for you," she said.

Josh took the instrument from her.

Amanda walked slowly toward the bedroom to give him some privacy, undoing the buttons of her long silk dress as she went.

"No, damn it, no!" Josh shouted.

Amanda turned quickly. Josh's face was suddenly distorted and anguished. His body crumpled as he shouted into the phone. Amanda was frightened and came quickly to him, putting her hand on his arm. But he shook her off impatiently as he kept shouting at whoever it was on the other end, the number he had gotten from the operator and punched into the phone.

Amanda stood silently watching him, her shock turning to horror as Josh sank into a chair, grasping the arms for support. He clenched the receiver close to his face, listening as tears streamed from his eyes.

Amanda stood stock-still, as if she were rooted to the floor. It was like being in a nightmare, witnessing something terrible and incomprehensible, yet being powerless to move, to do anything at all but watch helplessly.

"I'll be there on the first plane," she heard him say at last. He put down the phone without seeing it, staring straight ahead as though not seeing anything at all.

Amanda ran to him, kneeling, holding his arms, looking up at him beseechingly. "What's wrong, darling?" she asked. "What's happened?" she pleaded.

Slowly he turned and looked at her. "Dutcher's been killed," he said.

"Oh, my God!" Amanda's hand flew to her face as she heard the words, covering her mouth, pressing her knuckles against her face as if to protect herself from hearing any more. She didn't understand. The race wasn't until Sunday; they were going to fly to Long Beach Friday night. How could it have happened?

Josh seemed to read her mind. "He was in a practice run, his car went off the street and into a stone wall. It was a head-on collision. He never had a chance."

"Josh, I'm so sorry," Amanda said, her eyes full of tears, her arms reaching for him again.

"I should have been there," he said savagely, and the anger was all directed at himself. "Goddamn it, I should have been there!"

Amanda felt the enormity of his guilt. She hung her head, unable to look at him. The implication was too clear. Josh would burden himself with his brother's death, with the fact that instead of being in California he had been in Texas—with her. "What can I do, darling?" she asked plaintively. "Is there anything I can do?"

"No," he said dully. "I'll get all my stuff together and get out to the airport."

"There might not be a plane, not for hours," Amanda said. "Let me find out. I can do that much, and I want"—she hesitated, brushing back the tears, trying to put some strength in her voice—"I want to come with you."

"No!" he said, getting up and striding to the bedroom.

Amanda followed helplessly.

"You don't have to go through this alone, darling," she pleaded. "Let me come, let me help you. I'll—I'll call the airport and see when the next flight is."

"No!" he said again. "I'm going alone. If there's no flight, I'll charter a plane."

His voice fell on her ears, cold and unbearable. "Don't blame me for this," she cried, "and don't blame yourself. Only let me be with you. Let me help you, Josh, please!"

He turned from where he was pulling his clothes from their hangers and throwing them heedlessly into his bag. His expression softened just the barest degree as he looked at her. "I'm sorry, Amanda. It has nothing to do with you."

She put her face in her hands as if to quell the flood of tears that overwhelmed her. Her body shook and trembled with the wracking sighs that convulsed her.

Josh came over and knelt beside her, grasping her arms, burying his own tearstained face against her breasts. "I've got to do this alone, Amanda," he said softly. "It's going to be very ugly, and I don't want you to see it. Not yet."

"I'm part of you, Josh, and whatever happens, I want to be with you. I want to help if there's any possible way I can." She brushed the tears from her cheek and pulled back her hair out of her eyes. "We need each other more than ever now," she said simply.

Josh shook his head. "No, not yet." He held her tightly. "I can't bring you into this yet, and not this way. Besides, there's too much I have to do."

"Your mother," Amanda said falteringly. "Does—does she know?"

"Yes." The word was a deep groan erupting from him. "They had to call her immediately so that she wouldn't hear it on the news. They've been trying all evening to reach me here."

Again Amanda felt guilty and helpless. "What are we going to do?" she asked.

"You're going to finish here tomorrow as you're supposed to," Josh replied, "and I'm going to do what I must in California. I'll bring the body back—if there is anything to bring back—to Connecticut." The agony in his voice was overwhelming, but he didn't break.

Amanda found her own tears unstoppable. A dozen questions crisscrossed her mind, each one unbearable. *I've got to control myself,* she tried to take command inwardly. *I'm no help at all, no wonder he doesn't want me with him.* She pulled her shoulders tight, as if to dam up the reservoir inside. She touched his face lightly, gently pressing his head down till she cradled him in her lap. A few shuddered sighs escaped her body, but somehow she got herself still. "Are you going to call your mother before you go?" she asked.

Josh sighed. "Yes, I'd better do that right now." He got up.

Amanda rose too. "I'll finish packing for you," she said. As he moved away she reached out and grasped his arm again. "Please let me come with you, Josh," she begged. "Please let me help you."

"No, darling." His voice was soft, and she could hear at last his love in it, amid his anguish. "Not this time."

She had his bag ready when he came back into the bedroom. He kissed her briefly, his emotion showing mostly in the firm grasp with which he hugged her to him. "You do whatever you've got to do here," he instructed softly, "and I'll call you in New York as soon as I'm back home in Connecticut."

Josh kissed her again at the door of the suite, insisting that she stay there and not even come to the airport with him. Then he was gone.

The vast, luxurious suite seemed like a prison to her now, or worse, a mausoleum. Amanda checked herself crossly, reminding herself that the presence of death was all too real in their lives now. She had the ache and the loneliness and the last day tomorrow to get through after this anguished night, but the burdens on her were nothing compared to what Josh was going through.

She felt as alone as she ever had in her life. Dallas was, for all of its excitement and friendly welcoming, a strange city where she didn't know anyone well. She thought of calling her mother, but a quick glance at her watch told her it was the dead of night in New York. There would be time enough to tell Sylvia without scaring her out of sleep.

There was really no one to turn to, no one she could talk to. She thought of Josh's friends, the Cateses, but she had no right to unburden herself on them. Besides, they were just that, Josh's friends, not hers, and it was not her place to tell them of the tragedy.

Amanda paced around the suite, unable to go to sleep, not knowing what to do to make the awful hours pass. She stopped in the living room and stared at the fresh flowers arranged in a large glazed vase. How beautiful they were, how perfect and strong each fragile blossom seemed. Beautiful, yet out of place here, now, she thought bitterly. The petals should have been seared, the fragrance faded, the the stalks drooping and wilted, like all of the other bright things that had faded in these rooms.

Chapter 8

The day of the funeral was bright with sunshine. Amanda got off the train and found herself in a small, picture-perfect, typical New England town of the finest vintage. Large trees shaded the streets. Beautiful Colonial and Federal houses, in perfect restoration, sat solidly on sloping lawns and behind carefully trimmed hedges. Strong oaks and graceful willows stood everywhere, like silent guardians of the town and its traditions. *It's beautiful,* Amanda thought, but she knew its quiet conservatism was a world away from the scream and frenzy of racing. She wondered if the very smallness and solidity of the town had helped motivate the McKay men to break out of the confines of its slowly moving life and seek the excitement that was so foreign to this home of theirs.

The cab stopped in front of the slender-spired frame church. Amanda paid her fare and joined the people who were moving up the gray stone steps and through the open door.

She took a seat in a pew near the back, looking over the heads of the people sitting randomly in front of her, making the church about half full. She tried to recognize Josh, but the front rows on either side were dark in the dimly lit interior. She sat back, folding her hands on her lap, and waited patiently. She glanced around to the walls of the church and the altar. It was as precise and spare as she had expected it to be, of a piece with its surrounding

Connecticut countryside, with its design as lean and direct and straightforward as the people it served.

There was a sound from behind her as the doors to the church were closed, and the white-smocked attendant hurried down the aisle. The minister had already assumed his place at the head of the nave, and now the unmistakably somber tones of an organ sounded the beginning of the service.

Amanda concentrated on the words of the service, much of it biblical and familiar. She recognized the Psalms that were intoned by the minister. Then the minister began to speak in words that Amanda knew at once to be his own. He had known the McKays for a long time and was talking about them to the rest of his audience, before addressing himself directly to the family and their grief. He spoke simply and earnestly, and Amanda found herself caught up by his recollections of the McKay brothers when they had been small boys. He traced his remembrances of their growing up, their school years, their boyish pranks. He spoke of the closeness of the family, especially after the loss of the father, and how the brothers had always been a great source of strength to their widowed mother. Amanda felt her heart breaking as the minister addressed himself now directly to Josh, praising him for the model and support he had always provided for his brother, and telling him how his mother needed him now. He saved his final words of solace for Mrs. McKay.

He opened a large, leather-bound Bible and read another short passage. Then he indicated that everyone was to rise. The organ started up, the regular congregants stood, and the pallbearers moved quickly to hoist the coffin.

Amanda, with tears in her eyes, searched the faces

of the men as they slowly passed. Josh was not among them. But then she saw him, his arm supporting his mother as he helped her walk behind the coffin. She had a large handkerchief pressed against her face and was sobbing quietly but uncontrollably into it. Amanda's heart was flooded with pity as she watched. Then Josh saw her. Their eyes met briefly, and Amanda saw all the helpless agony and rage against himself she had anticipated. She turned away, unable to bear his hurt.

They moved past, and the other people started filing slowly out of the church. Amanda felt dizzy as she stood at the threshold, her eyes unused to the strong sunshine outside after the dark interior.

Josh came back from the limousine where he had left his mother. "Thank you for coming," he said simply, looking deeply into Amanda's eyes.

He turned and went back inside the long black limousine. The uniformed chauffeur slammed the door behind him. The limousine followed the flower-laden hearse, and the slow procession to the final resting place of Dutcher McKay began. Amanda was helped into another car. She was introduced to members of the McKay family.

"So different from his last ride," a man who introduced himself as an uncle said gloomily. "Dutcher, so young and full of life." He sighed heavily. "So mad for his car and speed, speed, always more speed." He turned to Amanda. "Did you know him?" he asked.

"No," Amanda said sadly. "I only know Josh."

"Ah, Josh," the uncle said, "he took such care of his brother, took such pains with him, tried so hard to prevent something like this." He shook his head.

"Are you a racer?" Amanda asked.

"No," came the reply. He gestured. "But the cars and the races are fascinating."

"It's so dangerous," Amanda said. "So many accidents, so many young men killed. Why do they do it?"

"That's the question everybody asks," he said. "They do it, quite simply, for excellence. To be the very best a man can be, pitting himself against the race and the other drivers, becoming a part of his machine, needing to give everything that a man can give of himself for those few hours."

"They give their lives," Amanda said darkly.

"Sometimes, yes," it was conceded. "But while they are alive they feel as fully alive as a man can be, perhaps more so than any other being in the world. Everything is at absolute peak. Their bodies, their minds, their nerves and reflexes, everything honed to perfection." He gave her a quick sidelong glance. "There are not many situations in life that afford the opportunity for a man to know himself and what he can do quite so well."

"You make it sound almost mystical."

"In a way, yes. A racer is as finely attuned to his performance as a great musician or dancer. He has conditioned himself as superbly and has given himself over to it completely. Yet he is putting himself into a danger that no one on a stage is confronted with."

"You seem to admire them very much," Amanda said.

"Yes, very much," he replied. "The same intensity they bring to their profession marks them off the track as well." He paused to look at her again out of the corner of his eye. "You must have noticed that."

"Yes, I have," Amanda said.

They drew up alongside the other cars parked at the cemetery entrance. He offered Amanda his arm as they walked across the sloping lawns that led to the grave site.

Amanda kept her eyes downcast, not daring to look over at the pit or up where she might meet Josh's gaze. She listened, unhearing, as the minister read the concluding words from a small Bible. Then the cemetery men began their work of lowering the coffin and covering it.

Amanda turned away.

"Will you be coming back to the house now?" The voice startled Amanda, and she jumped slightly. But her questioner was the uncle, named Nelson, who had driven out with her and was seemingly taking her in hand. Amanda nodded. He led her back to the car for the short drive through the green countryside, stopping finally at the large, rambling stone-and-wood house that Amanda knew must be the McKay home.

Once inside, Nelson led her gently into the front parlor, where quietly murmuring relatives and neighbors were drawn in an informal semicircle around Mrs. McKay.

The older woman, her gray hair in soft waves about her face, cried silently into the large white handkerchief she clenched against her cheek. Josh, somber but dry-eyed in a dark suit, stood behind his mother's chair, his hand on her shoulder.

Amanda took a seat at the end of the curve of chairs, not wanting to intrude on the intimacy of their grief. It was for Josh's sake that she was there, and even more, for the bright and beautiful young brother she had so wanted to meet and never would.

Amanda didn't know how much Josh had told his mother about her, or if the stricken woman even knew that she was there. Amanda's heart ached for Mrs. McKay and for all of them. It wasn't only Dutcher she had wanted to know, but Mrs. McKay and all of Josh's family. But she never expected it to be in circumstances like this that she would make their acquaintance. She imagined instead great holiday gatherings, Christmas in the country with all of the clan gathering, and herself and Tommy a part of Josh, part of them all.

More people were arriving, and the room was getting quite crowded. Mrs. McKay had stopped crying as she greeted new consolers, and the tension had broken somewhat, although the air of grief and gloom that permeated the entire house was as tangible as the furniture.

Mrs. McKay was deeply engrossed with a woman who was crouching in front of her and grasping both her hands. Josh broke away from his station behind her and came around the back of the other visitors to where Amanda sat. It had been five days since they had seen each other in Texas, and Amanda's heart was breaking at the change in him. Josh was as handsome as ever, and he stood ramrod straight, not slumping even when he bent over to whisper to her; but there was a difference in him that marked his features and bearing as though five years had passed since their last meeting, and not five days.

"I want to take you over to see Mother for a moment," he whispered to her, helping her up as he spoke, "and then I'll take you back to the city."

Amanda was surprised, but she didn't question him. He led her to where Emily McKay sat in the center of the semicircle, and Amanda bent down and softly voiced her condolences to the grieving mother.

Mrs. McKay nodded, and Amanda knew that she was still too overcome to speak. She said good-bye, grateful for Josh's arm to lean on as she got up and he led her back through the room. She nodded good-bye to Nelson and the others whom she had met. Then they went out.

Josh backed out slowly, and within minutes the soft, rolling hills of Connecticut were banking the highway going south.

"You don't know what it means to me for you to be here today," Josh said, keeping his eyes on the road.

"I want to be with you through everything," Amanda said. "I don't know how you could have gone through all of this alone."

His knuckles whitened as he gripped the steering wheel. "Most of what I have to go through in life, I have to go through alone. That's something you're going to have to get used to."

"I understand," she said, "as long as I can be with you most of the time, and especially those times when you most need me."

"You'll be with me in England," Josh said. "I promised you that. After this, we're going to need it. Besides, I promised Haskell that I would take care of that business for him, and I've got to do that first."

Amanda was puzzled. "First?" she echoed. "I didn't know that there were other things you planned to do."

"You couldn't have known before this, darling, because I've just decided," Josh replied. "There is something I've got to do now."

The determination in his voice frightened her without her knowing why. "What is it, Josh?" she asked.

"I've got to do what Dutcher didn't get to do," Josh said grimly.

"What are you talking about?" Amanda asked wildly.

"I'm racing."

"Josh! How can you? You're—you're not in training or anything," she finished lamely, her mind full of the things his uncle had been talking about on the way to bury Dutcher: all the conditioning, the fitness, the fiercely competitive frame of mind the drivers had to be in.

"I've got to do it, Amanda," Josh said. "I owe it to Dutcher, and to my father, too. There's got to be a McKay who's going to make a Grand Prix circuit."

She was astonished beyond belief as she listened to him talk about the obligation he felt incumbent on him, to do what his father and brother had tried. "It killed them, Josh," she pleaded. "How can you take such a chance? How can you do this to yourself, or to me, or to your mother, God help her? Whatever would become of that poor woman if something happened to you now, after all she's been through?"

"That's also part of why I have to do it." His lips were set in a thin, firm line, his eyes locked on the road ahead. "I knew it wasn't going to be easy for you, darling, that's why I wanted to tell you as quickly as possible." He took his hand off the steering wheel and put it gently on her knee. "That's why we're going to have England together. I want to show you the easier, happy side of my life before I go back on the circuit."

"Before you go back on the circuit," Amanda echoed softly. "Where does that leave me, Josh?"

"You'll come back to New York, to Tommy and your work, until after Monte Carlo. Until I know what I'm in for. It will be right for you to be with me, but not yet. This is something I have to do, and do alone."

"And after Monte Carlo?" Amanda questioned.

"By then I'll know exactly where I am," Josh answered. "I'll have had enough races under my belt to feel confident about having you with me."

"I would think that your need for me would come before that," Amanda said almost bitterly.

"It just doesn't work that way, darling," Josh said. "I know how much you want to help me, and I hope you know how much you mean to me and what you've added to my life. But there are some things that a man has to do alone, and dammit—racing is one of them. I can't impose my limitations on you, Amanda. I've got to do it myself first. Then, and only then, can I come to you. Try to understand."

"I am trying," she said, "but it isn't very easy for me. All of the times when I think you'd most need me are the times you don't want me around. I can't understand why it will be all right for me to be at one race or one track and not others."

"It's not just a race or a track or a car," Josh said, "it's a way of life. Until I've gotten myself accustomed to it again, I can't bring you into it."

"Accustomed!" Amanda exploded. "Can you be concerned about me adapting myself to what you call a way of life when you're going to be putting your own life on the line and you're not even prepared for what you're doing?" Her voice had the pitch of hysteria.

"I've got to do what I've got to do." His voice was as firm as his unwavering attention to the highway. "We've got to do this my way or not at all, Amanda."

"You're talking about principles when your life is on the line!" she cried.

"It's one of the things you're going to have to get used to," he said grimly, glancing at her quickly and turning his eyes back to the road again, "if you still want to."

"Of course I want to, Josh!" she exclaimed. "Only I want to in a way that's going to be best for you."

"Then do it my way, darling," he said softly. "I know the life, and you don't. I know you're trying to give me everything you've got and I love you for it, but you've got to give in. No matter how you feel about me, you can't know what's best, and I do."

"For both of us?" Amanda asked.

"For both of us," Josh said. "Exactly that."

She was silent for a moment, then shook her head. "With all of this hanging over us, how can we possibly go to England and be happy?"

"Because we have to." There was almost a trace of a grin on his face. "We have to go to England because all the same reasons that applied before, still do. We've got to learn to be happy again, because life goes on and all the tragedies we go through must serve to strengthen us for the ones ahead. We can't dwell on the past. We have to look to the future to help heal our grief."

"That's part of the life too, isn't it," Amanda said.

"Yes," Josh answered. Then, as if to prove the truth of what he was saying, he began to talk about England and the trip they had been anticipating so, about the good times they had shared in Dallas and his friends there, drawing Amanda slowly but surely back into the comforting circle of his love.

Before long she admitted to herself that he was at least partially right, that they had to focus on all the happy and positive aspects of life. She realized how much it would mean to Josh to have her not burdened and gloomy with worry about him, but loving and open and helping him to relax, the biggest part she had to play in his life, at least for the time being. It was to take his mind off Dutcher and the inadequacy of his own preparedness for racing, to fill him instead with all of the love and hope and confidence that a man needed from his woman, to keep his mind on the bright side, the future, the winning. It was a role to be played, and a crucial one. It was what Josh needed from her now, and Amanda resolved to gather all her strength together to give it to him. No matter how much she trembled with fear for him, or how shaken her heart was, she had to play it his way or risk losing him, losing him in the deepest, most final way.

Chapter 9

The happiness that Amanda had anticipated from introducing Josh to her friends never materialized. Although he was busy with picking up all the threads of Dutcher's life, Josh was still in deep mourning. Neither he nor Amanda wanted any social life other than the quiet hours they managed to spend together the few times Josh was in New York. Usually he was away from her, deep in conferences with Dutcher's sponsors, convincing them to protect their enormous investment by having Josh make the rest of the circuit.

But she contented herself with the knowledge that

she was doing exactly what he wanted, and she busied herself when she wasn't at the store with preparations for the trip to England, which now had an even more important purpose in her mind.

Much had to be accomplished in those two weeks besides helping alleviate the pain of Dutcher's death: she could make Josh so happy that he would never want to be apart from her, and the business for Haskell Cates could be so intriguing that Josh would give up the idea of racing and continue on instead with the business that would be so much more conducive to their lives together. She would be smiling and cheerful while praying for that to happen.

The day for their departure arrived. Amanda smiled endlessly, pushing the nagging doubts from her mind, determined to concentrate on making Josh happy.

They took their seats on the 747 that would carry them across the Atlantic. Amanda was delighted that there was no one seated with them. After the takeoff they unbuckled their seat belts, snuggling toward each other and giving themselves up to the lovers' conversation they'd missed in the rush of events that had overtaken them since the first realization of their emotions for each other. They talked about all the little things there hadn't been time for and found that the answers suddenly mattered. They ignored the movie that kept most of the other fellow passengers enrapt, and when the disembodied voice on the public address system announced that they would be landing in half an hour, Amanda was amazed. She hadn't taken her eyes off Josh long enough even to look out of the window at the sight of the green Irish countryside below, which had been the first land visible since takeoff. The trans-Atlantic flight seemed shorter than the one that had taken her to Dallas; but Josh was with her now, and he hadn't been then. That was what made all the difference.

He handled their luggage and immigration formalities with the same ease that, it seemed to Amanda, marked everything he did.

A black Bentley, the first Amanda had ever ridden in, was waiting for them at Heathrow to whisk them to the riverside suite reserved for them at the Savoy.

Amanda walked around the two rooms that would be their home for the next week, marveling at everything, from the English antiques to the magnificent view of the Thames and historic London from their window.

She turned to him, her eyes blazing with excitement. "It's perfect, Josh, just perfect!" And she turned back to the window as if trying to take everything in all at once.

"So are you," he said softly, coming up behind her and putting his arms around her. "Are you feeling any jet lag?" he asked. The flight that had originated at ten o'clock in the morning in New York had brought them to an England that was clothed in the darkness of early night.

"I think I'm too excited to feel anything," Amanda confessed.

"Let me call room service and have some tea sent up," he said, letting go of her at last.

While he ordered, Amanda went into the bedroom and unpacked. She had just rejoined him in the living room when the door to the suite opened and a waiter wheeled in a large round cart with a tea service and small sandwiches. Amanda was taken aback for a moment. She hadn't been in England in years and had forgotten that hotel staff never bothered to knock when they came into guest rooms.

Another one of the social rules I've forgotten, she thought, remembering an earlier time when Josh had teasingly accused her of having no sophistication at all. She wouldn't have been able to argue that point with him now, she realized. She was as giddy as a schoolgirl on her first time away.

They made love that night with the lights of London shining all around them. There was something bewitching to Amanda in the brand-new surroundings; even though the room had all the earmarks of long tradition, it was fresh and exciting to be someplace with Josh they had never been before. She had to admit to him, laughing at her own sentimentality, that being in a strange place with him put a decided edge on their lovemaking.

It was just something extra, something more. She kissed his open mouth, teased a lock of his hair around her finger, pressed herself against the length of his body with an ardent freedom that delighted him. She was no longer the woman who had feared the relationship, who had held herself away from him, denying not only him but herself as a woman, as all the woman she could be. They made love swiftly, again and again, as though all the world's supply had to be replenished through their tireless, demanding, ecstatic bodies.

At last they stopped, spent with exhaustion, almost embarrassed by the first glow of morning lighting the skies outside. She lay in his arms almost trembling with the aftermath of the desire that had raced through her and finally been mastered.

"How do you feel?" Josh asked tenderly.

She tightened her arms around his neck and squeezed herself to him. "As if I'm home," she said dreamily. "As if I've finally come home."

But it was a far cry from the life she had become so used to. They spent their days in a whirl of shopping and sight-seeing, avoiding the tourist buses that circled around the well-known landmarks, preferring to walk the streets of London, for once sunny and warm, poking into old shops and new, buying toys for Tommy. Amanda loved the narrow, often crooked streets that radiated from the larger squares and traffic circles. The city's ambience and antiquity enchanted her, and she would have spent all the time walking if Josh had not instructed the hotel's front desk to provide them with tickets for a wide variety of theatergoing.

The staggered curtain times, so different from the rigid New York pattern, let them see many more plays than they would have been able to squeeze into a similar week on Broadway. One day they managed to see three different performances. After the third play, when they stumbled back to the Savoy, Amanda at last had to admit they were overdoing it slightly. But the conflicts in the dramas, classical or contemporary, kept her from dwelling on her own problems. She knew that this week would end all too soon. Much as she looked forward to traveling through the countryside, there was an elegance and glamour to London that she was going to miss. The city was like a heady tonic for her, giving her the change and excitement that visits to faraway places are supposed to, convincing her that everything would always be this wonderful. How much of her happiness was due more to Josh than to London itself, she very well knew. But the city worked its magic on her and helped her forget, and she was determined to live and enjoy every minute of it.

Josh took her for Scottish smoked salmon at the

Connaught Grill and gambling at Annabel's, to the Royal Ballet in Covent Garden, in addition to the legitimate theaters in the West End and the famous repertory acting companies. He took her to Conduit Street, to the Rolls-Royce showroom, to see some of the most magnificent automobiles, old and new, ever made. They bought each other matching pale beige cashmere sweaters at N. Peal's in the Burlington Arcade, and tramped through Harrods as if they were going to buy everything in the world, which was exactly what the giant department store offered.

It was a tonic for Josh, too, Amanda thought, busying his mind and buoying his spirits, taking his thoughts off the tragedy.

On their very last night in London they didn't go out at all. Josh wanted to get an early start in the morning, and Amanda wanted to spend as much time as possible in the rooms where she had found the greatest happiness she had known in her life. They ordered a sumptuous but typically English dinner, steak and kidney pie, to be served to them in the suite.

After dinner Josh pulled two armchairs over to the window, and they sat and watched the lights of the boats going back and forth on the river.

When he took her to bed, they made love all during the night, so many times that Amanda lost count. Yet, for all the gratification her body felt, her mind was not at ease. She lay back, waiting for him to say something about her going on to Spain and Belgium with him, but he was already asleep, leaving that open question nagging at her mind. She wanted to go with him, but even more, she wanted him not to go at all. To turn his back on the mad and dangerous fixation about racing. Perhaps when he got involved in Haskell's business it would happen.

In the morning she could hear the waiter rolling in the breakfast table of tea and toast. She roused Josh moments before the front desk rang up, as instructed, to let them know that the garage had sent round the car they would drive to Coventry. When they were packed and ready to leave, Amanda cast one last fond farewell glance around the suite. A porter had already taken their bags down to where the car waited at the oval curb of the hotel's front courtyard.

When they got down there, Amanda was pleased to see that the vehicle, which would take them through England during the next week, was like the one in Dallas, belonging to Haskell, that she had driven in with Josh.

Once the bags were loaded, Josh maneuvered the car skillfully through the intricacies of the teeming London traffic. Their trip would take them into a northward loop, first directly to Coventry, then on to the Carrington works on the northwest coast below Liverpool, then along the Welsh border, and down through the Cotswolds and back to London.

" 'Oh, to be in England now that April's there,' " Josh said as they left the grayish outlying suburbs behind them and saw their first stretches of the thoroughly greening countryside.

The color was soon a blur as they sped along the M1 highway. They were laughing and talking, reminiscing about their first trip together in a Jaguar, when Amanda realized that the landscape was slipping by in a wash of color that made trees and fields indistinguishable through her side window. She glanced down at the complicated dashboard, trying to figure out which dial was the speedometer, her confusion increased by the fact that all of the controls on the dash were registered in kilometers and liters rather than miles and gallons.

"How fast are we going?" Amanda asked.

"Darling, I'm sorry," Josh apologized. "I didn't realize I was going too fast for you." His grip on the wheel tightened, and the car slowed down perceptibly.

"I didn't say you were going too fast," Amanda said. "I only asked *how* fast."

He reached out and squeezed her knee. "You're also not used to sitting on the left," he reminded her. "That makes a difference too."

There wasn't very much to see from the highway, but Amanda had been a little unnerved by how fast it had sped by. Josh could see that she was slightly shaken. "I'm a little hard to control when I get behind the wheel of one of these," he confessed. "I guess something inside me will always be racing."

Amanda laughed. "Right now, something inside me is too," she said. "My heart."

They both laughed. "I'll try to be good, I promise," Josh said, squeezing her knee again and letting his hand come to rest on her leg.

"That isn't much evidence of it," Amanda observed, looking down at the strong fingers.

He laughed, but didn't move his hand. "I had to write a very lengthy letter to these people I'm going to see," he said, "explaining how I damaged their prototype so badly that first day I met you. I think they might want to meet you, but I'll ask them not to press charges."

"You mean I'm part of your report?" Amanda asked in surprise.

"You had to be," he said. "I needed a scapegoat to

hang the blame on. I never had that kind of mishap in testing a prototype before."

"Well," Amanda said, "frankly, I like this one we're in now much better." She was beginning to develop a fondness for the cars they drove in, not because of anything technical she knew about them; she really hadn't put her book learning and her driving experiences with Josh together. All she knew was that she loved the feeling of leaning back against the luxurious upholstery of the vehicles he drove. There was a wonderful sense of security in the way he handled a car—even, she had to admit, when he was driving it too fast—coupled with the outfittings that any woman could appreciate. She enjoyed more Josh doing the driving than when they were being chauffeured in the New York limousine or the superb Bentley in London. There was just such a beautiful compatibility between man and machine when Josh held the steering wheel in his capable hands. She felt as though he could drive them to the moon and back in blissful luxe.

She didn't mind the monotony of the highway. Josh had told her it would have been a far more picturesque drive if he had avoided the ultraefficient M1 and taken the older back roads, but business was business, and he had a definite appointment to keep in Coventry. Once that was taken care of, they would go on to their next destination in the northwest, and their pace could be more leisurely and interesting. Also, he promised, the return trip through the beautiful Cotswolds would give her more than just a passing glimpse of what many considered to be the quintessence of the English countryside. She tried to concentrate on that, on the car, and on Josh.

"I think I love the Jaguars best of all the cars," Amanda said.

"Even after the Rolls-Royces we saw the other day?" Josh asked.

"Uh-huh," Amanda replied. "I've never been in a Rolls with you, so I really can't say. But I'm sure these will always be my sentimental favorites." She rubbed the rich leather seat with her fingertips, before touching them to his cheek.

"There's a Lamborghini you might like," Josh said. "It costs $125,000 or so and looks as if it should be hanging in the Museum of Modern Art."

"In shiny bright red, I imagine," Amanda said, laughing. "Somehow I get the feeling it wouldn't exactly fit in with our present surroundings." She wanted him to talk on about race cars. To exorcise the demons of Long Beach, to let his feelings about Dutcher not be repressed inside him. She strained slightly, waiting to hear the invitation she was sure he would make now. But he said nothing, concentrating on his driving and the road ahead.

She was deeply disappointed but tried desperately not to show it. Perhaps his mind was on Dutcher again. When Josh asked if she would like to stop for some breakfast she shook her head. They drove on some more miles in silence, Josh remarking on some aspect of the car or countryside from time to time, and Amanda acquiescing.

He seemed to sense the quietness of her mood, but not the cause of it, and he didn't push the conversation. He let her be alone with her thoughts, since that seemed to him to be what she wanted. The preceding week had been as brilliantly full for Josh as it had been for Amanda. He treasured the nonstop, twenty-four-hour-a-day lives they had led together, and took deep joy in her enthusiasms.

The future stretched in front of them, like an open roadway but with far more complications than any straightaway superhighway.

Before they could take up their lives together he had to get through his agonizing crusade, the pressures and toil and dangers of the Grand Prix. Only after all of that was behind him would he feel himself in possession of the answers to all the questions that were pounding him, answers he desperately needed before he dared involve Amanda with his visions for both of them.

Amanda was hurt, but grimly determined not to let her disappointment mar the possibilities of the full week that they still had in front of them. She lifted her chin and turned to Josh with a smile. "I'm going to be hungry just as soon as you are," she promised brightly. "You get full cooperation on this journey, sir knight."

"Maybe we should wait until we get into Coventry," Josh said, "unless you're really famished. It's really quite an interesting old town."

"Isn't it where Lady Godiva took her famous ride?" Amanda asked.

"Right," Josh said. "More to the point, our point at least, it's also where the first bicycle ever built in England was manufactured. And"—he stopped for emphasis—"also, where the first English automobile was built. Except for the war years, it's never really stopped."

"Did it take a lot of damage during the war?" Amanda asked. "It seems to me I remember something about it being practically devastated."

"Yes, it had to be almost completely rebuilt in some

areas," Josh told her. "The automobile manufacturers were making vital war equipment. It was the center of manufacture for armed vehicles, engines, and so forth. That's why the Nazis gave it the worst pounding of any city in England. Even the old medieval cathedral was demolished and had to be rebuilt from the ground up. Thousands were killed."

There would be lots there to keep her interested, he assured her, while he had his meetings with the car company executives. She could poke around and explore Coventry much as they had done London. They would stay overnight, to give Josh a rest from all his driving and to give them some hours in the morning for anything they might want to do together in Coventry before heading north.

After the sterile monotony of the highway the outlying industrial areas of the city looked cluttered and grimy. Amanda was glad they were stopping at their hotel first, so she could have a quick bath before their lunch.

She wanted to change her clothes, too, from the sweater and jeans she had worn for the road into something more suitable for a city. But when she got out on the streets, she was surprised to see almost everybody, men and women alike, in jeans, looking quite incongruous against the backdrop of the medieval-looking streets and buildings of the older part of town.

People were hurrying and bustling everywhere around her. If not for some of the half-timbered houses and the crooked, winding byways that were scarcely wide enough for a car to enter, she might as well have been set down in any small manufacturing city of the American midwest.

But Josh had been right about there being enough

of interest to absorb her for an afternoon. Amanda was surprised, when she thought to check her watch for the first time, at how late it had grown. She had to finish browsing in the antiquarian bookstore she was in before she made her way back to the hotel to meet Josh.

He was already in their room when she got there. "I'm glad I didn't have to present you as exhibit A after all," he said jokingly as he scooped her up in his arms. He whirled her around the overfurnished bedroom that was scarcely roomy enough for them both to walk around in at the same time, let alone indulge in any gymnastic displays of affection. "Where have you been?"

Amanda sat down on the bed, kicking off her shoes and rubbing her suddenly tired feet. "Just walking and walking," she said, "browsing in some perfectly lovely old stores. It's such a beautiful place. I didn't realize how late it had gotten."

"Here, let me do that for you." Josh sat down on the bed beside her and began massaging her feet in his large, capable hands.

Amanda lay back on the bed, legs dangling over the side while he continued to caress her feet. "Oh," she drew out the syllables. "Oh, that feels so good."

"Then tell me how this feels," Josh said, relinquishing his hold on her toes and lying down next to her. He kissed her full on the mouth, and when she lifted her head to meet his, he held her at the nape of the neck until her head was cradled in his hand, and he crushed her upper body against him. They lay in close embrace on the still-made bed, until it became impossible for either one to be contained with mere kisses. Amanda undressed quickly, not waiting as she often did for the joy of his doing it for her. Now she wanted him to be ready as quickly as she was. Her need spread like wildfire all through her, sparked by the touch of his lips on hers. Even that was more than she needed to want him and want him to take her. Just being with him was cause enough for every lovely thing that followed.

"I want to stop every night someplace different," Amanda told him when they had finished.

"Why?" he asked.

"Because I want you to make love to me in as many places as possible," she said simply. "I want you to make love to me all over the world."

"At least I can guarantee you England for now," he said, taking her face in his hand and kissing her again.

"Tomorrow, the north," she murmured. "The coast."

"Some day, darling," he whispered back, "the world. I want to love you every place there is. And even those that aren't."

"We'll name them ourselves," Amanda said, "and they'll become important just because we've made love there."

They stopped for lunch the next day in just the picture-postcard village Amanda had been hoping for, ancient cottages and all. The town, no more than a village really, had the kind of hyphenated name that spelled England. The weathered board hanging outside the inn looked as ancient as its surroundings. Josh parked the Jaguar neatly in front, on a stretch of road paved with the cobblestones that they had come onto unexpectedly when they left the highway and began meandering about the byways of the countryside.

He took the innkeeper's recommendation and ordered a hearty repast of roast beef and Yorkshire pudding, to be accompanied with a tall glass of ale. Amanda protested, saying she could not quite possibly eat that heavy a meal so early in the day. She settled for a rather untraditional salad, one made with the greens of the surrounding countryside. She exclaimed over the tiny pitcher of cream that was served with her coffee, thick and rich and almost yellow.

When they had eaten their fill, they thanked their host and Josh revved the Jaguar as townspeople came out and watched. It seemed extraordinary to Amanda that the car, which was manufactured relatively nearby, should nonetheless be an object of interest to the villagers. She attributed it to the place being rather off the beaten track—she couldn't remember just how many miles they had come in search of this perfect spot. But Josh reassured her it was the inbred interest of the people in fine craftsmanship and first-rate motorcars that drew them.

"How lucky I am!" she said happily. "I have everything anybody in the world would want."

"Especially a Jaguar," Josh said modestly.

"Especially you," Amanda corrected him with a badly planted kiss on the cheek.

"Hey, stop that!" Josh protested. "A few more like that and I'll drive us right off the road!"

Amanda laughed. His mood was generally even, but since his meeting in Coventry, he had seemed very pleased. The cloud, for once, seemed gone. She felt more strongly than ever the joy of being with him. It was the closest she'd been to him at a time when he was occupied with his work, and now Amanda could understand how much it meant to him. If only, she prayed silently, if only it could be everything.

His mood stayed high all during the hours they

drove north toward their next destination, Maidenborough, a name Amanda thought far too poetic for a city whose main attraction was heavy manufacturing. But this was where the Carrington plant was located. Josh had warned her that it was not very pretty, and that there wouldn't be a great deal to absorb her interest during the long hours he would have to spend at the factory. They were going to be there for at least two days, but once that business was taken care of, he promised her, they would be as free as the wind to make their way slowly back down to London.

Amanda knew how important these next two days could be. Josh could be diverted and involved enough with the plant to cancel his plans to race. But she couldn't push it. Although the lovely-sounding town of Maidenborough was a small gray replica of Liverpool, in whose shadow it almost sat, Amanda had to find enough to do to keep her spirits up while she waited. She didn't want her uneasiness affecting Josh.

Yet, after they had settled in at the hotel and Josh had gone off to meet with the company officials, Amanda couldn't help feeling herself depressed. She dressed and left the hotel, to find that the weather had turned as bleak as the city itself. The people, huddling against the raw air as they walked quickly by, seemed to be almost exclusively middle-aged and very working class. She wondered if there was even the geniality of a bookstore like the pleasant, musty place she had found in Coventry.

She walked a few more blocks. Maidenborough was near the Irish Sea, but the coastline, she knew, was mostly given over to shipping and there wouldn't be very much in the way of scenery, even if she could manage to borrow a car and drive out herself.

Then she remembered all about English roads and cars, and driving on the right. She was sure she couldn't handle it.

At last she went into a tobacconist and bought a few British women's magazines. The rest of the day she spent back in the hotel room, listlessly looking through the periodicals, turning the dials of the TV set.

Josh came in at last looking rather grimy. Amanda looked at him with mock reproach, while he explained that he had been poking in and out of machinery all day.

She asked all sorts of questions, showing her interest, but Josh had little to say about it.

"It couldn't have been any deadlier than my day," she declared finally. "Poking in and out of the dreariest streets and finding absolutely nothing."

"I was a little afraid of that," he said sympathetically, "but we'll try to scare up some fun tonight to make up for it."

He stooped down to kiss her lightly, but Amanda pushed him away. "Go and have your bath," she ordered playfully, "and then come and see me."

It wasn't the dullness of Maidenborough that was getting to her, she knew; it was the double stress of Josh's not yet asking her about going on with him or dropping his notion of racing completely, and of her trying to maintain a happy attitude in spite of it. Time was passing, and passing fast, even if the slowness of this afternoon had been no indication of it; and if he were going to ask her, there wouldn't be too many more opportunities. She was ticketed to go back to New York in six days.

Josh came back from his bath scrubbed clean, with

nothing on but a huge bathsheet wrapped around his waist.

"Tonight we'll do something exciting." He leaned over to her to whisper in a conspiratorial tone.

"Like what?" Amanda couldn't help but catch his infectious mischievousness in spite of herself.

"Like tooling over to Liverpool and going to a disco."

"Oh, Josh, really!" Amanda exclaimed.

He spread his hands. "It's about the best I can offer you," he said. "This corner of the country isn't exactly noted for its gastronomy, either."

"Well," Amanda said philosophically. "At least if we're making some headway on Haskell's behalf, then something is happening."

"Yeah, something is happening." Josh kissed her. But not enough, Amanda thought despairingly.

He made love to her then, Josh lying down and rolling her onto him, and Amanda giving in with cries of delight, no longer quiet as her mood had been. She gazed down at him as he held her aloft; it was her turn to hover over him, to explore him as he usually did her, to delight in the openness of her newfound freedom, her total trust in him and the feelings he aroused in her.

"My lady is a woman now," Josh teased her gently, gathering her in his arms, "and quite a woman."

Amanda laughed ecstatically. When he praised her sensuality, her happiness in their lovemaking, it was the greatest compliment he could give her, the one she valued most among all the lavish flattery he poured on her. It made her feel real, and alive, especially since her newfound feelings of physical joy had all come from him, were all due to him and the way he made her feel.

She circled in on him now, feeling heady with confidence, knowing the glory of her body and the strength of its effect on him. When, without words but only with motions, she wanted him to move, he moved; his body did her bidding as though he were the well-tuned racer and she the controlling driver. Then they raced together, and accelerated, and slowed down together after the burning laps of the fast-flying embraces.

At last she curled herself against him, spoon-style, and they drifted off into a lazy, short-lived nap that rounded out the afternoon. Josh urged her awake to get ready for the evening ahead, an interlude to divert them for a few hours before they tumbled back into bed again.

They dressed and drove the few miles to Liverpool, the hub of all northwest England.

Amanda was amused rather than attracted by the nightlife district with its caverns and dens and clubs. They stopped in at a few of the most invitingly named, Josh drinking mugs of Guinness and seeming to fit right in with the noisy young crowds.

Almost every club had live music, and although they weren't, strictly speaking, to Amanda's taste, there was a liveliness and sparkle to the bands she could enjoy.

"They didn't quite build Jerusalem in this green and pleasant land," she paraphrased after they had ducked out of one of the clubs just as a brawl was beginning. "At least I understand now why I only saw older people on the streets this afternoon," she said. "The young ones probably sleep all day saving themselves for this sort of activity."

"Mostly they're working," Josh said. "Assembly-line

jobs that pay them just enough to manage their few pints and some fun at night."

Amanda was glad to get back to the quiet stability of their hotel. It was staid and conservative, plain and rather inelegant, but still a welcome haven after the rowdy youthquakes of the nightclubs. Maidenborough and Liverpool were small enough price to pay for the chance that Josh would change, she hoped fervently. Then they would leave Maidenborough behind them.

But, as Josh had feared, the two days stretched into three. There was just too much he had to see at the plants in order to provide the total, and totally balanced, picture Haskell needed to make his decision. Josh, it seemed to a hopeful Amanda, didn't terribly mind the extra day. He would spend it in the company of the engines and other parts he had to inspect, but even more, with the workmen he loved to talk to. Many of them were survivors from the early, classic days when the country supported a dozen different independent marques, each vying with the other not only in sales but in making the fastest and finest motorcars possible. Josh loved to talk about those days, before his time but an important part of the legacy, adding so much to what he had learned about building cars from his father. Amanda knew that he loved the folklore and legends of the business as much as he did the technical side, and being able to talk and reminisce with the workmen was a golden opportunity for him. An opportunity, Amanda thought, that could fortify the right decision.

Although he was an American, Josh was accepted by the English workers as an insider because of his knowledge and feeling for the cars. And when he could add something to their storehouse of data, he was even more appreciated. As, he recounted eagerly to Amanda, when he had corrected the mistaken notion many of them had that the word Lagonda, the car used by British royalty on many state occasions, was Italian in origin. They had listened wide-eyed when he explained that it was actually the name of a small creek in Ohio, meaning, in some Indian language, "silent running water," and that it had been brought to England by an American engineer, who had come over to study opera but had succumbed to his love of automobiles to start the famous marque early in the century.

Even Amanda loved that story. Then and there she decided to be more productive with her time. Even Maidenborough must have a hairdresser, she decided, and she went off to find one and have her hair and her nails done.

The simple way she wore her hair was easy enough for the delighted owner of the shop to do. She fussed endlessly over Amanda, exclaiming that she had never had an American lady as a customer before; indeed, she seldom saw anyone outside of the circle of her usual lifelong clientele.

Amanda tipped generously and left the shop feeling refreshened and better.

She wasn't back at the hotel for very long when Josh appeared.

"Let's go!" he shouted. "We're all finished."

Amanda ran to hug him, but he held her at arm's length. "You look beautiful," he exclaimed. "Not that you don't look lovely all the time, but something's happened."

"I went and had my hair done," Amanda said sheepishly. "I have to admit it was a good idea. I feel so much better."

He hugged her tight. "Let's not wait until tomorrow," he said. "Let's pack and leave now. I want to take you along the Welsh border. It's magnificent, wildly beautiful, and we still have most of the day left."

"Super!" Amanda exclaimed, wanting more to hear about Maidenborough than to stay there. But Josh's mind was on other things.

"Then we can bed down someplace almost as remote and romantic as the one you were talking about the other day," Josh said. "My raven-haired beauty," he added softly.

Amanda turned saucy. "My highwayman," she shot back at him, and they both laughed.

Josh settled the bill quickly, and they piled back into the car. Amanda set her sights firmly southward, anticipating the next few days even more eagerly than she had before. It was her last chance to be asked to join the start of his racing circuit, but he would have to bring it up.

Josh took a road that hugged the border between England and Wales. Amanda was immediately struck by the great bleak beauty of the craggy mountains, which turned from black to purple to green in the changing sunlight. Almost as fascinating were the long and unpronounceable names on the road signs.

"Well," Josh reminded her. "You wanted us to make love in all sorts of exotic places, what about trying Llangollen? According to the last sign we passed, it's only two miles away."

"Shame on you!" Amanda cried. "We've only been out of bed for a short time and you're trying to get me back in already!"

"All right, have it your own way," Josh gave in. But he really was teasing her. The banked border road was not one that he had taken before, and he was enjoying the challenges it presented. Amanda was absorbed in the scenery and peppered their sporadic conversation by calling out the equally cumbersome names of other towns they passed and announcing that they weren't going to stop at any of those, either. Hours later they were feeling hungry, and both car and driver needed a well-earned rest. They had been exhilarated as they passed such storybook places as the River Dee. Amanda agreed to stop to eat in Wales, even though the next spot they had reached was perfectly ordinary and disappointingly named Welshpool.

As they ate simple but hearty country fare, Josh pored over his detailed road map. He looked up at her. "Do you think you've seen enough of Wales?" he asked.

"I guess so, if you have," Amanda said.

"Well, I think we should start moving more southeasterly than straight south," he said. "We'll be coming into some beautiful countryside soon, and I think we're ready for a change of scenery."

"What does your map show?" Amanda asked.

"We can head for Hereford," Josh said. "That will give us a long, leisurely drive into the Cotswolds."

"I'm for that," Amanda said, getting up out of her chair and coming behind him, resting one hand lightly on his shoulder while she peered over it and studied the map. "This sounds even more picturesque," she said delightedly, "and we can understand the names."

"Is that so, smarty," Josh teased her. "Tell me what this means?" He pointed to a spot on the map called Wyre Piddle.

"Oh dear," Amanda said. "Is that where we're going?"

"Not quite, but very close to it," Josh said. "As a matter of fact, we'll probably drive right through."

"Why?" Amanda had to know.

Josh had settled the bill, and they were walking back to the car. "It's near a place called Evesham that I've heard about," Josh answered. "It's supposed to be breathtakingly lovely at this time of year, and I thought it would be beautiful to see it together." He returned her hug as they stood on the cobblestone curb before getting into the car. Josh found the road he was looking for quickly, and soon a totally different landscape was setting itself out before them.

Lush green pastures and tidy cultivated farms formed a patchwork quilt of varying shades of greens, yellows, and the graceful beiges of stands of rye and barley. Even the villages retained the air of ordered serenity that pervaded the entire country. The roads were smooth and modern, but they stretched through countryside that seemed as if it had been the same for centuries.

"Look!" Amanda exclaimed. "There's a thatched cottage."

Josh was about to ask her if she wanted him to pull up so they could see it more closely, but she realized that it was not an isolated sight. Within yards of their first seeing it there were several others, constituting if not a village then at least a crossroads of some local importance. Amanda studied the map. "It all sounds so delightful," she said, "but I know we can't stop everywhere. There's so much I want to see."

Evesham turned out to be as beautiful as Josh had been led to expect. It wasn't the town itself that drew their attention. By the time they got there they had passed through several equally picturesque places, but Evesham was set jewel-like in a surrounding dale that had been planted from time immemorial with orchards. Now the trees were in full blossom, and the whole area seemed to be clouded over by a mist of tiny white and pink flowers. On all sides the vale was enclosed in this mist. Amanda was transfixed by the sight. For the first time in days her heart was at ease. She felt rooted to the spot where they stood, looking over the miles and miles of unbroken blossoms. "I want to stay here forever," she whispered to Josh. "It's the most beautiful and romantic place I've ever seen."

"But we're only a little way from Stratford," he told her. "I thought you'd like to spend the night there."

Amanda felt bewildered by the endless choices of things to see. It would be unthinkable to miss a visit to Shakespeare's birthplace when they were so close by, but she made Josh promise that after seeing Stratford they would continue on to only the tiniest, most untouristy, beautiful places, like Evesham. "I don't want to go any place I've ever heard of until we're back in London," she declared .

"You must make one exception," Josh insisted, and Amanda looked at him quizzically. "That is," he told her, "you'll never forgive yourself if we don't go to Bath. It's gorgeous and sumptuous, and besides, it's not far out of our way."

Stratford was interesting, but Amanda was glad she insisted on going back to the lesser-known countryside. The flowering lilacs, the majestic yew trees, the cottages and houses that were as often roofed in the tile of the area as in thatch, delighted her endlessly.

The villages, too, like Broadway and Chipping Campden, had rows and rows of medieval houses that still stood in perfect condition. Bath, when they arrived there at last, was as stately and elegant with its Georgian houses as she had always imagined it to be. She was glad of the nights they had spent in the rural inns with their warm hospitality and wonderful breakfasts, but the elegance of the former spa was a perfect combination of architectural and natural beauty.

The shops and the flowers were lovely in a nineteenth-century way, and Amanda felt as though they had been transported back to the romantic Regency era. They visited the new shops and the old ruins that dated back to Roman times. Everything had been perfect during this part of their trip, and nothing more so than this resort where their fairy-tale existence of the past few days finally had to come to its inevitable end. It was hard to believe it wouldn't be the ending she wanted.

Amanda washed the dust of the road off in a large steaming tub, and she scented and dressed herself with an elegance that hadn't seemed appropriate earlier but that their present surroundings demanded. She put on a velvet Bill Blass dress that she had packed carefully in tissue paper, and a choker of her own design at the base of her throat.

Josh had gone down to the dining room first. When he saw her, he lifted his glass of pale ale in a mock toast. "Our last night together," he said.

"Why?" The word was blurted out before Amanda knew what she was saying. She bit her lip, but it was too late.

"Because I have to go on to my work," Josh said carefully, "and you have to go back to yours. It's that simple."

"There's nothing simple about it," Amanda said, a touch of bitterness in her voice. "I thought everything had been so perfect. Why can't we go on together?"

"There are things ahead of me right now that I can't expose you to," Josh said slowly. "You knew this was coming, Amanda. We had said two weeks in England, and I think we've had as glorious a time as anyone could."

Amanda could not hide her disappointment. "Up til now."

He reached for her hand. "It's not even going to be six weeks that we'll be apart," he said. "Monaco is the last week in May. I'll catch the first plane back to New York and be waiting for you when you come back from your Memorial Day weekend."

"Why would you assume I'll be going away?" Amanda asked stiffly. "There'll be so much for me to catch up on at the store."

"That's all to the good," he said, squeezing her hand. "It'll make the time that I'm away go so much faster for you."

"That's right," Amanda said coolly. "I'll bury myself in my work just as you're buried in yours. I'm sure I won't have any more difficulty than you will in shutting all of this out of my mind."

"Amanda, don't," he said. "Don't spoil what we've had. I can't take you where I have to go now. This is how it must be. Someday I'll be able to explain it better. Trust me until then."

"I'll try, Josh," she said, but there was only politeness in her voice, nothing of the commitment he wanted to hear.

They ate their dinner silently.

"It's getting late," Amanda said, after refusing the waiter's offer of another cup of coffee. "We have to be at the airport rather early in the morning."

Josh held her chair back for her and they went up to their rooms.

"Amanda—" he began, reaching for her, but she shook her head and moved away from him.

She undressed herself, washed, and slipped into bed, first putting on the one nightgown she had brought on the trip and had only bothered to use once before, on an especially cold night near the Welsh border when they had had no fire in their room.

Josh didn't say anything, only leaning over to kiss her gently on the cheek when he got into bed.

The wake-up knock came sharply at their door the next morning. They got up and got ready for their departure. The same silence prevailed as throughout the evening before. Amanda couldn't stand the lack of communication, but she was too hurt and angry to try to make the small talk that could break it.

Driving to Heathrow from the northerly outskirts where they had spent the night kept them from going through London itself. Amanda was sorry not to have a farewell glimpse of the majestic city where she had known some of the greatest happiness in her life. *Perhaps it's just as well,* she thought bitterly. It would only restoke those lovely memories and make things worse.

Josh led her to the departure gate for her flight. They still had half an hour before boarding time to spend together; it would be another two hours for Josh alone in the airport before he flew to Spain.

He sat down on a bench; Amanda followed.

"Darling, please talk to me," Josh said. "It's crazy for us to be parting like this after the closeness we've known. It's only a month or so, Amanda, it isn't the end of the world."

"Yes, it is!" she cried.

"You can't be with me for what I have to do," Josh insisted. "You knew that before we left. Nothing's changed. I've got to go. That's all there is to it."

"You took care of all of your work in England without my ever having been in your way," she retorted. "Why have I suddenly become a hindrance?"

"You're not a hindrance, Amanda," Josh said. "I love you, goddamn it, but there are certain things I have to do, and certain decisions I have to make. You have to learn to accept those."

"I don't have to learn to do anything you say!" Amanda shot back. "You've made it perfectly clear that your life is your own concern. Well, so is mine. You don't have to dictate anything to me about what I must and mustn't do. Not ever again." She turned sharply away from him as she uttered those last three words so he couldn't see the tears spilling out of her eyes.

Josh put his hand on her sleeve, but she shrugged it off angrily. He wasn't going to change his mind, no matter what she said or did, and it was obvious she wasn't going to change hers either. He looked blankly at her turned back. She was wearing the same bright-red coat she had had on when he had first found her that November day that now seemed half a lifetime ago, not the few short months during which they had been together and separated, separated and together, like alternating squares on a chessboard.

He couldn't expose her to the rigors and possible dangers he faced. Not till he was sure of himself and his ability to race. Damn! He was almost as angry with Amanda for not understanding as he was already with himself for not being able to explain to her.

The clipped accents of a cultivated English voice came over the public address system. Josh smiled, almost wincing. "This has to be the only airport in the world where you can actually understand the announcements," he said. "This is you." He picked up Amanda's carry-on bag and held her lightly by the elbow as they walked to the boarding gate. "I'm sorry it has to end like this," he whispered in her ear.

"It didn't have to," Amanda said.

Josh shook his head and looked straight into her eyes. "Our trip had to end here," he said, "but it didn't have to end like this." He bent over to kiss her.

Amanda stood frozen until he lifted his mouth from hers. She couldn't look at him. She waited until he relinquished his grip on her elbow, then she turned and joined the stream of passengers heading for the plane.

She strode along briskly. It didn't feel like the end of a vacation, or even the end of an affair. It felt more like the end of a lifetime, as though she were leaving a part of her life there in the terminal.

Chapter 10

The flight home, so unlike the one to England, was tedious and endless. Amanda tried to get comfortable in a dozen different ways, but none of them worked. She tried to fall asleep, to read a magazine, to listen to music, to watch the movie. Nothing helped. The endless ocean, moving thirty thousand feet below, was a dark mass punctuated with minute whitecaps, barely visible in their motion. It was dull and monotonous, with not even a flash of color to catch her eye. She sighed deeply, relieved when at last the announcement came that they were only an hour from New York. But her relief was short-lived. This last hour seemed to stretch out even longer than the four that had preceded it. At long last they were on the ground. She got through customs, and then got angry at herself for neglecting to make arrangements for a car to take her into town.

She walked through the International Arrivals Building lobby to find a cab, moving as quickly as she could through the crush of people.

There was a sudden explosion of flashbulbs that made her jump back. Someone was clutching her arm. She tried to shake him off, turning in amazement to find that she was at the center of the pushing photographers and the crowd of people shouting questions at her. The strange man gripped her more firmly, hurting her.

"What are you doing?" she demanded, not realizing that he was trying to shield her and move her away from the crowd of photographers.

"Get in quickly," he said tersely as he helped her into a big car. "We'll try to lose them." He slammed the door behind him and barked quick directions to the driver.

Amanda looked at him in amazement. His features were strong, his face chalk-white and drawn.

"Who are you?" Amanda demanded. "Where are you taking me?" Her surprise had turned to fright when he forced her into the car, to terror when she saw she was sandwiched between him and yet another strange man.

"Don't be afraid, it's going to be all right," he said evenly. "We're FBI."

"What's happened?" Amanda screamed.

"Calm down," he said, his voice low but firm. "Your son's been—he's been taken."

"What do you mean?" Amanda felt something rising inside her that was about to choke off her breath.

"He's been kidnapped," the agent answered quickly, "but stay calm and don't be frightened. We're going to have him back soon and unharmed."

"When? How did it happen?" She was pitched to a state of hysteria. "Where is he? I want my baby!"

"We don't know where he is right now, Mrs. Parrish," he said carefully. "We're doing everything possible, and they've promised we'll have him back in a number of days."

"I can't believe this," Amanda said, "I can't believe this is happening." She slumped back in the seat, trying to contain the hysteria that still threatened to overwhelm her. "How could it happen?" she cried hoarsely.

The agent grasped her hands, trying to steady her, and explained how the boy had been taken from in front of their apartment house as he waited for the school bus to pick him up. The doorman on duty was new, a young replacement for the usual morning man. He had been questioned time and again but insisted he hadn't even seen the boy standing there. Sylvia had been called by the school when Tommy failed to appear. She was now back at her own apartment, hysterical and heavily sedated, blaming herself for everything. It had been impossible to locate

Amanda when the kidnapping had occurred, because she had left no definite itinerary behind.

"We're going to Tommy's father's country house," the agent said. "That's where they want to keep contact. I spoke to the boy this morning. He sounded fine. They won't hurt him. They'll call again at eight." He looked at his watch. "We'll be there in plenty of time for you to talk to him."

The dark outskirts of the city were a blur as the big car bore them at high speed north to Westchester. Amanda felt as though the breath had left her body. She bit her lip, trying not to cry out. Why had she gone and left him, she thought bitterly. This never would have happened if she had stayed home with Tommy, where she belonged. And Alan—where was Alan? The agent hadn't even mentioned him.

"You can't go blaming yourself for this, Mrs. Parrish," the agent said, as if he could read her thoughts. "Your mother explained that she followed exactly the same procedure that you have for the past year. It would have happened exactly the same way even if you or the boy's father had been here."

"I can't believe that," Amanda said. "I can't believe it. I'll never forgive myself for this. Or—if anything happens to him." Her voice ended in a sob.

"Chances are good nothing's going to happen to him," the agent, whose name was Fuller, tried to reassure her.

"How can you be so sure?" she demanded. "He's in the hands of criminals. Kidnappers! How can we know what will happen?"

"You've got to trust us," he said. "Everything is being done that possibly can be. We want him back as much as you do."

Amanda nodded. "I know you're doing everything

you can. I feel so guilty. And so—so helpless. If anything happens to Tommy, I'll just die."

"Stop it," Fuller said forcefully. "That kind of talk isn't going to help anybody. Not you or us or your son. You've got to keep a grip on yourself for his sake."

All she could do was nod in the darkness of the car.

"You're going to be talking to him in a little while," Fuller went on. "You've got to sound confident and unworried. If he hears any fear in your voice, he'll become frightened and upset himself. Up until now he's borne it very well. He's quite the little man, this son of yours. The kidnappers have promised to call twice a day, and they seem likely to keep to that plan. I told them you wouldn't be in until late this evening, and they agreed to make tonight's call later so that you could speak to him."

"I've got to be grateful for that at least," Amanda said. Then something in her mind clicked. "You said if his father were here. Where is he?"

The agent shrugged. "No one is quite sure. It seems he decided to take an extended trip to the Orient. Told his office he'd be out of touch for two weeks. Some kind of mountain-climbing retreat."

Amanda nodded. Alan had often spoken of seeing Katmandu someday. How could he have picked such a time—when she was already out of the country?

They rode the rest of the way in seldom-broken silence, Amanda tortured by her unspoken fears, until at last they were on the circular driveway of the sprawling house. She could hear the crunch of gravel under the car, but the sound did not hold the promise of a happy homecoming as it used to, so long ago it seemed another lifetime.

Gathered in front of the steps was another small mob of photographers and reporters. Amanda tried to shield her face as Fuller and Saunders, the agent who'd driven the car, guided her past them and through the front door.

The house had not changed in the two or more years since she had been inside. The only difference was yet another version of the tall, crew-cut agents who rose to greet her. "They've called with their demands."

Fuller looked at his superior, the question unasked.

"A million dollars."

Amanda looked at him fearfully, unable to say anything. She didn't have that kind of money; Alan, who might, was somewhere in India. She thought the floor was rising up to meet her.

Lackland, the chief agent, led her quickly to a chair. "The phone is going to ring very soon," he said. "You'll be able to speak with your son. Why don't you sit down now and compose yourself?" he suggested. "We want you sounding perfectly normal and natural when you talk to him."

Amanda nodded and sat down on the small flowered settee. She tried to get a grip on herself, tried to calm the nerve endings that were jolting her body, tried to get control of herself by thinking of everything that possibly could be done. But when the phone rang, she jumped up as if she had been hit with an electric shock.

She started toward it, but the agent put out a restraining hand.

"I've always answered the phone before," he said. "We don't want to do anything that's the least bit different from the routine they've come to expect. We don't want to give them any reason whatsoever for thinking that anything is different."

Again Amanda could only nod as she stood spellbound, watching him reach for the phone and pick it up.

"Hi, Tom," he said, and Amanda marveled at the firmness and friendliness in his voice. "How are you doing? Are you feeling okay?"

Fuller turned to face her, nodding as the chief agent listened to the small voice at the other end. "Hey, Tommy," he said finally. "I've got a nice surprise for you. Your mommy is here."

Amanda felt her heart drop as she took two enormous steps to take the receiver from him. She grasped it firmly in both hands, trying to use the instrument through which she would talk to her son to steady her as well.

"Hello, darling," she said in a bright voice, "how are you? I miss you so much."

"Where were you, Mommy?" She thought her knees would buckle under her as she heard his voice on the other end, sounding as natural as if he were speaking from home.

"Did you forget, baby?" she said eagerly. "I went to England? Remember?" She felt idiotic bantering with him like this, as if nothing at all were wrong, as if their world might not at any moment crash and crumble beneath them.

"I remember," Tommy said. "Did *you* remember about the car? Did you bring me a new car?"

Everything went blank as Amanda collapsed to the floor. The small wooden table that held the phone and a lamp went down with her. That was the only thing to break her fall as she dropped to the woodplanking floor. Fuller rushed over to pick her up as

Lackland grabbed the telephone and spoke into it quickly.

"Hi, Tom, are you still there?" he asked. "Mommy is very tired after her long plane trip. It's hard for her to talk anymore," he covered up quickly.

"I wanted to ask her about the car," Tommy said, sounding disappointed. Before Lackland could say anything, the phone was taken from the boy and the voice that the agent had learned to both anticipate and dread took over again. The unseen abductor on the other end of the line gave further instructions, which were readily agreed to, Lackland looking up at Fuller, who jotted down Lackland's repeating of everything the kidnapper said.

The other agent, Saunders, was on the floor, holding Amanda's head up and trying to force a little brandy into her mouth to revive her.

When she came to, Amanda looked totally blank and abandoned. She turned to Lackland, the expression in her eyes begging for reassurance. She knew she had passed out, but she couldn't quite believe it.

"He sounded fine, Mrs. Parrish, just fine," Lackland said, reaching down to help her get back into a chair. "You could tell he was perfectly all right by his voice, couldn't you?"

"Yes," she agreed slowly. "He sounded just like himself." But her faltering voice and trembling hands were saying the opposite about Amanda herself.

"This can't be happening, it can't be," Amanda said, holding her head in her hands and dissolving again in a flood of tears. "I can't believe this is happening to us. Why can't we get him back?"

"They want a million dollars," Lackland said. "They've already been told that Mr. Parrish, their intended payer, is away and out of touch."

"Do they believe that?" Amanda asked.

"Yes, they do," he assured her. "They know they can have it as soon as he gets back, and they tell us where to bring it to."

"I think Mrs. Parrish should have a sedative," Fuller said.

"Mrs. Parrish is having nothing of the kind," Amanda snapped, wheeling around in her chair to face him. "My son's life is at stake. I'm not going to rest until we have him back!"

"There's really nothing you can do," Lackland said sympathetically.

Amanda turned the other way to face him. "Perhaps not, but it certainly won't do anybody any good for me to have my mind turn to jelly. It is just possible, you know, I might be able to contribute something." She stared dejectedly at the floor, unable to keep her gaze up. "Besides, Tommy's going to want to talk to me, and I've got to sound all right for his benefit. When will they call again?"

"Eight o'clock tomorrow morning."

"Twelve hours," Amanda said. Twelve hours of torture and anxiety. She looked up at him again. "My God, you don't think they are doing anything to hurt *him,* do you?"

"No, I'm sure they're not, Mrs. Parrish," Lackland said quickly. "The boy sounds just fine, and I'm sure they're doing everything they can to keep him quiet and content. It's easier for them that way."

"They really spoil the kids a little bit," Fuller said earnestly, "so that in case they are caught they can get some favorable testimony."

"From the victim!" Amanda was furious. "What audacity!"

"I quite agree with you," Fuller said, "but you

should be happy for every bit of positive action in the situation."

She was sure he was right about everything, and conscious of his policemanlike use of the word "situation" as a substitute for the hard ugliness of "kidnapping."

Not that that made it any easier, nothing would until Tommy was back in her arms again.

"What was he asking you about a car?" Fuller asked, trying to put her at ease.

"He wanted to know if a gift I brought him from England was a model sports car," Amanda said. "He's gotten so awfully fond of them."

"He must have left this one on his last time here," the agent said.

Amanda stared in disbelief at the shiny toy Ferrari that Fuller took out of a desk drawer.

"Well, at least you'll have it here to give him when they bring him back," Fuller said sympathetically.

It was the first time since she got off the plane that Amanda's mind leaped back to Josh. Now her self-anger redoubled itself. She got up and started pacing back and forth across the narrow living room. She didn't dare look at the clock. Not more than a quarter of an hour could have passed since she had talked to Tommy, and the rest of the night wouldn't pass any more quickly or easily. She could tell from the glances of the men that her pacing was making them nervous as well. "Perhaps I should go upstairs," she said. "I won't be able to sleep, but at least I'll keep from driving you crazy."

"Try to get some rest," Lackland said to her, "just stretch out and don't fight the tiredness if it comes."

"If it comes," Amanda echoed hopelessly.

"Remember, you've got jet lag working in your

favor," he added. "That may just do the trick. You really must be exhausted."

Amanda shrugged her shoulders. "Perhaps I am," she sighed, "and I'm just too numb to feel it." She said good night quietly and walked heavily up the polished old stairs, leaning hard on the banister for support. She was glad for the darkness of the bedroom, grateful to be able to be alone and agonize privately without having to share her grief with strangers.

She lay in the darkness, insensible to the light April, almost May, wind moving through the oak trees that reached as high as the second-story bedroom windows, not breathing in the scent of the high-climbing lilacs she always loved and looked forward to each spring.

There had been lilacs in England, she remembered. A paler shade of lavender than they were here, and white ones, almost green in their cast as the first young blossoms pushed their way out. The rich forests, the rolling green meadows, the clipped and cared-for dark green hedges of the English countryside, now all that seemed so long ago, so much farther away than when she had left Josh at the airport.

Josh again. She had to push him out of her mind. He had been able to do that to her easily enough. Disengaging himself, he had called it, cutting himself off physically and emotionally from anyone or anything that could interfere with his racing. There had been lilacs, and it had been on a night such as this that he said it.

No time to think of that, she scolded herself. But an answering voice inside her made her realize that the only comfort she was likely to find this night was in recalling the beautiful rolling countryside, its complete and eternal serenity. If she could concentrate on that and try to ease her fears for Tommy from her mind, perhaps she could find some semblance of peace, something from which to draw the strength she was going to need to get her through.

She wondered suddenly what made Lackland and the others so sure that everything was going to be all right. He had told her they were working on many different levels, but he had never explained it to her. She wondered about it now, and started to get up, to go downstairs to ask him to explain it, to add something perhaps to the measure of hope she had for getting her son back. But if he had not discussed it with her, then perhaps it was of a nature that he didn't want her to know.

Amanda shivered in the darkness, dizzy as well as frightened. There was such a labyrinth of terror and concealment, one could get lost easily in the intricacies of what was known and what wasn't. A frightening maze of possibilities and consequences spun endlessly around each other and in her mind, trapping her in terror of someone's making a mistake that could be fatal.

And the core of all this, the very center on which it was all spinning, was her small, helpless son, so innocent of what was happening to him that all he could think of was another toy car.

She slept fitfully, waking with sudden starts, thinking that she had been asleep for only moments. Once, she thought the sky outside was getting lighter, where it was brushed by the treetops on the horizon, but then she was sure it was her imagination.

She slept again, waking with a start in bright daylight. She jumped when the phone rang, her arm freezing in midair when she reached for the nearby extension. She remembered the agent saying something about routine. She hurried into a robe, and a soft, quick tap on the bedroom door assured her that she had done the right thing.

Fuller gestured toward the living room downstairs, and Amanda hurried past him in her anxiety to get to the phone.

Lackland handed her the receiver without saying anything.

She spoke to Tommy again, the same sort of bright, meaningless chatter as the night before. She felt all of her emotions bottling up inside her, threatening to spill out. She longed to ask Tommy where he was and what they were doing to him and all the other countless questions that tore at her heart. But she knew she didn't dare, for the safety of this precious child of hers and the hope of getting him back.

"I have to say good-bye now, Mommy," Tommy said.

Amanda's heart stopped. She could hear the growled directive behind her son's words. Now it all became more terribly real than it had been since she got off the plane. Now she had heard for herself the man, or one of them, who had her son. The contact made shivers race through her, and she felt her whole body trembling uncontrollably. She gulped hard, quickly remembering that Tommy was still on the other end of the phone. "Good-bye, darling," she said, her voice choking as her throat constricted. "I'll talk to you later tonight. Be good."

She pressed her ear against the phone and listened, hearing nothing more from Tommy, only the sound of the phone being taken away from him and communication broken off with a final click.

She sobbed hysterically, falling into the nearest chair.

"You've got to take it easy, Mrs. Parrish." Fuller admonished her with more gentleness than she'd expect from a man in such a calling as his.

"How can I?" she demanded, looking up at him, her eyes narrowed. "Are you married?" she asked.

"Yes, ma'am, I am," he replied.

"You have any children?" As soon as the question was out, Amanda recoiled in horror at what she had asked. She could have bitten off her tongue. This man, and the others, were trying to get Tommy back for her and being extraordinarily concerned for her during the process. It was wrong, so wrong of her to bait him like that, when all he was trying to do was help. She lowered her gaze in shame. "I'm terribly sorry, Mr. Fuller," she murmured. "That was uncalled for. Please forgive me." The last words came out in a strangled sob as she put her face in her hands, crying uncontrollably.

She had never felt so helpless, so imprisoned by the doings of other people before. Her hands were completely tied. She had nothing to contribute, nothing she could say or do that would add anything to the law officers' task of getting her son back safely. Even they had something to do, or so it seemed, between the 8:00 A.M. and 8:00 P.M. phone calls. They were constantly on the phone, getting calls or making them. They were in contact with their headquarters and with other agents in the field. Every time the phone rang and she automatically reached for it, she had to stop herself. It was as though she were constantly in the way, getting underfoot. None of them said anything to her, but it seemed obvious they had a job to do and she didn't. It made everything worse, the whole tragedy of the kidnapping magnified in her mind not only by her having been away when it happened, but by her inability to do anything now. Amanda would never have believed herself ever to feel so completely weak and helpless.

"Although no one is exactly sure where Mr. Parrish is, his office does know when he's expected back." Fuller's voice broke into her anguish. "Until then, we'll just have to wait it out, I'm afraid."

"There's always the possibility of a break, Mrs. Parrish," Lackland added.

"Break? What kind of break? What do you mean?" Amanda asked.

"Some surprise element that will help us crack the case before the deadline they've imposed," he replied.

Break. Deadline. All of the words, even the ones that signified help, were so threatening-sounding to Amanda. It was all conjecture anyway. There were only three things that she knew: that Tommy was taken, that his kidnappers wanted a million dollars for his safe return, and that the source of the ransom would not be there for almost two weeks. Two weeks in which the kidnappers could change their minds, or grow frightened or impatient, or any number of other ideas could enter their crazed minds, ideas that could bring harm to her child. And all she could do was sit here helplessly, wringing her hands, her body wracked, unable to do anything to protect Tommy or bring him any closer to home.

A million dollars, she thought. *What do I have that could possibly be worth that much?*

The front door opened suddenly. Amanda jumped at the sound. But it was only Saunders, the other agent, reporting in. He nodded to her politely but directed his remarks primarily to Lackland, his chief.

"The reporters are still hanging around at the apartment, at headquarters, too, and I tried to discourage the contingent out here," he indicated with the shrug of his shoulder, "but they're just hanging in. I told them there's no hard news and that we didn't expect any for a while, but they figure maybe they can get a few words or some pictures of Mrs. Parrish."

Amanda was startled. She looked up at Lackland beseechingly, silently pleading with him not to let her be subjected to such a thing.

"No way." The FBI agent shook his head, reassuring her. "If we give them anything at all, we'll never get rid of them. This way they may be a little discouraged, at least the ones whose papers can't afford to keep them out here indefinitely."

Amanda's shoulders sagged with relief. "Thank you," she whispered gratefully. She sank back against the cushions of the settee. *That* was her value, she thought grimly, news value. That wasn't anything that would help get Tommy back, even if she had felt up to it. There was nothing she had that was valuable enough to get him home safely. The most precious thing in her life was her son himself.

Chapter 11

Josh gazed up at the burning blue sky above him. It seemed to stretch out to infinity, unbroken by even the punctuation of a single cloud. He didn't mind the heat and elevation of Madrid, but it would take some adjusting on the part of the car, and then the car would have to readjust again quickly as they moved to the more temperate climate of Brussels in the north.

But he had to make it happen here in Spain first. He had to make it through this race. Still, he couldn't help thinking of Belgium and the new pistol-shaped autodrome near its capital.

He thought ruefully of the old Francorchamps circuit where earlier Grand Prix had been held, knowing that he would have had far less of a chance of finishing on that old killer track. Located high in the Ardennes, it had been the site of the Belgian Grand Prix since 1925, but after severe crashes, and pileups had continuously occurred there, the drivers refused to race unless certain safety precautions were instituted. One dispute led to another and, finally, in 1969, to the track being scratched from the Grand Prix circuit. The new track, farther north toward the capital, was a delight, set near a beautiful spa and the elegance of medieval Brussels. Josh felt a pang at Amanda's not being with him. How she would have loved the soaring cathedrals and the lacy architecture of the gallery houses that fronted the imposing squares.

He had set himself a precondition, even before he had left New York: He was going to complete the race at Jarama or withdraw from the remainder of the circuit. He wasn't crazy enough to have supposed he could be among the winners. Just being able to finish would have to satisfy him, and his sponsors.

He tried to put Belgium from his mind, just as he made himself stop thinking about how Amanda could have filled her days in Madrid at the Prado and been with him at night. But he had made a decision, and he had to stick with it. No matter that wherever he was there was amusement and distraction enough for a woman of Amanda's taste and resources to occupy herself with, just as she was woman enough for him to want the closeness and luxury of her beside him when he went to sleep. But that was all extraneous, he reminded himself; he had come to Europe to race, and in his condition there could be no distractions, lovely or otherwise.

He was satisfied with his performance, ecstatic with the car, and grateful that the sponsors were going along with both of them. He had set the goal for himself here at Jarama: finish. He wanted the same for Belgium and Monaco; then he could start setting goals that would bring him closer to the winner's circle, quicker to the checkered flag of the remaining races. Then, Amanda could join him.

He put his hands on the hood of the car and straightened himself from the squatting position he had been in, ignoring the slightly cramped feeling in his legs, telling himself he had stayed in the position too long. On his feet, he arched slightly back and then forward again, testing his balance, stretching his muscles, assuring himself that the twinge in his limbs was just that and nothing more.

He glanced at his watch. It was time to wash and dress for his luncheon meeting at the hotel with his sponsors and the head of the crew. He walked past the pits toward where he had left his rented little green Isabella in the parking lot, his eyes caught by the unmistakable red of the Ferrari racers. Then he felt glad that Enzo Ferrari had stopped attending races years earlier. Otherwise the reaction to Josh's driving for another carmaker might cause him more trouble than the competition Ferraris would for him on the track.

He wondered when he would get a chance to see Enzo again. Perhaps after the Italian Grand Prix in Monza there would be time to pay a short visit, and homage, to the great man whose acquaintance was one of the great privileges of his life.

Right now, though, there were other things for him to know, a lot more pressing than his desire to call on the man behind the Ferrari greatness. Jarama was new to him; all he knew about the track was that it was named for a small river that flowed nearby, and that although it had a fairly long straightaway, the rest of the road was a collection of jarring twists and turns. The course was 2.11 miles long, and there would be 50,000 screaming fans in the grandstand.

He thought about the crowds as he drove slowly on the sun-drenched highway toward Madrid. There would be double that number of people in Monaco, not only in the grandstands there but spilling out everywhere, on the streets, at windows and balconies and terraces and choice viewing spots throughout the twisting streets of the tiny principality. There would be a profusion of flowers everywhere, and—Josh cut off the thought in midsentence. There was no point in thinking about Monaco now. Jarama came first. There were only two days left. This race, *this* one, required all of his conscious moments from now until the checkered flag waved gracefully in front of him.

The sun beat down relentlessly. Josh thought about the Rader's sensitive wiring. Josh had helped engineer and build the Rader for Dutcher and had inherited it from him to race in. Josh had great confidence in the Rader, but now he was most worried about the notorious climate of Madrid, where the temperature could drop from where it was hovering now, in the nineties, to thirty degrees colder—within the course of a single day. He eased the rental car off the highway and into the city proper, heading for the hotel on the Puerta del Sol, the imposing square that was the hub of the city's activities. Normally, he would have resented the intrusion of a business meeting at such a crucial time only days before a race. But he had to admit to himself that the brutal heat was taking more of a toll of him than of the superb car he had left in the pit at Jarama but that occupied his mind wherever he was.

Although the time trials wouldn't start for another day, the city already crackled with the excitement of Grand Prix. It seemed to be in the very air as Josh parked the Isabella and strolled across the lobby of the hotel where most of the racing people were staying. He could see the appraising glances that greeted the sight of his identifying coveralls, and the accompanying murmur of acknowledgment. The people did not in all likelihood recognize him personally, but they could tell he was a racer, and that was all that mattered.

As he stepped into the elevator and pressed the button for the third floor, he kept his eyes straight in front of him and tried to maintain a very serious expression, as though he were completely oblivious of the two young girls who had ducked into the elevator right after him and were whispering and giggling in the fashion of adolescents everywhere. If they attack me, Josh thought to himself, I'll threaten to tell their duennas. This was Spain, after all, and certainly some traditions were still maintained.

He was amused in spite of himself to see that after he got out, the elevator went straight back down to the lobby. The cute señoritas had only hitched a ride for the glory of being ensconced for a few minutes with a racer.

Josh pushed open the door of the sprawling suite. It was like a small enclave of America in the midst of the overwhelmingly Spanish atmosphere that prevailed everywhere else. They'd done everything but hang a flag, Josh thought jokingly. But really, there was no need. No one would have mistaken the occupants of the suite, or their purpose, for anything other than what they were. American businessmen promoting American products, international salesmen recognizable anywhere on earth. It gave Josh a good feeling, as if he were back in Connecticut or New York or Indianapolis or California. Merchandise of all types, from copies of the racers' uniforms to souvenirs and posters, were displayed on every unoccupied piece of furniture in the main salon of the suite. The men representing all of the blue-chip corporations who had combined to sponsor Dutcher were there waiting for Josh. They included one of the giant tire companies, a producer of automotive additives, an oil company, a cigarette manufacturer, and the century-old company whose blue jeans had moved from the old American West to become an international fashion.

Josh greeted them all, receiving handshakes and broad, beaming smiles all around. It had taken a lot of salesmanship on his part, as persuasive as the best that they themselves were capable of, to get them to go along with his desire to carry on in Dutcher's place. The early meetings after the death of his brother had been almost monologues on Josh's part, pleading and rationalizing, begging them, almost, to support him in his quest to finish the circuit in his brother's place. Josh never thought for a moment that their final agreement was based on anything other than the very substantial amount of dollars that each of their companies had already spent on the Formula I Raders and was committed to spend for the rest of the year. He knew that sentiment played no part in their decision, yet when it came in the affirmative, every one of them assured him of his company's and his personal desire to back him and the McKay name all the way.

None of them expected him to win the championship or even place close, but what he was doing was a great human-interest story, and that could generate nearly as much publicity, at least in the American press, as a victory.

Now that he had completed the first time trials without any mishaps, the mood among the sponsors was higher than it had been since before the tragedy in Long Beach. If Josh continued to race as well as he was, and continued to garner the attention and affection of the racing press and public, their combined investment would be more than protected. It would pay off handsomely.

Josh had no misgivings about the commercialization of racing. The days when a daring, innovative young man could put together a racer in his backyard from discarded parts held together with strings and tape had long gone. Racing was big business, like any other professional sport, and without the sponsorship of the companies and the continued interest of the fans, it could not exist. Daring young men, primed on their need for speed and the glory of winning, were still the crux of it all. But without the supporting teams, the sponsors and the expensive crews that they also provided for, it would all be for naught. The willingness of these men and the giant corporations they represented to go along with him would have in itself erased any negative feelings Josh may have had about the racer as merchandiser. It was part of the job, as much a part as any of the mechanical or technical or athletic skills a driver was called on to display.

This American enclave, although beautifully organized and wonderfully efficient, was scarcely the most experienced group on the circuit. The cars, as well as many of the drivers, were predominantly from England and Italy, and the Rader was one of only two American-made marques currently in Formula I competition. The other one, a car called the Eagle, did not race every year, and Josh's group's primary thrust was to create the nucleus of a permanent American presence on the Grand Prix circuit. The loss of Dutcher, their number one driver, had been a staggering blow. Their number two driver, although very talented, was not generally considered to be quite as strong. When Josh appeared, pleading to take his brother's place, the men in the room and the corporate boards behind them had been even more dubious. Josh, although generally acknowledged as one of the finest racing car innovators and engineers in the world, was totally out of training. It was possible although not highly likely that his early experience as a driver could help make up for that. It was a chance they had finally agreed to take with him. Now all of their judgments were about to be put on the line at Jarama.

Josh knew that even if he went on to complete the entire circuit successfully, he could never accumulate enough points to even get close to being the world champion. Too many of the others were already too far ahead of him. His chances for winning or coming in among the first six cars, and thus earning points in any of the remaining races, was extremely unlikely. But that was not what he was racing for. Nor was it what the other men in the room wanted to talk about.

Theirs was the business end of racing, and the promotional and publicity aspects that Dutcher had been very good at. In fact, Josh had to admit that he had often wished Dutcher was as committed to the mechanical side of the car as he was to publicizing it.

Josh admonished himself sternly as he only half-listened to the discussion flowing around him by the men comfortably seated, relaxed, in the deep, cushiony chairs of the semicircle. Dammit, if Dutcher had been so good at this sort of thing, Josh could do no less.

There had been a flurry of interest in the automotive trade press back in the States when they had announced Josh's intention to take his brother's place on the circuit. But much as the sponsors wanted publicity, they had moved very cautiously, not bringing his story to the attention of the general media. It was wrong to play on the public's feelings so soon after the tragedy of Dutcher, and premature to give people a potential sports idol before Josh had gotten a couple of races successfully down and proven his staying power.

Here in Europe the situation was already different. Grand Prix racing was a much more popular spectator sport than it was in the States. The European journals were hungry for everything they could get on the racers driving for the world championship, and here was a brand-new entry, and a brand-new angle to boot.

It wasn't only the Spanish press that was anxious to get to him, one of the sponsors explained to Josh, but journalists from all over Europe, leading newspapers and magazines from France, Italy, Germany, Scandinavia, and the Low Countries, the Netherlands and Belgium, especially since their nations were figuring so prominently on the circuit.

"If we hold a press conference, we've got some degree of control," Stevenson, who represented the cigarette company, explained. "If we don't, they'll be hounding you from now till after the race, and there'll be nothing we can do about it."

Josh reflected quickly, appreciating what Stevenson was saying. Hell, he was grateful for the enormous financial support of the giant tobacco company. "It's okay with me," he said, "if you're all agreed that it's our best course."

The other men nodded or murmured their agreement.

"Of course, some of their questions may be very painful," one of the men reminded him. "Even within the confines of a press conference, we'll have no control over what they ask you."

"I understand that, naturally," Josh said. "I anticipated that there would be some amount of sensationalism about my decision. I hate it, of course, but it didn't stop me from doing what I had to, and it won't stop me from facing them now."

"How about five o'clock, then?" Stevenson asked, glancing down at the expensive Santos watch on his wrist. "That will give you plenty of time to relax after lunch."

"Which should arrive at any moment," one of the other men joined in. As if on cue, there was a discreet knock at the door of the salon, and two white-jacketed waiters wheeled in a serving table laden with food and beverages. Working almost as swiftly as a pit crew, Josh thought admiringly, they silently and efficiently set up luncheon for the five men.

Josh confined himself to an appealing-looking salad of fresh greens and vegetables, drinking only mineral water, refusing any wine or other alcoholic beverages. He joined in the easy banter of the other men, but was grateful when they had at last finished and he could excuse himself to retire to the privacy of his own room on another floor.

Tomorrow would be a full, hard day of time trials and work at the track with the pit crew. Tonight there would be the press conference to face. He had asked Stevenson to confine the number of reporters to as small and manageable a group as possible, letting in all of the local press, of course, and only the major publications of the other countries. Then there would be dinner, again with the sponsors' committee, and socializing mostly for promotional purposes with various European business connections of the sponsoring committee. Josh scowled slightly. That was the part that Dutcher had been so very good at. He found himself wishing that he could be as naturally and easily extroverted as his younger sibling had been. *Stop thinking about it,* he ordered himself, stretching out on the bed whose cool sheets, after he had thrown the blankets back, were a sweet relief. He would sleep easily now, then get through the press conference, dinner, and the business bantering afterward until he could plead the necessity of an early curfew. That was more than enough to fill the time until he would allow himself a few moments, before falling asleep for the night, to think about Amanda. That was all he would permit himself; he had decided on that before they parted in London. It would be a bittersweet luxury. As busy and hard as the next few days were going to be, he was sure to drop quickly into deepest sleep, even with visions of Amanda swirling about in his mind.

A wake-up call signaled that it was time for him to get ready, to wash and dress for his confrontation with the press in the sponsors' suite. Josh, looking and feeling revived and businesslike, got there ten minutes before the reporters were due to arrive.

One of the men tipped him off about the publications, other than the Madrid dailies, that would be there: beside others he didn't know were *Paris-Match, Der Spiegel, L'Uomo,* and the European edition of the old *New York Herald Tribune.*

"I hope that last guy has a current copy of the paper with him," Josh said. "I haven't seen any news from home in weeks."

He glanced around the salon, noting how efficiently the rather formal room had been quickly converted to accommodate the press conference. He would be in a large, comfortable chair, in front of the sponsors and facing two neat rows of folding chairs that the hotel staff had brought in and arranged.

The door to the suite opened. Josh looked up expectantly, but it was only one of the sponsors and not the deluge of reporters he was anticipating.

The man walked over to Josh. "No need to try to bum a paper off a reporter," he said jokingly. "I've brought this up for you." He handed Josh a folded newspaper.

Josh thanked him, but before he could open it for

even a cursory glance, there was a knock, then the door flew open and eight or ten reporters were shepherded in by the team press representative.

They took their places on the hardbacked chairs. The sponsors sat down at the same time the reporters were taking their seats. Then, when everyone was settled, Bob Edwards, the press representative, got up and addressed the reporters briefly on Josh's credentials and contributions to racing, and why he had chosen to return to the Formula I circuit.

It was like a grenade.

"Mr. McKay, do you have a death wish?" a reporter shouted.

Josh was startled, but he kept his voice even and his expression relaxed. "No, I don't," he answered pleasantly. "I am the same age as most of the other drivers, and I think I can say, in all modesty, that I know as much about the workings of a race car as almost anyone in the world. I've engineered and built not only the car I'll be driving but, among others, Jaguars and Ferraris."

"Why aren't you driving a Ferrari, then?" he was interrupted with the demand.

"Because they didn't ask me," Josh replied, forcing a smile. "No, really, I wanted to drive the car I had helped construct for my brother. I believe very strongly in the Rader and in a continuing American presence in Formula I racing."

He steeled himself for the continuing barrage; somehow it was tougher than he had anticipated. The opening question, alluding so cruelly to Dutcher's death, had nearly thrown him out of kilter, but he determined to stay steady and turn their questions, however rudely or crudely they might be worded, into answers that would allow him to expound on the car and his feelings about racing.

"Are you going after the world championship, Mr. McKay?" The question was almost a smirking taunt.

"I'm going after everything I can get," Josh answered, stifling the compulsion to get up and punch his questioner. "In this car I think I stand a pretty good chance."

The next question was more of a technical nature, asking Josh for intricate details about the Rader's specifications, as if meant to test Josh's intimate knowledge.

He was able to field the question beautifully, the answers being as familiar to him, almost, as his own name. His obvious technical expertise seemed to calm the reporters, and the next several questions were easy to handle. He had successfully smothered the flames of sensationalism that some of the more aggressive reporters had tried to fan, and the questioning soon petered out almost anticlimactically, until Bob Edwards rose and brought the conference to a close.

The reporters filed out of the salon, only a few remaining to partake of the offerings at the bar. It reminded Josh that the suite would serve as a hospitality center during the rest of the time trials and the race itself, its other purpose, in addition to being the off-track nerve center for everything they were doing.

He turned away from the remaining reporters, talking instead in quiet tones with a few of the sponsors, glad to get their reassurances about how well he had handled the meeting.

"Hey, don't forget this," Bob Edwards said as Josh

started to return to his own room until dinner. "The paper you wanted."

Josh beamed his thanks and tucked the folded journal under his arm as he rode the elevator back to his room.

He took off his coat and tie, loosened his shirt collar, and stretched out on the bed, spreading the paper in front of him. There was a bold banner, three-column headline, the usual oil-increase crisis. He started to read about what motorists were going to have to be paying to gas up their cars, when a blurred but still unmistakable photograph caught his eye. He was stunned. Under the caption "Kidnap Victim Unaccounted For" was a startled, distraught-looking Amanda.

Josh scanned the column rapidly, his throat constricted. He read the account of the continuing vigil of little Tommy Parrish's mother and the inability of the authorities to come up with even a single clue concerning the apparently well-planned and perfectly executed kidnapping.

Dazedly, almost not knowing what he was doing, Josh reached automatically for the phone. He despaired of getting an English-speaking operator and somehow managed to make himself understood in his limited Spanish. At last he was connected with an overseas operator and managed to relate the urgency of his call. It seemed like hours after he had given her the number of Amanda's apartment that he finally heard the phone ring at the other end. He counted twelve rings before the operator interrupted him. "I'm sorry, there doesn't seem to be any answer. Will you place the call again, please." It was more of an order than a request, and reluctantly, angrily,

Josh hung up the phone, slamming the receiver down so hard that the jarred instrument sounded as if it, too, were ringing.

Where in the world could she be, he wondered. Why wasn't she at home? The usual procedure was for abductors to contact the parent with instructions about ransom, or was it just that way in movies and novels, Josh wondered. He had to get through to her somehow. He had to tell her how much he loved her and ask what, if anything, he could do to help.

The idea of catching the next plane back to New York raced into his mind. The hell with the circuit, he thought. That was a wild, mad dream of his. What Amanda was facing was real. Dutcher was dead and gone and no amount of heroics on Josh's part could bring him back, but Tommy, he hoped, was still alive, and anything that could possibly be done to get him back into the safety of his mother's arms had to be done.

But how would Amanda react to Josh after the bitterness at the airport in England? Would her emotions be able to even cope with the sight of him at a time like this, he wondered? Where could she be, if not in the Fifth Avenue apartment, and where was the boy's father? Josh read the newspaper's pitifully scanty account again. Although Tommy was described as being the son not only of the famous socialite designer but of the rich and powerful industrialist as well, there was no direct mention of Alan Parrish being part of his ex-wife's tormented wait.

Josh's puzzlement was almost as great as his alarm. He picked up the phone again, demanding the overseas operator. Again there was the wait and the crackle of static pervading the background hum before the operator's voice broke through and made contact. He repeated the number and listened again to the endless rings, picturing in his mind the sounds vibrating off the cool, familiar walls of her apartment. The operator broke in with her request to place the call again, and Josh hung up before she could finish.

What was to have been his much-needed rest became his own tormented vigil. He tried to keep himself from picking up the phone as quickly as he put it down, finally forcing himself to focus on the small traveling clock on the nightstand, allowing a full ten minutes to pass before trying to call again. *This is going to drive me crazy,* he thought. He knew that he needed sleep and utter calm. Tomorrow morning the time trials would start again. If he didn't qualify, he wouldn't be able to race two days later.

He had no way of knowing, of course, where Amanda was, or that Sylvia, who up until that morning had remained cloistered in hysterics in the Fifth Avenue apartment, had finally been ordered by her doctor back to her own home, where one of her Palm Beach friends had flown up to watch over her as she drifted in and out of the heavy sedation her physician had insisted on. And Josh knew no more about Alan's whereabouts, only that the painfully short article he had read and reread at least fifty times seemed to indicate that Alan wasn't there. It was only the mother's anguish that had been duly recorded and not the father's. Josh remembered that when Tommy had had visitation with Alan, he usually went to the country house in Westchester that Amanda had told him about. Perhaps they were all there, Josh thought, Amanda and the FBI and Alan. Or maybe it was only Amanda and the lawmen.

It wasn't more than four minutes after he had tried the call that he picked up the phone again. He wracked his brain while waiting for the overseas operator to come on the line, but he could not remember, if indeed Amanda had ever told him, which town in Westchester the house was in. He gave the operator the 914 area code and told her he would need information. He spelled out Alan's name carefully and answered, no, he didn't know the address. He sighed with relief when he heard, thankfully, the unmistakably American accent of the information operator answering. He tried to talk to her directly without the interference of the obviously European overseas operator, explaining that it was an emergency situation, a matter of life and death, and he had to get through to the Parrish residence.

But it was no use. The information operator insisted she could not help him unless he knew a more precise location.

In vain he tried to extract more information from her supervisor, whose voice came on, older than the operator's, kindly but adamant. She explained, as if she were talking to a child, about the impossibility of locating someone merely by name in an area that included several heavily populated counties. She sympathized officially with Josh's anguish, and assured him that the telephone company had done everything they possibly could to help him, but that unless he had more information, there was nothing else they could do.

He hung up in perspiring frustration, the cords in his throat stretched and angry. He realized that he had been yelling at the anonymous voices he had been connected with during the ten minutes the clock told him that he had been trying to get to Amanda in Westchester.

He was wringing wet inside the chilled, air-conditioned room. He was angry and upset, not only at his inability to reach her but at admittedly not knowing what would happen if he did.

He thought briefly of getting connected with the Westchester operator again and asking for the police.

But then, he rationalized, how could he explain himself? A friend of the family, stranded in Europe and unable to leave, concerned about the boy and anxious to contact the parents? If he tried to pose as a close friend or relative, they would expect him to know where the house was, let alone the phone number. In all likelihood he would be dismissed as a more than usually disturbed crank, calling all the way from Spain to hound the suffering victims.

And even if he were to get through, to get past suspicious police officers and inept telephone operators, suppose Alan—or one of the FBI men, which seemed more likely—answered the phone, how would he then introduce himself? A Grand Prix racer, lover of the suffering mother?

It was hopeless.

Toss and turn as he might, there was no way he could think of to get through. He yearned for Amanda, for nothing more than the chance to be able to reach across the cruel miles to comfort her with a word or a gesture or whatever heartfelt trifle she would heartbrokenly take from him.

He thought of calling the American embassy. Madrid was, in addition to being the location of a racetrack, the capital of Spain, and there would be a fully staffed embassy. But another glance at the clock assured him that it would no doubt be closed for business for the day, with perhaps a security force of caretakers left to guard the doors and answer the phones.

But it was better than nothing, he thought, grabbing the phone again and telling the hotel operator to put him through. But the masculine voice answering after only a few short double rings was about as helpful as Josh had anicipated. He replaced the receiver in its cradle slowly this time, instead of banging it to express his anger to the inoffensive caretaker at the other end. *I'll take your advice, Pop,* Josh thought bitterly, *I'll call again tomorrow after nine in the morning, when the embassy is officially open. Thanks for nothing.*

His mind twisted and turned, trying to remember some other connection, some other person who knew them both who could help him get to Amanda. Her mother! Why hadn't he thought of Sylvia before, he berated himself, Of course! Eagerly Josh reached for the phone. But he froze with his hand on the receiver, not lifting it. Idiot, he swore at himself savagely. He couldn't remember Sylvia's last name. He was sure that Amanda had mentioned it in introducing them, but before he was able to address her as Mrs. Somebody, the older woman had broken in with the jauntily voiced injunction to call her Sylvia. Whatever other name she had, it was as unknown to Josh as the town the country house was in, or any of the other million and one things he should have known about his Amanda but didn't.

He cursed himself again for a fool, and flung himself outstretched on the bed. The only other possibility that crossed his mind was Willis Haviland. He didn't even know if the great man was accessible to strangers. Even if he was, as with the embassy, it was sure to be during business hours and not the middle of the night, which it was in New York.

Meanwhile, in Madrid, it was time to shower and

dress and go down to dinner and the circulating, semisocial, semibusiness, that would follow. Amanda was somewhere on the other side of the ocean, and he didn't know where. But he knew that she was doing whatever she had to do. For his part, until he was able to help her, he could do no less. The night in front of him was mercifully short, but it would be difficult trying to keep his mind on business when his heart was someplace else. He had to force himself to bed and, more importantly, to sleep early that night, to be up at dawn and ready for the time trials. Maybe by the time the trials and the race itself were over, Amanda's trials would be over as well. At this bleak moment, it was the best that he could hope for.

He made his way through the crowded dining room toward the large table where his team sat waiting for him. He nodded briefly to some of the other drivers he knew. Mario Andretti, the greatest American racer. Jody Scheckter, the champion from South Africa. Ted Clifford, Kim David, and Talbot Knox: a couple of Aussies and an Englishman, young, lean, and hungry, all of them new on the circuit.

Josh knew and respected them all, but more than ever before he was grateful that the locker room camaraderie that prevailed among athletes in other sports was not part of Grand Prix racing. The men generally knew and regarded each other well, but except with the members of one's own team, it was too sharply competitive, too much a matter of life and death, to foster friendship among rivals. He remembered the admonition of the ancient Romans to their athlete-warriors never to make friends with another gladiator. It still held true.

He let the other men at his table carry the bulk

of conversation and was grateful when two hours after dinner, they had removed themselves to the bar-lounge and he was able to excuse himself on the basis of his wholly acceptable curfew. The men wished him a good night's sleep, the importance of which they all realized. They had a lot riding on Josh and this race. None of them would be up when he was, at the crack of dawn, he knew, but it was just as certain that they would all make their appearance at the trials during the day.

Before turning out his bedside light Josh tried Westchester information again. Something might have changed over the hours and might bring him a more sympathetic and helpful compatriot at the other end.

It was still impossible.

He closed his eyes and willed himself to sleep. Tomorrow he would put on the familiar Nomox fire-retardant racer's uniform from the skin out. He would step into the waiting Rader and put his life on the line.

It was a battle in which his only weapons were his own resources. Right now sleep was the fuel he needed to fire that ammunition, and sleep he had to get.

Chapter 12

Amanda awoke with a start. The day outside was colorless gray, giving no hint of what time it was. What matter, she thought bitterly. She didn't even know what day of the week it was, or how many days before this one she had awakened abruptly from her torn, tormented sleep to stumble through just more hours of anguish, punctuated by the twice-daily eight o'clock calls when she was permitted to speak briefly to her son. Everything ran together in her mind now, the days, the nights, the number of times she had spoken with Tommy. They were hopelessly scrambled and impossible to separate.

She splashed some water on her face in the bathroom across the hall from her bedroom and stared at her haggard reflection in the mirror over the sink. Her face was chalk-white, its pallor accentuated by the deep circles under her listless eyes. She dragged a comb through her hair, the result as indifferent as the little care she gave it. Was this really Amanda Parrish, the sleek, impeccable image of perfection she had lived with for so long? She didn't know, and she didn't care. She knotted the belt of her robe more tightly around her and went downstairs, as oblivious to the men around her as she was to the way she looked.

"There was a phone call for you, Mrs. Parrish, we didn't want to wake you," Saunders said quietly and with evident sympathy.

Amanda blanched. "Was it my son?" she asked.

"No, no, it's much too early for that," the agent said, glancing down at his watch. He looked up at her. "You know we would never let you miss Tommy's call."

"Yes, I know," Amanda murmured, slipping into a chair. "Who was it?"

"Mr. Willis Haviland," the agent said.

"Willis?" Amanda was puzzled. "What time is it?" she asked.

"It's just past seven o'clock, ma'am," came the polite answer.

"I thought I heard something, but I thought I was

dreaming," Amanda said. "Willis called me this early . . ." Her voice trailed off, puzzled.

"He said that we weren't to disturb you, but as soon as you woke up and were able to call him at the store," Sanders said. "He said you would know the number."

"Rather." There was a touch of irony in her voice. She couldn't imagine why Willis would be calling this early and whether she'd even be able to reach him before the switchboard opened. Then she remembered that he had a direct line into his office. She dialed quickly, and she straightened her slumped body almost unconsciously at the sound of his familiar and so-welcome voice.

"Amanda, my dear," Willis said, "how are you bearing up?"

"Not very well, I'm afraid," Amanda admitted. "I—I don't know what's happening to Tommy or to me."

"You must keep hold of yourself," came his gentle admonishment. "Everything is going to be all right."

"How I wish I could believe that," Amanda said beseechingly. "If only I could be certain."

"I think you will be, dear," Willis said evenly. "That's the reason I'm calling you. You sound much stronger than you feel right now, and I know you're going to be all right. I want to bring you the ransom money."

"Willis!" Amanda was stunned. "I can't let you do that."

"Yes, you can," he replied. "It makes no sense to wait until Alan gets back. He'll repay this loan at once, I know, and you and the boy won't have to go through any more of this." He spoke almost routinely, as if this were Pembroke's business they were discussing.

"Let me speak to the agent in charge, Amanda," Willis ordered softly. "I think the gentleman's name is Lackland."

"Yes, it is," Amanda replied, frowning slightly, wondering how he knew. "I'll see if he's here." She put her hand over the mouthpiece and looked around. "Is Mr. Lackland here?"

"In the other room," Saunders said, getting up out of his chair. "I'll go get him."

When Lackland strode into the living room, Amanda nodded briefly and handed him the phone. She listened as he spoke to Willis, fists clenched, at the edge of her chair until the chief agent said a quick good-bye and hung up the phone.

She looked up at him pleadingly and was rewarded with a warm, steady smile.

"When the eight o'clock call comes in, Mrs. Parrish," he said, "there's going to be good news all around."

Amanda was stunned. She didn't know what to say. She buried her head in her hands, not knowing whether the outpouring of emotion was for the joy of getting Tommy back quickly, or the unexpected, unparalleled generosity of Willis.

"It's not over yet, Mrs. Parrish," Lackland said gently. "But I think it will be, and soon. When they call, we'll tell them that the money can be readied as soon as they give us, or Mr. Haviland, the instructions on how it should be delivered."

Amanda looked up at him. "But I can't expect Willis Havilland to put himself into this kind of danger!" she exclaimed. "Surely he won't have to make the payment himself?"

"I hope not," the agent said, "although the courier is seldom in any kind of danger."

"Willis Haviland is not a young man," she said. "His helping me like this is more than I could ever have expected. I don't know how I'll ever repay him, but to ask him to be in *any* kind of danger—that's impossible!"

"Mr. Haviland made his offer because he wanted to spare you any unnecessary emotional outlay."

Amanda shook her head in disbelief. Tommy could be back in another day instead of another week, it *was* possible. How incredibly dear of Willis to help this way. Alan's money would replace Willis's temporary outlay, as he said, but how would she ever pay him back for this unprecedented kindness and concern? Certainly not by placing him in any danger. That was unthinkable.

When Tommy was back and safe, she would resume her life as it was, devoting herself primarily to him and secondly to Pembroke's. It had made her happy enough before, and she owed Willis Haviland at least that, if not much more.

The minutes were dragging longer than hours now, when for the first time the expected call would be not one of mere routine and relief but an actual break in their agony. Amanda would talk to Tommy, not telling him anything or sounding overly hopeful, but she would be able to speak encouragingly, for once with her heart in it. Lackland would discuss the ransom and its delivery with the kidnappers.

This agreed on, they sat quietly in the living room, nothing breaking the silence except the barking of a dog from a nearby estate and the sounds of the newspaper people arriving for their own daily doorstep vigil. Lackland had cautioned Amanda that they had to be more careful than ever at this fateful juncture. Amanda nodded, but the words were really unnecessary. She had no intention of going anywhere within sight of the reporters, let alone talking to any of them. Their initial assault on her had been more than enough. She was not going to face them ever again, except maybe after she had Tommy back, and even then it would only be for the briefest time possible. She knew that thousands, even millions of people were following the case, not with morbid curiosity or sadistic pleasure but with the heartfelt concern of real people. It would be nice to reward their good wishes just briefly with a smiling photo of Tommy in his mother's arms.

But all that was so premature, Amanda reprimanded herself. The phone call hadn't even come in yet, nor had the arrangements been presented and agreed to. She knew from gists of conversation she had heard between the agents, and from some of the pointed remarks they had made to her, that the FBI was less than pleased at having to cooperate with criminals. Even though Tommy's safe return would be the end of it for her, they were duty-bound to try everything they could to track down, and help prosecute, and punish, the kidnappers.

Pointed silence pervaded the room. Each occupant was engrossed in his or her own thoughts. When the phone rang at last, they all jumped, like puppets suspended from strings in the hands of an unseen master.

Lackland grabbed the phone. He listened for a few moments, then he spoke, Amanda hanging on every word. "Let the boy speak to his mother," he said, "then I'll get back on the phone with you. We have your money."

There was silence while he listened again. Amanda was reaching out of her chair as if she could no longer bear sitting in it. She looked pleadingly up at Lackland, who found her poised for the phone before he even turned around to hand it to her. He didn't say anything, but there was a world of caution in his face as he held it out to her.

Amanda nodded briefly, then spoke into the phone. "Tommy, darling," she said breathlessly, "how are you, my angel? Are you okay? Is everything okay?"

The deep sigh of relief that welled within her was almost choked back again as she heard his voice. "I'm okay, Mommy," he said, almost as matter-of-factly as if he had just come home from school and was calling her at the store while he had his milk and cookies. "Am I coming home soon?"

He had asked the question once before and had nearly torn Amanda's heart out, but at least this time, thank God, she could say yes with some degree of belief and relief. "I'm going to have you back very soon, darling," she cooed softly into the phone, her voice sounding as it did when she tucked him into bed at night, her free hand almost moving to straighten the hair that tumbled over his forehead as if he were there. She tried to keep the breaking sobs out of her voice as she rushed to reassure him that they would be together soon, that she and his cars were all waiting for him. She trembled as she heard the harsh male voice in the background signaling Tommy that his time was up.

"Bye, Mommy," he said, "see you soon."

Amanda handed the phone wordlessly to Lackland; she didn't want to hear the abductor's voice again.

She listened, trembling, as Lackland briefly explained that a friend of the family had the cash ready. He scribbled fiercely, repeating all of the instructions for the ransom delivery aloud so that Fuller could hear them and transcribe them as well. Amanda listened, none of it making much sense to her as far as where the drop was to be made. The area sounded deserted and unfamiliar. The discussion of cars and transfers confused her as she tried to wait patiently for Lackland to be finished and explain everything to her.

At last he put down the phone.

"I think this should be fairly routine," he said simply.

Amanda stared at him. She waited for an explanation.

"As soon as the money is ready, they'll tell whoever you designate as the courier where it should be brought. He promises that Tommy will be there and that as soon as they verify that they've got all the cash, they'll leave and your man will have Tommy. He must wait fifteen minutes with the boy before bringing him here. And, of course, there can't be any lawmen within a half hour's drive to the site, from any direction."

Amanda felt bewildered. "How can we be sure we'll have him after we give them the ransom?" she asked fearfully. "How do we know they'll keep their end of the agreement?"

"That's always the chance that has to be taken, Mrs. Parrish," Lackland answered. "The question for us is how we can get some of our people in place after we have the boy. Of course, we'll need an agent who cannot possibly have been seen by the kidnappers, to make the actual transfer and pickup."

"No!" Amanda shouted. "You can't think of doing anything like that! How can you even think of putting my son's life in jeopardy by disregarding their explicit instructions?"

"Mrs. Parrish, you're forgetting that these men are criminals. They are in violation of federal law," Lackland said firmly. "That's why we're here on this case."

"No," Amanda insisted. "You can't do anything to endanger my baby." For the thousandth time she found herself wishing that Alan were there. He would know, a man would have to know, more about handling these things. It was too important a decision to let her emotions rule her, yet regardless of what Lackland said, no matter how right he might be technically, she could not stand by and allow the letter of the law to be used against her son. "How would one of your agents even know for sure that it was Tommy?" she demanded.

"Every agent in the country has seen his pictures," Lackland reminded her. "They've been wired to every branch of the Bureau as a standard procedure in case anyone spotted him anywhere."

Amanda shook her head. That wasn't enough. Her mind was spinning endlessly, with all of the heartbreaking possibilities. All the hope of moments before had dimmed, the offer from Willis that had seemed like the answer now seemed too fraught with dangers to be utilized. She couldn't expect Willis to act as courier in something so dangerous; she had realized that even before this phone call, but she hadn't had time to resolve the answer either. To determine who could be the one to get Tommy. If only his father were here—she cut off the thought quickly, knowing that wishful thinking was of no use here.

Then it came to her immediately. There was only one person who could get Tommy.

She looked up. "Mr. Lackland," she said evenly, trying to hide her hands gripping the chair cushion that was helping to steady her. "I'll get my son myself."

Now it was Lackland's turn to stare.

"I'll call Mr. Haviland to see if we can have the money here this afternoon," she said, "I'll even go into the city and get it myself, but that's not important. We can handle getting the money however you think best, but," and her voice rose in warning, "I am going to get my son myself. And I'm going to go alone, just as they've said I must."

"It's dangerous in the extreme." Lackland had a warning of his own.

"Nothing matters except getting my son back," Amanda answered in the same flat voice. "If they see me they'll know that it's no trap. If they see one of your agents, they could kill him—and my son."

Lackland looked at Fuller and then around at Saunders. Fuller shrugged slightly, saying nothing. The other man gave no indication of his thoughts.

"It would be too easy for them to recognize one of your agents," Amanda was arguing furiously now. "You all look"—she groped for the words, not wanting to anger or offend them—"somewhat alike, you know." She tried to manage a weak smile. "You are all well built, with crew cuts, you're—" It was hopeless. "You're all very much the same." If she insulted them, the hell with it. This was no time to quibble over the niceties. "Besides, if the kidnappers ask Tommy who the man is who's waiting for him, he won't know. It'll be an automatic tip-off to them that we haven't done what they've ordered."

There was no refuting that point.

"The money's got to be gotten without any reporters being wise," Fuller pointed out. "They could blow the whole thing quicker than anyone else."

Amanda was grateful for the remark. The way he said it made her think he was on her side.

"If Haviland himself brought it here, I don't think it would arouse any suspicion," Lackland said. After all, he's a friend of yours, Mrs. Parrish, he could be coming here to comfort you."

Amanda bit her lip. She didn't like the idea of Willis's being physically involved, but he really wouldn't be. Once he left the money and was gone, he would be totally out of it and out of any possible danger. "He would have to walk out with the same attaché case," Lackland pointed out. "All we would have to do was transfer the money to a bag that you could carry."

Amanda beamed. "Then I could simply leave here at the designated time, bring them the money, and bring Tommy back with me," Amanda said. "That shouldn't be complicated at all."

"Except for the reporters," Fuller reminded them. "If they saw you leaving, they'd have to figure that something was up. You haven't stepped outside the door since you've gotten here."

"It will have to be in the middle of the night or just before daylight," Lackland said.

"Do you think the kidnappers would agree to that?" Amanda asked fearfully.

"I don't see why not," Lackland answered slowly. "The cover of darkness would be to their advantage. It's the way they like to do things anyway."

"I would like to call Willis Haviland," Amanda said slowly. "Just to ask him how quickly he could bring the money."

Lackland nodded. "It should be done in a very businesslike way. I can tell him now, if you would like me to."

Amanda shook her head. "No, I think I can handle this." She felt more hopeful and more sure of herself than she had in a long time. Something of her old confidence was back, something that had started ebbing away from the time that she realized Josh wasn't going to take her to Spain and Belgium. The feeling had climaxed when she blew up at him at the airport and had turned to rage, horror, and hopelessness as she got off the plane and the flashbulbs and reporters started bombarding her.

Ever since she had been in this house she had been numb, feeling almost nothing but fear for Tommy. Now Willis had offered a way out. It wasn't Alan or his power or his money that was going to save their son, it was Amanda's friend, Amanda's employer and benefactor, a man who was acting generously out of his feeling and regard for *her*. She knew exactly what she had to do. There was not going to be any government interference, no possibility of fumbling on the part of the hopeful but uninvolved lawmen.

She had to do it herself. Suddenly she knew she could.

Talking to Willis on the phone spurred her confidence. He offered to be there within a few hours, driven by his chauffeur as he would in any routine situation, bringing her the ransom money in plenty of time before the eight o'clock evening call.

When he arrived, Amanda, watching from an upstairs window, couldn't help thinking that it was like a movie scene. The large stretch limousine pulled up in front of the door. Fuller and Saunders kept the reporters at bay, preventing them from swarming all over Willis and the impeccably uniformed chauffeur, who even carried his boss's briefcase and walked a few steps behind him.

Amanda flew down the stairs to welcome Willis as they entered. She threw her arms around him, hugging him close but forcing herself to remain dry-eyed and, she hoped, sounding a lot calmer than she truly felt.

There was something about Willis Haviland's being there that threatened to break down all her freshly built defenses. The whole world knew this man as a sophisticated, perhaps somewhat overbearing, aesthete, wanting to impose his own ideas of taste and order on what he considered a somewhat tacky, undisciplined universe. Amanda wondered how few others there were who were privileged, as she was now, to be touched by his humanity. He spoke with her quietly for a few moments, the FBI men tactfully withdrawing to the kitchen so that there was some privacy. Amanda told him that she was going to get her son back alone. Willis raised an eyebrow at that. Amanda spoke hurriedly, explaining that the preconditions for getting Tommy back had already been agreed to. The kidnappers did not know who the single person exchanging the boy for the ransom would be, nor had they designated the exact meeting place yet. Now that Willis had brought the money, all of that could be arranged when they called in a few hours. "I could have him back tonight," Amanda said, tears threatening again. "It's at least possible now that you've done this." She gestured to where the attaché case had sat momentarily on the floor, vaguely aware that the agents had taken it into the kitchen and were already stuffing the stacks of bills into a duffel bag. When Willis left, the chauffeur followed him, holding the attaché case exactly as he had when they arrived. Only the two men now back in the big car and the four people inside the house knew about the changeover.

She had tears in her eyes as she watched the limousine pull away, and she wondered for the hundredth time how she would ever repay the dear, sweet man who had proved himself no ivory-tower idol but had left the sanctuary of his protected life and position to join her, console her, and help her overcome the misery and danger she was caught in. Alan would make quick restitution of the million dollars, there was no question of that. It was the act of giving that Willis Haviland had performed that Amanda herself needed to repay.

Only when the limousine could no longer be seen did she turn away from the window. Nobody said anything. Amanda's eyes were caught, directed by the gaze of the three agents, on the medium-sized beige canvas duffel that stood in the middle of the floor. She didn't have to ask; the money was in there.

She wondered how heavy it was. She wanted to test her strength against it, against that which would bring her son back.

She hesitated. If she had trouble carrying it, she was sure that Lackland would use it as a reason for her not to meet with the kidnappers herself. But she had to try. She walked over to where it stood. Bending easily, she lifted the double handles and very nearly had to set it down again after raising it only inches from the floor. It *was* heavy, but Amanda was determined. She braced herself, summoning every bit of strength she had, and lifted the suitcase in both hands. She held it against herself for a moment and then put it down with as much grace as she could manage.

She looked around at Lackland. His nod was so

slight it was almost imperceptible. He didn't say anything or do anything negative, and that made her feel triumphant. She sat down, turning to Lackland. "When the phone rings tonight," she said firmly but softly, not wanting to ruffle his feathers, "I think that I should answer it and talk to them directly. Let them know that this is in my hands and that I intend to follow their instructions to the letter."

"It's not the way we like to operate," Lackland reminded her. "You're dealing with criminals."

"I'm dealing with the people who have my son," she replied evenly. "If what I'm doing is considered aiding and abetting criminals, then once I have Tommy safely back, you can feel free to prosecute and jail me if you want. I really don't care, as long as my son is safe."

"You know we're not about to do that, Mrs. Parrish," Lackland said. "Of course we want to see you get the boy back safe and sound. It's just that there's danger for you in doing it this way."

"There's danger to my son any other way." Amanda was determined.

She was afraid of only one thing, that the kidnappers would take the money and not give her Tommy. It was no game, there were no rules they had to obey. As long as they held her son they could do anything they pleased and she would have to comply. They could take the money, keep Tommy, and demand more. She had never heard of that happening, but the thought was there, and the thought terrified her. She tried to brush it from her mind, to think positively. She was doing everything that they would demand. They were only interested in getting the money. It had to work. That was what she had to concentrate on, keep telling herself, through the long hours until the call came.

There was little she could do as the day dragged slowly on. Amanda spent most of the time alone in the upstairs bedroom lying still, eyes wide open, thinking that the sun would never stop its relentless shining and allow the night, the precious hour of eight o'clock, to arrive. Never before had she hated sunshine, but now the bright light that filled the entire house seemed to mock her with its impudence, hitting on metallic objects and making them glare, holding back the shadows that anticipated nightfall. The days were getting longer, Amanda remembered, longer and longer until they reached maximum number of daylight hours only a few weeks away.

There were suitcases standing against the far wall of the room. She had never unpacked from London. She hadn't even thought of it. Not that there was any need to, she would only have to repack to go home again. Still, it would be nice to have a change from the pantsuit she had worn on the plane and the few pairs of jeans that she had found that had somehow remained in the house after she was gone. She had been wearing one of them for the past few days, topped with a shirt of Alan's. She got off the bed slowly and knelt on the carpeted floor, unlocking her carry-on bag. When Tommy saw her, it would be nice if she were wearing something clean and cheerful.

She sifted through the layers of carefully packed clothes, choosing and discarding, her mind trying to make itself up; but all the while she mockingly knew that what she was doing didn't make one bit of difference. It was only something to help pass the hours until she heard, until she could move, until she could do something.

She finally settled on a pair of black pants and a beige cashmere sweater; as unrelenting as the sun seemed to be, the night would still be chilly. She wanted to be able to move as quickly and efficiently as possible.

A glance outside at the lawn told her that the shadows of the day were at last lengthening and the sun's slow descent to the horizon was well under way.

She didn't want to look at a clock. She had stopped wearing her watch the first day. She had grown almost superstitiously afraid of checking the time during these endless days of waiting between the two daily phone calls. She would guess at the afternoon hours, being elated when she found out that it was later than she had thought, or being sunk in depression when there were even more hours than she had supposed, before the evening phone call.

Now she guessed it was about five. She went downstairs, suddenly hungry, realizing she hadn't eaten all day. She poured some dry cereal into a bowl and splashed milk over it, setting it down on the large butcher-block table they used for breakfast and informal meals.

"Is that all you're going to eat, Mrs. Parrish?" asked Agent Fuller, as he came into the room.

"I'm not really hungry." Amanda tried to smile. "I just want to have something to help keep my strength up."

"You know you're undertaking a tremendous responsibility, one that really isn't necessary."

Amanda looked up at him. "I think it is," she said. "You've been extremely kind and helpful, all of you, but this is the surest way to get my son back."

"I wish we could talk you out of it," Fuller replied.

"You can't." Amanda smiled again, feeling almost lifted by the strength of her own conviction. "It would be far more dangerous for Tommy if one of you people were to go."

"Maybe," he conceded, glancing at his watch.

"What time is it?" Amanda dared to ask.

"Almost six."

"Six!" Amanda echoed in surprise.

The agent grinned, in a friendly way. "You're just slightly astounded because you're just eating breakfast," he said.

"No, it's not that," Amanda said. "It's just that I'm just so happy because it's closer to the phone call then I had dared hope."

He nodded. "The time should go quickly now."

But it won't, Amanda thought, *it won't.*

She studiously avoided the large round clock on the kitchen wall as she bent over the simple fare that was her meal for the day. It would have been nice to have gone out of doors for a little while, to sit in the garden just outside the kitchen door where she had spent so many hours on her knees, planting and caring for the flowerbeds that she had designed to fill the space with such great charm. But she didn't dare. Even though all of the reporters who were still assigned to the case were gathered around the front door, there was no telling when one of them would come working his or her way around back. Amanda had almost a superstitious fear of the media people, thinking them likely to cause problems with getting Tommy back.

She looked at the cupboards and cabinets in the spacious country kitchen, wondering idly how much had been changed behind the wooden doors and how much had remained the same since she had stopped coming here. Alan wasn't much of a kitchen person, and she surmised that he had probably kept all of the cookware and utensils she had chosen so carefully very much as she had left them.

There was a definite stillness in the air now, a country twilight descending that would bring darkness quickly in its aftermath. *Now,* Amanda thought ironically, *the sun is going down quickly, but the clock isn't moving any faster. It won't be eight o'clock any sooner no matter what I do or don't do.* She drifted out into the foyer, nodded briefly at the agents talking quietly in the living room, and went back upstairs. It would be wonderful to fall into a nice restful nap before the phone rang, but she knew that that would be out of the question. She would be on tenterhooks until she heard Tommy's voice and until she got explicit instructions for getting him back.

Even then the torture would not be over. Since the reporters usually hung around well into darkness, the kidnappers would have to know that it wouldn't be wise for her to leave the house before midnight.

This wretched night will never be over, she thought painfully, but, she reminded herself, when it was, she would have Tommy back safe and sound. She couldn't even think of what she would do when she did have him—that seemed too far away. Once he was safe in her arms and in the car she could decide her next move, whether to come back here or run with him for the safety and security of the apartment, their real home. She remembered then that it was from there that Tommy had been taken. But that didn't matter, she told herself, that was in the past. Never again was her son going to be left alone. She sat up quickly on the edge of the bed and then stood up, stretching her arms in front of her and then overhead, pacing back and forth around the bed that took up most of the space in the squarish room. She hugged herself close, looking down to guide her footsteps as she paced ceaselessly. It was no use to lie down or relax, or even sit still. She was too nervous, too frightened. She would walk the time away until the phone rang.

Amanda thought of calling Sylvia, but then stopped herself. She had spoken to her two or three times since the kidnapping, not wanting to set up a pattern of calling her every single day. That would have been too demanding on both of them. She longed to tell her that hope was near, that Tommy's return was in sight, but her mother had been too badly affected by the whole traumatic incident to have her stirred up now, only to be disappointed if things were not to go right. It would be impossible for Amanda to talk to Sylvia and hold back the latest developments. It was better to let the phone call go until she had Tommy back with her. Then everything would be all right; the ordeal would be over for all three of them, and they would be able to be together as they had in the past.

Would that really be true? Amanda wondered. Would anything ever be the same for them again? Probably Tommy, the most affected now, being as young as he was, would get over the experience most quickly, children being able to heal as quickly emotionally as they did physically. So much of that, she knew, would depend on how they handled him once he was back. Once he was back. Amanda repeated the phrase over and over to herself, thinking those were the most beautiful words she had ever known. Once he was back, everything was going to be all right. The kidnapping would be nothing more than a nightmare from which they had all awakened, and a danger they would guard themselves against forever.

The phone rang. Amanda jumped up as if an electric shock had jolted her into consciousness, into a new awareness she had never experienced before. She ran out of the room grasping the banister as she fled down the stairs, automatically holding on to keep herself from falling.

The phone rang a second time, but she reached it and cut it off in midring. "Hello," she said breathlessly.

"Mrs. Parrish?" she heard the male voice at the other end.

"Yes, yes, this is Mrs. Parrish," she answered quickly. "How is my son? How soon can I get him?"

"You have the money?"

"Yes, I have it all ready for you in a suitcase," she said. "I can bring it wherever you tell me to, whenever you want, as long as I can have my son back."

"Very good, Mrs. Parrish." The voice sounded sarcastic now.

Amanda jumped with fear. "Is everything all right?" she asked, her voice trembling.

"Everything is fine." The voice was almost suave, almost too smooth and oily now. "But if you want to see your son, you're going to have to do exactly what I tell you."

"I know that," Amanda said, "and I promise you that I will follow every letter of your instructions. I promise you that with my life."

"Very good, Mrs. Parrish, smart lady," the voice replied.

"I'd like to speak to my son now," Amanda said, feeling suddenly brave, "and before you tell me what you want me to know, I think you should know that there are reporters here. They're usually gone by dark, but I wouldn't want to take the chance of their interfering with your instructions."

"Okay," he said. "I'm going to put Tommy on now, and then I'll tell you what you're going to do." There was a slight pause. Amanda felt her throat constrict. "I just want to tell you, Mrs. Parrish, that your son's been a real good boy, very well behaved." He ended with a chuckle.

"Thank you," Amanda was scarcely breathing. "Can I speak with him now?"

There was no answer, but after a slight pause she heard Tommy's voice. "Hello, Mommy."

"Darling! How are you?" Amanda's voice broke with relief.

"I'm okay, I guess. I think," and he lowered his voice a little, as if he didn't want to be overheard by anyone else, "I may be getting out of here soon."

Amanda bit her lip to keep from crying. "Of course you are, darling," she said, "very soon. I'm coming to get you. I hope it's in a very little while. You've been such a good boy and so brave. I'm so proud of you, I just don't know what to do."

"Can you come quickly, Mommy?" he asked plaintively. "I really want to come home soon."

"As soon as I possibly can, love." She knew she wouldn't be able to control the tears if they spoke much longer. "Darling, why don't you let me talk to that man now? The sooner we make the arrangements, the sooner I'll have you back with me."

She could hear the sound of the receiver at the other end being transferred from one person to another. She listened carefully until Tommy's captor came back on the phone again.

"Mrs. Parrish, are you ready?" he asked.

"Yes," her answer came quickly and simply.

"You're to wait until midnight, and be sure that there are no reporters or anyone else around. Got that clear?"

"Yes," she repeated.

"You're to get into your car alone, nothing but you and the money," he went on.

"I understand," she said.

"You are going to be followed, so there'd better not be any lawmen or anybody else around. We'll know it before you've gotten five minutes from that house, and you'll never see your son again."

"Please, don't say that," Amanda begged. "I've already promised that I'll do exactly as you say and nothing else."

"Okay," he grunted. "Start driving north on the highway. Just keep going. There'll be a car behind you. When he pulls up in front of you, you start following him. Just keep right behind him till he signals you to stop."

"Where will that be?" Amanda asked fearfully.

"That's nothing you have to know," he answered curtly. "When you stop and hand over the money, you'll get your boy. We're not taking any chances of anybody knowing where we are. Get it?"

"Yes, I do," Amanda said as firmly as she could. "I'm not going to repeat your instructions, because I don't want anyone to hear. I guarantee you that I'm going to be alone. Please, please, promise me that my son is unharmed and that I'll be able to see him when I stop the car and give you the suitcase."

"Fair enough," came the answer. "He'll be standing next to a car. The headlights will be on so you can see him. As soon as we know the money is okay, he'll start walking toward you."

"Can I come out and get him?" Amanda asked. "After I give you the suitcase, you'll want to check it, I know. But can't I come out with it and be with him? It's going to be so frightening for him."

There was a slight pause. "Well, I guess you know what you're doing," the man answered. "If there's anything wrong, we'll have both of you, not just the kid."

"You see," Amanda's voice rose triumphantly. "If everything wasn't exactly as you said it should be, I couldn't do that, could I?"

"You can stay with the kid while we count," he said, "then you'll wait there for ten minutes after we leave. I don't want you starting your car before that. If you do, we'll know it and backtrack after you. We'll reach you long before anybody else can."

"I'm sure of that," Amanda said softly, "and as long as my son is all right you don't have anything to worry about from me."

"Just make sure it stays that way," the voice snapped, as if he had grown suddenly impatient. "Just remember the time and the route. There won't be anything else you have to know or do."

"Thank you," Amanda said. "I'll get out of the car with the suitcase, give it to whomever you want me to, or just leave it and go to my son. I'll stay with him until you've been gone for ten minutes. I promise no one else will be with me."

The phone clicked off at the other end. Amanda was startled. She had expected at least a word to affirm her statement, but there was nothing. The line was dead. Now there would be nothing until it was time for her to leave.

"Well, that's it," Lackland's voice broke into her thoughts.

Amanda looked at him. "Will I be able to use one of your cars?" she asked.

"Yes, but I'd like you to tell me where you're going," he replied.

"I can't." Amanda shook her head. "I can't do anything that will jeopardize my child's life. You've got to understand that."

"Will you bring him right back here?" Lackland asked.

"I don't know," Amanda admitted. "I don't know whether I should bring him back here or go straight to our apartment. I can't think that far ahead, I don't know which would be better."

"I'd like you to bring him back here," Lackland said. "It'll be important for us to get as early and accurate descriptions of the men as we can. I would certainly appreciate it."

"Promise me you're not going to do anything while I'm getting him," Amanda pleaded. "Promise that you'll wait until Tommy is safely back before you try to apprehend them."

The agents looked at each other, "Mrs. Parrish, we're as concerned for your safety as for your boy's," Lackland said. "You want to go into this thing totally unprotected. We can't let you do that."

Amanda was horrified. "You've got to let me do that!" she insisted. "It's the only way!"

Lackland shook his head. "There is another way," he said, "that we could put into operation without your knowing anything about it. However, I don't want to do that to you."

"What are you talking about?" she demanded.

"We can put a device in your handbag that is no larger than a lipstick," Lackland explained. "It's a homing device that will tell us where you are and enable us to track you at a safe distance."

"There is no such thing as a safe distance!" Amanda's voice was shrill. "I won't be carrying a handbag either. All I'm taking are the car keys and the ransom money, if you don't mind."

"There are other ways," Fuller interjected, "if you're afraid of their searching you, although I doubt that they would even recognize the device."

Something she had seen in a movie once came suddenly into Amanda's mind. She knew the kind of device the agents were talking about. She had seen it in a film. She slumped back against the sofa, suddenly realizing how much there was that they could do. She wasn't as nearly in control of things as she thought. She looked up at Lackland. "If you put that thing any place in the car and they find it," she said slowly, "they'll kill me and probably my child as well." She glared at him.

"That's why we wouldn't do it without telling you first," Lackland said. "We want you to know all the possibilities. On the other hand"—he paused—"I'm sure you want to see these men apprehended as much as we do, if not more."

"I want to see my child home safe," Amanda said, "the rest is up to you, but you can't do this to me. You can't take the chance on Tommy's life." She looked around at all three faces in turn. "I'll bring him back here, if you insist, and you can question him, if that will help, and once he's back I won't mind telling you exactly where I went to if that will be of any help. But once I have my son back, I'm finished with it."

"Kidnapping is a federal offense, ma'am," Lackland said. "That's why we're here in the first place. The government will be the ones to prosecute the kidnappers, if and when they're caught. But we'll need your testimony and the boy's to convict them and to keep them from perpetrating the same thing on other innocent people."

"Of course we'll help all we can," Amanda said wearily, not caring what she agreed to. "So long as you don't interfere now with my getting him back. Please promise me that there won't be any devices or anything else. Please."

"You have my word," Lackland said.

"Thank you." She got up and walked slowly to the staircase to change her clothes and wait out the long hours until it would be time to leave.

She lay down in the darkness after putting on the simple clothes she had selected earlier, trying to calm her nerves and keep her mind alert. But she couldn't stop the trembling or the spasms that were overtaking her entire body. She had been in agony for days, with her child in the hands of those unknown abductors. Now, she realized, Tommy's life would be in *her* hands, and suddenly that was even more frightening. If she did the least thing wrong, if she lost control of herself in some way and failed to obey the instructions she had been given, her child's life could be forfeit. She was shaking so, she didn't even know if she would be able to keep the car under control. She was one woman, going out against an unknown number of men, wanting nothing more than to get her child back. *What are the odds against me,* she wondered, *what are the chances that we'll ever get through this night?*

Again she found herself cursing Alan's uncharacteristic choice to go out of the country. He had never done that before. And Josh, what of Josh, the man who said he loved her, the man who built and raced cars, where was he when she didn't know if she'd even have the control to drive a simple sedan several country miles? How was it that she was so alone at such a time as this?

Stop it, she told herself firmly. *You can't expect anyone else to do the things that you have got to do.* She should be grateful for all the help she was getting, like the vast amount of money that Willis had brought, instead of berating the rest of the world for not being there when she needed them.

When I needed them, she thought bitterly. *I'll never have to think of those words again. I'll never depend on anyone else in the world again. I'm going to take care of Tommy and take care of me and all of the rest can go to the devil.* It was bitter and cynical to feel that way, she realized, but somehow it was looking at someone outside herself who was saying these things, and like an observer she realized that the anger she felt had replaced the trembling fear of moments earlier. She almost smiled in the darkness. *If this is what I need to get through tonight,* she thought, *then this is what I'll use. If my anger can steel me to get my son back, so be it.* She felt stronger and more resolved than she had all day. *I'll get my boy back,* she said to herself in the darkness, *I'll do it.*

She got up and opened the top drawer of the dresser, where she had tossed in her watch days earlier. Now she retrieved it and slipped the narrow band over her wrist, fastening the clasp securely. Now time was going to be on her side as she got ready for the enormous task in front of her.

She snapped on a light and looked at herself in the mirror. She grasped her hair and with both hands wound it tightly in a bun over the nape of her neck, reaching into her bag for large hairpins to secure it. She didn't want her long hair blowing in the car, getting in her eyes, distracting or obliterating the road in front of her. Nothing extra, nothing extraneous on this trip, only the car keys and the ransom money, just as she had told Lackland. Getting there, getting Tommy back. That was it.

Some time later she heard a light tap on the door. "Yes," she called out.

"The reporters have all gone, Mrs. Parrish," Fuller's voice came to her. "We just thought that you'd like to know. It looks like it's going to be all clear from here on in."

"Thank you," she said. "I'll be right downstairs."

She rejoined them in the living room, asking Fuller again for the time. She wanted to set her watch so that she didn't wait a single minute too long.

At last it was time. Lackland and Fuller both preceded her out of the house, leaving only Saunders behind. Fuller opened the car door and fit the key into the ignition, showing her where all of the controls were on the bureau's unmarked vehicle.

She thanked them and closed the door, starting the engine and moving slowly down the driveway as the two agents watched silently.

She took a deep breath. It was the first outdoors air she had experienced in days. The car moved quietly forward on the gravel driveway, and then Amanda felt the smoother country road beneath the wheels.

She picked up a little speed, heading for the highway. She kept the car at a steady 40 miles an hour, her eyes dead set at the road in front of her, glancing only occasionally in the rearview mirror to see if she was being followed.

A shock went through her when she picked up the headlights of a black sedan bearing down close behind her. She gripped the steering wheel, telling herself not to panic, it was exactly as they had told her it would be. The car behind followed her closely as Amanda drove along the highway. She was tempted to increase her speed to see if the other car would follow, to see for sure that it was the right one. But she didn't dare. The way the car stayed steadily behind her, following so close, not trying to pass as an ordinary vehicle might, convinced her this was indeed the car she had been told about. Now all she had to do was continue driving until it overtook her and began to lead.

They drove for twenty minutes in almost unbroken darkness. Amanda could feel the headlights of the other car as if they were boring into the back of her head. She glanced at the clock on the dashboard from time to time, but the hands never seemed to move more than a few moments between glances. The worry had seized her entire being. She felt like a robot, going through the motions of driving reflexively, almost without thinking. It was as if her feet were rooted in place, her hands gripping the steering wheel with a life and a mind of their own. She stared at the road, trying not to think about anything but the unflagging white line in the center of the highway and the child who would be waiting for her at the end of it.

She forced herself not to look at her watch or the

dash until it was unbearable. When she looked, she was shocked. She had been driving for more than half an hour, and she guessed that the car had been trailing her for all but the first ten minutes of that. The other driver seemed to be in no hurry to overtake her. Amanda drove on, not varying her speed by as much as a mile faster or slower. The car continued to follow her, hugging her rear, not bearing down but staying close enough to let her know that he was there every second.

She picked up a little bit of speed, about 5 miles an hour, just to break the intensity. The other car picked up the same speed but gave no other sign. The highway was nearly deserted in the direction they were going. From time to time cars on the other side of the divider passed them heading south. Only twice did Amanda notice cars in the next lane going in the same direction. She realized that she was prolonging the agony for Tommy and for herself by maintaining 45 on this road. She was fearful of accelerating too much all at once, making the man following her think that she was trying to pull away or do something strange. She increased her speed again slightly and again after a few miles, repeating that pattern until the needle on the speedometer hovered between 55 and 60. She was not going to run the risk of attracting attention by speeding, but every faster mile would bring her that much closer to her son. The other car followed exactly, Amanda noted with satisfaction. If the driver had felt she was doing anything wrong, she was sure she would have been made aware of it soon enough.

Now that the miles were flying by more quickly, the time seemed to pass faster too. A glance at the clock told her she had been driving for almost an hour.

She didn't dare pick up any more speed, she knew that. She had to contain herself to drive just as she was, although the now deserted highway tempted her to make the car leap to 70 or 80. But she didn't.

Amanda jumped suddenly, grabbing the wheel and turning it quickly to keep from going onto the shoulder. The car behind had finally moved forward, and the unexpected movement had startled her as the roles were reversed in this desperate game of follow the leader. Now she had to be content with shadowing the car that had suddenly taken command. She wished she had some way of egging him on, of urging him to dare higher speeds than she had permitted herself, to get her to this unknown destination as quickly as possible. But the car maintained the same 60 miles an hour that she had, and Amanda had to press her spine against the back of the car seat to keep from overtaking him.

She leaned forward again as the front car signaled a turn, slowing down as it rounded an exit off the highway. Amanda breathed heavily. She glanced quickly at the heavy suitcase on the seat beside her, reassuring herself for the thousandth time that it hadn't somehow disappeared into thin air, that the means for the getting her son back were still next to her, solid and supportive.

She concentrated on following the small black sedan as it made its way onto yet another road. She took no notice whatsoever of any markings, not knowing or caring whether there were any street signs or route markers that she could follow to find her way out. None of that mattered. Once she got Tommy back, she would be in no great hurry to get back to the highway. She just wanted the security of having him with her. They would make their way home somehow.

The sedan's taillights were blinking again as it slowed down. Amanda decelerated and stayed right behind, her heart leaping as she knew they were slowing to a stop.

The car in front halted. Amanda braked quickly, startling herself by the screeching noise that she made in the quiet darkness. She didn't turn off her headlights. She looked around, trying to see her son.

Her vision was blocked suddenly. Again she jumped, almost screamed, then she realized that a man was standing at the window.

Trying to stay calm, she rolled the window down. "The money is right here next to me," she said. "If I can open the door, I can get it out and give it to you."

The man stood aside. Amanda opened the door quickly, again trying to spot Tommy before she turned to drag out the suitcase. She pulled it across the seat, moving nervously when she felt the man beside her, reaching to lift the heavy bag. As soon as he had it in his grasp she turned quickly, not caring about it, looking for her son.

There was another car at the far end of the clearing where they had stopped. She could barely make it out in the darkness. Then, suddenly, its headlights came on and she could see, faintly, a group of figures standing nearby.

She broke into a run, her arms flung out, unaware of what was happening behind her or any place else. She ran toward the small, familiar figure. "Tommy!" she screamed. "Tommy!" The ground beneath her feet was uneven, beveled with grass, and twice she felt herself falling. But she quickly righted herself, running and screaming.

Tommy came slowly toward her, moving uncertainly until he felt a small push from the man who had kept him all these days. Then he broke into a run, calling "Mommy, Mommy" as he recognized Amanda plunging toward him.

She reached him and fell to the ground, pulling him down with her, hugging him and kissing him as the tears streamed uncontrollably down her face. The mad momentum with which she had grabbed him propelled them both, making them roll and tumble on the wet earth, but Amanda knew nothing, nothing except the feel of her son in her arms. "I'll never let you go again, never!" she wept between the kisses that were landing everywhere on his small white face.

"Don't cry, Mommy, it's all right," Tommy said, his little body struggling to wiggle out of her tight grip. "I didn't even cry once the whole time."

His words brought Amanda back to reality again. She kissed him once more, not looking anywhere but at her son. She couldn't see the men who had taken her son. She didn't want to. All she wanted was to take Tommy home.

"It's all right, lady," a voice came down to her. "Don't look up. The money is all here. Now you and the kid just wait ten minutes. Then you can split."

"Thank you," Amanda breathed. She clutched Tommy, barely aware that the man was turning and walking away from them.

"The less you remember about all this, the better," the voice came again. "You've got a good kid there, sorry this had to happen."

Then he was gone. Amanda lay still, holding Tommy more easily now, looking down at him, not lifting her head until she heard the motors of both cars start and drive away. She didn't look up until she knew they were out of sight. Then she looked down at Tommy again and smiled for the first time in almost a week. "Come on, darling," she said gently, "let's go home."

Chapter 13

Amanda and Sylvia flew crying into each other's arms, all but smothering the little boy who was caught between them. Mother and daughter disengaged themselves at last, laughing amid their tears, holding each other at arm's length and promising that such a thing could never happen again.

Amanda put her arm around her mother's shoulder. "I don't want any recriminations about this," she said firmly. "We all could have been a little smarter, and from now on we're going to be. It wasn't your fault, and I won't have you driving yourself crazy with blame." Tommy went dashing into his own room, beloved silver car in hand, to check the safety of all of his other possessions.

Amanda turned to Sylvia, reminding her that the best recuperation now would be for all of them to return to their normal lives as quickly as possible. But Tommy would not wait alone for the bus ever again, though he would not be restricted from normal play, or overprotected. He would be staying home for the few remaining days of the school week. But come Monday everything would go back to a normal schedule. As normal as they could manage. The kidnapping had to be put as far behind them as possible. She would have to trust that the FBI would locate and arrest the kidnappers soon. Until then life had to go on as before, both generations agreed.

The two women stood facing each other. The living room was suddenly strangely quiet.

"Do you want to talk about it?" Sylvia asked.

"The kidnapping? No," Amanda said wearily, dropping into an easy chair.

"I meant about England," Sylvia said. "You're right about the kidnapping. The sooner we put this whole ordeal behind us, the better off we'll all be, especially Tommy. It won't do us any good to dwell on it."

"No, I don't want to talk about England either," Amanda said.

The fear that had seized Sylvia since Tommy's being taken was slowly dissolving in the happy aftermath of the reunion. Now she felt all of that emotion replaced by concern for her daughter. There was a haunted sadness in Amanda's eyes that seemed to dwell on something else. The agony she had suffered over her son's ordeal was over now. What remained was a residue, Sylvia guessed shrewdly, of something earlier. "I'm here when you're ready to talk about it," she said simply.

"I know it, Mother, and I appreciate it," Amanda said gratefully, but she could not bring herself to meet the gaze that was fixed on her.

"Nobody's perfect, Amanda," Sylvia said.

"Whatever that means," Amanda murmured.

"It means just what it means," Sylvia said. "You're not perfect, and you can't expect anybody else to be. You think he—"

"He," Amanda echoed. "What 'he' do you mean?"

"The young Lochinvar who came out of the west"—Sylvia's rejoiner was unexpectedly poetic—"with his shiny cars and his beautiful manners and the looks just bursting with love."

"It sounds to me like you're trying to make him sound perfect," Amanda said stubbornly.

"All I'm saying is that even he's entitled to a mistake," Sylvia amended. "If he made one."

"I don't want to talk about it," Amanda said again. "But if you want to know, he's made more than one. Not that it matters."

"Really?" Sylvia asked in surprise. "You could have fooled me."

"It doesn't matter, because I made an even bigger one," Amanda said. "I never should have listened to him in the first place, or agreed to see him or to go away with him. That's pretty obvious, isn't it? Damn near tragic, it could have been."

"Now, hold on a minute," Sylvia admonished her. "What did you just get finished saying, that I also agreed with. You know damn well this could have happened just the same if you had been here. Do you think the kidnappers were counting on your absence?"

"It doesn't matter," Amanda insisted. "I should have been here and I wasn't."

"Fiddlesticks!" Sylvia said. "I know what you're doing, Amanda, and it's wrong," she added shrewdly.

"It won't be the first time," Amanda said.

"No, but it doesn't have to be another time either," Sylvia countered. "You're going to take the blame for this, on your not being here when it happened, and you're going to use that plus whatever happened in England as an excuse to shut yourself up again and withdraw from life."

"That isn't true!" Amanda protested.

"Isn't it? Isn't it exactly what you did after your divorce?" Sylvia asked. "You buried yourself in your work and those friends of yours, and pretended that that was living." She paused to see if her harsh words were having any effect on her daughter. Her expression softened, and she felt her heart melting inside her when she realized how deeply unhappy Amanda was. "Don't do it again, darling," she pleaded. "Don't shut yourself off from everything in the world you could have."

"All I want is Tommy and my work," Amanda said slowly. "And the friendship of the very few people I value."

"Who?" Sylvia asked. "Laura Summers, the international butterfly? That old movie star who was mature when I was your age? Or going back to safe old Marshall, the walking museum piece?"

"There's Paolo," Amanda argued. "I feel very close to him, and he's been very good to me."

"One out of the many," Sylvia said. "There I agree with you. I think he probably has a lot more backbone than people give him credit for. But is that enough, Amanda? One friend, good though he may be, who can be just that, but no more, to you? You need someone who's going to fill the emptiness in your life."

"There is no emptiness in my life," Amanda insisted. "I have Tommy and I have my work. I have you and I have some good close friends. I don't need anything else."

"Stop fooling yourself," Sylvia pleaded. "There's a dead spot where your other emotions should be. You've got a heart, but you've got to use it. Otherwise it will dry up and disappear and so will you.

Then it will be too late, and you're much too young for that, Amanda."

She wished that Amanda would unlock somehow and tell her what had gone wrong in England. Joshua McKay wasn't the only man in the world, but he wasn't the everyday, run-of-the-mill kind either. If Amanda shut herself off from him, Sylvia couldn't imagine what kind of man it would take to open her up again. "I'm going to my room," she said. "I want to lie down for a while." There was nothing else she could do, after Amanda refused to say anything at all.

"Don't turn on the radio," Amanda said suddenly, "or the television. There's bound to be a lot on about us. I don't think Tommy should hear it. By the time he goes back to school, it'll be old and forgotten."

"That's a good idea," Sylvia agreed, "for now. But remember, darling, you can't protect him forever. The kids at school will all know about it, and they're bound to say something."

"But that would be natural," Amanda said. "Questions from his own friends will be a different thing for him to handle than a media bombardment."

"You're right," Sylvia said. "And I think you ought to call the school and tell them how you want them to handle it."

She walked into the guest room and closed the door behind her.

Amanda wondered how much publicity the kidnapping would be given beyond New York. There might be a mention of the case and its happy ending on the national news, but she wondered if the story would have been carried overseas as well. She realized with a sudden start how horrible it would have been if it had happened while she was still in London, leaving for home and seeing the newspaper at the airport, or hearing it on the radio. She shook the notion out of her head; still, she could not stop herself from wondering just how far-flung the story had been; if the story had reached Spain or Belgium.

Everyone at Pembroke's was full of sympathy and commiseration when she went back to work the following Monday. She and Tommy and Sylvia had spent the previous days together. Sylvia used the guest room and the two of them took him to the movies, the zoo, and other special treats on those carefully planned occasions when they left the apartment. It was important, Amanda knew, that Tommy not develop a fear about being outside, where the cruelty of his abduction had taken place. She was glad to see that he behaved as exuberantly and mischievously as any little boy his age would, as he himself always had before.

Before. Amanda wondered if that was the way she would count her days from now on, neatly dividing everything that had happened before the kidnapping from everything that would happen after it. It would be natural for the mind to work that way, she thought, but it would be far better to do as they had agreed and put the whole thing behind them as quickly as possible.

She buried herself in all the details that had accumulated during her two-week absence. The store seemed to have gone merrily along without her. The sales figures, both those from Pembroke's and the ones she was most eager to see, from Neimeyer's, looked very good. The Dallas report especially delighted her. Of course, she reminded herself, it was to be expected that the first week would show the results of all of the special promotion built around the opening and her being there, but the next week had leveled off at a figure not that much lower and better than the store had anticipated before the opening. That was very gratifying, and Amanda thought how wrong Sylvia had been in thinking that her work and her child weren't enough to build a good life around.

It was time to start thinking creatively again, to begin more serious work on the new pieces that would be unveiled after the summer, in time for the next holiday season. She pushed the sales reports aside and put a fresh large sketchpad on the desk in front of her. This was how she could best repay Willis, by creating something more exciting, more important, than anything she had ever done before.

She examined a few charcoal pencils to determine whether she had the variety of thicknesses she needed in order to get started. Started, yes, on what she hoped would be her masterpiece. The very best thing she had ever done, new and different and irresistible.

Basil, to her great relief, seemed very subdued in his manner and in his behavior toward her this morning. He, too, after having expressed his sympathy and relief at Tommy being returned, had been bent over his desk. The office was quiet, except for the scratching of their pencils, when the door opened suddenly.

Amanda looked up. It was Willis Haviland, and Amanda was certain at once that it was the very first time he had ever entered her office. Usually meetings were held in his far more spacious premises, and when he wanted to see her, he summoned her there.

"Willis, good morning," Amanda said nervously.

"Good morning, Mr. Haviland," Basil echoed.

Willis returned the greetings and sat himself in the visitor's chair at Amanda's desk. "I wanted to tell you how concerned we all were and how happy we are that your son is all right."

Amanda smiled. What he had done was in strictest secrecy, with only those directly involved aware of his participation. She felt her eyes brimming with the tears she had been able to contain for the last few days while she had Tommy back with her again. "I can't thank you enough for your kindness," she said weakly.

"Of course, we were all terribly concerned," Willis said, "I just wanted to be able to express that to you personally. Somehow," he said, looking carefully around the crowded room, "somehow it didn't seem appropriate for me to call you to my office to tell you. I hope you don't mind my having come here."

Amanda smiled. "You're welcome here anytime, Mr. Haviland," she said with mock formality and, turning slightly toward Basil, added, "I'm sure I speak for both of us when I say that."

Willis kissed her lightly on the forehead and left the office.

"Well, that's a first," Basil commented.

"Yes," Amanda said lightly, "it was." She looked back at her sketchpad, wanting to work but also wanting, for once, to prolong a conversation with Basil. There was so much she wanted to ask him about the publicity that the kidnapping had received—how intensive it had been, and how widespread. She knew why the question was burning in her mind. But she didn't know quite how to frame it so that Basil wouldn't think she had some sort of morbid curiosity about the publicity or was thinking of exploiting something so horrible for her own benefit. "It must have been quite a shock for everybody," she said. "The way the news broke, and all."

"We were absolutely panicked, but it couldn't have been as bad as it was for you," Basil said somberly.

"No, you're right," Amanda sighed. "When I got off the plane and found myself surrounded by all those reporters and those flashbulbs going off in my face and not knowing what in the world had happened, I thought I'd lose my senses, and then," she gulped, "when I found out why, it was even worse. I really came very close to losing control of myself." She paused. "There were even reporters and photographers waiting for us at the house. I couldn't believe that there would be so much interest in what had happened to us."

"It was front page news for the entire time Tom was held," Basil said, "and then, of course, his rescue made headlines. But I suppose you saw those."

"No," Amanda admitted, "once I had him back I wanted to forget that the whole thing had happened."

"That makes a lot of sense, but it's easier said than done. People are going to be questioning you about it until forever."

"Do you really think so?" Amanda asked. "Maybe I should plan on taking Tommy away for a while. His school term will be over soon."

"I don't know where you could take him to," Basil said. "You can't run away from it, Amanda, I think it made news worldwide."

Her heart sank. "Do you really think so, Basil?"

"You can't run away, Amanda," Basil said matter-of-factly. "Even if the story hadn't been sent all over the world."

"Do you think it was heard in Europe?" Amanda asked.

"I know it was. One of my friends just got back and told me he read about it in Paris, in the *Herald Tribune*."

There it was. Amanda rubbed her hands across her eyes. There was no escaping it. If the news had appeared in the European papers, there was no way for Josh not to have known. And there hadn't been a word from him.

Even if he had given up on her, she couldn't imagine that he wasn't concerned enough about Tommy to have called. He had seemed to be so attached to Tommy, having won the boy's confidence from their very first meeting. She remembered how frequently Tommy had asked about Josh. And then when he had reappeared after Dallas, Tommy wasn't the least bit sorry that he had come to take his mother away, he was so glad to see Josh again.

And Josh had seemed so sincerely fond of Tommy as well. It was Josh who had directed her to the elegant toyshop in London where they had selected the model cars that Josh had promised him; the promise had stayed so strong in the boy's mind that it was the first thing he had asked Amanda about, even when he was still being held by his captors. Amanda brushed the tears from her eyes. Josh could have been angry at her, and justifiably so, but how could he have not been concerned about Tommy?

Yet as the next week passed and there was still no word from him, she had to admit that unconcern had to be the kindest word she could apply. Sylvia sensed her mood and stopped asking questions. She urged

Amanda to expand her social life, but she stopped making any reference to Josh.

Tommy had been back in school for a week and they had relaxed the rule about not having TV on. Now, Amanda noticed when she came home in the evening, Tommy was often glued to the set, as if to make up for the time he had lost. She started to speak to him about it on more than one occasion, but always stopped herself. He had been through so much, so much that he didn't even talk to her about, that she didn't want to take away any of his little pleasures. God only knew how much the boy was still holding inside from his fearful experience.

The apartment was quiet. Sylvia had gone back to her own place a few blocks away two weeks after Amanda had returned to work and Tommy to school. It was as if it was difficult for her to take her eyes off both of them, but at last she relented. Amanda reminded her that she had a social life of her own to worry about, that she was in danger of becoming the same kind of recluse she accused Amanda of being.

Amanda knew that Tommy's kidnapping had had a severe effect on Sylvia, much more than her mother would have admitted if Amanda had confronted her with it. She seemed deeper and stronger than the flighty socialite she had been before, and Amanda found her quiet and reflective in a way she wasn't used to. She had gotten used to having Sylvia around, though, and it was with a little regret that she helped her pack up to go home, even though it was being done at Amanda's urging.

The terrible experience had brought them closer than they had ever been before, and Amanda was glad that some good had come out of it. She knew that soon she would be able to confide in her mother in a way she never had before. *If,* she told herself, walking around the living room and plumping up sofa pillows after Sylvia had left, *there'll ever be anything to exchange confidences about.*

Alan had returned, full of chagrin at having left the country on an impulse at a time when he knew Amanda was away, and anxious to make up for it with his son.

Tommy's alternative weekends with his father had been resumed, and since they were going to be together for the one upcoming, Amanda had accepted an invitation from Paolo to spend her weekend up in Connecticut with several other people from their old crowd. She had been working very hard at the store and at home, finalizing and perfecting the six new designs that would make up her next line. She was almost at the stage where she was ready to start modeling in clay, getting ready for the first casting by the workrooms. It would be nice, she had thought, to be getting back to the country just when the weather was turning so warm and wonderful. Just as she was picturing it, she reached for the phone and called Paolo, canceling her plans to go up there.

After she hung up she found herself staring at the floor, completely bewildered at herself and wondering what could account for such contrary, compulsive behavior on her part.

She thought of the lonely Christmas she had spent with an apple, and jotted a note to Naomi to lay in a nice selection of cheese, pâté, and other nibbles for the weekend she would spend with her work.

In trying to relax she turned on the small TV in her bedroom, but a blue-eyed Paul Newman racing cars was more than she could bear. She flicked the dial, but with no more success on any of the other channels, and she gave up. She didn't like to work when she was like this, when she was nervous and restless, especially if she was working on new designs. She needed something to calm her down and put her in the right physical and mental state for concentrating on the intricacies of a new jewel.

She went into the study and looked for a book, finally settling on a lavishly illustrated volume on Art Nouveau, a period she admired but didn't use in her work. There was something very beautiful and soul-satisfying about the graceful lines and opulent curves of that style, from the beginning of the century, that had influenced every aspect of design from furniture to fabrics and jewelry. Amanda carted the book back to bed with her, propping herself up and turning the pages slowly, letting her eyes linger on the rich blues and golds and purples of the period.

After a while she felt herself eased into the more relaxed feeling she had wanted. Pleased with herself, she put the book aside and went into the study to check out various materials she had assembled there. She adjusted the high-intensity lamp that sharply illuminated the objects directly in front of it but threw the rest of the room into darkness. This was exactly the way Amanda most liked to work. It was as if the concentration of light was directing and paralleling her own concentration. She was sorry she had not thought to turn on some music before she started, but now that she was well into it she didn't want to interrupt herself even for the few moments it would take to get up and select something. She worked on doggedly, letting time and the sense of the world around her slip away until there was nothing but the light and the materials and the work in her hands.

When she stopped at last, it was to get up with a satisfying stretch. She walked around to the other side of the table, propping up her elbows on it and peering down at the three clay models she had finished, examining them from a perspective other than that in which she had created them. She walked slowly around to the side, again taking her most critical gaze at her work. She came around front again, and at last admitted that she was satisfied. The models were ready for a first casting.

It was a nice bit of work, she congratulated herself silently, but a voice inside her rejected the praise. Instead it taunted her. *It's only Friday night,* it reminded her, *what are you going to do with yourself the rest of the weekend?*

Amanda took a long, pampering bath and decided she would give over the next two days to the making of the three other models. She had planned to do those during the following weekend; this would put her well ahead of schedule. Pleased with herself again, she let the warm air of the bathroom dry her, and she went to bed.

She was glad she hadn't stopped to watch the racing movie, she thought. Yet it would have been interesting to see how accurately some of the things she now knew about were being portrayed. But it was much too late, the film was long over.

By midafternoon on Saturday all six models—the last three for rings—were finished, and so was most of the cheese. Amanda picked up a magazine entertainment guide and wondered if there was a good movie around that she hadn't seen. It was a strange notion, to go to a movie alone, but just because she had never done it before was no reason she shouldn't do it now, she decided. She found a well-touted French farce playing not far away. She got into sweater and jeans, grabbed her bag, let the solicitous doorman hail a southbound cab for her, and took off for the theater.

The film was well made, and Amanda found herself thoroughly enjoying it, not needing the company of anyone with her to share it. On the way out she walked toward Madison Avenue, remembering that she had pretty nearly depleted most of her food supply. She didn't particularly like cooking, especially when she was alone. She walked a few blocks to a food shop famous for its unusual selection of gourmet items. Catching them just before they closed their doors, she loaded up with everything from fresh raw almonds still in their shells to a small tin of caviar that the proprietor assured her did not come from any of the nation's enemies, to a wonderful-smelling loaf of dark bread, whose uneven proportions signaled its home baking. She glanced about the well-stocked shelves of the store, the owners quite patient with her now that they saw how much she was buying.

At last she had all her things on the counter, ready for her purchases to be totaled up.

Opening her purse, Amanda realized that she had also surprised herself with the amount of buying she had done. She looked up at the owner. "I'm sorry, but I don't seem to have as much cash with me as I thought I did," she said. "Can I pay you by check?"

Had it been winter, the fur coat or other expensive covering she would have been wearing would have immediately established her as a woman of substance, but in the jeans and sweater that were everybody's uniform, there was no way for the usually astute shop-owner to know at a glance just what he was dealing with.

He fumbled for a moment, quite at a loss.

Amanda felt immediately sorry for him. "Look," she said, "I have personalized checks with my name and address. I can give you all the identification you want, and I'll write my phone number on the back. Will that be all right?"

The man was still hesitant. "Let me see the check, if I might," he said. Amanda handed it to him, watching as his wife peered at it also.

Then the woman spoke up excitedly. "You're the lady whose son was kidnapped, I saw all about it on television."

A flash of annoyance crossed Amanda's face, but she tried to erase it quickly. "Yes, that's right," she said evenly. "You can see by my address that I don't live far from here. I assure you it will be all right."

The couple did not look totally convinced, but at last agreed to take her check after Amanda had produced charge account plates from Saks, Bloomingdale's, and Bergdorf's, and her employee identification card from Pembroke's.

The woman dutifully noted down each of the store names and account numbers. After she wrote down all the identification on Amanda's Pembroke card, she handed it back to her without a murmur.

Amanda thanked them, wrote out the check, and took the filled shopping bag, amazed at how little it seemed to hold in comparison with the amount of the check she had written out and the trouble she had been put through.

But that wasn't what was bothering her, she admitted as she stood at the next corner waiting for the light to change.

The woman had known her immediately as the mother of the kidnap victim but had passed right over the card that identified her as Amanda Parrish of Pembroke's. Amanda crossed the street. She wondered if the worst experience she had ever had in her life was now going to be her major identifying factor.

Tired of walking, and angry, she hailed a cab for the few short blocks home. She got upstairs and dumped the groceries unceremoniously on the kitchen counter. It was a good thing she had finished all of her work, Amanda thought: the mood she was in now would certainly not have been conducive to doing anything creative or worthwhile.

She flung herself on her bed, eyes wide open, all the fun of the movie totally forgotten, the small adventure of going out and doing something on her own completely nullified.

No matter what she did, no matter how hard she tried to get the kidnapping out of her mind, there were going to be reminders of it every way she turned.

She remembered promising Tommy she would get a car for them to take short trips in. It had seemed a good enough idea at the time she had thought of it; then, in retrospect, it had seemed rather reckless, and she had put it aside. Now she thought of it again. She didn't have to get anything as glamorous or potentially fast as the cars that Josh handled. Just something that Tommy would be proud of and she would enjoy handling. It would be a good idea to get away from the city. It was probably too late to make a decision before the Memorial Day weekend, but Tommy was scheduled to be with Alan then anyway. They certainly could have a good time shopping around and making their choice and having the car for the Fourth of July. Then she could find someplace with great facilities for children where she would take him, and she herself would be able to unwind from the hectic pace she expected in the next several weeks.

Tommy, when he got home, reacted just as she thought he would; ecstatic at the news that they were going to have a car of their own.

"Not as big as Daddy's," Amanda cautioned him against disappointment. "But something that will be just right for you and me to have a lot of fun in."

The very next Saturday, true to her word, they started making the rounds of various automobile showrooms. Amanda was not at all sure about what she wanted, only that it be rather small and racy-looking, if not actually meant for competition. They collected splashy sales brochures from every show-room they visited, and Amanda was kept busy jotting down prices and costs for a bewildering array of options. She didn't want to make a quick decision, and she realized they had lots more ground to cover, but she promised Tommy that by the time the summer was in full gear they would be completely mobile.

She got to the store earlier than usual Monday morning, intending to make the workroom her first order of business. But when she stopped in her office to leave her things, there was a note from Willis's secretary saying that he wanted to see her as soon as possible. She hastened to his office, hoping that nothing had gone wrong. At this busy time the last thing she needed were complications of any sort. He waved her into a chair as soon as she came into the office. "We've got a slight problem of conflict of interest," he started in directly, without any preliminaries.

Amanda looked at him questioningly.

"Neimeyer's is opening in Westchester this fall," Willis said.

Amanda nodded. There had been general knowledge of that for quite a while. The Dallas-based company's first venture in the New York area was hardly news.

"We didn't get into specifics when we agreed to have your line carried in Dallas and the Southwestern branches," Willis went on. "We left this area pretty much open. Now the time's come to get it settled." He propelled a piece of paper across his desk toward her.

Amanda picked it up and read. It was a letter from Neimeyer's president, couched in the friendliest terms to Willis but containing a very businesslike statement that they expected to be able to order Amanda Parrish jewelry for the new store.

"You've always been exclusive with us in this area," Willis said, although he didn't have to remind her. "How do you feel about this?"

"They've been selling a very good amount of merchandise, haven't they?" Amanda asked.

"You're answering a question with a question," Willis pointed out. "Besides not answering specifically the one I asked you—how do you feel about it?"

Amanda had been stalling for time, and both of them knew it. "I really don't know what to say, Willis," Amanda admitted. "I'm perfectly willing to go along with your decision. Whatever your judgment is in this will be all right with me."

"If we say no," he warned, "they may get angry enough to yank you out of all their other stores."

"Can they do that by contract?" Amanda asked.

"Technically, no," Willis said, "but all they have to do is start hiding the merchandise and that would be the end of it, or at least a major slowdown. It would be a damn difficult thing to prove."

"Why would they want to do it, if they're making money with me?" Amanda asked.

"I'm not saying that they would," Willis said. "They're very honorable people and first-rate merchants. I wouldn't expect them to do anything to jeopardize that business, as healthy as it's been. I just wanted to point out all the possibilities to you."

"It isn't necessary," Amanda smiled. "Everything you've ever done for me has worked for the best, Willis. I leave the entire matter in your hands."

"Thank you for your faith in me," he said.

"Better a vote of confidence than a conflict of interest," Amanda said. "If we've got to make a choice between the two." She looked at him for a moment. "You know, I'm rather glad that that was the problem. I was expecting something a lot more troublesome, like their deciding at the end of May that they need something exclusive for September."

"What makes you think they haven't?" His eyes twinkled.

"Willis, you're kidding," Amanda exclaimed.

"Yes, I am," he admitted. "But it may yet happen. You have how many new pieces going into casting?"

"Six."

"Well, in a pinch I suppose we could select one piece and confine it to them for six months or so. I don't like offering less than the six new pieces we feature for ourselves every season, but if we must, we will."

"I could probably get something else done," Amanda said slowly. "There are a couple of other things I've been thinking of that I haven't put down on paper yet."

"Forget the paper," Willis said, "why don't you go directly to clay? Then when I answer this most gracious threat in my own gracious way, I can hold out the possibility of your giving them something exclusive, to celebrate our ecstasy at having them for close neighbors."

"Speaking of castings," Amanda said, "I'd better get to the workroom quickly. This is the first time I've sent so many new models in all at once." She blew him a good-bye kiss and took the elevator to the floor where the workshops were hidden behind the huge panorama of silverware.

The rest of the week found her in the workrooms for hours at a time, conferring with the silversmiths, making adjustments in her models, inspecting the castings, and waiting with bated breath for the first silver samples to appear. By the end of the week she was glad, even grateful, for the upcoming holiday. She had at last accepted an invitation from Paolo, reminding him that she had to get back to the city in time for Alan to deliver Tommy.

She took the train up, not wanting to bother with a car. Someone could always drive her back to the station on Sunday, or they could call for a cab.

The weather was blissfully warm, and Amanda was happy to slip into a bathing suit and enjoy the amenities of the wide wooden deck Paolo had had built around the pool. She was happy, too, that there were only the two of them, their other friends having taken off for the holiday weekend that opened the glamorous summer resorts.

On Sunday, Paolo offered to drive her back to town himself. "We've had a marvelous weekend, *cara,"* he said, "quiet, and nice. I'm as refreshed as I have to be, and besides, I rather like the dullness of New York when no one is there. There's a certain freshness to the city when all the people have left."

They loaded their things into the car and drove back leisurely. Amanda invited him to come up for a cool drink when they arrived at her door, but he declined graciously. He knew that Alan would be bringing Tommy back in an hour or so, and that Amanda wanted to spend time with Tommy alone.

Tommy came up by himself in the elevator after the doorman announced that he was there. Amanda hugged him and helped him out of his clothes, depositing what she knew would be the first but not the last sand of the season all over his bedroom floor.

When the phone rang, it was Laura, inviting her to a big party. *Just what I need,* Amanda thought, and accepted happily.

The glitter of Pembroke's was a welcoming cocoon the next morning. Amanda felt as though the store were a safe haven, wrapping itself around her, protecting her, and harking back to the old days when it was, along with Tommy, of course, the center of her existence and almost the first thing on her mind.

As soon as she got to her desk she picked up the sketchpad again. She was past, way past, the designing stage for the new line; all of the clay models had been approved by Willis the previous week and were in the workshop being cast. Yet there was something that drove Amanda to her sketchpad. The six new pieces were going to be beautiful, of course; but she wanted something else, something more, something different, something very special for Willis and all he had done for her. The idea of creating something really spectacular had been in her mind all of the time she was doing the work on the six new pieces. She knew she wanted something else, but so far the concept had eluded her.

Amanda thought hard. A piece of jewelry was an accessory, perhaps the most important one that a woman wore. Someone of taste kept jewels in proportion; a more important piece of jewelry called for simple clothes and attention-getting fashions were not meant to war with the wearer's jewels. Amanda wanted something beyond that equation. A piece of jewelry important enough to be almost the costume itself, and not accessory to it. She started sketching, using the smooth lines of a woman's bodice and torso as her background, the frame of reference for she didn't quite know what.

Suddenly she had it. Her pencil, sharpened to the finest of points, flew over the sketchpad. Her excitement mounted as she realized she was creating the thank-you she wanted for Willis Haviland, the most original new piece of jewelry in years.

It was a very simple idea, really. She visualized several strands of baby-fine gold chain and the idea of having great amounts of pearls, pounds of pearls, fixed at random places along the chain. A woman would have lengths and lengths of the pearl and gold to wrap around her in whatever way she chose. The fine strands could make an eye-catching bib that wound from the base of the throat almost to the waist, or could be twined in various lengths like the elegant opera necklaces of earlier years. A small, slim-waisted woman could work the chains into a belt, or they could be woven into a dramatic hair ornament. The possibilities were endless, and the luxury was total. Amanda's innate taste had fixed on the finest of chains and tiniest grades of quality pearls, so that the total effect, no matter what a woman did with it, would never be garish or overwhelming. Pearls-by-the-pound, as much or as little as a woman chose.

She couldn't wait to show the sketch to Willis, to hear his delighted reaction. It was not only superb jewelry, it was a great new merchandising concept that allowed the customer to buy what she could afford without compromising on elegance. Pearls-by-the-pound could be had for a few hundred or many thousands of dollars.

Willis was as lavish with his praise as Amanda had anticipated. He assured her it was going to be the most successful item Pembroke's had ever launched. He called in the workroom head while Amanda sat there, caught up in the flurry of excitement so unusual for the sedate store and its stately president, ordering everything else to be set aside to expedite the prototype model of Pearls-by-the-Pound.

The rest of the day was equally exciting as Willis called in executives one after the other to create promotion, advertising, and publicity campaigns, to coordinate merchandising and display plans, everything to make the new item the sensation of the year.

It was late when Amanda finally got back to the apartment. She had a light supper with Tommy, tucked him into bed, went into her own room, undressed, tumbled into bed, and cried herself to sleep without knowing why.

Josh shivered in the unaccustomed chill. Nivelles was beautiful, but the temperature change from Spain to Belgium was even greater than he had anticipated, an unexpected front having blanketed the Low

Countries with unseasonable cold. He hoped the Rader was adjusting better than he was.

He smiled, thinking of the car. It had performed beautifully at Jarama. They had finished the race, both of them intact. No points, but that would have been asking too much of their first race. Maybe here in Belgium . . . he let the thought go unfinished. It was too dangerous. But still, he didn't have the agony of Amanda's ordeal hanging over him as he had in Spain. The story of Tommy's safe return had been in the paper. Not nearly as prominently featured as the more sensational beginning of the kidnapping had been, but at least he knew that they were both all right.

He had thought again of trying to reach Amanda but doubted that she even wanted to hear his voice. Her rejection would be even worse than his frustration and anger in Spain when he couldn't reach her. He couldn't risk it. He sighed. It would just have to wait, like everything else, until after the big race, until they could be together again, until he could explain, and maybe they could resume the lives they had so barely begun.

He walked past the pits, crews busy with the brilliant cars of each team: the bright French blue Ligiers, the pristine white Hesketh, the two-tone red and white Surtees. He liked the color of the Rader: deeper than the blue of the French cars, yet not as inky dark as the Lotus or Shadow racers. He glanced at his watch. He had a meeting in a few minutes with Scott Peters, his Rader teammate. Scott had had some damage to his car at Jarama, and Josh wanted to take a closer look at it. They had given themselves an extra day before the time trials started at Nivelles, in order to take advantage of Josh's engineering expertise. Josh liked his younger teammate: he had the makings of a top-notch racer. He was glad again for the Formula I structure that placed two cars of each team in competition. Although they raced against each other as well as the rest of the field, they helped each other too.

He saw Scott heading toward him and waved him over. Now he was in his old role, teacher and mentor, advising a younger man, much as he had Dutcher. A twist of pain tore through his chest. *Stop it, stop it,* he ordered himself, forcing his mind back to the present and the important work at hand. Damn! How hard it was sometimes to keep emotions from crowding in and taking over. Dutcher, Amanda . . . *Later,* he admonished himself, *later.* There would be time enough to think later, and to remember. Right now he had to concentrate on Scott and the cars and himself. Making the cars perfect, keeping both of them alive.

In four days this race would be over. In two weeks Monaco would have been run. He had to get through those, and everything would be all right. It would be, It had to be.

He smiled at Scott. "Well," he drawled in the young Southerner's own accents, "let's take a look at this vehicle, boy."

Chapter 14

Since she had driven up to Paolo's the previous weekend she had tried not to think about Josh at all. Now, as she retraced that route, Amanda could think of no one else. The last night's party had been the climax of a week-long spree of outings that Amanda had worked hard to convince herself she was enjoying. She admitted now how empty it had all been and how less than honest she had been with herself. And with Josh, in her thoughts or lack of them.

The parties had been fun, some of them, in some respects, that much was true, but she had worn herself out, and having given so much of her time and energies to such meaningless activities left her distressed instead of elated. And what was the point of parties, if they brought you down instead of up? No point at all, Amanda reprimanded herself, and she sighed deeply. She hoped that this weekend wasn't going to turn into more of the same.

Paolo opened the door, the famous red door, when she rang.

"I'm so glad you're the first to get here," he said, kissing her on both cheeks. "Poor darling, after that fiasco last night I was half afraid you were going to change your mind."

"The only peace and real pleasure I've had in a long time is being here with you, dear," Amanda replied. "Even though this weekend will not be as serene as the last one once the troops arrive, I'm sure it's going to be lovely."

"I hate to see you so unhappy," Paolo said as they walked into the yellow-and-green-patterned summer living room.

"But I'm not!" Amanda protested. "Since I've got Tommy back and that awful ordeal is behind us, everything has been terrific."

Paolo looked at her testingly, not saying anything.

"Look at my Pearls-by-the-Pound," Amanda went on, as if she were refuting this unspoken argument, "truthfully now, have you ever seen better work from me? And there are the six new items I'm getting ready for the fall."

"I'm not talking about your accomplishments, Amanda," Paolo said gently. "They have always been splendid, and I'm sure will be even more so. What concerns me is not your work but the unhappiness I see in your eyes."

Amanda tried to brush aside his concern. "Oh, darling, there's bound to be some residue from that awful week while Tommy was gone," she said. "We've agreed to discuss it as little as possible, to keep it as far behind us as we can, but of course that's easier said than done. I'm sure it's going to continue to haunt me for a long time."

'We never got to talk about England," Paolo said softly. "With all that happened since you got back . . ." His voice trailed off, leaving the sentence unfinished. He didn't want to revive bad memories, but it seemed obvious that something had gone very wrong. Otherwise the man would have been here with Amanda during the wrenching experience she had just been through. That she didn't want to talk about Joshua McKay was obvious, but Paolo knew only too well that sometimes the best way to exorcise demons was to bring them out and talk them away, rather than keeping them hidden deep inside. He didn't want to press or pry, but his sound instincts told him that there was something inside Amanda that was not only causing the unhappiness he could see, but threatening to explode and take her over completely.

Amanda turned slightly away, not wanting to meet the concern in her friend's eyes. He of all her friends would understand what she was going through and could be trusted not to treat her confidences like confetti, to be tossed everywhere for the amusement of others. She felt as though there would be some relief in being able to unburden herself, but she didn't feel quite ready to do it. Besides, she wasn't really ready to talk about Josh, not with anyone, even Paolo. She could barely express her longings to herself. Or admit they existed. She turned to Paolo with a half smile, ready to tell him that there was nothing for him to concern himself with, when the doorbell rang several quick times in succession.

Saved by the bell, Amanda thought, but she didn't voice the cliché; instead she simply smiled at Paolo, her eyes following him as he murmured to her, excusing himself, as he went to answer the door and greet the new arrivals.

"Dear Lord, I never thought we'd make it." Laura blew into the living room like a minor hurricane. "We positively closed that disco this morning! Amanda darling"—and the hurricane turned to envelop another part of the room—"you picked the absolutely wrong time to leave last night. The fun only really started after you were gone."

Since most of the talk centered around Basil Hemmings and his group, Amanda was hard put to keep from expressing her displeasure with Laura's mindless chatter. She was glad when the flow of words was interrupted by the arrival of Laura's escort for the weekend, a man introduced to Amanda only as Alberto, who had been busy parking his Alfa Romeo in Paolo's small garage.

"And then when I finally did get home," Laura's voice escalated to nearly a squeal of ecstasy, "the phone was ringing damn near off the wall." She looked straight at Amanda, her large blue eyes absolutely blazing with excitement. "And would you believe, it was Diego! He called me from Paris, on his way to Monaco."

"What a time to be going there," Paolo said, looking softly at Amanda. "It's a positive circus this time of year. I always avoid it like the plague."

"You mean because of the Grand Prix?" Alberto asked.

"Exactly," Paolo replied. "I have an apartment in Monte Carlo that's absolutely delightful, overlooking the harbor, and you can imagine the views. But I never go for two weeks before or two weeks after the races."

"Why ever not?" Laura wanted to know. "I would think that the height of the season would be the best time."

"I always give them the two weeks before to go crazy in," Paolo replied with mock seriousness, "and two weeks afterward to clean up the streets. Only then can I stand it."

Amanda was beginning to feel distinctly uncomfortable. She didn't know what was worse, Paolo's intuitive concern or the obliviousness of the others to her hidden feelings. Once again the doorbell caused a momentary pause in the flow of conversation. This time it was Colby Brookes, accompanied by two women, one of whom Amanda knew slightly and the other not at all. Once again introductions were made where necessary, and those already acquainted touched on mutual points of interest.

"But where is Marshall Strang?" one of the newly arrived ladies demanded. "I was sure he would be here."

Paolo stepped smoothly into the awkward breach. "Marshall is in Hong Kong," he announced quickly.

"He's with several of his merchandisers on a major buying trip."

"Oh, that's too bad," the woman, sleek and dark-haired, whom Amanda guessed to be in her early fifties, exclaimed. "I was so looking forward to seeing him."

"Don't feel too badly, darling," her friend, a tall, pale blonde, cooed, "he can't stay in Hong Kong forever. I'm sure you'll have plenty of occasion to run into him in town or out at Southhampton, accidentally, of course."

There didn't seem to be a subject anyone talked about that didn't have a painful reaction on Amanda. *Next, I suppose,* she thought bitterly, *they'll start reminiscing about the Lindbergh baby. Thank God they don't know about Josh.* She tried to shake the somber mood that was quickly enveloping her. *I'm getting much too thin-skinned,* she thought, *too sensitive and too quick to take offense when none is meant.* It was obvious that the women with Colby had no idea of Amanda's former connection with Marshall, nor did Alberto know about Josh. So the famous Grand Prix was the next weekend, she thought. It meant that Josh would be coming back soon or communicating with her in some way. She wished that she could tell him not to bother, there wasn't going to be any picking up from where they had left off. If spectators like Diego were already flocking to Monaco, then the drivers were probably there also. It wouldn't be too difficult to reach him and tell him it was over.

But neither would it be fair, she quickly realized. Amanda believed that Josh still harbored feelings of love for her. To tell him that it was over before he ran his most important race would be needlessly cruel and thoughtless. He had enough on his mind without any emotional burdens.

If he even thinks of me at all, she rebuked herself bitterly, remembering the detached way he had spoken to her in England about his racing and its needing his total and complete attention. They would both be better off not even thinking about each other. But, she had to admit, she couldn't stop. Could he? Had he?

"Amanda, you're thousands of miles away," Laura said accusingly. Her face took on a sly expression. "I'd give an awful lot to know just exactly where you were, but I've got the feeling you're not about to tell."

Amanda forced a smile. "You'd be disappointed, Laura, dear," she said, lying gently. "I was just thinking about all the work I have to do." It was the first thing she could think of, but it sounded plausible.

In any event it worked. Laura went into a vivid description of Amanda's Pearls-by-the-Pound, extolling her creative genius and informing her female audience that they could scarcely expect to survive without ownership.

"Oh," the blonde murmured, "so you're *that* Amanda Parrish."

Amanda wondered if there were another one around with her name, and whether the allusion was to her jewelry, the kidnapping, or her breakup with Marshall Strang. She didn't very much care. Her only reaction was annoyance at finding herself the center of a conversation that she could have done without altogether.

She cast a pleading glance at Paolo, as if begging him to rescue her from this conversational cobweb.

As usual he came to her immediate aid. "What a terrible host you must think I am," he exclaimed. "Here you are, in the house for three minutes already, and I haven't even brought you anything to drink."

Amanda smiled in spite of herself. It was so characteristic of him to draw attention by gently making fun of himself. She leaned back, somewhat more relaxed, watching as he busied himself with getting refreshments from his large country kitchen, and letting the resumed flow of conversation drift aimlessly about her without contributing to it.

She felt a little guilty. Every guest at a country weekend should contribute something to the ambience, something to keep the mood light and amusing, to keep the party going. She loved Paolo and his house. Several times it had been a refuge for her, and for that she was eternally grateful.

Never had she felt uncomfortable being there as she did now, surrounded by some people she cared for, but others she scarcely knew, all of them occupied with bits of chitchat that either mattered to her not at all or brought stinging reminders of everything she had rather not think about. She began to wonder how soon she could gracefully escape to the sanctuary of her own apartment, but it was only midmorning on Saturday and it would be unthinkable to leave before Sunday night. She would have to grit her teeth and just dig in.

She felt as though the walls were closing in on her. After all she had been through, she realized, she was still somehow caught in the kind of social web that marriage to Marshall would have meant. She knew she longed for the freedom she had so recently found and lost.

She stood up suddenly, stretching her arms out. "I think I'm going to change into a bathing suit and lie outside in the sun," she announced to no one in particular, hoping that no one would follow her example. At least not yet.

She changed into a rich brown one-piece, one-shouldered suit she had found at Saks and, taking a thick paperback novel with her, went out to the sundeck. She took a beach towel from a pile in the cabana, went back outside, and stretched out on a lounge.

She opened the book and tried reading, but the words were swimming in front of her eyes. She forced herself to concentrate, but that didn't help. She was reading the same paragraph time after time and making no more sense of it after the fourth reading than she had after the first. With a heavy sigh Amanda put the book down on the deck, dismissing the idea of reading as hopeless. *Perhaps I can fall asleep,* she thought, dozing for a little while in the not-yet-scorching morning sun. Almost instantly she felt a cooling presence blocking its rays. She opened her eyes.

"Amanda, darling, see what I have for you." It was Paolo, sitting down next to her carrying an ornate silver Mazzuccato tray, bearing only a small glass of frothy beverage.

"It's fresh *frullato,*" Paolo explained, "milk and ice and apples and bananas, with all the vitamins and everything else totally intact. Marvelous for you. We live on it. You know whose recipe it is, I'm sure."

Amanda took the glass and gestured toward him, toasting, "To you, and your grandmother." She drank it dutifully, refreshed, but feeling like a little girl under the watchful eyes of a parent. When she drained the glass, she looked up at him, but could not return his unwavering gaze for long.

"Amanda," Paolo pleaded in a low voice, "your child is back safe and sound, your work is going more beautifully than ever. What is it that's tearing you up so, my sweet friend?"

"Is it so obvious that something *is* the matter with me?" Amanda asked.

"Yes, *cara,* it is," Paolo said. "I was aware of it last week when we were alone. I didn't bring it up then because I thought you would, if you wanted to talk. I can't bear to see you agonizing the way you are, or as if you're punishing yourself for something."

Amanda smiled. "You make me sound like a figure out of tragedy," she tried to keep her tone light, "as if I'm playing Lady Macbeth or Medea or someone."

"No, it's not that at all," Paolo contradicted. "You're very composed, Madame Parrish, for those who love you and know you well, a little too composed. Only someone who feels about you the way I do could see the unhappiness behind that quiet exterior."

Amanda hung her head. It was easier to hide from yourself than from a dear friend who loved you. She looked up at him. "What can I say?" she asked pleadingly, her eyes searching his face frantically, as if starved for the compassion she knew she would find there. "I am unhappy, Paolo, terribly unhappy, but there's nothing I can do about it. Nothing."

"Now you are sounding like one of the tragic heroines," Paolo chided her gently. "If something is wrong in your life, Amanda, certainly you have the means for making it right."

She shook her head slowly. "No, I don't."

"Go to him."

Amanda looked up in astonishment. Paolo's shocking words were an order, not a hint or a suggestion.

"I—I can't. He doesn't want me."

"I can't believe that," Paolo said.

"Please, Paolo." Amanda's voice was low, entreating him not to press her any further, begging herself not to collapse into the tears that were threatening her. "I can't live my life—or Tommy's—at the edge of danger. Even if he wanted me to."

She couldn't say the name out loud, but there was no need, they both knew who she was talking about.

"I know what I went through the week of Tommy's kidnapping." Her voice was gaining some strength now as she relived that nightmare for her friend. "I know that I haven't got the strength, let alone the desire, to live my life under that kind of constant threat. I need more than that to build my life around."

"What *do* you want, Amanda?" Paolo asked gently, almost the way Sylvia had earlier.

Amanda glanced at their surroundings before she turned her head back to face her friend. "I want this," she said slowly, but with a steadiness in her voice, "I want the peace and security of a simple spring in a place like this. I want the smooth lawns and the sheltering trees and the clear air and the sense of order."

"Just add the lunatics inside," Paolo said with a gesture toward the house, "and you're given a perfect description of a sanitarium. Is that really all you want out of life, my darling? Don't say yes too quickly," he added warningly, gazing forthrightly into her eyes. "Because I for one will not believe it."

"What can I say to convince you?" Amanda asked with a sad smile.

"Nothing," Paolo said frankly. "Your white knight is charging off on his admittedly dangerous steed and you should be there, waving him on."

"No," Amanda disagreed. "Even Josh said that we couldn't be together until after the race at Monaco."

"You can still be there to encourage him," Paolo pressed gently. "And the 'together' can be right after he's finished. Who knows," he added with a characteristically Italianate shrug of the shoulders, "he may even win it, and you could have a marvelous double celebration."

"I can't do it," Amanda said.

"Can't, or won't?" Paolo asked.

"Either one, what does it matter?" Amanda wanted to end the conversation. She had no answers for Paolo or for herself.

Her friend recognized her reluctance. "We won't talk about it any more, *cara,*" he said softly, taking her hand and squeezing it gently. "Just think about it, Amanda. Everything is possible. You could be on a plane in a matter of hours and be there with him when he most needs you."

She shook her head. "No, darling," she said with the same wistful smile. "You make it all sound so simple, but it isn't. Even the logistics would be impossible. Monte Carlo is jammed at this time of year, you were all saying so only a few minutes ago. Even if I wanted to go, which I don't, the whole thing would be out of the question."

Paolo got up slowly, relinquishing her hand. "Think about it, Amanda," he said lightly. "Getting there would be no problem. A little complicated, perhaps. But no problem. And," he added, "my apartment is always waiting for you."

He walked quickly back to the house before

Amanda could answer or protest in any way. Paolo was an incurable romantic for other people, if not for himself. He had that Old World love of adventure and gallantry, the beautiful, even though ultimately meaningless, gesture that harkened back to the days of chivalry, whose expressions and images he constantly used, especially when he talked about her and Josh. Dear of him, and how sweet to picture her as a noble lady, cheering on the champion who wore her colors. Amanda closed her eyes. All the pageantry, knights in armor taking the field as their highborn ladies watched from the stands, was stirring indeed. But it was as long ago, as lost and forgotten, as those doll-like creatures themselves. Paolo's romantic wishes for her were as old-fashioned and reckless as those long-gone ideals. Camelot was dead.

She was not going to be swayed by anything as unsubstantial as pretty pictures painted in words, she thought. But even she had to admit that the comparison between the knights on horseback and the racers in their swift, smooth cars was not as farfetched as she liked to think. And if Josh wasn't wearing her colors, what else could one call the tiny silver horse she had designed for him, which had never left his neck since she had given it to him, not even in those hours in England when she had slept in the circle of his arms.

Amanda shook her head savagely, trying to brush that image from her mind.

Josh, she thought. The memory was like a weight on her breast, pressing against her, making her ache with a pain that was as real as if the assault on her had been physical. How could her heart hurt so? she wondered. How could an emotional pain be so real? She sat up suddenly, unconsciously covering herself with a beach towel as if to be hidden from the other people whose chatter and laughter floated in front of them, heralding their arrival at the pool. *Stop it, Amanda,* she scolded herself, *stop it.* She put on her huge sunglasses, grateful for the privacy they gave her, and added a welcoming smile for the others.

Lounge chairs were drawn up close to hers, animated conversation was punctuated by people throwing themselves into the pool, declaring it was too hot to languish on the deck, pulling themselves out of the water after finding that element too cold for their tastes. Amanda smiled through it all, the brittle, aimless chatter, the silly disporting in and out of the pool. She joined in the raucous laughter that accompanied some of the more outrageous antics and pretended to be fascinated by the equally outrageous gossip whispered into her ear from time to time.

Gradually the day drew on, and with it the night, and the next day, until it was somehow over. Amanda repacked her weekend case neatly, congratulating herself on her discipline in having gotten through the weekend without any of the others being aware of her unhappiness. Even Paolo had at last let her be, although the expression in his eyes as he kissed her good-bye Sunday night told her very clearly that their conversation was still very much on his mind.

The Fifth Avenue apartment felt like a welcome sanctuary when Amanda let herself in. In her bedroom she kicked her shoes off, grateful to be home, glad even for the little while of silence she would have until Tommy got in, even though she longed to see him again and hear his happy chatter about the weekend.

Amanda stared glumly at the toile pattern of her summer bedspread. There was nothing but Tommy to look forward to, she realized. The only plans she could get at all excited about were the ones she made for him. After that business at the disco she didn't care if she never saw the inside of a New York nightclub again. Nor did she look forward to any more social weekends such as the one that had just passed. Or, she thought grimly, the lecture that the dinner conversation with her mother the following evening was sure to deteriorate into.

What's happening to me? Amanda worried. *If people are so caught up in themselves that they don't notice what I'm going through, I'm grateful, yet I'm bored with them. If someone tries to help, like Mother or Paolo, I can't cope with their concern for me. No matter what people do these days, it just doesn't seem right. Yet,* she reminded herself, *I can't build* all *of my life around Tommy. It would be unfair to him, too much of a burden for a little six-year-old, forgetting about whether it's right for me or not.* Tommy deserved his childhood, she knew that: it would be brutal to turn him into an adult male at this tender stage of his life. She wanted everything in the world for him; the last thing he needed was an overbearing mother.

She paced the room, trying to keep up with her scattered, confused thoughts, trying to find the middle ground, the place where she could be comfortable and productive and, yes, maybe even happy. Amanda grimaced as she thought of that word. She started to tell herself off, but her thoughts were interrupted by the doorbell. Tommy was home! She ran for the front door. Burying herself in his world for a little while, she would be able to forget about her own.

She scooped him up in her arms, thanking Alan for bringing him up to the apartment, glad when he declined her invitation to come in for a while. She put Tommy back down on his feet, trying to ignore the flash of silver tucked under his arm that she knew was the little Ferrari. She helped him undress and substitute for the car a little red and yellow plastic boat that was his bathtub plaything. She let him wash himself, then helped him out of the tub, rubbing him briskly with the towel and tickling him into fits of laughter at the same time. She watched approvingly as he got into his neatly pressed pajamas, buttoning them carefully himself, needing her help with fewer and fewer things. *He's growing up beautifully,* she said to herself, *be careful. Don't ruin it. Don't spoil him or overprotect him or drive him away from the sweet closeness you have now.*

As he sat down on his bed, his face upturned for the customary good-night kiss, he looked at her carefully, his dark eyes round with wondering.

"What is it, son?" Amanda asked softly, sensing the unspoken question in his eyes.

"Will Josh come to see us any more, Mommy?" he asked.

Amanda pulled him close to her and hugged him again, rocking him with her body. "I don't know, darling," she admitted. "But if you want him to, I'm sure he will."

"He brought me my first real car," Tommy said, "and I know what happened to his brother. But I never got to tell him how sorry I was."

Children, Amanda thought, *they combine joy and sorrow in the same breath and take both in together. Perhaps somehow they understand things better than we do. In any event, they certainly handle it better.*

Her heart went out to Tommy, who didn't have his father most of the time, and to Josh, who no longer had the brother he had been like a father to. A flood of misery washed away all the questions that had been bedeviling her about why he hadn't called. She remembered the state of concentration he had been in when he had divorced himself, those last few days in England, from almost every other consideration but the oncoming races. She remembered everything he had told her about the concentration and the danger, and his gratitude for their two-week holiday together, and the sunshine they had shared, for her help in lightening the cloud of grief that had been hanging over him ever since Dutcher's death, that had helped him achieve the calm he needed before giving himself up to the racing. Josh had been right. How shallow she had been in not understanding. But it wasn't too late.

"Do you miss Josh very much, Tommy?" she asked, her voice husky.

"Don't you, Mommy?" The question was a shock, so direct and true to its mark. She started crying, completely unable to hold in the tears now, conscious only of the enormity of her unhappiness, only at the fringes of her grief somehow ironically aware that Tommy was patting her shoulder as she cried with her head in his lap, that the roles had been reversed and the child was comforting the parent. At last she stopped, horrified with herself at letting her young son see her like that, almost embarrassed at this young male solemnly watching her cry. It was as though he were waiting, patiently, for her to stop.

Amanda looked at her son expectantly. She had never seen quite that expression on his face before.

"Mommy, let's go to Josh," Tommy said. "Do you know where he is? Wherever he is," he added quickly, not waiting for her answer, "let's go to him!"

"Do you mean that, Tommy?" Amanda asked slowly "Do you really want so much for us to be together, son?"

Tommy nodded slowly, then more enthusiastically. His head bobbed up and down. "I want to be with Josh, Mommy. Let's call him right now!" His laughter bubbled over at his own boldness.

"I don't know if we can call him right now," Amanda said slowly, thinking, "but we can call someone else." She grabbed his hand, playfully pulling him out of bed and taking him along with her to the living room phone. She dialed Paolo's number in Connecticut, her hands almost trembling as she pressed the receiver to her ear and listened to the ringing. Her heart was in her throat when she heard the phone picked up on the other end.

"Paolo," she said, shaking with happiness, "when can I pick up the keys for Monte Carlo?"

Chapter 15

They had to settle for connecting flights, but Amanda was glad for any accommodations that would get them to Monaco as quickly as possible. The flight to Paris had a movie that kept Tommy absorbed most of the time, and Amanda, in spite of her excitement, even managed to doze off for a while. She hadn't called Josh to tell him they were coming. She didn't want to do anything that would distract his attention or, more importantly, she admitted only to herself, give him the opportunity to tell her not to come. What she was doing now was exactly in accordance with his wishes, she reminded herself for the hundredth time. She, with Tommy, would be in Monaco and would join him after the race was over, which was exactly when he wanted them to be together again. All she was doing, Amanda reminded herself joyfully as she snuggled under the Air France blanket, was saving Josh the time and effort of waiting to see her back in New York. That might have been days after the race; this way she could be in his arms almost as soon as it was over.

It was a lovely idea, and the consummation was going to be even lovelier. She was doing what he wanted her to do, and if she was taking a little extra initiative, what was that, after all, but an added measure of the freedom he had taught her to enjoy?

She was proud of herself for having moved so swiftly, making the arrangements, getting the tickets, and receiving the approval of the three people who most mattered—Sylvia, Paolo, and Willis. She smiled down at her son. She hadn't needed *his* approval; the whole madcap venture had been his idea.

She practically had to remind him of that as she hustled a drowsy Tommy through customs at Orly and they sat on the airport's hard benches waiting for the flight to Nice. Amanda knew that there were showers and other freshening up facilities for passengers between flights, but there wasn't quite time enough for her to avail herself of them, and no need, really, to put Tommy through the rigors of bathing before getting him on the next plane. Once their traveling was over there would be time enough to refresh, relax, and figure out her next step.

Along with the keys to his condominium, Paolo had given her the phone number of a domestic who took care of the apartment in his absence and who could come in to cook and clean while she was there. He had even written out the phone number of the Hôtel de Paris, where, he assured her, all of the racers stayed. She would be able to reach Josh, at least to leave a message for him, whenever she chose. Paolo had thought of everything, Amanda reminisced gratefully, sitting on the bench, Tommy propped up against her. She listened anxiously for all the announcements, fearful of missing the flight. But it came through loud and clear, and once again she was bundling Tommy up the flight stairs, this time of a smaller plane and, happily, for a shorter flight.

The airport in Nice was a mad scramble, eloquent testimony to the fervor of Grand Prix week in Monaco. Amanda tried everywhere to get a taxi to take her to the principality, dragging Tommy after her to the taxi stand in the terminal and out on the street, but it was no use. They were all gone.

She couldn't believe her bad luck. After having gotten the plane tickets so easily for connecting flights that were less than an hour apart, it seemed too ironic to be stranded in Nice, only about thirty minutes from Monaco and unable to get a taxi for this minuscule part of their journey from New York.

Amanda felt dejected. She couldn't think of anyone she knew in Nice to call upon, and certainly trying to reach Josh to come and pick them up was too silly even to be contemplated.

Suddenly Amanda laughed out loud. What would any simple person do in her situation, she asked herself? Surely not everyone who went from Nice to Monaco in the course of their normal lives did it by a taxi or limousine. She approached a man in dark blue airport uniform and asked him tentatively, in her best sophomore-year French, where to find the bus that went to Monaco.

Within minutes she, Tommy, and their baggage were settled in a streamlined vehicle. The driver nodded at the address Paolo had written out for her and assured her that he would advise them when to get off.

Happy with the simplicity of the solution, Amanda leaned back, one arm around Tommy's shoulder, the other hand pointing out various sights along the way. The sapphire blue of the water charmed her, and the swaying palms along the road reminded her that she would be able to take Tommy to the beach. She caught the scent of orange trees and was elated at the bright flashes of bougainvillea climbing everywhere. The bus was also climbing, she realized, making its way along the winding scenic highway from which they would soon see the glistening white towers of Monte Carlo, the city within the country of Monaco, all of it no larger than their own Central Park.

The city was suddenly in front of them, clusters of towering white apartment houses that stood above the magnificent port.

"Look at the boats, Tommy. Aren't they wonderful?" Amanda exclaimed. The port was a floating forest of masts against the sky, the billowing sails of the moored yachts secured in the late fading light.

"Nous sommes arrivés," the driver called out to Amanda, looking back as he drew the big vehicle to a halt. "We are here."

Amanda thanked him quickly, in English and in French, as she hastened Tommy and their belongings onto the street.

She looked up. The apartment complex was very much as Paolo had described it to her, its main entrance in the middle of a curved driveway only a few feet away. "Come on, Tommy," she said, adjusting her bag on her shoulder and reaching down to help him with his. She was anxious to get inside and get him tucked into bed after this tiresome day that had taken him more than three thousand miles away from home.

She introduced herself to the concierge, and explained that she was using the apartment of Monsieur Aldobrandini. The white-haired, stout-armed woman nodded and indicated the elevator that would take them to the fourth floor.

Amanda heaved a deep sigh of relief when the key fit the lock perfectly and turned at her touch. She herded Tommy inside and dropped their bags in the entrance foyer. There would be time enough for unpacking later. Right now all she wanted was to get him washed and to bed and to relax for a few minutes herself. She would make arrangements for Veronique, Paolo's housekeeper, to come in the next day. Then she would be free to decide how to handle this impetuous arrival of hers.

She turned on the light and even in her restlessness found a moment to admire the magnificent apartment Paolo had established in Monaco. She put Tommy to sleep in the smaller of the two bedrooms after giving him a glass of water. The kitchen cabinets held a few cans of juice and mixers, and she refrigerated those for the next day. Other than that, she thought ruefully, just like in the old nursery rhyme, the cupboards were bare. Veronique, if she could get her, could shop in the morning. Amanda was sure that everything necessary for a comfortable stay would be easily obtained. There was something about the understated elegance of the apartment that would admit no deprivation or discomfort of any kind.

Tommy fell asleep immediately. Amanda stood for a moment smoothing the hair away from his brow. Then she turned toward the main salon. She walked to the windows, an enormous wall of glass, that overlooked a swimming pool, set jewel-like on the roof of one of the lower wings of the building. Then her gaze went out to the harbor and the Mediterranean beyond. It was lovely, all lovely, almost enough to hypnotize the senses and lull the mind away from reality, the everyday, workaday world.

But Amanda was here for an important purpose. Perhaps the most important of her life. The luxury of the surroundings was only a fortuitous element. It was nothing that would distract her from getting Josh back.

She turned back to her own reality. Moving quietly so she wouldn't waken Tommy, she unpacked his bag and put his things away before unpacking her own things in the master bedroom. She found the telephone and dialed Veronique, and in a mixture of English, French, and Italian explained that she was a friend of Monsieur Aldobrandini's and was staying in his apartment for a few days. The woman on the other end seemed a little confused as Amanda described her situation.

Then the air cleared. "Ah, Paolo!" the woman exclaimed, and Amanda remembered with a smile that all of her friend the count's employees called him by his first name.

Veronique offered to come to the apartment at once if madame needed her, but Amanda assured her that the morning would be fine.

She drew a relaxing bath for herself, feeling that

she had accomplished everything she had set out to do. Now her mind was clear to concentrate on Josh.

She had to admit to herself that she was suddenly bone-tired. It was Friday night, and she had not really adjusted to the time change. In the morning, she told herself, she would be able to think more clearly, to find out what events were scheduled prior to the big race on Sunday. Then she could determine the best course of action.

It pleased rather than troubled her to think that Josh was probably falling asleep right now as well, in a bed only a few streets away. Perhaps a boulevard or two separated them, but surely no more than that. It was a peaceful, happy feeling to know that he was so close. Soon, soon they would be together, and just knowing he was near would make these two nights pass almost quickly. What else the days might bring she didn't want to dwell on, not yet. She fell into a deep, sound sleep.

She was awakened by Tommy pulling on her arm and shouting excitedly. "Mommy, Mommy, wake up. Look at the cars! They're right outside!"

Sleep still glazed her eyes, and she tried to focus as Tommy dragged her across the carpeted floor of the salon.

"Look!" he pointed excitedly, standing on the narrow balcony that ran the length of the glass wall.

Amanda stumbled out on it, not even remembering seeing it the night before. A sudden grating noise drew her sharply alert.

"There goes one. There goes one!" Tommy shouted.

Amanda grasped the terrace railing, looking down in amazement to see a cluster of cars streaming through the streets below them. "We'll be able to see the race from here!" she marveled. She studied the cars again, trying to recognize something, anything, that would connect with Josh. As the noise from the departing cars abated, she heard voices and laughter from close by and suddenly realized she had nothing on but a skimpy nightie. She fled inside, leaving Tommy to watch the cars.

But before she went into her room to dress, the telephone caught her eye. She remembered that when she had used it the night before she had seen a number that connected directly with the building management. She tried it now, hoping that whoever answered could speak English. Amanda's French, adequate for conversation and shopping, would never encompass the automotive terms she needed now.

Luck was with her. The man who answered said yes, he spoke English. Amanda asked him why the cars were racing now, when the race was set for Sunday afternoon, and how she could find out the number of a particular driver's car.

He seemed surprised that she was not thoroughly familiar with the schedule of time trials and races.

Amanda explained that she had only arrived the night before, whose apartment she was occupying, and that she wanted to watch the race from the terrace.

The man explained patiently that the cars going by now were Formula I racers on the last official set of their time trials, and he himself could tell her the number of the car she was interested in, if she liked.

Amanda felt almost giddy, "Yes, please," she said, "I need the number of the car of Mr. McKay."

"Ah, yes, of course," the manager said. "The American in the American car." He paused for a moment as he checked a copy of the weekend's program.

Amanda felt as though her breath had stopped too, but in a moment he was back on the phone.

"Your Mr. McKay is *numéro trente-cinq*. Number thirty-five."

"Thank you," Amanda could scarcely breathe the words. *"Merci."*

"Bonne chance." he replied. "Good luck, madame."

Amanda put down the phone. She went into the bedroom to change into pants and a shirt. A sudden noise at the door startled her, and she came running out.

"Bonjour, madame," a stout, dark-haired woman said, beaming at her.

"Veronique?" Amanda greeted her, glad that she had dressed so quickly. The maid knew her way around the apartment, was, in fact, far more familiar with it than Amanda, so there was nothing to show her. She explained that she and her son would be staying for a few days and their most important requirement would be food.

"Ah, yes, madame," Veronique agreed. "There is nothing here." She put her arms back into the sweater she had started taking off. "I will get the basket and go to the market immediately."

"That's fine," Amanda said. "Just wait a moment while I get my purse. I'm afraid I only have traveler's checks. Will they be acceptable in the stores do you think?"

"Ah, that is not necessary, madame," Veronique said. "Paolo has accounts with all the best merchants. There is no need for money."

Amanda smiled. How like Paolo to provide not only a haven for his guests but relief from having to struggle with any of the usual necessary details. Again she was lifted into feeling she had ascended from reality into this world of pleasure. For years she had associated Monaco with a certain magic that all its visitors seemed to bring from it, and now she was experiencing it herself. "Very well, Veronique," she said, "do as you think best." She walked over to the terrace, leading Tommy inside so that she could introduce him to the woman in whose provident hands they had been so happily placed. He worked hard at mastering the unfamiliar name, and then squirmed under his mother's eye until she laughingly realized that his mind was on the cars below and let him go.

When Veronique left to do her marketing, Amanda braced herself to rejoin Tommy on the terrace. She wondered if she would have the strength to watch the cars go by, Her stride toward the balcony was interrupted by a knock at the front door.

This time it was someone unexpected. Amanda was puzzled at the appearance of the uniformed young man at her front door. "Yes?" she said.

The young man bowed slightly, handing her a brightly colored booklet. "Compliments of the management, madame," he said. "Monsieur Girard sends this for your convenience." He saluted slightly and bowed his way out of the door.

Amanda closed it behind him, amused and edified by the manager's thoughtfulness. She peered at the brochure with its brightly colored photograph of a racing car above the heraldic symbol of the Automobile Club of Monaco. She turned the pages quickly, skipping over lists of committees, trophies, and full-page ads from a variety of manufacturers, unknown and quite familiar, until she was rewarded with the smiling face of a well-known racer. She flipped through the following pages quickly until she found number 35. There he was. Josh.

Amanda stared down at the page. He looks so wonderful, she thought, so serious and grave, yet his familiar half smile full of gentleness. It was Josh exactly. And suddenly it was all very real.

She scanned the text next to the picture. It was in French, and she could understand most of it, a recounting of the world-class races that Josh had won in the past, and mention of both his father and brother.

It was as if someone had slapped her across the face. The blue sea below, the glittering skyline of Monte Carlo, even the elegant room she stood in and the delighted squeals of her son on the terrace outside, all were just a dream. The reality was here, in this book, in the men and cars it pictured and the dangers it scheduled as prosaically as a railroad timetable.

She had convinced herself that because she and Tommy had come here and all the interlocking pieces of the jigsaw puzzle were falling magically into place, that everything was simply going to be all right. Josh was going to run his race, they were going to be reunited, and they were all going to live happily ever after. But that hadn't happened to his father, or Dutcher. Emily McKay sat alone in Connecticut, widowed and bereaved again. There had been no fairy-tale quality to her life, only the tragedy and loss of a husband and young son, and now all that she had remaining, and all that Amanda wanted, was out there someplace, five stories below, pitting his life against the broken dreams of the women he loved.

Amanda walked to the balcony. *Josh is a fool,* she thought bitterly *and the more fool I for following him here*. Her gaze rested on her son. Tommy was reaching up for a better view of the street, his hands clenching the topmost rail, his bare feet perched on the lower one, his heart and mind totally taken over by the scene below, where cars were still completing their time trials.

"Tommy."

The boy turned around, his eyes bright with wonder. "Mommy, this is the best place in the world!" he exclaimed. "The cars are still racing and I can even read the numbers on them! And look, there's a swimming pool right here in this building. They have everything here, Mommy, everything. I hope we never have to go home."

Amanda stepped outside, putting her hand lightly on his shoulder. "We must look for car thirty-five, darling," she said. "That will be Josh's car, do you think you've seen it?" She tried to keep her voice light, her tone unconcerned, but the nearness of the cars and the closeness to the start of the race were pulling in on her. This would be no cinch to get through, she corrected her earlier assessment, this would be probably one of the longest days of her life. Abruptly she remembered the long days of Tommy's abduction. Again she cursed herself for a fool. What was she doing here? What were they doing here, she wondered bitterly. She was putting herself through the same kind of torture she had not yet gotten over with Tommy. There she had no choice, the kidnappers had forced the agony on them. But now she was here of her own choosing. She had brought it on herself, this waiting and suffering that she had sworn she had wanted no more of in her life.

Amanda sat down on one of the wicker chairs on the balcony. The zooming cars had stopped, but the program told her that they would start again at one o'clock and run for another hour. She wanted to bring Tommy inside, perhaps take him swimming, perhaps take his mind off the races; she didn't think she would even have the courage to watch the second hour of time trials. Her mood had changed as swiftly as if a cloud bank had eclipsed the sun. Tommy still hung on the rail, absorbing the street scene below, fascinated by it even without the fast cars zooming past.

"Let's go inside," Amanda started to say, but she was interrupted by the arrival of a smiling Veronique. The housekeeper was carrying a tray, which she set out on the balcony's round table. An oval platter was filled with sliced fresh fruits of an amazing variety —oranges, pineapples, bananas, the luscious red strawberries of the French mountainside, kiwi fruit, and other tropical and subtropical delicacies. Veronique hummed as she busied herself fixing places for her two unexpected but no less welcome guests.

"Merci, Veronique," Amanda murmured. "Thank you." She handed Tommy a napkin, which he dutifully dropped in his lap before he began eating. Amanda asked Veronique to bring fresh juice for both of them, shaking her head at the offer of coffee.

"I like eating fruit without cereal," Tommy said happily. "It's much more fun this way."

"Luckily it's good for you, young man," Amanda said, "so go ahead and enjoy yourself."

"I knew we were going to have a lot of fun when you told me we would get a car and go places," Tommy said, continuing to eat, "but I didn't think it was going to be anything like this, Mommy, this is terrific!"

Amanda's eyes misted over from her son's happiness. "I want you to have a good time," she said, "the best time there is in the whole world."

"That will be tomorrow," Tommy said confidently, "when the real race begins. I bet Josh wins it," he added boastfully.

"I don't think so, darling," Amanda said softly, not wanting to see his too-high hopes dashed. "Josh didn't come back into racing with the idea of winning such an important one as this. Just getting through and finishing will be enough."

She wondered again if she should call him. There would be time enough after the two o'clock end of the trials. They would be able to talk, perhaps even see each other that evening. Would it help Josh to know that they were there, or would it be just the kind of distraction he had told her in England he couldn't afford to risk? Amanda gazed out at the beautiful colors where the blue Mediterranean met the sky at a cloudless horizon. She wished some of the serenity around her could seep into her bones and help her find, if not the answers she sought, at least the calm resignation to get through the next days.

She tried to think out the situation clearly. If Josh knew she was there, and the race went badly for him, she could very likely be the cause. On the other hand, not knowing anything, he would race uninfluenced by her, and the outcome would be unaffected by her presence.

Amanda decided the latter course held the least risk to all of them, especially Josh. Should he win, or finish gracefully as he wished to, she had no desire to share in the credit. If she were to hurt him, she would have to shoulder some of the blame. The best course was to do nothing, to wait until she was sure he had started racing the next day, to call and leave a message for him at the hotel, so that as soon as he got back he would know immediately that she was there, or, Amanda thought—even better—that she and Tommy could be waiting for him in the lobby. But she had to dismiss that idea as impractical. The Hôtel de Paris would be jammed with people, and Paolo had warned her that there was no entrée anywhere unless you had the proper badges and credentials. The best recourse would be to call, leave a message, and sit as calmly as possible waiting for him to call back.

"Can we go swimming now, Mommy?" Tommy asked, breaking into her thoughts.

"Yes, darling," she said a little absentmindedly, "let's just wait a half hour or so after you've finished eating. Then we'll change and go." She had to laugh in spite of herself, knowing full well there was no danger in Tommy's splashing around a pool after lunch, yet somehow unable to shake off this old rule of Sylvia's that had outlasted Amanda's own childhood.

She was glad of the diversion of the pool, though, it would mean missing the second hour of time trials, and Amanda was glad of that, wanting to take Tommy's mind off the cars for at least a little while. She had been all too conscious of how completely absorbed he had been, watching them earlier, and she was fearful once again of having instilled in her only son the love of fast cars that had destroyed the other McKay men and still threatened the one she loved.

They changed into bathing suits, and Amanda stretched out on a lounge, contentedly watching Tommy as he splashed around the pool, swimming and playing with the other children his age. It was remarkable how they were able to understand each other, even without being able to communicate in a common language. It was delightful watching them demonstrate and gesticulate and manage their little games.

How quickly childhood was over, she mused. How much she longed to stretch these happy years for Tommy as long as she could. The golden afternoon of the Mediterranean summer splashed its light and warmth on children and adults alike, charming those favored affluent few who could be as thoughtless as children if they chose. Amanda watched them, the quietly wealthy people who gathered in places like this, confident, protected, unworried. Ice cubes tinkled in large cocktail glasses as music filtered through the replanted palm trees that graced the pool roof. It was a golden existence, much to be envied, Amanda admitted to herself, but not one that she would be happy in for any length of time. It was good to be here on holiday or for a real purpose such as hers in meeting Josh, but to idle away one's life as if childhood were perpetual held no great charm for her. She was glad such people existed, she thought realistically; they were often the very ones who bought her jewelry. She felt smug for a moment; by this time next year probably half the women at this poolside would have bought their weight's worth of Pearls-by-the-Pound. It was a happy, if somewhat materialistic, thought, she knew, yet she was satisfied. It was better to be on the giving than the receiving side after all. Better to be able to create some of the world's gifts than merely to acquire them.

She wondered what was making her feel so philosophical. It wasn't her usual turn of mind; *perhaps,* she admonished herself, *it's just a defense mechanism, making me think about myself and other people, taking my mind off Josh and the race.*

A sudden noise from below, and everyone around the pool, as if drawn by magnets, went to look over the retaining wall.

"Mommy, they've started again!" Tommy shouted as he dashed out of the pool, as if she didn't know. "The time trials—let's look for Josh!"

Slowly, Amanda swung her legs over the side of the chaise. Reluctantly, she walked over to join her son. She hadn't wanted to watch, but it was impossible not to. She held Tommy's hand tightly, gripping his fingers between her own. The cars went by singly, their brilliant colors flashing in the sun. Their enormous numbers, painted on the front and side, were easily readable, even from this height. All the balconies had quickly filled with people, in this building and the ones that Amanda could see surrounding it. The air was full of the cheers of people on the ground as well. At the moment Amanda found herself more intrigued by the people than the cars. She thought of the hanging gardens of Babylon, those ancient terraces filled with plants that gave rise to the legendary image. Monaco seemed to be a garden of people, with human beings suspended everywhere in groups, flanking the buildings, crowding the terraces and balconies that were everywhere. It was as if the very walls were blooming with people, glistening faces laughing and smiling in the sunshine of a glorious day.

She could glance to adjacent buildings at the right and left, lean down over the retaining wall, or look up above it, and see people everywhere. How much more crowded would it be the next day she wondered, when the race actually started.

She looked down again as a deep blue car rounded

the turn at the farther end of her line of vision. The large black digits were unmistakable. It was going too fast for her even to try to see his face, but it was Josh. Number 35. Almost before her mind had a chance to readjust to what her eyes had seen, he was gone, the car a flash of cobalt blue disappearing around the next turn.

Amanda felt staggered. She clutched at the wall for support, unmindful of the rough masonry against the palms of her hands. She had seen him! That was all that mattered. That and getting through the reality of the race itself, when the course he was following now through the winding streets of Monaco would have to be crossed and recrossed seventy-eight times with other cars streaking in front of him, racing alongside him, backing up against him relentlessly in the 250-kilometer run for the precious championship points.

Amanda felt dizzy. She increased her grip on the wall scarcely hearing Tommy's excitement at having spotted Josh's car. *My God,* she thought, *if this is the way I'm reacting now, what in the world is it going to be like tomorrow when the real race is run?*

Amanda went back to her poolside lounge. There were other types of cars going through the circuit now. In the early evening, second in importance only to the great Formula I Grand Prix on Sunday, the Formula III race would be held. She knew there would be no way to tear Tommy away from watching that. It simplified everything. Veronique could prepare a light supper for them, and they could dig in for the rest of the night, Tommy to watch the Formula 3 race, Amanda to browse through the books on the few shelves in the apartment.

It was dusk when the Formula III race started, the

sky growing rosy above the darkening sea and the lights of Monte Carlo twinkling on the hillsides. Again the fairy-tale quality of the principality was taking hold, and Amanda could not deny the magnetic charm of the place. She was easily able to envision Paolo here; it was exactly his kind of setting. She wondered why he was so adamant about avoiding it at this time, when she remembered that since getting off the bus, a stone's throw from the condominium, she hadn't stepped out into the streets of the city. Between the balcony and the pool she and Tommy had gotten all the fresh air they needed. She had no idea how crowded and hectic the city actually was. Not that she was terribly tempted to find out. She was more than content to stay put, enjoying the apartment and its magnificent vistas. Tommy could cling to the balcony railing, scanning the streets below to see his beloved cars. His mother's eyes were more frequently set on the horizon to the west or the sweep of the city to the east of them.

When the last of the Formula III had sped past, Tommy was content to have a glass of freshly made orangeade and almond cookies before tumbling into bed. Amanda's eyes started to tear when she gave him his good-night hug. She had never seen him so happy and excited. The trip had been such a tonic for him, and the most important part, seeing Josh, hadn't even happened yet. Amanda felt eternally grateful. It seemed impossible that only weeks had passed since his kidnapping, even less than that since she had worried if he would ever be the happy, unscarred child he had been before the incident. Now he looked up at her with more contentment than she had ever seen on that dear little face. It was almost too good to be true.

She kissed him lightly on the forehead, smoothing the light coverlet across his little body, and switched off the light, tiptoeing out of the room and into the salon. It was much too early for her own bedtime, and she felt restless. Veronique had already left, promising to return early enough in the morning to prepare one of those big American breakfasts that Paolo's guests were so fond of and that were such a far cry from the usual coffee and croissants that Europeans were used to.

She browsed through the kitchen, curious to see what kind of food Veronique had tocked for their short visit. She rifled through Paolo's art books, concentrating on the magnificent photographs rather than trying to understand the German, Italian, and French texts. Three times she started to pick up the phone to call Josh, and three times she made herself stop.

Amanda couldn't help a bit of self-mockery. Here she was in the most glamorous city in the world, on the eve of its greatest event, for a brief period the center of the universe. And here she was, all alone with nothing but time on her hands, trying to make the hours pass till ten o'clock, when she could decently go to sleep. *If ever there was a case of world-weariness, you're it, my girl,* she told herself sternly. But she knew it wasn't true. She simply didn't want or need any of the things the world could give her. All she wanted was Josh, and that was a matter of waiting. Wait she would, no matter how tiresome or tedious it was, no matter how tempting to call him or go out and join the partying throngs spilling out of every café and hotel. In fact, she wouldn't even have to go that far to partake of the gaiety. From all around her she could hear music and laughter and people out on their balconies, dozens of private parties taking place right in the condominium. But none of that held anything for her.

By this time tomorrow she and Josh would surely have had their reunion. They'd be back in each other's arms and planning for the wonderful future she had so foolishly been denying herself. She had paid heavily for the happiness they were going to have together, and the waiting game she was trapped in now was just more payment in kind. Soon it would all be over.

Let it be tomorrow, she whispered to herself, *let it all be over quickly*. A glance at a small clock told her it was just minutes before ten. Time enough to go to sleep.

The roar of motors woke her in the morning. Pulling on a robe, she found Tommy already on the balcony. It was the last time trials for the Formula I cars, according to her program. The drivers each got to give their cars three final run-throughs without being timed.

Amanda was astonished to see that it was past noon. The travel and excitement had evidently taken their toll of her. She walked back into the salon, pleasantly aware of the sounds of Veronique moving about the kitchen. A big, bracing breakfast would certainly feel good, she thought.

She flipped on a small TV, finding that the camera eye was watching the cars as avidly as the thousands of spectators in the principality. Their own window was located nowhere near the finish line; they would only be able to see Josh as he went by one small segment of the circuit. But, Amanda realized gladly, she would be able perhaps to see him cross the finish line, thanks to the TV. She wondered if she could move it so that she could see it without leaving the balcony. She called Tommy in, explaining her idea, and the two of them went at it until they had a viable accommodation. "This way we'll be able to see just about everything," she explained, Josh live in front of their balcony, Josh on TV at the televised points.

The half hour of pretrials was over, and they sat down to their early afternoon meal. "In America we would call this brunch," Amanda told Veronique. "It looks just wonderful, thank you." The housekeeper had augmented the fresh fruits of the region with raw local vegetables, several varieties of hard and soft French cheeses, thickly sliced cold fish, plump black olives. Carved radish rosettes garnished the platters, which were worthy of the finest New York caterers.

"Eat something of everything, darling," Amanda urged Tommy. "It's all fresh and delicious and good for you."

Veronique shot Amanda a warning glance. "Do not tell *les enfants* that, madame," she said, "children, never will they eat what is good for them."

She went back into the kitchen, leaving the two Americans to their feast and Amanda to wonder once again how Paolo managed to find the best of everything and everyone, no matter where in the world he was.

It was almost time for the race to begin. Preliminary coverage had started. Amanda knew that the first lap was the most dangerous. She had begun familiarizing herself with some of the most prominent points of the circuit. Some of them were named for landmarks that no longer existed, like the horrendous hairpin turn at the site of the old gasworks factory. Others, as the course wove in and out of the narrow streets, banked around the Hôtel de Paris and the casino itself. The portion that they were able to see from their balcony was a section of straightaway that came soon after the drivers emerged from the seaside tunnel and before they approached the *Chicane* and the route that took them alongside the municipal swimming pool. Much of the circuit ran along the port. Amanda remembered Josh's telling her of the terrible crash that had been caused one year by sea-spray churning up and wetting the pavement.

Amanda turned back to the television set. At three fifteen, it was announced, their Serene Highnesses Rainier and Princess Grace would have an honor tour of the circuit. Fifteen minutes later they would be seated in their loge and the race would be started. Isolated as she was within the apartment, Amanda could not help but feel the rising tide of excitement. It was in the announcer's voice on TV, in shouts from the street below their windows, in talk from the balconies of other apartments. She felt herself trembling. For all of these other people it was a show, a gala sporting event. For Amanda it was an event that was totally outside of her control, but one on which her entire future life pivoted.

She tried to pay attention to the announcer, following the rapid-fire French. She longed to know how Josh had done in the time trials and what his starting position in the race was, but the combination of excitement and machine-gun rapidity made the words all but unintelligible to her. She finally gave up trying to comprehend, concentrating instead on the pictures that flashed on the screen, hoping to see either Josh himself or at least the numeral 35. From time to time she got up to join Tommy at the railing where he was watching the preliminary event, a challenge race for twenty drivers, all in the same French sports cars. She fidgeted with the TV set, coordinating what she could see from the balcony with the scenes on the set. As soon as she thought she had the timing worked out, she realized with a sigh that the Formula I race would be much faster, and that she'd be jumping up and back seventy-eight times in two hours. That last statistic pleased and amused her. She had been very negligent about getting to her exercise classes of late, and the bouncing back and forth would be the closest equivalent.

The sports-car race finally ended. Now all attention was focused on the imminent Formula I competition. Amanda scrutinized the TV now as the race commentator described each of the racers while an image of each filled the screen behind him. She sat nervously, jumping slightly every time the backdrop went dark before the next face appeared. It seemed to be taking forever to get to Josh, but there at last he was, his photographed likeness blown up larger than life-size, grinning at her while the commentator read out a brief summary of his career and background, only some of which Amanda caught.

But there he was, that was the important thing. He had made it to Monaco, just as he had dedicated himself to doing. Tears filled her eyes with pride. Josh had reached his goal.

Then, just as swiftly, he was gone from the screen, quickly replaced by another driver. Amanda counted the number of faces that followed after the one she loved, not paying any attention to their names, only to see how far back in the field Josh was.

Soon it was time for the opening ceremonies. Amanda drew Tommy to her, so that he could see the real-life prince and princess on the television screen. The royal couple took their seats, and the cars began lining up on the grid starting pattern that had been determined by the time trials.

Amanda and Tommy watched eagerly for number 35. Josh was toward the end, rather a bit past the center. She flushed with mounting anxiety as the cameras swept over the scene, now concentrating on the drivers waiting for the signal to begin, then scanning the crowded streets that constituted the circuit, then gazing upward at the crowds in the stands that were erected at various points along the circuit. Amanda tried to will the screen to focus on Josh, but he was only one of the two dozen men who were racing.

Then, all of the people in the royal loge were standing.

The flag of Monaco, half-red, half-white, was slowly dropped from a vertical position to a 90-degree angle, signaling the start of the race.

Amanda's throat went dry. She felt her heart jump as the noise and motion of the cars filled up the screen. Josh had told her that the first lap of the race was the most dangerous; that was why the time trials were held, to determine the fastest cars, the ones able to make the quickest start. Now they roared and leaped like a pack of hungry animals suddenly unleashed and after their prey. Only one could win, and the spectators could only hope that none of the others would be chewed to pieces in the fray.

She watched the TV fixedly until a louder roar told her that the cars were entering below. She nearly tripped the few steps to the railing, hugging it for support as she looked down at the surging mass of speeding metal below her. Quickly Josh's car came into view, the black number 35 looking to Amanda as if it were a signal for her eyes alone. The car moved steadily among the other roaring beasts, gaining some speed, she thought, along the short length of straightaway and then quickly disappearing out of sight.

She turned back to the TV, her fears drowning out the unintelligible shouting of the commentators, her eyes glued to the screen, searching for number 35. She caught a glimpse of him as the cars roared into the tunnel, then he was lost again as the cameras focused on the leaders making their way through the casino turn, past the overflow of cheering onlookers at the Hôtel de Paris.

Time and again she jumped from the pictures on the screen to the reality of the street below, forgetting to do what she had promised herself, counting the times the cars went by, so she could keep track of the laps.

It didn't matter, Amanda told herself. What was important was that every time Josh passed she knew that he was all right.

The outcome of the race itself was of no consequence to her. All that mattered was that he got through it, collected the laurels that he had promised himself, and turned his back on this madness they were both caught up in now.

Amanda had never been so aware of being caught in the grip of a relentless pattern before. The kidnappers had imposed their evil; racing was Josh's choice, which he had been forced into only by his own compulsion. No, she could not live with it, she knew, and watching the fury on the screen in front of her, she wondered how long he would be able to.

The accelerating roar of cars was building. Amanda rose almost mechanically to take her place beside Tommy at the railing. She watched almost unseeing as the first lead cars and then the great mass in the middle streaked by.

Something happened. She came quickly to awareness. Another car, number 32, had inexplicably stopped. Its front, instead of facing the direction of the others, abutted against a low brick wall on the opposite side of the street. Other cars were still racing by, a dark green one swerving expertly to pass the stalled vehicle. A bright blue streak came swiftly on. Amanda's heart stopped as number 35 swerved in the same pattern as the car that had preceded it. But he didn't go as wide of the stopped vehicle.

"Josh!" Amanda screamed. The sickening crunch of metal on metal pierced through the thundering roar of the other, still speeding, cars in front of them. Number 35 had stopped. Thin fingers of flame sprang suddenly upward from its hood. Thick smoke surrounded the front of the vehicle, first white, then quickly turning black as most of the car was enveloped. "Josh!" Amanda screamed again, not knowing if any sound had come out. She gripped Tommy's shoulder, unconsciously digging her nails into his skin.

Flames, larger now, more like sheets of fire, were engulfing the whole car. She saw the driver of the first stalled vehicle jump out and head toward Josh, but the smoke and flames drove him away. She saw him run to the safety of the narrow sidewalk in front of the condominium.

The TV announcer was shouting at fever pitch now, and Amanda could hear from the distance a shrieking of sirens and bells.

A fire engine drew up, and streams from its powerful hoses began playing over the burning car. An ambulance pulled up alongside it. Two men ran out swiftly, unencumbered by the spacemanlike suits and hoods they wore.

She could barely stand up as she watched the fire-shielded figures pulling a limp body from the blue car. They had gotten him out. But there was no telling whether they had been in time.

"Wait here, darling. Don't move!" she told Tommy. "Stay with Veronique. I've got to get to Josh!"

Tommy nodded solemnly, not saying anything.

Amanda ran from the apartment, jabbing at the elevator button in the corridor. She jammed her palm against it time after time, cursing it for being so slow. At last the doors silently opened and she smacked the button for the first floor. She ran through the lobby toward the glass front doors but was immediately stopped by a uniformed policeman who blocked her way, explaining that it was impossible to go out in the street due to the accident.

"But he's my friend!" she shouted, trying to explain in French.

The policeman only shook his head.

Amanda peered over his shoulder. Number 35 was a smoldering wreck, heavy-duty machinery mounted on a truck hauling it out of the way of the other drivers. The ambulance was nowhere in sight. "Where have they taken him?" she demanded.

"To the Princess Grace Medical Center, no doubt," the gendarme answered in halting English, "but, madame, you will not be able to cross this street or any of the others between here and the hospital until the race is over."

"When will that be?" Amanda asked, angry at herself for not having kept the lap count that would have told her.

"Perhaps another hour," the gendarme answered patiently.

Amanda's heart sank. Another hour! Another hour before she even knew if he were dead or alive. She slumped suddenly, only the quick response of the gendarme, leading her to a chair, kept her from collapsing on the floor.

Amanda thanked him softly, growing even more angry at herself. This was no time for her to fall apart. She would need every ounce of strength she could marshal for Josh. She had to think clearly.

She got up and walked slowly back to the elevator, hitting the button with much less force now. She got back into the apartment, picked up the slim Monegasque telephone directory, and dialed the number of the hospital. "The driver who was just brought in," she asked in faltering French, "is he all right?"

There was an unintelligible answer, then the sounds that told Amanda her call was being transferred to someone else. A man's voice answered, identifying himself, but Amanda cut him off quickly, repeating her question. She was shouting, in English, barely able to contain herself. The man was sympathetic, asking her to wait. The silence seemed to go on forever, but at last he was back saying that the American driver was badly hurt, unconscious, but still alive.

Amanda breathed a sigh of relief. She told the man where she was calling from and asked how quickly she would be able to get to the hospital. Like the gendarme he told her she would have to wait for more than an hour until the race was over and the streets cleared. Even then, he warned her sadly, he was sure she would not be able to see her friend. His condition was too critical. The doctors were already attending him, and it was impossible to say how long they would be or to predict the outcome.

"I just want to be there, close to him," Amanda said quickly, "to know how he is. I promise not to cause any trouble. Please, may I come as soon as possible?"

"*Eh bien, madame,*" he said, "very well."

"May I ask for you when I get there?" Amanda was thinking quickly now. She had precious permission to be there, she didn't want to get to the hospital only to be stopped by some underling.

He gave her his name, and Amanda thanked him breathlessly. She called to Tommy. "Josh is still alive, darling," she told him, putting her arm around him and pressing him close to her. "I have to wait until the race is over before I'll be able to get to the hospital. All we can do until then is pray."

"Can I come with you?" he asked.

"No, darling," she shook her head. "They didn't even want me to come, but I insisted. It would be much better for you to stay here with Veronique; there's no telling how long I'm going to be there. It'll be much better if I know you're here and safe."

He nodded gravely, and Amanda kissed him.

She couldn't wait the hour or watch the rest of the race, only pray over and over again that it would be finished quickly.

The TV was still blaring. She glanced at it quickly. The sovereigns were smiling at a man in racer's uniform who was holding an enormous cup. The checkered flag had been lowered, and the results were history. Amanda didn't want to know. Now it only remained for the stragglers to come in and it would all be over.

She picked up her purse and kissed Tommy good-bye. She could at least go down and be ready to leave at the first possible moment.

The street was strangely quiet, and she was standing at the curb, uncertain of which way to go, when she spotted a taxicab. She hailed it jubilantly, got inside, and uttered the single word *hôpital*. The driver nodded and took off quickly, but not nearly as quickly, Amanda thought grimly, as the cars that had just preceded them. How she wished for the speed of a Grand Prix car now.

She gave him a bill when they pulled up at the medical center, and she ran inside, not knowing or caring how much money she had given him. She stopped, out of breath, at a desk located centrally at the back of the large, austere reception area, asking for the administrator she had spoken to on the phone.

The nurse on duty, in modified nun's habit, picked up the phone. In a few moments Monsieur Lebrun appeared. He greeted Amanda, shaking her hand.

"I am afraid there is no more news about Mr. McKay," he said, "but some of his friends are also waiting. Perhaps you would want to join them." It was a suggestion, not a question, and Amanda recognized it as such. She nodded briefly and followed him down a corridor and up a flight of stairs.

He led her to a small waiting room, gestured briefly, bowed, and left.

Amanda was surprised. She had expected to see, if anyone, other drivers still in their racing suits, but the four men who rose quickly as she stood on the threshold were all middle-aged, dressed in conservative blazers and ties, looking like typical American businessmen. She realized at once that these were probably the sponsors Josh had been meeting with before they had left for England.

Even more surprising was the sight of a young girl sitting on one of the benches. Amanda took her to be no more than twenty or so. She had a pale, grief-stricken face and long blond hair streaming past her shoulders. She looked up at Amanda.

Something clicked in Amanda's mind. "Bootsie?" she asked.

"Amanda?"

The men looked uncertainly at each other and then at the two women.

"Sit down, please," Amanda said, trying to hide her awkwardness at finding Bootsie there. The men sat down obediently and Amanda took a seat facing them.

"Is there any news?" she asked. "Is he going to be all right?"

One man, who she would later learn was Donovan, shook his head. "It's too soon to tell anything yet, but"—he looked up at her warningly—"he has been hurt pretty badly."

"I know," Amanda said simply. "I saw it happen."

Again the men registered surprise. "Where were you?" Donovan asked quickly.

Amanda explained how she had watched the race from the balcony. She explained it simply, in a quiet voice, forcing herself back from the edge of the hysteria that threatened to overtake her.

The men were sympathetic, telling her to be optimistic and to hope for the best, but there was a deep despair in the room that the most hopeful wishes could not dispel. There was nothing to do now but wait.

Amanda gripped the edge of the hard wooden bench, trying to keep from crying out. She choked back the tears and turned to the others. "Has anybody called Mrs. McKay?" she asked.

"I don't know how to tell her," Bootsie said. "Actually, I didn't want to call her."

"Somebody has got to tell her," Amanda said simply.

"After what happened to Dutcher," Bootsie said, her voice rising almost to a wail, "who is going to have enough guts to tell her about this? We might as well wait a little while. Maybe he'll take a turn for the better, then the news won't be so bad. I feel so sorry for that woman, don't you?"

"Yes, I feel very, very sorry for Mrs. McKay," Amanda replied. Amanda tried to remember what Josh had told her about Bootsie Farr, but her mind was blank in that area. She had only remembered the name because it was such a striking one, and she knew that Josh's mention of it was only in association with Dutcher.

There were a thousand questions on her mind. How *did* Bootsie know who she was and what was she doing there? In the excitement of the race, Amanda had never called the hotel to leave her message for Josh. He would have no way in the world of knowing that she was even here in Monaco. None of that mattered, Amanda told herself forcefully. All that mattered now was Josh. Still, there was something uncomfortable in the air, and Amanda realized that the men sensed it and were made uncomfortable by it. She had no idea of whether or not they knew who she was. Probably not, but it must have been obvious that she was not a racing groupie like Bootsie.

"How long do you think it's going to be before we know anything?" she asked no one in particular.

Donovan seemed to be the spokesman. "There's no

telling that." He hesitated, as if waiting for something.

"Mrs. Parrish," Amanda supplied the missing information, "Amanda Parrish, how do you do?" She extended her hand as if observing the common courtesies might somehow bring this nightmare down to manageable size.

"Mrs. Parrish, of course," he acknowledged. "As I was saying, there is no way of knowing how long the doctors will be with him. However, we were able to contact one of our own men, an American, and the medical commission has agreed to let him assist."

"That's good." Amanda breathed a sigh of relief. "If he's conscious, at least there'll be someone he can communicate with easily."

Amanda glanced over to where Bootsie sat slumped on a bench. Again she could not help wondering what the girl was doing there.

Donovan stood up. "I'm going to see if I can get a call through to Mrs. McKay." He didn't look directly at Amanda, but there seemed to be a tacit agreement in the room that she was the one whose wishes must be adhered to.

She nodded. "That would be very good of you. It would be horrible for her to hear about it on television or in the papers."

He walked out, and again silence prevailed in the room. Amanda couldn't stand it. She wanted to be alone with her grief. To wait privately. To give herself over to whatever emotions flowed through her. It was too ghastly to have to expose her suffering for Josh to a roomful of strangers. She took a deep breath and then spoke up boldly. "There really isn't any need for everyone to wait here," she said. "As long as Mrs. McKay is being told, there's nothing else that any of us can do but wait. I'm sure you'll all be more comfortable back at your hotel. I'll be here, and I'll call you as soon as there is any news." She directed herself toward the men, not quite daring to look at Bootsie, although she would have been happier if the girl were gone too.

"I think that makes a lot of sense, Mrs. Parrish," one of the men said. "I thank you for the suggestion. As soon as Jack comes back we'll see if we can find out anything else. If not, we'll go and count on your being here."

Amanda nodded. She glanced at Bootsie, but the girl's face registered nothing, not acquiescence or denial, not any kind of emotion that might show what she was going through.

Jack Donovan came back unable to complete the call to Mrs. McKay, and Amanda repeated her intention of staying and the advisability of their all waiting to hear from her. Donovan praised her courage and thanked her for her courtesy, but Amanda could detect a tone of relief in his words. All the men shook hands solemnly with her as they said good-bye, leaving in a body, much the same, she was sure, as they had arrived.

Bootsie stayed. She seemed to ask neither permission nor anything else from Amanda. She just sat, silently.

There were a thousand things Amanda wanted to ask her, but they would all have to wait. She had neither the strength to frame the questions, nor the courage to know some of the answers. It didn't matter anyway. All that mattered was Josh. She couldn't focus her mind on anything else. If Bootsie wanted to stay there, so be it.

"Can I get you some coffee or tea?" Bootsie asked quietly.

Amanda smiled, shaking her head. "Thank you, but I really don't think I could stand anything right now," she said, touched by the girl's kindness. *Maybe that's why she wants to stay, to keep me company and help in some way if she can.* "Do you know the American doctor's name?" she asked.

Bootsie shook her head. "But I'd recognize him," she said. "He said he'd come to talk to us as soon as there was something to tell."

"How long are you going to wait?" Amanda asked gently, her feelings for the girl softening.

"As long as they let us," Bootsie said.

Amanda accepted the pronoun. *We're in this together,* she told herself. *Whatever Bootsie's reasons are, she's united herself with me in this vigil. Perhaps it will make it easier to have someone here with me, especially someone who knows Josh.*

Minutes went by in silence. No one came into the waiting room, although Amanda was aware of hushed activity in the corridors outside.

She got up out of her seat and paced back and forth. She walked along the perimeter of the small waiting room, glancing through the window at the opposite wall. The shadows were lengthening across Monte Carlo, the sun slowly heading for its shelter behind the hillsides. Soon it would be dark, and the long wait would extend into the night. Amanda knew somehow that she would see the dawn rising from this same window. She went back to her seat. She wondered how soon Veronique would be able to get Tommy to bed. She didn't want him staying up waiting for her to phone. *Perhaps,* she thought, *it would be a good idea to do that now.* "Is there a telephone nearby?" she asked Bootsie. "My son is back at the apartment, and he is terribly worried. He saw the accident with me."

"How awful," Bootsie said. "How old is he?"

"Only six," Amanda said. "He loves cars and races, and he was so happy when I brought him here."

Bootsie nodded. "I know about the cars," she said with a half-smile, "Josh told me."

Amanda was slightly startled but recovered quickly. If Josh had told Bootsie about Tommy and his playthings, the girl must know how they felt about each other. "I'd like to call him now," she said again, adding, "even though there really isn't anything to tell; but I'd like to talk him into going to sleep."

Bootsie showed her where there was a phone down one of the corridors and dove into her jeans pocket for some francs when Amanda admitted she didn't have any change.

She hurried off to make the call, talking to Veronique and Tommy both. She came back to the waiting room, telling Bootsie that everything at the apartment was under control. "Now we just have to wait," she said.

They alternated the hours between sitting rigidly and pacing the little room, punctuating the vigil by venturing occasionally to the nurses' station at the center of the floor to see if there was any news.

She didn't even have to ask. At the sight of Amanda's anxious face the on-duty nurse shook her head sadly. No word. No change. And Amanda would go back to the waiting room, wondering how much longer it could last.

After one such fruitless attempt she came back into the waiting room to find Bootsie curled up on the bench, asleep. Amanda envied her. She herself would find no such respite this endless night.

She was sitting in the chair, almost nodding, when a doctor came in. She jumped up.

"How is he?" she demanded.

"Are you friends of Mr. McKay's?" the doctor asked.

"Yes," she said eagerly, "how is he? Is he going to be all right?" She looked imploringly at the man in the creased greens of the operating room.

He was tall and lean, his white hair in a close crew cut. He was somehow older than Amanda had expected him to be, without her quite understanding why. They introduced themselves briefly. Much more important, and making communicating so much easier, was that he was English, and not French.

"I can get the X rays for you to look at," Dr. Whitman offered. "It might make his condition a little easier for you to understand."

"I don't think so," Amanda said quickly. "If you would just explain to me how badly hurt he is and what his chances for recovery are."

"I had figured his chances as being pretty good at first," the doctor said. "I've been in sports surgery for a good number of years, and I've handled about every kind of accident that can occur on the track. His fractures are severe, but mendable. It's this coma business that's got me frankly worried."

"Is he going to make it?" Amanda blurted the words out without realizing what she was saying.

"I don't know," was the equally terrible answer.

Amanda felt herself slumping, but the doctor realized it and grasped her arm, setting her back in her chair and nodding to Bootsie, who had wakened. They all sat in silence until Amanda felt more in control of herself.

She looked at the doctor. "I'd like to see him now," she said. "May I?"

Dr. Whitman was ambivalent. "I know that he was asking for you and that you've come a long way," he said hesitantly, "but we can't allow any visitors. There wouldn't be any communication anyway, with the state he's in. Also, he's swathed in bandages. It might be better if you didn't go in."

"I want to," Amanda said. "I must."

"Very well," Dr. Whitman said. "But only for a moment. I'll go with you, but I'm going to bring you right out again."

Amanda nodded and stood uncertainly, letting the doctor lead her back in the direction of Josh's room.

He opened the door quietly, nodding to the nurse who sat at the bedside. "Any changes?" he asked.

The nurse shook her head.

Amanda wondered if the doctor had been right in trying to spare her. Josh was unrecognizable. His face was completely covered and so were the visible portions of his arms, in mummylike gauze wrappings. The machines monitoring him almost completely covered one wall of the room, a bank of instruments that gave off bleeps and signals that frightened her. Various tubes were attached to his wrist, which lay totally motionless outside of the sheet that covered the rest of his body. The whole bed was encased in a clear plastic tent. Although it was transparent, it made everything within it look distorted.

Amanda turned her head, unable to look any longer. She felt as though the sterile whiteness of the room was closing in on her. The machines were like grotesque caricatures out of a science fantasy; even their bleeps and wavering lines were more alive than the human body to which they were attached.

The doctor took her arm and led her outside the room. Amanda followed unseeing, stopping only to stand against the corridor wall, wondering if she had the strength to take another step. She had never seen a human being so devoid of life, so seemingly suspended between the stretches of what was still possible and what was finite and done with. The man who was encapsulated in all the gauze and plaster and tubing and tentwork was the man she loved. He was Josh.

It didn't seem possible. Nothing could have snapped the vital being that was Josh McKay and reduced him to this. *Not possible.* Amanda shook her head. She had seen it and sensed it, but she could not accept it, she could not believe it.

"There must be something we can do," she burst out suddenly.

"Would you like me to give you a sedative?" he asked kindly.

"No!" Amanda shouted.

Several white-uniformed attendants passing in the corridor stopped to look at her uneasily.

Amanda brushed the hair back from her face. "I'm sorry, doctor," she muttered. "You must think I'm becoming hysterical, but I'm not. I'll be all right."

"I wish you would let me give you something, Mrs. Parrish," he said. "Nothing strong, only something to relax you." He looked at her keenly. "When was the last time you had some sleep?"

"I slept last night," Amanda said, stumbling over the words as she thought back. *Last night, a year ago,* she felt like saying. It would be a more accurate description of the way she felt.

"Please let me prescribe something," the doctor said kindly.

Amanda shook her head. "No, thank you, but no," she said. "I've got to be awake to know what's happening. I've got to stay strong in case he needs me."

"Very well," Dr. Whitman conceded. "Let me take you back to the waiting room. I'll ask the nurse to see if she can do anything to make it more comfortable for you and the other young lady."

In her horror at seeing Josh's motionless form, Amanda had completely forgotten about Bootsie.

The girl looked up expectantly. "Any change?"

Amanda shook her head.

Bootsie sighed. "Do you think we should try again to call his mother? She should know about his condition. . . ." Her voice trailed off tearfully.

"I really don't know," Amanda said. "I don't know what to think." She was too shaken by what she had seen to rely on her own judgment. She tried to push the sight of the hospital room from her mind and reason out the best thing to do about notifying Mrs. McKay. If they called her while things were so bad, it would put a terrible burden on the already bereaved woman. If Josh didn't pull through–Amanda couldn't complete the thought, but it was that Mrs. McKay would have some peace until she had to be told. On the other hand, if Josh got better–and there was every chance, every hope, that he would–then the phone call to Connecticut might not be so devastating, and the older woman would have been spared a great deal of unnecessary anguish. It was a difficult decision, and it agonized Amanda to have to be the one to make it. Amanda wondered suddenly if Sylvia had heard. She would have to recover some of her strength before she could think of talking to Sylvia. But sometimes, she reflected, even knowing the worst is better than knowing nothing at all. Besides, this wasn't the worst. Things could still improve. Josh could be all right. She suddenly wanted her mother very much. Wanted the comfort of her voice and the strength of having her pulling for them.

"I'll be right back," she whispered to Bootsie, "I have to make a phone call."

She found the booth, certain she had done the right thing in calling, when Sylvia's voice came over the line, even before the first ring had been completed.

"Mother, it's very bad," Amanda said tersely. "He went into a coma just before I got to the hospital. His other injuries can be healed, but right now he looks so–so lifeless. There's no telling when he'll come out of it. We can only wait and pray."

She heard Sylvia's voice break in a sob.

"Oh, Mother, don't," Amanda pleaded. "If you break down now, I'll just fall apart. I need you, Sylvia, I need you." It was the first time in years she had addressed her mother by her first name. She didn't even realize she had done it.

"We'll all pray for him, Amanda," Sylvia said. "Now pull yourself together. You're going to need every drop of strength you've got."

Amanda could tell how much effort it had taken for Sylvia to speak. "I'm going to be strong," she heard herself saying. "I've got to. I'm going to stay right here near him until something happens," Amanda said. "I'll call you back as soon as there's any change. Tommy is with the housekeeper. He's all right."

"Good-bye, my darling," Sylvia said. "God bless you and help you both."

They hung up. Amanda walked slowly back to the waiting room. There was nothing else to do now but wait.

"Can I get you something?" Bootsie asked as soon as Amanda made her reappearance.

"No, dear, thank you." Amanda said. "Why don't you get something for yourself? You've been here even longer than I have."

"That's all right," Bootsie said. "I've had to make do in even tougher places than this." She cast a sidelong glance at the bare green walls that were almost as pale as the whitewash of the room Josh lay in. She looked at Amanda again. "Are you in love with him?" she asked.

"Yes, very much," Amanda replied, staring back at her.

"I'm glad," Bootsie said, "I mean, things are so tough for Josh now; at least he has someone like you in love with him. If he gets better, everything will be perfect. I'm sure you will be very happy."

"Thank you," Amanda murmured. Bootsie was pushing for Josh to pull through and had remained in the hospital ever since the accident. Amanda admired her loyalty, and told her so.

Bootsie lit up happily at the words of praise. "I wouldn't have left for anything," she said, "not until I know everything is all right. You sure you don't want some coffee?"

"No, not really, but thank you," Amanda said, trying to manage a weak smile.

"Do you smoke? Do you want a cigarette?" Bootsie asked, eager to be of some help.

Amanda shook her head. The girl was like a courtier, trying to please or be helpful in any way she could. It was sad, Amanda thought. She had probably followed at Dutcher's heels like a little puppy dog, wanting to be close to its master but only succeeding in getting underfoot. It seemed so hollow an existence; like an empty pitcher, serving no purpose at all on her own, she came to life only when there was some function to perform for someone.

She was exceptionally pretty, Amanda thought, young, with a lovely straight nose and pale blond hair that hung almost to her waist. Her eyes were pale too, a light blue shade, with a vacant cast to them, almost as if they didn't see from within but waited for what was reflected from other people. Amanda surmised that Bootsie felt lost without Dutcher and had somehow connected herself to Josh as a surrogate. Amanda wondered what it was that had brought her to Monte Carlo for the race.

Don't think about things like that, she told herself crossly. She was there to concentrate on Josh and what she could do for him, not worry herself thinking about other people, especially, she thought, looking over at the girl again, a helpless, mixed-up waif like this one, who didn't seem to have any direction in her life and had lost Dutcher, the leader she had tagged along behind. Now she followed Josh, it seemed.

But Josh was not lost, not yet, Amanda swore to herself savagely, and there was no mistaking that now that she was there, Bootsie's role was greatly diminished. It would be Amanda the doctors brought their reports to, Amanda whom Josh would be looking for when he woke. She forced herself to think "when," not "if," she couldn't let "if" cross her mind.

A glance at the one window in the room told Amanda that it would soon be daylight. Yet the turn of the night into day promised no change in their vigil. It could go on forever.

She felt her tiredness at last overtaking her. Putting her handbag under her head as a pillow, Amanda stretched out on the bench. She was too worn out to mind its hardness, and she found herself curling up and drifting off.

When she woke up many hours later, it was with a start at the unexpected surroundings. The waiting room was almost completely darkened, as if someone had switched off the day that in her complete exhaustion she had slept through. The large, open rectangle that served as a doorway faced out into the dimly lit corridor, which was almost completely still. Amanda had a sense of somebody being out there, probably at the nurses' station, but everything else was hushed and forbidding.

She struggled to sit up, rubbing her eyes, thinking what a wreck she must look like. She glanced over at the other bench. Bootsie was curled up and sleeping. Amanda could make out her huddled form in the little light that was cast into the room. She tiptoed out, not wanting to wake the girl. She walked up to the desk. A solitary nurse sat there, writing.

"Excuse me," Amanda said. "I'm asking about Mr. McKay. Has there been any change in his condition?"

"Are you the lady who's sleeping in the waiting room?" the nurse asked in careful English.

"Yes, I am," Amanda said. "Is there anything you can tell me?"

"Dr. Whitman was here before," the nurse said. "He didn't want to wake you, because you were so obviously exhausted. He said to tell you the patient is still in coma, but there are some signs of movement in the extremities."

"That sounds hopeful, doesn't it?" Amanda asked, not quite sure.

"Yes, it does," the nurse confirmed. "It's the first sign of activity returning."

"But that doesn't have anything to do with the coma, or does it?" Amanda asked. "Has that changed any?"

"No, I'm afraid not," the nurse said. "I'm sorry, but that condition is still the same. Just stable."

"He's holding his own," Amanda said.

"Yes, he's holding his own," the nurse repeated.

Amanda looked around. The deserted hospital seemed almost like a mausoleum. The floors were polished to an unnatural brightness, imitating marble. The few lights that had been left on in corridors were eerie in the distant dimness. There was nothing to do but go back and wait some more, try to sleep some more, and wait some more. Amanda wondered if it would ever end. She glanced up at a large clock on the wall. It was eleven thirty. Everything outside the hospital lay in deep darkness.

She wandered back to the waiting room. Something inside her felt empty and hollow—a strange feeling, almost like getting sick. Amanda realized it was hunger. She picked up her purse and went back to the nurses' station. "I don't suppose the hospital has any place to eat, does it?" she asked.

"There's a restaurant in the basement, but it's been closed for hours," the nurse said. "But there's a vending machine just down the corridor behind me." She pointed with her pencil. "And you can also get something to drink."

Amanda tried to remember the last time she had had a Coke. Probably at the zoo with Tommy, although she remembered that she usually opted for one of the watery orange drinks that Central Park seemed to specialize in. She got the soda from the machine, feeling grateful for this reminder of home among the unfamiliar French soft drinks. Then she got some crackers, also unknown to her.

She went back to the waiting room but didn't go inside. There were a couple of chairs in the corridor, and she sat down in one of them, afraid she might wake Bootsie. She drew the makeshift meal out for as long as she could. Then she went in search of somewhere to deposit the remains and, she hoped, to find a water cooler where she could wash the unaccustomed tastes out of her mouth.

It had made her feel better to eat, she admitted, and the strangely sweet taste of the Coke had been a real pickup. If she got thirsty during the night, she could go back for more. The walk to the machine seemed like the only activity.

She didn't want to go back to the waiting room. She walked along each of the similar four corridors, just for the sake of stretching her legs. It might have been nice to talk to the nurse for a while, she thought, but it wouldn't be fair to interrupt the woman while she was so obviously busy, and Amanda herself didn't feel up to providing conversation. She stretched her arms out a few times and then bent over, reaching her hands to the floor. She did a few more exercising warm-ups, feeling better but wishing she had thought of it before she had eaten. It didn't seem wise to do any more. The best thing was to go back to the waiting room and curl up and try to sleep again.

She realized she was in the corridor where Josh's room was. She walked quietly toward it, and opened the door slightly. There was a small lamp lit, and the nurse for the night shift was knitting. She glanced up warningly at Amanda, but Amanda shook her head. She looked at the perpetual machines. They were making the same lines and noises they had earlier. She knew that meant that everything was the same. She tried not to peer into the darkness where he lay immobile under the oxygen tent. She nodded slightly at the nurse and slipped out again.

She walked back to the waiting room and curled up on her bench. She stared at the darkness outside and felt terribly far from home. It was as though she were suspended somewhere in limbo, not one place or the other, just as Josh was hanging so tenuously between life and death. How long the dual wait would go on, no one could say. Certainly no answers would come from the dark and unfamiliar landscape outside. Amanda turned her head and looked the other way, wondering how long she would have to accommodate herself to this interminable waiting.

She almost had the answer when she woke up in the bright, sunshiny morning. The hospital looked so much better in daylight than it had at night, that she actually felt better. *Maybe it's a sign,* she thought, *maybe the parallel does exist. Maybe Josh will be better too.*

She almost felt superstitious about asking at the desk, but she had to stop, to hear the same report again: Nothing had changed.

She went back to the waiting room. Bootsie still slept. But by the time Amanda got back from washing, the girl was up also.

"Are you feeling better for having slept?" Bootsie asked.

"Yes," Amanda said. "Better, in fact, than I thought I would. How are you feeling this morning?"

"About the same," Bootsie said noncommittally. "How's Josh?"

"No change," Amanda said.

Bootsie, noticing Amanda's apparent freshness, went off to make some changes of her own.

A few minutes later Dr. Whitman looked in. Seeing Amanda, he came into the waiting room and sat down beside her.

"Has anything happened?" Amanda asked quickly, her heart jumping.

"No, everything is about the same," the doctor said. "But that in itself, at this stage of the game, is a pretty good sign. He's stable, and maintaining all of the vital functions. His breathing is regular, and his blood pressure has steadied. The picture is a little brighter, but there's nothing much else I can tell you."

"But at least he hasn't gotten any worse," Amanda said.

"You're absolutely right," the doctor agreed. "He hasn't done anything to cause us any more concern."

"Do you think now that he'll pull through?"

"There's every chance that he will, Mrs. Parrish," the doctor said. "But it's just too early to tell. You'll have to be a little more patient, I'm afraid."

"That's exactly how I feel, doctor," Amanda said glumly. "Afraid."

"Hope for the best," he said, patting her hand and going out.

He had intimated to her earlier that when an improvement came, it could be at any time and without any prior indication. They would have to live minute to minute, and now Amanda tried to block out her day, hour by hour. She wanted to call Sylvia again, but thought that if she waited until she had been awake for another hour, the phone call could break the monotony of the morning. If she called sooner, the morning would stretch as endlessly as the afternoon that loomed just beyond it. Bootsie came back and offered to go for coffee, and this time Amanda accepted. She paced up and down alone in the waiting room, barely aware of the sounds of the hospital as it came to active life. She was standing and staring out of the window. The trees that had been only masses of black during the night were green and visible now. How long would it be before Josh could see them, before they could exclaim over the simple pleasures of nature the way they had in England?

That time seemed so long ago, and as magical and perfect as if it had never happened but had only been imagined. What wouldn't she have given to be back there, in those quaintly named villages of the Cotswolds that they had driven through and exclaimed over and delighted in! All the golden days and silvery nights of that magic time came flashing back to her, she remembered. And perhaps the loveliest where they had only stayed for a few moments, hugging each other, was Bourton-on-the-Water, where the main street was set right on the beautiful and beautifully named river, the Windrush. So many others, all lovely in their own ways, so many towns she never would have been able to remember if she hadn't insisted on marking Josh's road map, making little notes and keeping it so that she could remember all of it forever.

But even more important than being back in those places would have been the chance to be back in time, just to prevent all the unhappiness and misunderstanding that had led, finally, to this.

"Are you Amanda?" a feminine voice asked in accented English.

Amanda spun around at the question. "Yes!" she said.

"Come with me quickly," her questioner, a nurse, said. "He's asking for you."

Amanda flew behind her, down the corridor to Josh's room, her heart skipping beats with every step. She didn't even know if the nurse had meant that it was only the doctor who wanted to see her. But it had to be Josh.

She opened the door to the room and walked to his bedside. The oxygen tent was still placed over the bed, but even through its distortion she could see that his eyes were open. She went around to where she could be closest to him.

"Josh," she called out softly. "I'm here."

She would never forget the look in his eyes when he saw her. She yearned to throw herself on the bed, to lift the tent and give him breath of her own, but she knew she couldn't. She stood staring down at him, tears rolling unchecked from her eyes as all she could see of him were his.

"I can't talk much," he said. His voice sounded as though it were coming from someplace else, but each word was music to her ears.

"Don't try, darling," she said, putting a finger to her lips. "I'm here and I'm going to be here for as long as you are. Everything is going to be all right."

His eyes signaled a look that said he knew how badly hurt he was.

"You've had a long sleep, darling," Amanda went on in a rush of words. "But you've started to get stronger already. The doctor told me that this morning."

His eyes flickered.

"I'm never going to leave you, Josh," she said, not

caring if the nurse or the doctor or the whole hospital staff could hear her. She suddenly knew that his life was all that mattered. Whether he made a complete recovery or not, she could never leave him. Whether he raced or not didn't matter anymore.

His eyes closed again, and Amanda jumped.

"Don't be afraid, dear," the nurse said quickly. "He's very tired and he's sleeping again. I'll call you as soon as he's awake, and you can talk to him for a few more minutes then." She beamed at Amanda, who could have embraced the white-garbed, motherly figure. "Each time he'll be getting a little stronger," the nurse added, reassuring her.

Amanda gazed lovingly at the still figure in the bed. A movement in the room made her look up. It was Dr. Whitman, who also beamed approval.

"I think you're the best medicine he can have, Mrs. Parrish," the doctor said. "I had a feeling he was going to be coming around this morning, but I didn't want to say anything to get your hopes up too high."

"Thank you, doctor." Amanda could hardly breathe the words. "Thank you for everything."

"How long are you figuring on camping out in the waiting room?" he asked.

Amanda was surprised at the unexpected question. "I know it's not exactly according to rules," she said. "If it's impossible to remain there, then I'd like to take a room for myself, as close to this one as possible."

"You'll find it's more expensive than a hotel, even without providing you any services," he said. "But you're welcome to stay if you want. We have a room close by that's just been vacated, and enough empty beds to be able to offer it to you."

Amanda went back to the waiting room, where Bootsie held out a lukewarm container of coffee.

"I just spoke to him, Bootsie," Amanda said exultantly. "He's gone back to sleep again, but he's out of the coma."

"Gee, that's great," the girl replied.

Amanda was amazed that that was the best Bootsie could do, but in her own happiness she didn't care. "I'm taking a room here," she went on, "I'm going to move in. You're welcome to sit in there with me if you like. I'm sure it's going to be a lot more comfortable than this place was."

"Do you think you'll be needing me for anything else, really?" Bootsie asked.

"No, not really," Amanda replied. "I just thought you might want to see Josh later."

Bootsie bit her lip. "I'd only be in the way," she said. "You're the one he wants to see. I was just waiting until you came."

"Of course, I understand entirely," Amanda said. "I'm going to get settled in and wait till he's awake again," she said. "I want to thank you for everything you've done, Bootsie, and for being here in the first place. I'll remember you for it as long as I live, and I'm sure Josh will too."

The girl blushed but said nothing.

"Shall we say good-bye, then?" Amanda asked, reaching out her hand.

Bootsie took it and they shook solemnly, and then she left.

Amanda knew she would never understand anyone like Bootsie, but it didn't matter. She busied herself in the room they gave her, opening doors, glad to see that she had her own bathroom and more closet space than she would need. She telephoned Veronique and Tommy, and told him that she would be back as soon as Josh was better. Meanwhile Veronique was to take Tommy to the pool and around the city and anywhere else he wanted.

Josh's room was still off-limits to visitors, but Dr. Whitman agreed that an exception would be made for her, and the nurses were instructed to come and fetch Amanda whenever Josh woke up.

She called Sylvia to tell her the good news. Of course, she explained, there was still a great deal about his condition left unanswered. But as long as the injury to his head proved to be no cause for concern, the rest was a question of time.

Sylvia breathed a sigh of relief. "How are you feeling?" she asked. "You must be ready for a hospital bed yourself by now."

Amanda was able to laugh. "Would you believe, I have one," she said, telling Sylvia the arrangements she had made for staying close enough to Josh to be able to see him every time he was awake. "I even have a phone number where you can reach me," Amanda said. "Call whenever you like. I doubt that you'll be interrupting anything."

"What if you're with Josh?" Sylvia asked.

"He isn't awake for more than a few moments at a time," Amanda explained. "Then I'd be right back in here." They spoke for a few more minutes before ringing off.

The ordeal was far from over, for Josh or for her. Amanda was just beginning to realize the terrible emotional toll the shock had taken from her. She didn't want to think about it. She didn't want to think about anything, not Pembroke's, not anything that existed beyond the four walls of the hospital.

That wasn't perfectly true, she reminded herself.

There were her mother and her son and a couple of other people who were important to her. But right now and for the foreseeable future, it was Josh who was at the core of her existence.

There was a light knock at the door.

"Yes?" Amanda hurried to see who it was.

The motherly nurse beckoned Amanda to follow her down the hall back to Josh's room. He was awake again.

This time he was able to speak a little longer. "I love you," came the strange sound of his voice, "I don't know how you got here, but I don't want you staying here killing yourself."

Amanda signaled to him not to exert himself. "Stop worrying about me," she warned him. "Or I'll stop worrying about you."

"Okay," he agreed weakly.

She knew how much her being there meant to him, but she wondered if he realized that wild horses couldn't have taken her from his side.

That was all. He had fallen asleep again. Amanda went back to her room. The next interruption was from Dr. Whitman, who came by to tell her that Josh's breathing was enough improved for them to plan on removing the oxygen tent the next morning. Once more Amanda was filled with a rush of gratitude. "It's going to be all right, isn't it?" she asked.

"I think so," he smiled encouragement. "Every day a little bit more, every day a little bit better."

Amanda had her meals delivered to the room. She didn't want to go even as far as the restaurant, in case he should wake. He was conscious for a few minutes, three or four times a day: the doctor came by half as frequently, but also with more encouraging news.

Amanda lost track of the time. Her life was reckoned

not in days and hours but in the visits she made to Josh's room and the reports the doctor made to her. She was able to sleep at night, the night nurse refusing to wake her but assuring Josh that she was close by.

One morning the doctor came in as she was gazing out of the window, watching people coming and going.

"Josh is awake," the doctor said. "Come and see him."

Amanda didn't even stop to think that it had always been a nurse who summoned her. It wasn't until she was in his room that she realized there had been a change in the routine and a reason for it.

The oxygen tent had disappeared days ago, and now the bandages that had covered his face were gone too. There were no more barriers. Amanda could reach him and touch him and kiss him. He was sitting up in bed, propped back on pillows, but although he greeted her with the smile she loved, he wasn't quite ready for her onslaught.

Amanda could barely keep from hugging and kissing him. Her arms and lips were everywhere on his face, her tears falling heedlessly on his still-bandaged chest.

"Take it easy, take it easy," Josh said softly. "You're going to tear me up worse than that damn car did!"

Amanda stood back to look at him. There were a few bruises still showing on his face, but he was Josh, unmistakably Josh, and she loved him.

She touched one of the black-and-blue spots gingerly with an exploring fingertip. "You look just the way I did when you smashed into me," she teased him. "Now we're even-Steven." She blushed at what she had said, wondering from what recesses of her mind she had dredged up the childish expression.

Josh laughed. Then he grew serious again; the sparkle in his eyes seemed to diminish, and the clear blue color deepened. "I'm going to be completely well, Amanda," he said. "You're not going to be stuck with a helpless invalid for the rest of your life."

"I know that, darling," Amanda said, her eyes brimming again, "but even if it weren't so, it wouldn't have made any difference. You still wouldn't have been able to get rid of me." *Soon, soon,* she wanted to tell him, *we'll be back to normal lives and burning nights.* She loved him so.

"We still have so many problems to settle," he reminded her. "How is Tommy? I tried to call, I couldn't get through. I can't begin to tell you what I was going through."

"Not now," Amanda said gently, remembering what Sylvia had told her about being there. She was to help him, and all of the questions, all the uncertainties, and everything else, could just wait.

"How soon do you think you'll be able to drive again?" Amanda asked.

Josh looked at her in surprise. "Why?" he asked. "I didn't think you'd ever want me in a car again."

"Nonsense," Amanda said lightly. "I want to go back to the Cotswolds on our honeymoon."

"You really loved England, didn't you?" Josh asked, smiling.

"I'd love any place with you, but, yes, England was very special," she said.

"I think we should go someplace else for our honeymoon," Josh said. "Maybe South America, maybe the Jersey shore, someplace different."

Amanda laughed. "Okay, but I thought I'd like to

go back to England to make up for my bad behavior there," she said.

"You may get a little tired of England." Josh couldn't suppress a grin. "We're going to be spending an awful lot of time there."

"What are you talking about?" Amanda asked.

"Haskell bought the company," he said, "one of the greatest deals in the history of deals. But he wants me to spend some time there every year, checking the operation."

"See how soon they can start racing again," Amanda hazarded a guess.

"I won't be racing, Amanda, I promise." Josh's voice was serious.

Amanda believed him. "Does that mean we go back to Maidenborough?" She wrinkled her nose, wanting to keep the conversation light, not ready to go into those deeper aspects of their lives. Not yet.

"That's the best part," Josh said. "I was waiting till I got back to New York to tell you. But you might as well know now. I've convinced him to move the entire operation to just outside Coventry."

"That lovely countryside!" Amanda exclaimed. "Oh, Josh, how perfect." She smiled at him.

A thousand details came running through her mind, a thousand things that had to be taken care of, a thousand questions that had to be answered. At last she could call her mother with the good news, and Josh's mother to say that he was all right, skipping over the details so she wouldn't know how long they had waited to tell her. She looked at Josh. His eyes were closed again. She bent over, kissing him lightly on the forehead, and turned to tiptoe out of the room.

But she felt him grasp her arm and pull her back.

"Josh, be careful." Amanda was alarmed by his sudden and energetic movement.

"Sit down and kiss me," he ordered, "hard, and long. Just watch out for the bad parts."

"I hope we're not going to have to get you any replacements," she said, gazing at him with all the love she had ever felt in her life.

He shook his head. "No, just some rest and rehabilitation and the love of a good woman."

"You have that, darling, I promise you," Amanda said. "Everything else will have to wait."

"I don't want to wait," Josh said. "How would you like to have the honeymoon in Monaco?"

"And the ceremony here in the hospital, I suppose?" Amanda retaliated.

"It was only a suggestion," Josh grinned. "We're not getting married until I can carry you across the threshold, any threshold."

She kissed him then, the way he had wanted her to kiss him, the way she wanted to kiss him, as if there were nothing in the world but the two of them, locked in embrace, no ticking of a clock on a wall, no roads winding anywhere, just this.

Just this, forever.

"THE MOST ROMANTIC NOVEL SINCE LOVE STORY."
—Good Housekeeping
Change of Heart
SALLY MANDEL
Once in a long while, a story is so bursting with tenderness that its charm is irresistible.
That story is Sharlie and Brian's story, Change of Heart—a love story for a lifetime.
A Dell Book $2.95 (11355-5)